A Changing

At Home and At Sea,

1805 - II

by

John G. Cragg

©2019 John G. Cragg

A Changing War: At Home and At Sea, 1805 -- II

Copyright © 2019, 20221 by John G. Cragg

All rights reserved.

Dedicated to

Charley Cragg

Table of Contents

Chapter I	1
Chapter II	15
Chapter III	27
Chapter IV	39
Chapter V	49
Chapter VI	59
Chapter VII	73
Chapter VIII	87
Chapter IX	105
Chapter X	125
Chapter XI	143
Chapter XII	159
Chapter XIII	177
Chapter XIV	199
Chapter XV	221
Chapter XVI	241
Chapter XVII	261
Chapter XVIII	283
Chapter XIX	301
Chapter XX	317
Author's Note	337
Glossary	339

Preface

This book is a work of fiction. It follows on from the first four volumes in this series, *A New War: at Home and at Sea, 1803*, *A Continuing War: at Home and at Sea, 1803-4*, *A War by Diplomacy: at Home and at Sea, 1804*, and *A Stalemated War: at Home and at Sea, 1805*. They are available at Amazon.com and other Amazon sites by searching for my name or the title. The present tale takes place in 1805. A great many things have changed in the more than two centuries that have elapsed since that date, including items and phrases that may be unfamiliar to many readers. To help those who are curious, a glossary is provided at the end of the book. Items that appear in the glossary are flagged on their first appearance in the text by an * as in, for example, tack*.

As always, I am indebted to my wife, Olga Browzin Cragg, for encouragement and meticulous help in trying to make a readable manuscript.

List of Characters

Adderly, Graham — Man hired by Daphne to manage Moorhouse and Son

Amery, Mr. Justice Titus — Judge and mysterious fixer for the government. Knighted in the novel

Arbinathy, Mr. — Solicitor who handles George Moorhouse's affairs

Beamish, Mrs. — housekeeper to George Moorhouse

Bottomly, Hugh — Yard foreman at Moorhouse and Son

Burns, Sir Thomas — Representative of Lloyd's insurers

Bush, Captain Tobias — Captain, Royal Navy. Knighted in the novel

Beamish, Mrs. — Housekeeper to George Moorhouse

Bush, Randolf — Midshipman on *Glaucus*, nephew of Captain Bush

Creasy, Captain — Master of the smuggling craft, *The Ruddy Fox*

Dalton, Sir Humphrey — Society portrait painter

Dugmore, Mrs. — Initial Caregiver for George Moorhouse

Edwards, Mr. — Giles's prize agent

Findlay, Michael	Younger painter more skilled at landscape painting than Sir Humphrey Dalton
Gardiner, Sir Thomas	Representative of the East India Company
Geoffreys, Admiral Andrew	Replacing Admiral Carnarvon in a squadron based on Portsmouth
Giles, Daphne	Wife of Sir Richard Giles
Giles, Sir Richard, Viscount Ashton, KB	Captain of H.M. Frigate *Glaucus*
Gordonston, Lord	First Lord of the Admiralty
Granger	Groom at Dipton Hall, former cavalry man
Griffiths, Mr.	Stablemaster at Dipton Hall
Hatcherley, Sir Metcalf, later Baron	Replaces Lord Gordonston as First Lord
Hazelton, Geoffrey	Solicitor in London, an expert in entails
Hopley, Mrs.	Replacement for Mrs. Dugmore

Lassiter, Mr. — Sailing master of the East Indiaman *Gloriana*
Macauley, Latimer — Lieutenant of Marines on *Glaucus*
Maclean, Dr. — Surgeon on *Glaucus*
Macreau, Etienne — A Frenchman, Second Lieutenant on *Glaucus*
Miller, George — First Lieutenant on *Glaucus*
Mohammad, Mr. Sidi — Translator, supplied by the East India Company
Moorhouse, Daniel — Father of Daphne Giles
Moorhouse, George — Daphne's uncle, a mill owner in Birmingham
Moorhouse, Geoffrey — Daphne's brother, a bookstore owner in Winchester
Moudley, Captain — Captain of the East Indiaman *Gloriana*
Quincy — Butler to George Moorhouse
Shearer, Geordie — Head clerk at Moorshoud and Son
Snodgrass, Mr. — Solicitor in Ameschester
Snodgrass, Mr. — Previous Earl of Camshire's London Solicitor, cousin of the lawyer in Ameschester
Steves — Butler at Dipton Hall
Stoner, Major — Giles's half-brother-in-law

Struthers, Lady Gillian	Giles's maternal aunt
Struthers, Lord	Her husband
Stuart, Daniel	Acting lieutenant on *Glaucus*
Tapley, Graham	Representative of the East India Company
Throgmorton, Admiral Sir Thomas	Replaces Admiral Casterton blockading Brest

Chapter I

The old, red-brick gatehouse of St. James's Palace in Pall Mall, Westminster, must have seen thousands of carriages pass through it since it had been built by Henry VIII, though with less frequency now, in 1805, than in earlier times since the palace was no longer the *de facto* residence of the King, George III. However, the more formal duties of the sovereign still took place at St. James's Palace, and its many servants were as highly trained as any in the country.

The carriage arriving that morning had the marks of one that was used mainly for traveling significant distances on country roads rather than the more sleek appearance of ones used only in town, and the horses had been chosen more for their ability to pull the carriage than for the splendor of their gait. The footmen who were on hand to open the carriage door and set out the footstool for its passengers to use were too well trained to show any surprise either at the inelegance of the vehicle or their lack of familiarity with the coat of arms painted on its doors. It was the crest of Viscount Ashton, but it had rarely been seen in London in the past year or so and never at St. James's Palace.

Had any passerby been interested in yet another carriage bringing people to the Palace and been aware of the distinguishing aspects of the dress of various notables, they would have seen that the first occupant out of the vehicle wore the dress uniform of a Post Captain of the Royal Navy of more than three years seniority. He was wearing the star of the Order of the Bath and a sword with a jeweled handle, undoubtedly the gift of some patriotic brotherhood, possibly of merchants whose vessels he had protected. To the considerable chagrin of the attendant footman, the captain had bounded unassisted from the carriage and had immediately turned to assist the next passenger to descend. Again, a post-captain appeared, though a notably more junior one, for he had only a single epaulet on his shoulder. What was more notable was that one of his legs and one of his arms had been shortened by the surgeon's knife and had been replaced with a peg-leg and a hook. Despite these disabilities, he emerged confidently from the carriage holding the hand of the first captain lightly to steady his descent. One could now appreciate why his companion had offered assistance, for he might well have been afraid that the footman would not be aware of any special needs of those who had lost limbs.

The first captain descending from the carriage was immediately recognized by the attendants who had been stumped by the coat of arms. The man was Captain Sir Richard Giles, Viscount Ashton, whose feats and pictures frequently featured prominently in the newspapers. They also knew that he was about to be made a Colonel of Marines. His companion was undoubtedly Captain Tobias Bush, a war hero in his own right, who was about to be created a baronet. The attendants had been given instructions to be extra attentive to the disabled captain, but Viscount Ashton had anticipated any needed aid that they might have offered. If they had been surprised by the senior captain's assisting his junior, they were astounded to overhear Viscount Ashton's remark to Captain Bush.

"Steady on, Bush. No need to be terrified. After all, the King is just human, you know, and this is just routine for him. No need to worry. I was scared when I was given the Bath, but it really wasn't bad at all. Anyway, cheer up. It will soon be over."

A flunkey led the two men into the palace and through a series of corridors, stairs, and rooms to a richly decorated drawing room where they were consigned to a fussy factotum, who explained in considerable detail what would occur. He spent a lot of time on the details of how they were to approach and leave the throne, requiring the men to bow deeply three separate times in approaching the monarch and an equal number of times withdrawing. The organizer of the ceremony also went over what they should do when they were in front of the King. Giles would be receiving a parchment scroll appointing him to his honorific position as a Colonel of the Royal Marines and was to give a half bow as before after taking it. In Bush's case, as in the case of others who were to be knighted, he was to kneel, after which the king would tap him on the shoulder with his sword in the time-honored ceremony. After their third bow as they retreated from the King, those who were being honored were to remain in the room standing near the wall until all had been presented to the king. The men would receive their awards in the order determined by their existing precedence. Those for whom this principle did not establish when their turn would come would line up in alphabetical order based on their last names. As a result, Viscount Ashton would be the first to be honored, and Captain Bush would be third. Giles felt that the man was belaboring the obvious, but held his tongue.

As the fussy official was concluding his instructions, Giles spotted Mr. Justice Amery among the men waiting to be honored. He was wearing the voluminous robes of his judicial position. Giles, whose nanny's teaching about precedence had not included judges, had presumed that a judge would precede a courtesy-title viscount, but, apparently, that was not the case. Would Mr. Amery be going second because he was a judge or because his name started with 'A'?

Giles was about to go over to greet Mr. Amery when the court official started getting the men to line up in the designated order in front of a door leading to the next room.

They waited a few moments before the door was opened from the other side, and Giles was motioned forward. The king was sitting on his throne, with several attendants on either side of the dais. Further back, there were groups of well-dressed men, probably important members of the government or court functionaries.

Giles had been through this ceremony before and performed his three bows as he advanced without any missteps. The King rose from his throne and presented Giles with a scroll that an attendant had slipped into the royal hand. "Captain Sir Richard Giles, Viscount Ashton, we hereby appoint you a Colonel of the Royal Marines," he announced loudly. In a much softer tone, he added, "It's the very least we could do. Your service has been invaluable."

Giles made the first of his three bows to indicate he was retreating and backed away, smoothly executing the other two as he went. He was relieved when he reached the door. Walking in reverse while wearing a sword could be tricky, he knew, especially for someone who hardly ever wore one. Even in battle, Giles did not usually wear his sword, having discovered that, as a weapon, a cutlass did a much better job in a boarding* melee than a sword. His servant had never been amused by having to be on hand in a battle with the sword in case things went the wrong way for his ship so that Giles could hand it over in defeat.

When Giles passed through the entrance, he was hustled away to another door where he could slip into the room where the levee was being held. Mr. Amery was just completing his third bow to the King when Giles again could see the proceedings.

"Mr. Justice Titus Amery, by this letter patent, we make you the holder of a baronetage," the monarch intoned. "Kneel, Mr. Amery."

King George then drew his sword and tapped the kneeling judge on the shoulder. "Rise, Sir Titus," he ordered.

Mr. Amery, now Sir Titus Amery, stood up, bowed, and started to walk backwards. It was not something he had practiced, nor had he noted that the carpet had a line leading from the throne to the doorway. By the halfway point, more or less, where he bowed again, the path he was taking, if continued, would have him crash into the wall rather than going through the door.

The factotum in charge of the orderly presentation of those being given awards at the levee whispered loudly, "Over here, Sir Titus." He had to repeat himself quite loudly since the newly honored judge had yet to realize that this was now how he would be called. The new baronet altered his track enough so that his third bow took place in line between the King and the doorway.

Captain Bush was next. Giles had offered to accompany his friend, but Bush would have none of it. He was fiercely independent and only made the most necessary accommodations for his disabilities. He stumped his way towards the King, making quite elegant bows along the way. He even succeeded in kneeling at the appropriate moment, although one hand was holding his parchment scroll, and he had only the hook on his other arm to make sure he did not trip over his sword. His first bow in retreat went without a hitch, and he had no difficulty in keeping to the line to the door even while stumping along backward. However, disaster threatened when it was time for the second bow. With his nervousness and the unbalancing effects of his sword, he was in danger of losing his balance. Giles had been afraid this would happen and had made his way to be as close to his friend at that point as was possible. He stepped forward and steadied the other captain, and then the two of them proceeded towards the door with Giles's arm on Bush's elbow to steady him. The third bow was a joint one, and then they were no longer facing the King.

Giles and Bush made their way back to the levee room by the other door in time to see the knighting of the next baronet. He was a corpulent man who looked uncomfortable wearing a sword. He almost fell over when he knelt to receive his honor, forgot to make the first bow afterward, and then got tangled in his sword when straightening up from the second bow. He performed a little dance as he tried to maintain his balance. He then turned and almost ran from the room.

Sir Titus Amery joined Giles and Bush. It seemed to be a feature of a levee that the various groups of men were conversing in low voices, paying little attention to what the king was doing. Sir Titus greeted his two acquaintances with another bow and said, "Congratulations, Viscount Ashton, Sir Toby."

"And congratulations to you, Sir Titus. Do you know, I had never heard your Christian name before today," replied Giles. "I still do prefer to be addressed as 'Captain,' and just 'Giles' by friends. I still think of 'Ashton' as the name of my disreputable brother."

"I'm afraid that you will have to get used to it at Court," replied the newly named Sir Titus. "And you, Sir Tobias. Do you also want to be called 'Captain Bush'?"

"I don't know. I have never liked 'Tobias,' but 'Sir Toby' has a nice ring to it. Since it matters to my fiancée, I think I would prefer 'Sir Toby' to 'Captain Bush' at least when I am on shore."

"So be it, Sir Toby. You will be the second most famous 'Sir Toby' who has ever been at court."

"Second most?" queried the newly-minted Sir Toby.

"I suspect that Sir Titus is referring to Sir Toby Belch even though you have quite the opposite sort of personality," laughed Giles.

"I hadn't thought of that," said Bush, with a blush. "I know why you were honored, Sir Titus, but what about these other men? Are they keeping up the more traditional way of becoming a baronet?"

"What are you referring to?" asked Sir Titus.

"The rank of Baronet was revived under the Stuart kings as a way to raise money. The recipients paid very hefty sums of money to obtain the title."

"I didn't know that, but you are quite right, Sir Toby. Except for you and I, the people being knighted today are all wealthy men of business who have contributed financially either to the Government coffers or, in most cases, to Government members. Of course, they are men of some merit in their own fields. For example, the man who just made such a charade of retreating from the King is a wealthy mill-owner from somewhere in Lancashire."

The last of the baronets had been honored. The King descended from the dais to mingle with the men attending the ceremony. Giles noticed that the monarch was waylaid by several people, one of whom was Lord Gordonston, the First Lord of the Admiralty, but King George broke away from each of them after only a minimal greeting and came towards Giles's little group.

"Captain Giles – I have been told how you prefer to be addressed when in uniform, Viscount Ashton – it is a pleasure to honor our military heroes. Your exploits in Ireland were remarkable. You certainly have been doing down the French in your recent voyages. I can't think how much of a black eye it must have been to Napoleon to lose a regiment of soldiers and two ships-of-the-line to you. And you did that after you rescued a whole group of captured sailors from his own troops. Maybe we should have done better than making you a Colonel of Marines, but you have no idea how strong the dislike for anyone connected with the Earl of Camshire is. I suppose that naval politics must have had something to do with it.

Sir Tobias, your service has been more than exemplary, most exemplary. And I am astonished that you did not rest on your laurels after your last trip, but instead, I am told, you took a big hand in our efforts against those horrid smugglers. Well done!"

Bush was already red in the face and stammered a few words about how much he appreciated being honored. He looked as if he would rather face a French broadside than converse with his sovereign. Luckily, King George was used to such reactions from people he met for the first time at one of his levees and turned to Mr. Amery, as Giles still thought of the third member of their group.

"Sir Titus. You also have richly earned your title. I presume that you will continue your judicial duties."

"Of course, Sire, I will continue to devote my energies to the bench unless your Government has other pressing needs for my service."

"Yes, I know how many in the Government do value your efforts. Splendid work, Sir Titus, splendid!"

The King subtly turned his shoulders so that it was clear he wanted to converse with Giles. "Lord Gordonston mentioned to me that you take a keen interest in agricultural progress, Captain Giles. I want your opinion on a problem that my steward has told me exists at Windsor. Has to do with a marshy area that he thinks could be productive."

The King was sometimes referred to as "Farmer George," so Giles was not entirely startled by his statement. What did surprise him was that the monarch knew about his interest in farming and especially his fascination with drainage.

"I'll offer any help I can, sire, but the real expert in our family is my wife, Lady Ashton. In fact, when I first met her, she provided me with a lot of information on the subject. She will be presented to you later in the day at your audience."

"Good! However, I am not sure that I will have time to talk with Lady Ashton properly. I am required to converse with so many politicians, and the men that they claim absolutely must have their feathers smoothed by me. The result is that I rarely have much time to talk uninterrupted with anyone about anything, even matters in which I am truly interested. I am annoying those people a bit right now, and I'll do more of this evening by talking about what interests me. Now the problem is this."

The King proceeded to outline his drainage difficulties to Giles, much to the visible annoyance of the prominent men attending the levee. Giles had no choice but to express his views, though he warned the King that his ideas might be quite inappropriate since he didn't know the area in question. His wife, Lady Ashton, was the real expert, he emphasized again. That warning resulted in an invitation for Lord and Lady Ashton to visit Windsor soon. Giles could hardly refuse the King and was interested in the problem even though he would much have preferred to spend his time at Dipton before next having to go to sea. Would Daphne be thrilled to be invited to Windsor, or would she also have preferred the less exalted time they would spend together at Dipton? Of course, with any luck, the invitation might never be firmed up.

The King wandered off to another group. The newly minted Sir Tobias Bush seemed to be completely overwhelmed by being recognized by the monarch, rather as if HMS *Victory* had suddenly opened fire on his small frigate. Sir Titus, by contrast, was trying to treat the encounter as a matter of no consequence, though he had never met the King before and was stunned to realize that he had already come to His Majesty's attention.

When the King left them, Lord Gordonston then sidled over to the group. "Captain Giles, Captain Bush, congratulations. You have both eminently deserved your awards. Sir Titus, I am sure you have earned your baronetage by exceptional service. I have heard about you from the Prime Minister and the Foreign Secretary, though I confess it is probably just as well that I do not know of the details of what you have accomplished.

"Giles," he continued. "This is not the time to discuss your next assignment, but it will need to be started soon. In my role as First Lord of the Admiralty, I need to see you tomorrow morning at eight o'clock."

With that cryptic remark, Lord Gordonston left to trail after the King. Nobody else at the levee seemed interested in conversing with the three men after the King, and his accompanying toadies had moved away from them. When Giles suggested that they repair to a coffee shop before returning to wherever they would be having dinner before the royal audience later in the day, the other two agreed at once. It was for all of them something of a relief to escape the stilted affair that was a levee, especially since they were in for a very similar experience when they again attended the Court later in the day.

"Sir Titus," Giles opened the conversation when the three friends had received their coffee, "you are a bit of a mystery to me. I know you are a judge, but you strike me as being more a government fixer than a judge."

"I suppose that recently that has been true. I was asked, as you know, to look into the election at Dipton as a matter of urgency since it was about to be stolen from you using a completely fraudulent electors' list. That would never do; the whole system of electing parliament would be at hazard if people could get away with setting up their own schemes for naming members of parliament that did not correspond to the law. I went down and set things to rights and returned to the bench. I, of course, met Lady Ashton and her father, Mr. Moorhouse, on that occasion and formed a close bond with him. After that episode, I simply returned to the bench. However, partly because I had visited Ameschester Assizes as part of my duties, I was drawn into putting down the smuggling activities that Lady Ashton had uncovered in the area. That task rather snow-balled out of control, so I have taken a leave from the bench. Now that business is completed, I will return to the courts as I told the King."

"So, putting the election to rights was your first bit of settling things outside your court?"

"Well, no. There have been several other occasions where the government thought having a judge look into putting things to rights would be advantageous. I like to think that I have made many important contributions, though they have to remain hidden."

"You seem to be very good at it. I am surprised. Quite frankly, I would expect that someone trained as a barrister would have little understanding of the illicit inclinations of the gentry, which seems to have been at the heart of the smuggling."

"Well, I was trained as a barrister, of course, but my route to the bar was a bit unusual."

"Oh?"

"Yes. I am the son of a marquis, and my mother was the governess of his children. Needless to say, they were not married. My father must have had some genuine feelings for my mother, for he didn't just turn her out of doors when she became pregnant, as so often happens. Instead, he got a solicitor in Buckingham, named Amery, to marry my mother and to treat her baby when it was born as if it were his own child. The marquis also, I think, must have provided funds explicitly for my education as well as for inducing Mr. Amery to marry my mother.

"With my mother's skills and my father's money, I received a gentleman's education. I was slated for the bar and, at the appropriate time, went to Grey's Inn to become a barrister. I did well and was successful at it, which is how I came to be a judge. But my most useful education in the law and its quirks came from my stepfather rather than from my formal training.

"As I mentioned, he was a solicitor. He had the usual sort of business, wills, property transfers, and that sort of thing, but he reveled in advising clients about matters of law and especially how to avoid getting afoul of it. He was quite adept at devising schemes for others to follow in evading the law. He always did it in a form that would not come back on him if things went wrong. He was also very good at briefing skilled barristers who were not averse to sailing close to the wind* in representing his shadier clients. I learned a lot from him, which has been invaluable both when I became a barrister myself and especially when I became a judge. I could see through and understand a lot of the tricks that were being played and see where unscrupulous lawyers were trying to pervert the law."

"I guess that all that experience helped you to nip Sir Thomas Dimster's plot to steal the Dipton riding in the bud," remarked Giles.

"Yes, the minute I heard about it, I knew exactly what was going on. I must say, Sir Thomas was very clumsy in executing his scheme, but we frustrated him by Lady Ashton's initiative as by anything I did. When I was trying to determine how the smuggling ring which she discovered operated, thinking of how my father would structure the plot helped me to unravel it, though I wouldn't have had anything like as much success without Lady Ashton's help."

"Will you now rest on your laurels and go back to the bench, Sir Titus," asked Sir Toby.

"That's my immediate plan, but the government will likely call on me again. Of course, I am honored to have been made a baronet, but I won't be happy until I am a marquis, like my real father, though hopefully a more honorable one. I have heard rumblings that there is something rotten in the East India Company. I may be called upon to root it out."

"I wish you well in that, Sir Titus," said Giles, "though I don't understand the desire for titles. I will become Earl of Camshire when my father dies, but I would prefer just to be Captain Sir Richard Giles, titles I have earned. Now, Bush, we must get back to my aunt's house for dinner, and I need to see how Lady Ashton is faring with getting dressed for presentation to the Queen. When I left this morning, she was not happy about the sort of dress that is *de rigeur* for such an event. She was threatening to be too ill to attend, even though she is a perfect vision of health. I suppose that we have to attend, and that applies to you too, Bush. Your fiancée, Lady Penelope de Roi, will never forgive you if you don't appear after all the pressure she has put on her father to get an invitation to the event and come to London for the first time in years."

"You are right about that, Giles, dammit. I would be happy never to be in Court again as long as I live. Will you be there, Mr… Sir Titus."

"These new titles will take a bit of getting used to, won't they, Captain Sir Tobias Bush?" chuckled the new baronet. "Yes, I'll be there. In my case, being seen at court and other haunts of London Society is my best way of making important people remember what a help I can be to them."

They left the coffee shop. One of Giles's footmen had had the task of seeing when his master was ready to depart. The trio had hardly been bowed out of the coffee shop before the conveyance appeared. The two naval captains got in, leaving Sir Titus to find his dinner before attending the royal audience later in the day.

Chapter II

Daphne Giles, for that is how she thought of herself – not as Lady Daphne Giles, Viscountess Ashton, though she was entitled to use that name if she wished – was in a tizzy. She had come to London with her husband expecting to attend some sort of reception, called an audience, at St. James's Palace. It would be held to celebrate her husband's being made a Colonel of Marines and to recognize other men who would be rewarded at the King's levee. The colonelcy didn't strike Daphne as being much of an honor since the position was only a sinecure yielding £200 per annum with no duties attached. She and Giles certainly didn't need the money, and Daphne believed that her husband was entitled to a much more prominent form of recognition.

Unfortunately, she would not be allowed to be present at the levee. That was a serious business, which only men could attend. Daphne's only participation in her husband's honor would come at the audience. There Daphne would be presented to the Queen, the signal that she was now recognized as being among the most important ladies in the realm and that she was a full member of London Society. In the past, she had pooh-poohed Society, but she did recognize that criticism of it would be more appropriate if she were a member who rejected its values rather than as an excluded stranger resentful of not being part of the glittering scene. Daphne was honest enough to know that her attitude might change after participating in the initiation ceremony.

The visit had been made more attractive since, at the same levee, two of her good friends, Captain Tobias Bush and Mr. Justice Amery, were to be made baronets. These rewards were based partly on activities in which she had participated.

Mr. Amery, she was sure, would take becoming a baronet in stride as just another event that came his way when he was not acting as a judge. Captain Bush was a different matter altogether. He was very shy in unfamiliar company, so she welcomed the chance for him to overcome some of his reluctance to take part in ceremonies that he was almost bound to loathe.

The visit to the capital had become even more enticing when, soon after the initial announcement of Giles's need to attend Court, Daphne had received a letter from Lady Struthers, Giles's aunt. The message announced that Daphne and Giles *must* stay at her house in Mayfair when they were in London. Giles was enthusiastic about the idea since Lady Struthers was a great favorite of his. To Daphne's surprise, he immediately wrote to ask whether Captain Bush would be welcome too, though he knew full well that his friend would be.

Lady Struthers's house in Mayfair was spacious and decorated in the best taste. Lady Struthers had been a lady-in-waiting to the Queen earlier in her life while Lord Struthers was the secretary of something or other in the Government. They were close to the Court. Insofar as anyone was willing to admit that there were factions other than Whig and Tory, they were on the King's side rather than the Prince of Wales's one. Nevertheless, they were welcome at events put on by Prinny, as everyone in the know referred to the heir to the throne. What Daphne had not been expecting was that Lady Struthers would turn out to be warm and unpretentious as well as being fully acquainted with the various subtleties of Court etiquette and what was proper everywhere in London Society. That very knowledge was the source of Daphne's pique at the moment.

Daphne had had no time to order a new wardrobe for the visit to London. Luckily, she had recently acquired a summer ball gown in the latest fashion, embellished by some improvements she had suggested herself. That should do for the main event, and she had some other clothes of a stylish nature that should suffice for other gatherings.

Daphne had shown Lady Struthers her wardrobe to check that it was suitable. It was fortunate that she had asked.

"This summer gown is perfect, my dear," declared Lady Struthers. "It will do very well for the Prinny's rout*. Now, Daphne, where is your Court dress?" Lady Struthers had insisted that, in informal situations, she would address Daphne by her Christian name while Daphne should call her "Aunt Gillian."

"My Court dress? I thought that gown would do for the audience."

"Oh, no, Daphne. Court clothes are completely different. At least they are for us women, and the gentlemen would never think of appearing in anything but breeches at Court no matter that they may have adopted trousers to wear the rest of the time. Court dress harkens back to earlier times. Some would say that it is stuck in the past. However, as long as the Queen does not say otherwise, we all have to have proper Court dresses at Court functions."

"Are they so completely different from other clothes?"

"Totally. None of what you have can be adjusted, and I am afraid that we are such different shapes that none of mine could be adapted. Let me think… I cannot get a Court dress made for you in time for the audience. However, Miss Amberly, Lady Amberley's daughter, came out this year and was presented at Court in a lovely gown. She is about your size. Not as good a waist, I would say, even though you are expecting."

Lady Struthers had guessed that Daphne was pregnant within the first ten minutes of their meeting. "I know," she continued, "that Lady Amberly is prepared to sell the gown at a very good price; the Amberlys are quite hard up, and the dress did its job of finding Miss Amberly a fiancé. I think that, with some little changes, it would not be recognized as having been worn earlier at Court, and it can be altered in time. I'll look into it at once, and I'll have my seamstress take your measurements right now."

On the day of the audience, quite a long time before their early dinner, Lady Struthers suggested that it was time to dress. Daphne thought it was a bit early to start getting ready for the next activities, but, of course, she went along with her hostess. That is when she scrutinized her Court dress for the first time. It was indeed very different from anything she had ever worn before. The gown had quite ridiculously full skirts and a very abbreviated top section. How in the world was she supposed to walk or dance in this garment? She was about to discover that the gown presented more challenges than that one.

Daphne's maid Betsy was on hand to help her mistress into the gown, together with the seamstress who was present in case any last-minute adjustments were needed. Getting dressed started normally enough with new, white stockings. That was almost the last normal part of the procedure. The shift to go under the dress had very narrow and widely spaced straps over her shoulders. It did nothing to cover her breasts. It made Daphne think of the harlots she had encountered when dealing with the unpleasant aspects of Giles's inheritance from his half-brother, the previous Viscount Ashton. An ordinary petticoat followed. After that, her garments changed radically from anything she had worn before. Betsy produced a pair of stays*, a beautiful, scarlet garment with widely spaced shoulder straps and a bodice that cupped her breasts but left her nipples exposed. Betsy, rather happily, announced that stays were an essential part of wearing the gown. Yes, they did have to expose Daphne's breasts as if they were being presented on a platter.

Daphne had never worn stays. When she reached the age when young ladies would typically be subjected to the garment, she had objected forcefully to her governess, who declared that Daphne must wear stays from then on. The new, flowing fashions from France were starting to be illustrated in English fashion periodicals, even though these clothes reflected the godless, revolutionary blight that had taken over the French. Daphne thought that those fashions were much more appealing, whatever one might think of the French. She certainly did not agree with her French governess that wearing such garments was to enter into the clutches of Satan.

Even if Daphne wasn't to wear the outrageously loose gowns that her mentor declared were the height of decadence, she was not going to wear stays, whatever her governess thought. It was a standoff, the first one they had ever had of such severity. Neither Daphne nor her governess agreed to back down. In the end, they appealed to Mr. Moorhouse, Daphne's father. Her mother had died some time previously, so he was the final arbiter of any disputes in the household. To Daphne's surprise, he sided with her. The governess resigned in a huff, and Mr. Moorhouse had been persuaded by Daphne that there was no need for another one since he was quite capable of undertaking her education. Any more personal questions which it would be inappropriate for Mr. Moorhouse to answer could always be dealt with by their housekeeper. Now Daphne was faced with real stays, much more severe and constrictive than had been the garment that would have been suitable for introducing young girls to the modes of dressing that were appropriate for ladies of wealth.

Betsy presented the garment to her mistress to slip her arms through the appropriate holes. The lady's maid then went behind Daphne to start lacing the stays in place. She was taking secret joy in this task. Though not as rigid as the ones her mistress would soon be wearing, stays were a part of a maid's uniform. It had never occurred to Daphne or Mrs. Wilson, the housekeeper at Dipton Hall, that they could be dispensed with by the female servants. Betsey wondered if the experience might make Lady Ashton open to the suggestion that the servants at Dipton might be relieved of this part of their uniform.

As Betsy drew the laces tighter and tighter, Daphne was discovering that stays were no laughing matter. They pulled in her waist sharply, but their main effect was to make her upper body rigid and to pull her shoulders back so that her breasts stood out. She had frequently seen sketches of women who must have been wearing such garments, but she had always presumed that the artists were exercising a great deal of artistic license. Now she realized that the pictures had been accurate. She also recalled how not very long ago she had had dealings with the keeper of a house of ill repute whose dress had rather shocked her. Now, it seemed, she was about to be dressed in the same ludicrous way. She had heard that some high-quality harlots frequented the Court, or at least the Prince of Wales coterie, but did all the women dress similarly?

What in the world had she got herself into? If this was the price of being presented at Court, maybe she should decline the privilege. She could claim a sudden severe headache or something similar. Giles would understand, but he would be disappointed, though not very disappointed. It would be she, herself, who would be very dissatisfied. All her life, she had heard of girls being presented at Court as part of a fairy tale. She had presumed that it would never happen to her, but she had dreamt of being presented anyway. Now she would be living the fairy tale. Was she going to refuse because of these stupid stays, which very many women wore as a matter of course? She would see how much worse the costume got before she feigned illness. Quite possibly, there would never be another opportunity for her to be presented. Anyway, if she did have another chance, it would entail the same awful garments.

A set of hoops held together by linen cloth was Daphne's next garment. Betsy laid it out on the floor, and her mistress had to step into it so that the elaborate petticoat could be tied around her waist. The hoops swayed most alarmingly when she moved. Would she have to learn a different way of walking when dressed in them? She had never appreciated the skills that women of the earlier generation must have mastered so that they could be at ease in these costumes. Was it hoping too much that she wouldn't make a fool of herself tonight?

Betsy and the seamstress gathered up the gown and slipped it over Daphne's head. They smoothed it down to fit at the shoulders and then arranged it so that it was draped smoothly over the hooped petticoat. It was a gorgeous gown, despite its ridiculous shape. Daphne would be quite enamored of it were it not for the dress requiring stays. She would be quite happy to wear it that evening just as it was. Unfortunately, the seamstress, egged on by Betsy, declared that it was not tight enough at the waist. Miss Amberley must have had a larger midriff than did Daphne. The gown had to be taken in at the waist. It occurred to Daphne that the easy solution might have been to loosen the stays. However, when she suggested this, the seamstress protested that the gown would not look right without the shape that the tight stays produced. Only a little more time was required for the changes to be finished. Betsy again buttoned up the back, effectively trapping Daphne in the clothing.

Daphne was delighted with her appearance. As a very young lady, she had been intrigued by fashion sketches, and, in those days, gowns similar to the one she was now wearing were the style. She had dreamed of wearing such a dress and being the center of attention at a ball where she would be swept off her feet by a charming prince. Even back then, she had realized that that was not really at all what she wanted. Still, it was a sweet dream, even though it was unrealistic both in the likelihood of any such thing happening or in her genuinely wanting it to occur. Thinking of those daydreams now, Daphne realized that, in a way, they were all coming true. She had been swept off her feet by a charming man, though he was a sea captain and not a prince, and she had married him before the royal ball, not after. However, for the first time, she was becoming excited about appearing in this garment and being presented to the Queen.

Betsey and the seamstress had not yet completed their work. The final part of the costume was a headdress made of long feathers that had been skillfully fastened together so that Daphne could wear them even though they towered above her head. She would now have to keep her head up so that the weight of her headdress would not topple her over, or so Daphne thought ill-temperedly. She was about to insist that she did not need this addition to her costume when Lady Struthers came to warn them that the early dinner would soon be served. She admired Daphne from all angles, cooing about what a stunning sight she was and how elegant was the arrangement of the feathered headdress. It was quite *de rigueur* at Court functions. Daphne, Lady Struthers declared, was bound to outshine everyone else at the audience. Daphne took the compliments with a grain of salt. She had become aware, even in the short time she had been with her, of how generous and enthusiastic her aunt-in-law could be.

That generosity was displayed when Lady Struthers produced a diamond necklace for Daphne to wear.

"It was my mother's," she declared. "I am now much too old to wear it, and it has been going to waste for years. I know that she would want Richard's wife to have it. He was a great favorite of hers."

The necklace was a beautiful piece of jewelry, quite unlike anything that Daphne had ever seen. She hadn't even thought of the need for gems if she was to be presented at Court, and her own collection was minimal for a viscountess. When Lady Struthers fastened it around Daphne's neck, Daphne realized that it called attention to a feature of the dress that had been alarming her. The gown had a very low neckline, and with her breasts forced up by her stays, their rounded tops were on display in a way that was foreign to Daphne's inclinations. Now the necklace highlighted that feature. She had been thinking to ask if there wasn't some kind of kerchief she could wear to prevent the display of flesh, but now that would be impossible. All she could do was to ooh and awe at the magnificent gift that Lady Struthers had bestowed on her. Deep down, however, she was delighted with how well the necklace went with her clear skin.

Giles had never given Daphne any significant items of jewelry. She wondered if seeing how this necklace enhanced her appearance would make him consider such a gift. Then she felt guilty about even having such a thought flit through her mind. She didn't need costly jewels to know that her husband adored her.

Daphne's words of gratitude to Lady Struthers were cut short by Giles bursting through the door. He had just returned from the morning levee and his visit to the coffee shop with his two friends. As usual, he had not thought to find out if his wife was presentable before entering because, in his view, she always was. He was quite taken aback by the spectacle that greeted him but soon recovered enough to announce that Daphne was the most lovely creature he had ever seen. If he would have preferred her in the latest styles, he was wise enough not to say so. Daphne was delighted. He had left so early that morning that she had not fully appreciated how he had dressed for the levee. Now he was here, splendid in his full-dress uniform, with the Star of the Order of the Bath glistening brightly from the left side of his chest. He might not be a prince, but he was undoubtedly the present-day equivalent of a knight in shining armor, and his heart was all hers.

Daphne noticed that Giles's eyes had been drawn to her bosom. Was it because of the necklace or because of the wanton display of the tops of her breasts? She suspected from the way they lingered and the slight flush on his face that it was the latter. If so, he recovered immediately. Maybe there was something to be said for the stupid display!

"You look stunning in that gown, Lady Ashton," he proclaimed. "Is the necklace new?"

Daphne explained how his aunt had given it to her, and his thanks were added to her own. The Baroness's acknowledgment was typically modest and was followed by a suggestion. "You really should have your portrait painted in that outfit, Daphne. With Richard, of course, if you want. It would look splendid and be just the thing to hang in the staircase at Dipton Hall. If you can be here for a few more days, I am sure I can arrange for you to sit for Sir Humphrey. I am a great favorite of his, even though I am myself quite undistinguished."

"We will have to see, Aunt," Giles replied. "I have to see the First Lord of the Admiralty tomorrow, and I don't know how soon I shall have to return to my ship."

"I'll just have a word with Sir Humphrey if he is there tonight," replied Lady Struthers. Her confidence in getting the very fashionable painter to do as she wished suggested to Daphne that Giles's aunt was a much more formidable member of Society than she had realized. Sir Humphrey Dalton was not only the most fashionable painter presently working in London, but he was also one who was at the top of Daphne's list of artists to make portraits of her whole family.

Lady Struthers' casual reference to being acquainted with a leading artist brought home to Daphne how much richer living in London might be in terms of meeting celebrated people than her existence in Dipton. Society at home was limited and genuinely remarkable people few and far between. Maybe she and Giles could visit more often and spend more time in the capital. That hope ignored the fact that he had to be away at sea most of the time while this war continued.

26

Chapter III

The rest of the day and the evening passed in a blur for Daphne. There were so many new experiences that she could only sort them out partially in the days following the audience. She remembered that she could eat little before the event both because of excitement and her dress's tightness. She had no idea what dishes had been served or of the conversation during dinner. Then they were off to the Palace, Giles and Captain Bush and herself in one carriage and Lord and Lady Struthers in another, through the still-crowded streets of London in the late afternoon, summer sunlight.

Daphne could remember almost nothing of the events that must have occurred between leaving Lord Struthers's residence and her presentation to the Queen. Strangely, her clearest memories of the evening only began when she was in a sort of anteroom with Lady Struthers at her side, waiting for the presentation. They were shown through the door and walked to the throne as gracefully as they could before making a low curtsey before the Queen.

Lady Struthers had mentioned that the ceremony would be but a poor cousin of the presentation at which the young ladies who were 'coming out' were presented. That event, she said, was filled with excitement since it involved dozens and dozens of young ladies and their sponsors. The ceremony marked the start of the marriage market in which many aristocratic matches were arranged or confirmed, either through family alliances or, more rarely, through attraction between the young lady and her beau. For the ladies presented at that event, it marked their leaving childhood, though, of course, they remained subservient to their fathers until they were married.

The occasion was different for Daphne, of course. Still, she was excited because it marked the explicit recognition that she truly was a viscountess, soon to be a countess, unquestionably part of the uppermost echelons of society. What a change from being simple Miss Moorhouse, daughter of an unpretentious, though well-off, country gentleman of no notable lineage!

The presentation went without a hitch, despite Daphne's worries about it beforehand. She sailed up the carpet smoothly, like a ship under full sail in quiet waters, the gown hiding any suggestion of her walking as usual. Lady Struthers presented her to the Queen, and Daphne sank into a deep curtsey. She had practiced the ritual several times but without the court dress and flamboyant feathered headdress. She was amazed at how the gown spread out about her as she bent her knees while holding her body straight. Even the ridiculous feathers above her head cooperated. Daphne realized that she must be presenting a lovely picture for the Queen and bystanders. Maybe there was something to be said for this ridiculous costume, after all. Perhaps she should have her portrait painted while wearing it.

Lady Struthers had warned Daphne that Queen Charlotte was likely only to nod in acknowledgment of the presentation and might at most utter a few bland words. Instead, Her Majesty announced in a thick German accent how pleased she was to welcome a lady who had stood up so effectively for herself in difficult situations to aid the rule of law. The Queen must be referring to the brawl in which Daphne had defended herself with a chair-leg during a riot opposing the enforcing of smuggling laws. Lady Struthers had warned her that her exploits were not unknown at Court, but

Daphne had hardly expected the Queen to be aware of them, let alone comment on her activity. Lady Struthers later told her that, while the Queen's notice had flustered Daphne, it had caused far more of a stir amongst the ladies surrounding the throne. Such remarks from the Queen were exceptional.

Daphne succeeded in gliding backwards from the Queen without tripping and with her headdress still pointing upwards without waving as if it were in a gale. Lady Struthers then accompanied her to the main room, where many groups of aristocrats were chatting together. Daphne was introduced to one after another titled ladies. Ladies Struthers had warned Daphne that there would be a few minutes of inconsequential conversation with each one before going on to the next group. However, Giles's fame and Daphne's notoriety, as she regarded the reputation that she had gained, meant that many people wanted to talk to her longer than was usual for a newcomer, so her progress was slow. Finally, the parade of introductions was over, and she could join Giles, where he was standing with Sir Titus and Sir Toby.

Their little group was soon joined by Lord Gordonston. Daphne was not pleased to see him since he usually met with Giles only when he had an assignment for her husband that would take him from Dipton. She also did not like him since she knew that his reputation as a libertine was entirely deserved. The First Lord was displaying that aspect of his character by dwelling most appreciatively on her décolletage.

Lady Ashton," the Baron started the conversation, "It is good to see you in London society at last. I hope that we will see more of you in the future." His leering at her bosom placed a clear double entendre to his otherwise vacuous message – he would enjoy seeing Daphne's bosom even less well covered.

"I am afraid, my Lord," Daphne replied, "that I only come to London when we have pressing business here. That very rarely happens when Captain Giles is at sea. As you well know, that has been the situation almost always recently. With this threatened invasion still in the offing, I expect to be fully engaged at Dipton for a while."

"I am sorry to hear it, my lady. Regrettably, the country does require Captain Giles's services again. In fact, Captain Giles, I hope I can get you to slip away with me from this crowd to meet some men about the next assignment. I think it would be good for you to come with us if you would, Lady Ashton. People are less likely to guess what Captain Giles and I are doing if you disappear at the same time as us. Among other things, you have the reputation of being a most devoted couple who are likely to prefer each other's company alone at times during the course of an evening."

Lord Gordonston led them through a narrow doorway and along a series of empty passages before entering another room. It was clearly the library. Though the King was not noted as a reader or bibliophile, there were well-stocked bookcases against the walls of the room and between the windows. The furnishings were dark brown. In the center of the room was a large globe. Three men rose to greet them.

"Lady Ashton, Captain Giles," said the First Lord, "let me introduce Sir Thomas Gardiner and Mr. Graham Tapply, both from the East India Company, and Sir Edward Burns from one of Lloyd's insurance syndicates. They represent the businesses most interested in the losses of East Indiamen that Captain Giles will be investigating. I have asked Lady Giles to be here because if she is missing along with her husband, no one will suspect that we are meeting somewhat surreptitiously.

"It is news to Captain Giles, which I will make formal tomorrow morning, that part of his next assignment involves going to the West African Coast to help the East India Company. Now, Sir Thomas, I think you would be the best person to explain the problem."

"Thank you, my lord, for arranging this meeting. For some time, Captain Giles, we have been having some of our ships – they are usually referred to as East Indiamen – intercepted by pirates off the coast of Africa, a short distance south of the Canaries. That is beyond where the warships guarding our ships leave us, and convoys are used only on outward-bound voyages. All the vessels in question have been homeward bound, so they would not be accompanied by warships anyway. We cannot even get the captains to sail together from Cape Town because of the desire to be the first to land a new cargo.

"The pirates operate in a pack of several ships. They use a cross between a lateen-rigged ship and a galley so that they can maneuver as galleys. They mount a single cannon, roughly a nine-pounder, we believe. The pirates attack from the bow and the stern, with several ships in a coordinated attack. While our East Indiamen are armed and indeed can usually see off square-rigged pirate ships and even enemy frigates, they are very vulnerable to the craft used by these people. The predator ships can stand off where our guns cannot reach them and pummel our ships into submission. They can also defeat us by boarding in a swarm of their ships. Usually, our ships have surrendered before much damage could be done, partly because of worry about the safety of passengers, partly because defiance seemed hopeless. It helps, of course, that the ships are insured through Lloyd's. Indeed, for some time, there has been a well-established pattern that we could live without requiring more extreme assistance.

Recently that has changed. Possibly Sir Edward Burns can explain what has happened better than I can."

"Well," said the member of an insurance syndicate in a broad Scottish accent. Giles wondered idly why a disproportionate number of men of learning and business were Scots.

"There have been precisely two of these incidents a year, oddly enough. The pirates would capture a ship and take her into the port of Kamlakesh. The Bey of Kamlakesh would inform our agent in Marrakesh of what had happened, demanding a ransom for the release of the ship and its passengers and crew. When the funds had been transmitted to the Bey's agent, he would let the ship and its people go. Their captives had not been mistreated. Indeed, some of the passengers seemed to have enjoyed their stay in the town. From the point of view of our syndicates, the ransom was a predictable cost of the East India trade, so we charged for it in our insurance premiums. The East India Company still made a very healthy profit, even on the vessels for which a ransom was paid, which helped keep our premiums down."

"So, has something changed that requires the Navy to intervene in this business?" asked Giles.

"Yes," Sir Thomas Gardiner replied. "Two things. First, some very prominent people were on one of the captured vessels, and they very much objected to their enforced stay at Kamlakesh. They are people with enough influence and persistence that the government has been moved to look into the matter. Much more serious, and the reason this is now a priority for the government, as I understand it, is that the nature of the piracy, or at least of their treatment of their spoils, has changed radically in the last year."

"Oh, how?"

"For a while, we had thought that no vessels had been taken this year, though a couple has gone missing between Cape Town and the Canaries. It was puzzling, for no storms had been reported at the right times to account for their disappearance. Then, surprisingly, one of the missing ships, *The Star of Madras*, showed up under a different name in a little-known Portuguese port. It was listed as being for sale by a very shady agent in Lisbon. On board* was only a small Portuguese harbor watch hired to look after the ship, and all the agent in Lisbon claimed to know about the vessel came from correspondence with another agent in Tangier. At the urging of the representative of Lloyd's, the money was paid, and the ship was recovered."

"I should explain why our man took that action," Sir Edward interrupted. "The amount was about half of the sum for which we had insured *The Star of Madras* itself. He thought, quite correctly, that if this was to be the new version of piracy, we should induce the pirates to restore our ship while at the same time taking steps to prevent its reoccurring. We do not know if the second missing ship, the *Gloriana* met the same fate as *the Star of Madras*.

"Finding the ship told us nothing about the people who had been on board the *Star of Madras*." resumed Sir Thomas. "However, shortly after we acquired the ship, the Company received word from the British Consul in Casablanca that at least some of the people were in Kamlakesh. He supplied a list of the names and the amounts that were being demanded to release them. These demands were on an individual basis, the Consul stating that the people who had drawn up the list were quite willing, if the Company did not wish to rescue any or all of the captives, that their families or they could pay the money themselves to secure their release. The Consul had determined that the people were being held captive in Kamlakesh, but the Sultan declined to take the prisoners from their captors and restore their freedom. He would be willing to ensure that the captives would be released when the money was paid in gold. Otherwise, the individuals would be sold into slavery or be executed by the Bey of Kamlakesh. The Sultan, however, would guarantee that the captives would indeed be released when the money was produced.

"The Directors of the Company, I am glad to say, decided that they would pay the ransom demands this time, but they would convey to the pirates through their agents that they would not do so again. I am skeptical that this will do much good in solving the problem in the future. That is why we have come urgently to the government for help."

"Excuse me," Daphne interrupted. "What happened to the ordinary seamen?"

"Oh, they have been sold into slavery, I imagine," said Sir Thomas, airily. "They were not mentioned in the list. They were mostly lascars," he added contemptuously. "The same was true of servants, which is more distressing. While many of those were also Hindus, some English ladies-maids in the group were not included in the list to be ransomed. I might mention that only the British and European seamen and servants were returned."

"That is shocking!" said Daphne. "About all of them, not just the English women."

"Well, yes, I suppose it is," said Sir Thomas, though he clearly thought that it was a matter of no concern. "Capturing important people for ransom, however, is beyond the pale. I trust, Lord Gordonston, that the government will take action for us."

"Yes, that is where Viscount Ashton comes in," said the First Lord. "Your orders, Captain Giles, after you have dealt with another matter which we will discuss tomorrow, are to go to Kamlakesh and find out what you can about the pirates. With any luck, you will be able to sink a few of the pirate craft. I doubt that you can stop the piracy. Instead, what is needed is a report on the situation so that we can send the appropriate resources to stop it. Of course, with the present threats to us from Napoleon, we cannot spare a sufficiently large fleet to deal with the Sultan of Casablanca properly or even with the tin-pot Bey of Kamlakesh. We can only hope that your presence and refusal to pay ransom may scare them off or get them to return to the previous arrangement."

"Aren't you afraid that the pirates will be able to use their agility to avoid Captain Giles's guns and treat him in the same way they use on our ships?" asked Sir Thomas.

"That is where we are lucky to have Captain Giles. His ship, *Glaucus*, uniquely among our frigates, has powerful bow and stern chasers. They are against Admiralty rules and regulations, but we turn a blind eye to them because he has been remarkably successful in using them. As a result, I believe that Captain Giles will be quite capable of dealing with any pirate ships that try to attack him."

"It is possible that Captain Giles will find that the pirates have another of our ships when he gets to Kamlakesh. What is he to do about it?" asked Sir Edward Burns.

"He will have to use his initiative since we know very little about Kamlakesh, not even its size or fortifications. If he thinks it is worthwhile and if he can do it without danger to *Glaucus* or himself, he can find out what will be required for the Company to recover the ship."

"That's not very satisfactory."

"It's the best I can do, and, even then, I am hesitant to encourage any direct contact with the pirates of the Bey."

"Is there an English Consul in Kamlakesh?" Giles asked.

"No, there isn't. The nearest one would be in Casablanca." Lord Gordonston replied.

"I suppose that we are finished now?"

"Yes. I will have to see you tomorrow, Captain Giles, to give you the rest of your orders."

"Very good, My Lord."

Giles and Daphne said goodbye to the men in the room and made their way back to where the crowds were. Though the gathering had not been touted as a ball, there seemed to be dancing, for they could hear the orchestra playing before they found the ballroom. Giles immediately asked Daphne to take to the dance floor. Her annoyance at Lord Gordonston's disrupting the festivities faded away as her fairy-tale evening continued with Giles, Bush, and some other men asking her to engage in her favorite social activity. Giles claimed her on many separate occasions.

Lord and Lady Struthers left long before Daphne and Giles were ready to depart and had taken Captain Bush with them. Daphne wished that the magical evening would never end, but, eventually, they called for their carriage and arrived back at the house in Mayfair to find the public areas empty except for a footman who had been ordered to lock up after they came in.

Betsey was dozing in Daphne's dressing room and was shocked when her mistress dismissed her because Captain Giles would help his wife to undress. The maid was sure that her master would not know what to do, entirely forgetting that the buttons on a lady's dress were no obstacle to a man who had practiced in the dark by undoing knots that had jammed. Giles did make some rather crude remarks about tearing the gown from her so that he could ravish her, which Daphne found quite charming, and about how others had only been given a glimpse of one of her attractions while he would enjoy the full package, a remark that Daphne interpreted as referring to her revealing bodice. Although she had been offended by Lord Gordonston's lewd comments, she was more than content to let Giles carry out his wicked intentions. In fact, in the morning, Betsey found that the gown, stays, and other garments had been neatly folded. Somehow her mistress seemed to have forgotten to wear her nightdress.

Chapter IV

The Ashton carriage swept into the Admiralty courtyard at ten minutes to eight exactly. Based on his previous visits to the center of Britain's naval might, Giles had calculated that ten minutes were required to get from the courtyard to the First Lord of the Admiralty's room. His arrival was designed so that he would not have to wait, nor would Lord Gordonston. His careful plan was upended when he was ushered into the notorious waiting room. Despite the early hour, it was already stuffed with men with early appointments or others who had no allotted time to see one of the Admiralty officials. These poor men were the ones Giles had hoped to miss. They were captains and lieutenants who had come to see if, somehow, their presence could inspire the Admiralty to assign them to a ship so that they would no longer have to suffer the boredom of half-pay and penury.

Only two chairs in the room were unoccupied when Giles entered. They were on either side of two older men, each one dressed in the uniform of a rear admiral. Giles was thankful that the Admiralty was almost the only place in London where naval officers were not expected to wear civilian dress, for, in this instance, the uniforms told him that he was about to sit next to two senior officers. He would have to guard his tongue if anyone else in the room raised any of the common complaints about senior officers.

Giles did not recognize either of the admirals but rapidly found out who they were when one turned to the other and said, "We are likely to have a rather long wait, Throgmorton, when even the hero of the hour, Giles, is kept cooling his heels here."

"That's unfair, Geoffreys, decidedly unfair. Lord Gordonston has always been rather capricious about the order in which he sees people, and, in our cases, he may be arbitrarily demonstrating yet again that he is in charge."

The Admirals were Sir Thomas Throgmorton and Andrew Geoffreys. Both had long careers as naval Captains who had been in command of ships of the line when the Peace of Amiens had unwisely led to cuts in the strength of the Royal Navy. Their promotion to flag rank had been reported in a recent Gazette, but with no indication of their being given any assignments. Both men had solid reputations for ship handling and maintenance but had had little if any, battle experience since the American War when they had been in smaller vessels. Giles had presumed that they were among the many yellow admirals*, men who had been promoted but would remain on half-pay while someone junior to them was given the next available admiral's command,

He was startled when Admiral Throgmorton deigned to recognize him. "You are Captain Giles, are you not, sir? I have been following your exploits with a keen eye. Very good work, Captain Giles! Splendid!"

"Thank you, sir. I have been lucky in the chances that have come my way."

"Luck? Luck?" Admiral Geoffreys intervened. "It's not luck when you take the initiative to destroy a French bastion and rescue a lot of our seamen! It's not luck when, instead of turning tail in the face of a far superior ship, you instead blow her to Kingdom Come! Especially when you had to escape the clutches of that fool Casterton before you could exploit the information you had gained. Well done! I would say, well done!"

"I agree, Captain Giles," added Admiral Throgmorton. "Frankly, I have envied you. I haven't even had an independent command since my first one in a schooner in the West Indies. Tied to one fleet after another when there was war, and even in peace whenever I was lucky enough to have a ship. First, an errand boy in a brig* and then a frigate for some admiral in peace and later in a 64 as part of a line that never formed. The same in the last war. Even missed all the fleet actions by being assigned to the wrong fleet."

"Let's hope you are given a better command now, sir," Giles said diplomatically.

"Not likely. Even if I get one, it will undoubtedly be subservient to some other admiral waiting for a chance to form a line of battle. I missed out on all the big battles in the last version of this war."

"I was at the Glorious First of June," interjected Sir Thomas, "but only just. I was rejoining the fleet after being sent away on convoy duty. The battle then was almost over. What a shambles that fight was, though somehow I did get knighted for my tiny participation in it. Largely because I seemed more competent than most of the captains – and maybe I was. I also missed the mutinies, being in Jamaica, and did nothing useful for the rest of that war. Now, tell me about your Irish adventure."

Giles tried to keep the account to the minimum, but neither admiral would let him. All around the room, others were listening and whispering to each other when one or another failed to catch crucial words. He finished his account with his return to Portsmouth and his relief at not having to worry anymore about taking too many captured ships across the open ocean.

"Good God, man," Sir Thomas broke in, "are you telling me that your group of three warships and two transports got all the way up the Channel without being challenged?"

"I am afraid so, sir. Admiral Carnarvon mentioned that his part of the Channel Fleet was only at anchor to get supplies."

"I expect that he was no help to you at all, what?"

"Admiral Jerrycot, the port admiral, was very helpful," Giles replied diplomatically

"Good man, Jerrycot!" interjected Admiral Geoffreys. "Knew him in the Mediterranean in '93. Pity he doesn't know anyone with real influence. Then he would be afloat, maybe, instead of those men you ran into, Captain Giles."

"That's true of all of us here, I am afraid, Geoffreys," stated Sir Thomas.

Giles was spared the need to comment on this remark by the arrival of a messenger who summoned him to see the First Lord. He was brought into the Board Room of the Admiralty, where he met Lord Gordonston and another man whom he did not recognize.

"Ah, Giles. Here you are. I gather that you two men have not met before. Sir Metcalf Hatcherly, may I present Captain Sir Richard Giles, Viscount Ashton. Sir Metcalf, as you know, Giles, is the First Naval Lord. The only seaman among the top officials at the Admiralty, though in recent years he has been navigating the dangerous waters of the House of Commons rather than the oceans."

"Like everyone else, Captain Giles, I have been following your career with great interest," Sir Metcalf said. "Now we have some more very important matters for you, I am afraid," he continued without a break, relieving Giles from having to stumble around the fact that he had never heard anything at all, neither good nor bad, about this particular First Naval Lord.

"First, however, Giles, we have some news for you, and we seek your advice,' Lord Gordonston broke in. "I have to tell you that this is my last day as First Lord, and Sir Metcalf will be taking over. The Prime Minister has asked me to step aside while this nonsense about impeaching me is being debated. Utter poppycock, especially as the difficulty comes from the Naval Board, not the Admiralty, but there you have it."

"I am sorry to hear it, my Lord," Giles said. "I am surprised. Everything I have seen about the Admiralty has filled me with admiration."

"You are too generous. What we want from you, to begin with, is your opinion on a couple of admirals whom we are thinking of replacing. I know that it would usually be considered outrageous for a junior officer to comment on a superior one, but our needs are great."

"Sir?" was all Giles could think to say to fill in the pause.

"Sir Metcalf read your reports on your last voyage, Captain Giles," The First Lord started the serious part of the conversation. "He spotted something about the way you referred to two of the admirals you encountered that raised some concerns, or rather reinforced some concerns, that we have had about them."

"Sir?" Giles had thought that he had been remarkably restrained in mentioning his encounters with admirals during what turned out to be his Irish adventure.

"Yes. We'll take Admiral Carnarvon first. I gather that he was not very helpful."

"Not really, sir, no. The main difficulty was that he did not immediately dispatch forces to help me when Captain Bolton reached him with news of the French expedition to

Ireland. Captain Bolton finally felt that he should come on his own to help. His presence was invaluable in getting the prizes to Portsmouth, but he had to leave Portsmouth alone and on his own initiative when Admiral Carnarvon saw no need for haste in following up the news of French involvement in Ireland."

"And when you arrived in Spithead? Was he helpful in dealing with your captures?"

"No, sir. Admiral Jerrycot took the initiative in dealing with the French prisoners."

"As I thought. I told you, Hatcherly. Carnarvon's taking credit for any of Giles's accomplishments was completely bogus. He likes to sit around doing nothing while waiting for someone to do something notable for which he can claim the credit. He's got away with it in the past."

"I am surprised, Gordonston. I am still hesitant about relieving him. He has an immense amount of influence."

"He does, but it will be considerably less with the changes in the Government. He should go.

"Now, Giles, you also encountered Admiral Casterton on your last trip. I sensed a lack of respect in your report when you mentioned him. Why was that?"

Giles was too lacking in guile to deny the allegation, even though criticizing senior officers was a good route to losing his command. Of course, he might well prefer to be put on half-pay since then he would be free to enjoy his life at Dipton.

"I had the sense, my Lord, that he was primarily interested in running his command to obtain the greatest amount of prize money rather than to harass the French most effectively."

"I've felt that for some time, Gordonston," said Sir Metcalf broke in. "But do we dare relieve two admirals of their commands at the same time? That will be two sets of influential men whose noses will be out of joint."

"True. At present, however, the best defense of the realm should for once take precedence. I am sure the Prime Minister will find ways to smooth the ruffled feathers. If you want, I can sign the orders relieving them of their commands. Then the Prime Minister can point out that I have had to step aside."

"I would appreciate that. Do you think that Throgmorton should replace him, Captain Giles?"

"I think that Sir Throgmorton would be better replacing Admiral Casterton, sir. He has seen fleet action, and he had some sensible ideas after participating in the Glorious First of June about how battles should be managed. Geoffreys would be better replacing Carnarvon. He had the reputation of being an efficient and effective captain."

"So be it. Giles, you have not heard any of this, do you understand?"

"Yes, my lord."

"Now, that is not why I asked you to come today. I did call you in early, even though everything is at sixes and sevens, to get your opinion on the admirals. As I told you, this is my last day at the Admiralty, but there are two items I would like to have you undertake. Since I have urged them on Sir Metcalf, who is a bit skeptical about each of them, I will take the responsibility of assigning them to you.

"The first is connected with your Irish venture. The logs that you sent in with Captain Bolton mentioned something that you probably didn't notice when you examined them, but which one of the lieutenants, whom

Admiral Carnarvon set to examining them, spotted. It indicated that the merchant vessels that were on the way to Ireland were loading in the Golfe du Morbihan. I confess that I had never heard of it, but officials here tell me that it is in Britany somewhere between Brest and Nantes. Have you heard of it, Captain Giles?"

"Yes, sir. One of my smuggling connections mentioned it. There is a town there called Vannes, I believe, that he sometimes uses to acquire cargoes, though he also mentioned that the tides and currents make it difficult to get into and out of the Gulf of Morbihan."

"Interesting. I confess that neither I nor Sir Metcalf nor, surprisingly, Newsome here," the First Lord pointed at the Second Secretary of the Admiralty who seemed to be taking notes, "had ever heard of it, but luckily this lieutenant had and realized the significance. It appears that the French once tried to invade England using Vannes, which is at the end of this gulf, as the embarkation point. The Battle of Quiberon Bay, which I had never heard of either, but the others knew about, put paid to that endeavor. Hearing this made me start thinking that what the frogs had tried once, they might try again. Even though you interrupted Boney's attempt to aid the Irish rebels, I thought it might be a good idea to find out what he might be up to in Vannes now.

"I dispatched orders to Admiral Casterton to look into the Gulf of Morbihan, warning him that there might be enemy ships in the area. I presumed that he would detach a ship of the line, or at least a frigate, to look into the situation there. Instead, the fool reported that all his frigates were on duty watching Brest or off harassing enemy shipping, so he sent a brig of war, under some newly promoted master, to investigate. This chap reported that he could not enter the Gulf because of a very severe tidal current. As a result, he was unable to explore further. Besides, his lookouts reported the presence of a French frigate at anchor nearby in Quiberon Bay, so he had not been able to explore more extensively. That fool, Casterton, thought that getting this report discharged my order and did not even send a stronger ship to investigate the frigate. He claimed that he presumed that the frigate would have been long gone before he could send one to attack it. How that man ever became a Post Captain, let alone an Admiral, I will never know. Usually, privilege does not produce results quite this outrageous. The brig's master will be on half-pay from now on, though I think Admiral Casterton should suffer Admiral Byng's fate*.

"Anyway, Sir Metcalf could order Rear-Admiral Sir Thomas Throgmorton to explore the area properly, but that would take time as the command of that fleet has to be shifted before Sir Thomas could comply. It would also criticize Admiral Casterton needlessly, and he has too much interest for us not to step warily about his dismissal. I want you to take *Glaucus*, sailing again under Admiralty orders, to find out what is going on. You can give your report to Admiral Sir Thomas Throgmorton to forward to us if you find nothing immediately threatening. If something needs a fleet's attention, he can deal with it. After reporting to him, we want you to take on a special assignment that we discussed last night. Sir Metcalf is fully aware of it, though he is not entirely happy about diverting you to investigate East India Company messes. I'll want you to go down to Spithead to start your voyage just as soon as possible because your task at Vannes is urgent."

Giles was ushered out of the room promptly and met Admiral Sir Thomas Throgmorton being escorted to the Board Room. He couldn't help wondering if Admiral Geoffreys would have been sent for first instead of Admiral Sir Thomas Throgmorton if his opinion of the two admirals with whom he had been chatting earlier had been different.

Now, Giles had better stop at Fortnum and Mason's to arrange for cabin supplies that would be suitable for the voyage that Lord Gordonston had mentioned and then return to Struthers House. Daphne would not be pleased to learn that he was going to sea so soon. He wondered how long this business in Africa would take. Would it allow him to return to England before the baby was born? That was unlikely to happen since the baby was expected in a few months.

Chapter V

Daphne had made plans for what to do while Giles was at the Admiralty. She was going to go shopping, especially for some things she knew that Giles would appreciate on his voyage and which he might not have time to get himself. She would go first to Piccadilly to see what new books Hatchard's had that might interest him,

She was just about to leave when she met Lady Struthers in the entranceway.

"My dear, I spoke to Sir Humphrey Dalton yesterday. He will be able to see us at one-thirty. I see you are about to go out."

"Yes, Aunt Gillian. I was hoping to get a few things in Piccadilly."

"May I come with you? And then we might go to a tea shop before proceeding to see Sir Humphrey. We can walk if you wish, rather than take the carriage. It is all within easy walking- distance of us, at least it is if we go to Gunter's tea shop. Were you thinking of going to Hatchard's by any chance?"

"Yes, after I have visited Fortnum and Mason's."

"Oh, good. I want to visit it to get the new novel by Miss Helme, *The Pilgrim of the Cross*."

The two ladies set off with their maids. It was only a short distance before they came to the hustle and bustle of Piccadilly. Daphne stopped at Fortnum and Mason's to order some cabin stores for Giles, asking for items suitable for the tropics. Then she went to Hatchard's, where she bought some serious volumes for Giles and a couple of novels for herself.

She was disappointed that they had no music for pianoforte and violin that she and Giles had not already played.

When they left Hatchard's, Lady Struthers suggested that they proceed to the tea shop via Bond Street. It quite outdid Piccadilly as a place where the *ton** shopped and paraded up and down to see and be seen as much as to spend money. The narrow street was very crowded with hoards of elegantly dressed people, as many men as women, strolling along or looking in the shop windows, which were a feature of the street. Daphne was not happy with being in the crowd. It was impossible to avoid being jostled. The stores were exciting, but the hoards of people stifled much of her interest. The smells at Dipton were also much more appealing.

Then Daphne spotted Blakett's. It was a music shop. Peering through the window, she saw that they had shelves and shelves of music and many instruments for sale. On display was a set of sonatas for violin and piano by Beethoven. Daphne had heard of them and that these works were an advance on any previous compositions. Could she and Giles play them? Daphne went into the shop without even asking Lady Struthers if she wanted to.

They were greeted at the door by an obsequious attendant, who turned out to be very knowledgeable. Yes, Herr Beethoven was a remarkable composer, but some found him a bit difficult. The sonatas about which madam inquired had only just arrived in their shop even though they were dated 1803. The delay had something to do with the wretched war. The sonatas were challenging, but if madam and her partner could navigate Mozart successfully, as she had indicated, they might well find these sonatas rewarding. The pieces were not well known in England. Madam need not worry about others having heard them if she and her partner were to attempt them. Did she really want *two* copies? She was in luck. That was precisely the number they had on hand, and heaven only knew when the next lot would arrive.

As Daphne was about to arrange for her purchase to be delivered to Struthers House, the sound of a violin being tuned came from the back of the shop. Daphne was struck by what a beautiful tone it had. This judgment was confirmed moments later when the unseen violinist launched into a lively jig. He was very accomplished, but Daphne was struck more by the violin's sound than by the player's skill. Giles needed a new violin, and he never seemed to have a chance to buy one. His instrument was the one he had used since his days as a lieutenant. It had had some rough treatment in the various men-of-war in which their owner had traveled, and Giles's instrument did not have the sweetest of tones.

The attendant noted Daphne's interest. "That is Mr. Jacobs, who is a violinist in the Covent Garden Opera House."

"It is more the instrument that struck me than the performer," Daphne stated. "It makes such a lovely sound."

"It does, doesn't it?" the attendant replied. "It is an excellent instrument, made in Cremona in Italy. The best violin we have had in the shop in all the time I have been here. I must warn, Madam, that it is very costly. Does Madam play the violin?"

"No, I am the pianist in our duo. It is my husband, Captain Giles, who is the violinist."

"Indeed, Lady Ashton. I have, of course, heard of Captain Giles, but I was not aware that he is musical."

Daphne was amazed at how quickly the man had picked up on who she must be and so the proper way to address her. "Oh, yes. He plays. Not as well as Mr. Jacobs, of course, but enough that it is a pleasure to hear him and to play with him. He gets quite a good tone out of the violin that he has, even though it is hardly a fine instrument. How much does that one cost?"

"Madam has to know that such a fine instrument, made by one of the world's best violin makers, is expensive. It has been waiting for someone who knows a great violin when he hears it and has the funds to express his appreciation properly."

"And how much is it?"

"Mr. Blakett would not part with it for less than two hundred and sixty guineas."

Daphne was about to accept the price without question since she wanted to give Giles something special, and she was well aware that they could afford the amount. It was less than what she had spent for hosting the Ameschester Hunt Ball when all the costs were tallied up.

Before Daphne could accept the figure suggested, Lady Struthers intervened, "That is outrageous, my man. It is a fine instrument, I agree. Indeed, I have rarely heard better at the many concert venues in London. Nevertheless, it is not worth anything like two hundred guineas. I would say it would be overvalued at twenty guineas. Daphne, I suggest you offer that if you really want it."

"Lady Struthers, I could not accept such a low price. Indeed, I think this is a matter for Mr. Blakett," replied the attendant who had surmised who Lady Struthers must be only from her accompanying Daphne. Daphne later would recall the incident and realized that knowing all the Court gossip was part of the stock-in-trade of Bond Street attendants.

Mr. Blakett was summoned. A stout, elderly man, dressed more like his customers than his shop-attendants, with a slight Germanic accent. In the most polite of terms, he and

Lady Struthers started haggling. Daphne was amused. Bargaining, especially at places where horses were sold, was a fine art. After she and Giles had acquired a horse-breeding farm, she had seen their stable master engaging with very proficient adversaries. Though the tone was more elevated, Mr. Blakett and Lady Struthers were as adept at the game as any horse traders whom she had observed. It took a good quarter of an hour, but, in the end, an agreement was reached. Daphne almost expected the hagglers to spit on their palms before shaking hands on the deal, as they would if they were at a horse auction.

Mr. Blakett personally made sure that the transaction was completed to everyone's satisfaction. Though the sum was not inconsiderable, Daphne was surprised that he was quite content to be told to present his bill to Mr. Edwards while the instrument would be delivered promptly to Struthers House.

Both ladies were well stimulated by buying the violin and adopted a jaunty pace as they made their way to Berkeley Square. Gunter's Tea Shop quite outshone the establishment in Ameschester, in the decor, in the elegance of the customers, and in the marvelous cakes that were presented to enhance the wide selection of different types of tea. What struck Daphne as most remarkable, however, was that the establishment offered a service where coaches could pull up, and steaming cups of tea would be brought to their passengers together with whatever cakes they desired.

All too soon, it seemed to Daphne, Lady Struthers said they must leave if they were to keep their appointment with Sir Humphrey. Off they went to Albermarle Steet, where Sir Humphrey Dalton had his house. They met with him in the drawing-room on the first floor, one whose furnishings were in expensive good taste, which announced that they were in the abode of the most fashionable portrait painter to the aristocracy.

Sir Humphrey would be most pleased to have Lady Aston and Viscount Ashton sit for him. Yes, he could combine them in a single portrait even without them sitting for him at the same time. Could he incorporate some of the features of Dipton Hall in the picture, and would he be interested in visiting Dipton Hall? Not really; that was not his practice. They really would want someone like John Constable, who was beginning to make his name, but Sir Humphrey could not recommend him as a portrait painter. There were far better ones for what Lady Ashton wanted. Possibly she could persuade the newly prominent painter, Michael Findlay, to undertake her commissions. Findlay was a first-class man, though little known as yet. That was one of his pictures on the wall in the corner.

Daphne and Lady Struthers examined the picture, which showed a charming view of a mill stream as a background for a nymph and satyr engaging in suggestive dalliance but portrayed in the very best taste. Daphne was charmed by the way the landscape was presented and by the vitality that the painter had put into his models. Yes, this man might do since Sir Humphrey was not available.

In short order, Daphne and Lady Struthers found themselves in Albermarle Steet again, with an introductory note from Sir Humphrey in Lady Struthers' reticule. The address was in Old Bond Street, so the ladies returned to the site of their morning's triumph. Almost exactly so, for Mr. Findlay's address belonged to the house directly across from Blakett's music store. Access was by a small door at the side of the shop that led to a staircase. The first floor blossomed into less cramped rooms, one of which was a drawing-room into which the slatternly maid, who had opened the door, ushered them, saying that she would let the master know that they were here. Several minutes later, she returned to say that Mr. Findlay would see them in the studio at the top of the house.

The 'studio' turned out to be in the attic with sunlight pouring through grimy windows set in the roof with, like the store-front below, one-foot squares of glass. Scattered about the walls were several paintings, some not yet finished, while three others were on easels ready to be worked on some more. Two of those were covered with paint-smeared sheets.

Mr. Findlay appeared to be in his late twenties. He had unkempt hair and was wearing a smock, which was smeared with a startling number of different colors. A paintbrush in his hand suggested that he had been interrupted as he worked on a picture, probably painting the background of the portrait on the third easel, but she felt that he was posing theatrically as an artist interrupted during the creative process. The picture was of an admiral, supposedly seated before the stern windows of a ship with a view of other vessels in the distance. The admiral's portrait was well executed, especially the face, which gave the impression of a lively and kindly leader taking a moment's rest with a book in his hands. Daphne had no idea about how good was the likeness of the admiral, but it was a picture she would be happy to hang on one of her walls as a study of a seaman. Giles, she knew, would be less favorable. There was no plausible source for the light that illuminated the subject's face, and Daphne knew from her own experience that such a source simply would not exist in a cabin on board a warship.

"Viscountess Aston, Lady Struthers, Sir Humphrey mentions in this note that you might want me to paint some pictures. What did you have in mind?"

Daphne explained what she wanted.

"I see," said the painter rubbing his chin and adding a streak of vermillion to it. "I would, of course, have to visit Dipton. It would be best if I painted the landscape aspects of your portraits there, as well as the country scenes you have in mind. The paintings would also be better if they were designed to hang in particular places in your residence. When did you have in mind for the commissions to be executed?"

"I hadn't considered that matter. I expect to be at Dipton all summer. That might be the best time if you are available. Unfortunately, Captain Giles is likely to be at sea, so when he could sit for you has to be left up in the air." As Daphne said this, she realized that she had decided to have Mr. Findlay make some paintings. Shouldn't she think about it and at least consult Giles? However, if he was opposed, she could cancel any arrangements she made now, and heaven only knew when she would be in London again to see other possible painters.

"That is understandable. Admiral Trunkett there sat for me in this room, but he wanted me to go down to Portsmouth for the background. He is well pleased with the portrait so far, though I confess I am not happy with the impossible way the light falls on him. It is at the heart of the picture, of course, but you would never get that illumination in the cabin of a flagship. It is quite easy to work the subject into a chosen background without him posing in the place shown. I could sketch a man into the picture for you and then have Captain Giles pose when it is convenient. Of course, you will have to think the matter over, but let me see what times I have available in the next few months. What have I done with my appointment book? I may have left it on one of my easels when you were announced. I, of course, covered the painting before you arrived since it is not finished."

Mr. Findlay went to the first covered easel. In trying to feel under the sheet for his book, he somehow pulled the sheet off the painting. It was a portrait of a middle-aged woman of very ample proportions dressed in an elaborate Court dress. Daphne thought that the woman looked vaguely familiar, though she could not quite put a name to the face. Lady Struthers had no such problem.

"I see, Mr. Findlay, that you have been very generous to Lady Simmons. Ten years younger, at least, and smoothing out all those frown lines that I can assure you have been a prominent feature of her countenance these twenty years. I am not sure that I have ever seen her smile."

"My lady, you must know that usually we painters have to embellish our subjects and paint not what we see but what the subject wishes that others could see. That will not be necessary with Lady Ashton, of course. In that case, I shall be hard put to it to catch her full beauty. Lady Simmons was very pleased with this portrait. Sir Maxwell was, too, though he pointed out that I had given his wife a much more amiable countenance than he had ever seen. He did commission a gentleman's portrait of his wife."

"Gentlemen's portrait?" Lady Struthers asked for clarification.

"Yes, my lady, it is a nude portrait of a woman that is hung in a gentleman's bedroom or dressing room. I understand that it tends to make a marriage more – how shall I put it? – passionate when he can study the picture before visiting his wife in a darkened room."

"Well, I never!" Lady Struthers exclaimed. It was not clear to Daphne whether her aunt meant that she had never heard of such paintings or that she had never posed for one herself. "Did Lady Simmons pose for the picture in a state of undress?"

"No, in her case, I substituted a rather voluptuous model for her body. Lady Simmons believes that she has been posing for a picture for her drawing-room, which Sir Maxwell also commissioned. But now, I mustn't keep you. The appointment book must be on this easel."

It was, but in retrieving it, Mr. Findlay revealed a painting of a reclining nude with a most lascivious glint in her eye.

"Good heavens, isn't that Lady Martin? Is that another gentleman's picture?" asked Lady Struthers.

"It is, my lady, but it was not commissioned by Sir Gerald Martin. Indeed, he is not aware that his wife has sat for this picture, and I don't suppose that one would do him much good, being rather ancient and afflicted with gout. No, it is intended for the Hunter's Club. I really shouldn't have let you see it."

"Everyone knows that she has no morals, but to flaunt herself at that den of libertines does surprise me. No, I won't mention it, but I can assure you that Lady Ashton had quite a different sort of portrait in mind to present to Captain Giles, as well as the painting of the pair of them that we have been discussing."

Daphne was a good deal less shocked by the painting of a naked lady than she should have been and did not feel that Mr. Findlay was rendered unsuitable for the pictures that she wanted by the less than proper ones he also painted. With the appointments book found, she rapidly made arrangements for the painter to come to Dipton in two weeks' time when he could better evaluate the possibilities.

They left the artist's studio and returned to Struthers House in time to change for dinner and the Prince of Wales's rout that evening. As they walked along, each engrossed in their own thoughts, Daphne found herself wondering if Giles would like a revealing painting of herself. It would not hang in his bedroom, of course, since he did not have one, but could he keep it in his cabin on *Glaucus*? He certainly was a marvelous lover – not that she had had any other experiences. She really knew very little about men and why they found naked women or even the hint of what lay beneath women's clothes so attractive.

Chapter VI

Struthers House was a large residence in Grovesnor Square, much larger than Lord and Lady Struthers needed. Daphne and Giles had been assigned four rooms for themselves: a bedroom and a dressing room each. When Daphne and Lady Struthers returned, the butler informed them that Giles had gone for a walk until it was time to change. However, Daphne had just reached her dressing room when Giles appeared.

He had news for her about the other purpose of his visit to London. *Glaucus* was to investigate whether the French had further surprises about possible invasions of Ireland and then go on an assignment arising from piracy problems involving the East India Company's ships.

Giles was more eager to hear about Daphne's day than to speculate on what was in store for himself. She happily told him how she had gone shopping with Lady Struthers in Piccadilly and Bond Street. When she commented on the fashionable crowds and the wonderful shops, especially in Bond Street, Giles interrupted her.

"I know some of what you did."

"Oh?" Daphne asked, not wishing to tell Giles about her purchases until she had his full attention.

"I went to Fortnum and Mason's. They told me that you had already ordered my cabin supplies. Thank you very much. It was only because I had time on my hands that I thought to go there. I might well have been kept longer at the Admiralty so that I would not have had a chance to visit them. Without your thoughtfulness, I would have to do with whatever was available in Portsmouth, where the chandlers are better known for their prices than for the quality of their offerings. At the shop, the attendant mentioned that you had specified things suitable for a warm climate in summer. That reminded me that I would need hot weather clothes for this voyage, so I went and ordered some from my tailor. He is in Bond Street. I ordered a few things, and they will be ready and sent to Portsmouth as quickly as possible. The tailor swore that my purchases would reach me before I sailed. As I was leaving my tailor's shop, I noticed that there was a music store nearby. A place called Blakett's. They sell instruments and music scores. You know that I have had my violin ever since I was a midshipman, and it wasn't a particularly good one then. So I went into the shop and ended up being very disappointed.

"I first asked about music, hoping to find something new for you and me to try. The attendant showed me various works which they had on hand. We already have some of them, and there were many which I didn't want because they were too easy or trivial. There was nothing I wanted. The shop clerk mentioned that he had just sold the last of a set of sonatas by Herr Beethoven to a very knowledgeable woman, who took their last two copies. Of course, he could not divulge her name.

"I don't know why, but from the attendant's description of the pieces, I had set my mind on getting those sonatas. Having got used to the works of Mozart and Haydn that we have been working on and hearing that Herr Beethoven's sonatas could be regarded as the next step in writing for our instruments, nothing else that this store had on hand seemed worthwhile.

After this disappointment, I asked about violins. I learned that they had had an exceptional one that had also just been sold. What they had at present probably wouldn't satisfy someone who played the sort of music that I had mentioned at a satisfactory level. I might have said that many people say that you and I are pretty good at playing together and that we would sound better if my violin were of better quality."

"Pretty good? Everyone says our performances were outstanding."

"Yes, but what else could they say when we were playing in our own drawing-room? Or were guests in theirs. Anyway, after that lead-up, I wasn't pleased with a couple of violins that I tried, even though they were quite a bit better than the fiddle I have now. Of course, I thought it might be me, but a professional violinist there said the problems were the violins. I had been getting as sweet a tone out of them as they could produce. He told me that Blakett's had had an exceptionally fine instrument that he couldn't afford. A lady had bought it just that morning, even though she didn't play the fiddle herself. This musician was very annoyed with her. If she hadn't stepped in, the violin might not have sold for some time, so possibly Mr. Blakett would be willing to part with it for the sum this chap could put together. He would have to select an inferior instrument for himself since his one had been damaged in the theatre.

"The situation was very frustrating. I suppose I should have settled for what the shop had on hand, but I didn't like the thought of there being much better instruments available. Chopping off my nose to spite my face, I guess. What they did have was a great deal better than the one I have, but I was affected by the frustration of the man who had been unable to acquire the best one. He might have to settle for second best, but why should I? Well, I'll have to pay for that reasoning by using the same old violin on my next voyage. Why are you grinning at me that way, Daphne?"

"Two reasons. First, surely getting to Portsmouth is not so urgent that you can't stop by Blakett's in the morning, or I could get the violin for you. Second, I have already done just that."

"What?"

"Well, how many women do you know who are interested in violins and violin duets with pianos?"

Giles had a very puzzled look on his face until he realized what his wife was getting at.

"Oh, Daphne, it was you!"

"Yes. I don't think the shop has delivered my purchases yet. I do want to hear you play the new fiddle, of course, and we will both have copies of Herr Beethoven's sonatas to work out how the parts go together as well as to work on mastering our own parts of them when we are apart."

"I certainly am eager to try the violin, now that I know that you have bought it for me. Do you think we could skip the Prince of Wales's rout in the hope that the shop will deliver your purchases later today?"

"Don't be silly. You have to go, and I have heard so much about the Prince and his circle that I wouldn't miss the rout for anything. I will probably never have a chance to see that side of life again."

"I don't know about that. I am sure that anytime you want to go, we can get an invitation, or Aunt Gillian can get us one. Of course, we would have to come to London to attend such a function, and I know how you love the city. Anyway, I have something I did succeed in buying in Bond Street, so the trip to Blakett's was not a complete loss."

"Oh?"

"Yes. I noticed a shop called Phillips. Did you see it?"

"Not as I recall. What did they sell?"

"Jewelry. I was intrigued by the shop window because of some notable blue stones in it. Lapis lazuli, the attendant told me when I asked. I had never heard of it. But that is not what truly excited me."

"Oh?" Daphne was starting to think that Giles might have bought her some trinket. They would be the first jewels she had ever received from him.

"Yes. They had a display of sapphire jewelry, which was even better suited to your eyes than the lapis lazuli. So -- well -- so I bought something for you."

Giles pulled a small leather box from his coattails and presented it to Daphne. She opened it to find a necklace, two earrings, and a semi-circular comb that she recognized as a jeweled embellishment to wear in her hair when it was put up. As Giles had indicated, sapphires were the principal stones, but their brilliance was enhanced by the many small diamonds in the settings. In one step, Daphne was going from having hardly any jewelry to having an elaborate display. As luck would have it, for Giles had had no idea of what she would be wearing that evening, her gown would be of just the right color to wear with the sapphires. After staring at the box for a short while, Daphne launched herself at Giles to exuberantly express her surprise and gratitude at receiving the gift. Luckily, he had braced himself at the last minute for his wife's onslaught, for he had previously discovered how Daphne would express enthusiastic joy. She soon, however, shooed him out of the room so that she could have Betsey arrange her hair in a way that would bring out the beauty of the comb while at the same time the comb enhanced her hair.

The Prince of Wales's rout took place in Carlton House, his residence near St. James's Palace. Daphne thought it a much more impressive site for a royal reception than the older palace. The rooms had higher ceilings and were painted in lighter tones, while the scene was more glittering and splendid than the one hosted by the King the previous night. She didn't need telling that, in her new gown and her new necklace, she stood out as one of the brightest ornaments to the event. Although many of the people she had met the previous night were at the Prince's rout, Daphne had the impression that it was, in general, a younger and more lively crowd. The gossip was the same insipid and back-biting talk that had dominated conversations at the King's assembly. Daphne realized that these two experiences would last her for quite a while, even though she liked attending these functions. The only reason for her to want to stay was the hope of dancing later in the evening. Giles did not look at all comfortable.

"What's the problem, Giles?" Daphne asked.

"I am not comfortable with what is happening here."

"What do you mean?"

"It is some of the women. They are just …just …just concubines – courtesans – I don't know the right term. But they are mixing with respectable people."

"How do you know that?"

"Lord Struthers told me so that I wouldn't make a *faux pas* in talking to the ladies here. And some of these … these…people are notorious women whose sketches have shown up in some of the magazines that come into the wardroom* or the gunroom*. The Prince of Wales is with Mrs. Fitzherbert over there, and there are several others who everyone knows are mistresses of men who are not their husbands.

"My uncle pointed out to me several of these relationships that I believe should be outside the pale. See that woman in the dark green gown that you can see through. She is a courtesan, said to have been the mistress of several younger men, including the Marquis of Landendough, who is one of her current lovers. It's both what I know about them and the indecent way that they are dressed that troubles me."

"That's the way things are now, Richard. It's modern times, and we have to accept things that do not appeal to us. Are those diaphanous gowns any worse than the exposure of bosoms that we encountered last night, including mine?"

"I don't know. I suppose that it shouldn't bother me, especially if it doesn't bother the ladies present. I just hope you are not going to dress that way."

"Of course not. There is only one man I want to attract, and that is you. I don't think I need a suggestive gown to get and keep your interest."

Daphne was about to suggest that they slip away when Sir Titus Amery came up to them.

"Lady Aston, Captain Giles, I have something of importance to discuss with you. It is very private, so we have to go into the next room."

Giles responded immediately, saying to Daphne, "Let's go."

Sir Titus led them through a nearby, narrow doorway and then to what must be a card room, though it was not in use as such this evening.

One man was already there, Sir Thomas Gardiner.

"Sir Thomas," said Sir Titus. "I think you should start."

"Yes, well, I have had Mr. Tapley looking into any information we can glean from our records about why the pirates have been able to take a regular number of East

Indiamen. Two a year for the last few years, neither more nor less. It was particularly puzzling since the ships should have been quite far away from land at that point in their voyage. However, judging by how long it took them to reach Kamlakesh after being captured, they were much closer to Africa than they should have been. Mr. Tapley has been going through the logs of the ships that were taken and of their captains and comparing them with voyages that arrived home safely. He wanted to see if there was any hint in these records of what may have been going wrong.

"We started to see a pattern. The captured ships had all recorded that they met with some fishermen from whom they had bought fish a day or so before they encountered the pirates. In itself, buying fish was not remarkable; most vessels that meet fishing boats try to get some fresh fish. The strange thing was that these fishermen were unusually far from shore according to the ship's location, as recorded in the logs. Ships that were not taken had had no contact with fishermen in that area.

"Mr. Tapley discovered another oddity in the log of Captain Murray Simmons. He had commanded one of the ships that the pirates had captured, the last one adhering to the pirates' previous pattern. Captain Simmons is a very experienced seaman who has left the sea following that incident. No one thought much about it at the time, but after he returned to England, he purchased a large property in your part of the country, Lady Ashton. Keeling House, it's called. It came with extensive lands, so it must have cost a pretty penny. Looking into it, we were surprised that he had acquired such riches, especially as he had not seemed to have made very much out of his ventures on earlier trips. He and his wife lived modestly, about how one would expect for one of the Company's captains who was not into speculating rashly. That made me look at his logs more carefully.

"I did find one thing odd. Captain Simmons regularly entered the ship's position after the noon sighting. In several instances in the passage from Cape Town to where the ship was captured, he added that he had adjusted the chronometers. In each instance, he had crossed out the notation, but I could still figure out what he had written. I originally took the phrase to mean that he determined the longitude by reference to the chronometers and realized that entry was redundant in the log.

"Then it occurred to me that Captain Simmons might be indicating that he had changed the chronometers, which would also account for his scratching out the entries. If he were altering the chronometers to make it appear that they were farther to the west than they were, they would adjust their course correspondingly. The upshot would be that the ship would be off course, closer to the coast of Africa than it was supposed to be, while the false reading on the chronometer would indicate nothing was amiss in its longitude. Meeting the fishing boats was a way of confirming to the pirates that his ship was approaching so that they could apprehend it. Changing the ship's recorded position so that pirates could capture them would have been a grave crime, but I had no real evidence of it. I took my suspicions to Sir Titus Amery."

"I'm glad that you did," Sir Titus took up the tale. "I had become suspicious of the East India Company and how it was abetting smuggling through the work I had done establishing the duty-paid alternative to the free trade through Harksmouth. Of course, I had been assisted in the work by Captain Giles and Lady Ashton and several of their friends. I had also realized that records in financial houses are not quite as confidential as one might expect. At least not if one is a government agent. It is amazing how suggestions of government displeasure can loosen tongues and open books. I used such sources to investigate Sir Thomas's suspicions.

"The first thing I did was to examine Captain Simmons's account at Child's Bank. It provided very suggestive material. His wages were paid regularly into the account by the East India Company. In addition, there were a few entries that suggested he had been trading on his own account in his voyages since they came soon after he arrived back in England. There were also a few transfers from India, suggestive of small ventures from England to India. All of these were of a nature and magnitude to be expected. They would not have made him rich.

The very questionable items in the account were some transfers from a bank in Lisbon. It was the same bank that had handled the ransom payments for the ships taken at Kamlakesh. That already made me suspicious. Much more indicative was the fact that soon after the ransom for Captain Simmons's vessel was paid, a transfer came from the same source to his account. The amount was exactly fifteen percent of the payment, less the standard fees charged by the two banks. When I checked other transfers from the Lisbon bank, I found that they all occurred shortly after payment had been made to the same correspondent bank to recover other pirated ships and crews. In each of these cases, the sum amounted to five percent of the money paid to get back the East Indiaman.

"I then looked for accounts at Child's for other captains who commanded East Indiamen, which the pirates had taken. Two of them dealt with Child's. They each had a payment amounting to ten percent of the amount paid. Four other captains banked at Barclay's Bank. They had also received the same sort of payments. I concluded that there must have been a conspiracy to arrange for East India Company's ships to be diverted from their courses so that it would be easy to capture them. Captain Simmons must have been a ring leader and recruited the other captains. Even ten percent of the value of the ship and its cargo would be far more than a captain could earn legitimately.

"Did you have Captain Simmons arrested and tried?" Daphne asked.

"No, Lady Ashton. I have nothing that would stand up in court. Charging him prematurely might mean that he could destroy any evidence that might be in his possession. Then, if these criminals stay mum, they might get away with it."

"So, what are you going to do about it, and why are we here?" demanded Giles.

"I have discovered that Captain Simmons likes to keep his own log or diary, nicely bound with separate ones for different years. If I can get my hands on the ones for the appropriate periods, I am sure that we will have Captain Simmons and his henchmen trapped. But there is the problem of how to do so.

"I have investigated Captain Simmons and the estate that he bought with the proceeds of the crimes he committed. It is quite a large place, and the Captain has a full set of servants. There is a local public house where some of them drink on their afternoon off. Captain Simmons is not a popular or respected master to his staff, and I hoped to persuade them to help me. The trouble is, of course, that if it is known that they are helping me, the servants will lose their positions without a character. Most of them are not very good, anyway – not surprising for a newly minted gentleman who does not know how to win his servants' loyalty. He wasn't very good at endearing himself to his crews when he was a sea captain, either.

"I did find one man, a second footman, who is a cut above the others. Well trained at another house and let go when his master got into debt and had to reduce his staff. Captain Simmons's establishment is a cut below his previous place. He would be willing to help me because he despises his present master. However, he needs a safety net in case Captain Simmons finds out about what he has done. My pointing out to him that he will be dismissed whether he helps me or not, if Captain Simmons falls on hard times, may have persuaded him to assist me, but only if I could find him a place.

"Captain Giles, Lady Ashton, I know that you may not have any positions available, and it would be asking a lot to have you guarantee a place, on a trial basis, for this man if he helps me. I know that I should have talked to you alone, Captain Giles, and I hope you will forgive me presuming that it is Lady Ashton who probably has the last word on such matters."

Before Daphne could protest that Sir Titus was mistaken, Giles laughed. "My wife is much more competent in dealing with all such matters than I am. If you spoke to me alone, I would have asked her anyway."

"Well, Sir Titus," said Daphne, "The first footman at Dipton Manor – my father's house – has recently given notice because he has secured a place as a butler at another estate. So there is an opening for a footman. My father would certainly take my recommendation for filling the position. The footman, of course, would be on a trial basis before we could make it a regular appointment. It must, of course, be understood that my father and I would expect complete loyalty. That is my one reservation. I am skeptical of someone who might be as willing to broadcast our secrets as he seems to be with Captain Simmons's ones – not that we have any serious ones. However, this seems to be a rather unusual situation."

"I think that it is. Providing the position is very good of you, Lady Ashton. I will let you know how the attempt to get information goes and whether I need to take you up on your offer."

"Thank you both. Now we had better slip back to the rout separately. We don't want any wagging tongues. I don't know how deep into the Company this conspiracy may have gone."

Daphne and Giles found their way back to the main rooms. They soon found Lady Struthers.

"There you are, you two," she exclaimed. "It is almost time to go into supper. You really must stop disappearing together that way," she added with a grin. "It is considered bad manners in certain quarters, particularly at Prinny's routs, for a man *not* to abandon his wife if they have been married more than a few weeks."

Daphne was amused. She had noticed that when Lady Struthers was not engaged in introducing people to one another, she was always with Lord Struthers. Lord and Lady Struthers might be welcome at the Prince's functions, but they certainly were not members of Prinny's fast set.

Supper did not last long, and Daphne was glad to leave right after it. She was not used to the late evenings that seemed to be the rule in London Society, and she wanted to discuss the day's events with Giles. It seemed so unfair that he should have to leave again so soon on his next adventure. It was a shame that she couldn't go to sea with him; she was sure that she could sail a ship as well as any of his lieutenants. The baby reminded her with a hearty kick of the other aspects of her life that would prevent her from going to sea, even if she were able to join the navy.

Chapter VII

Glaucus slid effortlessly along the south Breton coast, sufficiently offshore that it would not be evident that her mission involved anything in the immediate vicinity. The light wind was from the southwest, ideal for her course to the southeast. The breeze was just strong enough to make the frigate heel a bit. She was entering a wide passage between the end of the Quiberon Peninsula and an island about nine miles to the south of the mainland. Mr. Brooks, *Glaucus*'s master, had been able to copy a recently captured French chart of the area. The island to their starboard* was called Bel Île de Mer. Two smaller islands lay ahead to starboard, and shoal water was shown close to all three islands, but the chart indicated deep water on the course they were sailing. The master was confident enough in the chart and the reports he had received from other masters that there was no need to have a man in the chains with a lead-line*.

Quiberon Bay would soon open up to larboard* of *Glaucus*. Giles climbed the mainmast and joined the lookout at the crosstree. Most captains, he knew, would have sent a midshipman, or possibly a lieutenant, to supplement the lookout's reports when action might be in the offing. However, he had found that for fully appreciating the tactical possibilities, there was no substitute for seeing for himself. He told the lookout to keep looking all around while Giles pulled out his telescope. He slowly scanned the bay, starting on the left at Quiberon and working his way around to the east.

There was little to see. A few inshore fishing boats were the only maritime activity. At a town at the far end of the Quiberon Peninsula, Giles thought that he could spot some masts in what must be a small harbor, but there was no ship large enough of interest to him. He continued to move the spyglass rightwards, quite unphased by everything seeming to be upside down and backwards. He had learned long ago how to adjust for the distortions of a telescope. Years spent aloft while he was a midshipman, sometimes as a punishment and sometimes to gain information, had made him an expert in handling the instrument. That reflection sent a guilty wince through him. How could he expect his officers to become proficient at various skills if he insisted on doing them himself? Now would be a good time to start to teach one of them.

Giles leaned over to bellow to the deck to send Midshipman Fisher to come aloft with a telescope. Then he turned his attention again to larboard as the far side of the bay came into view. The first thing he noticed was a frigate at anchor on the eastern side of the bay. A small one, a thirty-two, he would guess, one that had already seen a lot of service and was not at all smartly maintained. She was at anchor a cable or so from the shore and very open to the ocean, the offshore islands being too far away to give her any reliable protection from bad weather. The telescope revealed a few men on deck, none of them seeming to be engaged in urgent tasks. A tricolor flag at her masthead confirmed that the frigate was French. She was a complication that would have to be dealt with somehow if he were to complete his mission.

To the north of the French frigate, Giles could make out the entrance to the Gulf of Morbihan on the northeast side of the bay. Several small ships -- fishing boats and little coasters -- were scattered in an arc about the entrance while a few similar craft were coming through the gap between two low headlands. Behind each of the points, he could see churches marking small settlements, likely fishing ports. The chart noted them but did not indicate either their names or any remarkable features. It also stated that the current through the entrance could run nine knots. Giles wondered how accurate the translation from French of the speed had been, not that it mattered. It would be wise only to attempt the passage at slack water. He suspected that he was watching various craft waiting outside the entrance for the tide to turn while the ones in the narrow passage were coming out with the last of the ebb.

Giles followed the unfolding coast with his telescope as Glaucus's progress opened up more of Quiberon Bay. Halfway around, he spotted something that made him pause. A ship-of-the-line was nestled close to the shore where there was a shallow cove. A glance told him that she was no danger to him at present. She was anchored, and even if she tried to pursue him, his frigate was far more maneuvrable and could easily outsail her on this wind.

Giles's gaze kept coming back to the warship even as he concentrated on what other surprises might await him as more and more of the bay was revealed. As he was doing so, Midshipman Fisher settled himself on the crosstrees*. It would be crowded with the lookout there as well, but the seaman moved to sit on the yard, yielding the platform to the officers.

"Mr. Fisher," Giles said, "do you see that ship off the larboard beam."

"Yes, sir."

"Have a really close look at her. Tell me everything you see about her when you have finished."

"Aye, aye, sir."

Giles also trained his telescope on the seventy-four. Since he knew exactly what he was looking for, it did not take him long to complete his survey. He was not surprised that it was taking Mr. Fisher longer to complete in his mind his catalogue of what he was examining, especially as the midshipman knew that his captain was about to grill him on what he was seeing.

Giles took the time until the midshipman was finished to look more closely at the French frigate. She was a thirty-two. Her sails were furled tightly as if she expected not to use them for some time. He could see that she was moored by a single anchor with neither a spring* attached to its line nor a stern anchor to control how the ship lay. She was close enough to the entrance to the Gulf that the current was affecting her so that she was not lying bow to the waves. Instead, she was turned a bit by the current to take the waves on her larboard bow in a corkscrew pattern. It must be more uncomfortable for everyone on board than if she had been bow to the wind. A lot of crew members were on deck, but they were not engaged in any naval tasks. Giles guessed that they had been given a "make and mend" watch, suggesting that the frigate had been at anchor for some time but was ready to set sail at short notice.

"Was this the frigate that had been reported earlier?" Giles wondered. Surely the French had not dallied about whatever they were up to so that word could get to the Admiralty, and *Glaucus* could be sent to investigate. When Lord Gordonston had reported the situation to him, Giles's reaction had been that whatever ships had been sighted in the Gulf of Morbihan would not still be there weeks later. But maybe he was encountering the French equivalent of Admiral Carnarvon. The French might be no more efficient than the British, no matter what Napoleon's reputation might be. Giles would have to do something about that frigate if he were to do anything about what was happening in the Gulf of Morbihan.

"So what have you seen, Mr. Fisher?" Giles asked.

The midshipman rattled off some obvious features. Giles was delighted that he had not just gone by the nominal rating of the ship as a seventy-two but had counted the canon and the carronades* and noted which parts of the armament he had not been able to see and so was guessing. He had not noticed that she appeared to be extremely new. He said that most of her crew were on deck, which brought a rebuke from Giles since Mr. Fisher did not know how large was her crew. All he could say is that a large number of men were on deck, too many for him to count reliably. Were there many officers on deck? Now that Mr. Fisher thought about it, he realized that he could see what appeared to be four lieutenants, but he had not spotted anyone who looked like the captain. How was she anchored? Was the anchor buoyed, which would indicate that she could get underway very quickly? Would Mr. Fisher have used a spring line if he were in charge of that vessel?

Giles was even-handed in praise for things noticed and in rebukes for items missed. Finally, he summed up for the midshipman what he might be able to infer from what he had seen, especially when augmented with the details that he had missed. The ship was very new. They could deduce it from observing that the wood was not weathered and that what they could see of the canvas and rigging was very fresh. The sails were furled tightly but not as evenly as expected from an experienced crew working with familiar material. The officers and petty officers seemed to be frantically trying to get the sailors into the right positions to work effectively. What were the crew members doing? It appeared that they were trying to lower the mizzen topgallant-mast, x they were bending on a new topgallant sail in his mind. Neither task was proceeding smoothly. On deck, they were engaged in basic gun handling, loading, and running out. The gun crews also did not seem to have a good idea of what they were supposed to be doing. Mr. Fisher had observed one man having his foot crushed by the gun carriage as it was being run out.

Giles then asked Mr. Fisher to make conclusions from his observations. The French seventy-two was newly commissioned. She was possibly built in Lorient nearby, but that was relevant only to the belief that she might have little experience at sea. One could guess that she was on a training cruise and was anchored to make it easier to conduct the initial drills. She would not be a significant threat to *Glaucus* if Giles took his ship into another part of Quiberon Bay.

Since the French seventy-two was engaged still in elementary aspects of seamanship, it would not be surprising if her crew had been inadequately drilled in repelling borders or similar actions. Giles could ignore the French battleship because he had been ordered to do other things, but he might not find her much of a challenge to capture if that were not the case. Giles elicited all these conclusions from Mr. Fisher by giving him many hints.

The French frigate was another matter. She might well interfere with any attempt to explore inside the Gulf of Morbihan and to extract any captures from it. But would attacking her warn the French so that it would be impossible to discover what the enemy might be doing in Vannes? For the moment, all he could do was sail by as if it was only idle curiosity that had three people on the crosstrees. Giles turned his telescope on the French Frigate again. The lookout had been joined by an officer who was studying him through a telescope. Giles was wearing an old coat, but it did show that he was the captain of *Glaucus*.

"We had better pretend that I am conducting more extensive instruction on what to look for from the masthead,"

Giles said to Midshipman Fisher. "Let's return our attention to the seventy-four. You start pointing out particular features to me using your arm to make it clear what you are doing, and I'll pretend to be also pointing out things to observe. We don't want the frigate to realize that we have more than a passing interest in her."

Giles looked again at the frigate and waved to the officer who was observing him. Such a cheerful, friendly gesture would not be expected if he intended to attack the ship, which was precisely what he was thinking of doing. He continued the charade with Mr. Fisher for another ten minutes while *Glaucus* kept to her course before the two officers descended to the deck.

"Mr. Brooks, we will continue this course until we are out of sight of Quiberon Bay," Giles ordered. "I'll be below."

In his cabin, Giles started to pace back and forth. He was better at making quick judgments when the situation required them than when having a long time to sort through the alternatives. He had to get to Vannes and see what was going on there. It would be suicidal for him to take *Glaucus* into the Gulf of Morbihan. He hadn't realized how narrow was the entrance and how limited would be the times when it would be feasible to take his frigate through it. *Glaucus*'s cutter would have to do a lot of hard rowing if she were to get to Vannes and back between one or even two slack waters, and much of such a trip would be in full daylight. The situation would be even worse if he used his barge or the jolly-boat. If they could do it at night, they might get away with going to Vannes. In daylight, the distinctive shape of any of his boats would tell the world that the English were there.

Various possibilities were going round and round in Giles's mind, but he was getting no closer to a strategy that did not have a high probability of their being caught. Maybe, he should lose himself in music for a while. Sometimes playing his fiddle seemed to clear his mind. He got out his new violin, tuned it, and started to play a Haydn adaptation that he had always found very calming. He was amazed again at what a difference the beautiful instrument made to his enjoyment of the sounds he was producing. Thank heavens that Daphne had bought it for him. He had wormed the cost out of her. It was high, but it certainly was worth it. He would not have spent that much money on himself, even though he knew as well as she did that they could afford it, and a dozen like it had the fancy struck them.

All this while, there had been calls from the masthead that he had been aware of without paying attention to their contents. There were quite a few small vessels about and some larger ones, but he was not interested in possible prizes on this mission.

One cry did penetrate his consciousness: "The lugger two points off the starboard bow is *The Ruddy Fox*."

The Ruddy Fox was a smuggling vessel that Giles had had dealings with on earlier occasions. He had caught her red-handed, as it were, and was able to turn her captain into a useful source of information and of smuggled goods on which duty would be paid. It was a profitable arrangement for the smuggling captain. Only co-operating with Giles would ensure that it continued. A plan to use the lugger was forming in his mind.

"Close* with *The Ruddy Fox*, Mr. Miller. I want to speak with Captain Creasey," Giles ordered his acting first lieutenant, who happened to be the officer of the watch*. His previous first lieutenant, Mr. Hendricks, had been promoted to commander as a result of *Glaucus*'s past successes. Giles had used his influence at the Admiralty to secure Hendricks a sixth-rate immediately, so that promotion would not leave his former subordinate sitting on the beach at half-pay. Mr. Miller had become his first lieutenant, and Giles had promoted Midshipman Stewart to acting lieutenant. He would do everything in his power not to have another lieutenant appointed since Mr. Stewart had passed his lieutenant's examination but would not receive the rank until he turned nineteen. He was a much better lieutenant than Giles could hope to have appointed by the Admiralty. He had taken Randolf Bush, the fourteen-year-old nephew of Sir Toby Bush, as his new midshipman.

The two ships closed with each other. When they were less than a cable-length apart, *Glaucus* backed her mainsail while *The Ruddy Fox* lowered her sails. She glided up to the side of the frigate where they rafted* together, Mr. Miller making sure that adequate fenders separated the two ships. Captain Creasy stepped across to the frigate and came onto the quarterdeck* in a happy mood.

"Captain Giles. Good to see you again. Your doings in Ireland were all the rage when I was last in Harksmouth. I have brought you a bottle of the best French brandy as a reward."

"Thank you, Captain Creasey. Let's go to my cabin and have a glass."

The two captains went below, and Giles opened the bottle and poured generous glasses of the brandy. While Giles nursed his drink, Captain Creasey showed little restraint as he savored the liquor. Giles poured him a second glass and waited for him to take a gulp before proceeding to business.

"Captain Creasey, I need you to take me to Vannes."

"Whatever for? I am not going there. I already have a good cargo."

Giles explained what his problem was and how *The Ruddy Fox* and Captain Creasey could fix it.

"You want me to go to Vannes just so that you can see if the French are up to something?"

"Not something. It's a question of whether the French are making preparations for invading Ireland."

"And you think that they might be loading troops there?"

"We have heard rumors to that effect, and there is a French frigate right at the entrance to the Gulf, anchored as if she is waiting for something to emerge from it."

"Captain, you will have to get someone else. I cannot go to Vannes when I have a cargo already. What do I tell them? I just wanted to see what your army might be doing here?" Sarcasm dripped from Captain Creasey's mouth before he took another swig of brandy. "Oh. I just heard that you have the best lasses in Britany, much better than the ones in Nantes. I had to come and try them. Is that what I am supposed to tell the frogs when they see that I am already fully laden? Seize one of the other luggers that are around here, Captain Giles. Use that."

"Those ships are all French. The minute we got to Vannes, someone would smell a rat. No. It has to be you. I can transfer your cargo to *Glaucus,* and then we can proceed, or I can still seize you and your boat for smuggling."

"All right, but I'll want my cargo back if we don't get ourselves killed in this crazy venture. I suppose that you will be sending some poor sacrificial midshipman on this crazy voyage."

"No. I'll be taking Lieutenant Marceau with me. He talks French like a native since he is."

"You'll be coming?"

"Of course. Now we had better start to get ready."

Giles wasted no time getting the lugger's cargo transferred to *Glaucus*'s hold. It was, as he had guessed, made up of wine and brandy. Good wine, he noticed. Creasey had picked it up at St. Nazaire. The Loire valley produced some excellent wines, he knew. Giles hoped that Major Stoner or whoever was in charge of distributing cargoes in Harksmouth would set some aside for Dipton Hall.

Mr. Miller was not happy about taking the wine and brandy on board. Like all sailors, *Glaucus*'s crew could not be trusted around alcohol. He was only partially mollified when Giles ordered Mr. Macauley, the lieutenant of marines, to set a watch over the hold.

The cargo transfer was quickly finished. Captain Creasey asserted that there was time for another glass of brandy before they set off because they would have to wait for slack water to enter the Gulf of Morbihan. He had found some ordinary seaman clothes that would fit Giles and Lieutenant Marceau since their uniform coats, though worn, would stand out like a necklace on a whore, nor would clothes of the seamen of the Royal Navy make them look like they fitted on a coastal lugger. They were supposed to look like crew members of an English smuggler; with Captain Creasey's contribution, they did, except that they were too clean-shaven. That would change somewhat by the time they reached Vannes.

Since *The Ruddy Fox* never had more than five crew members, Captain Creasey announced that Giles and Lieutenant Marceau would have to help with handling the lugger while two of the lugger's crew would stay on *Glaucus*. Captain Creasey made sure that those remaining on *Glaucus* had their exemptions* with them.

It was clear that the lugger's captain enjoyed the prospect of ordering about a post-captain. If he thought that he would be humiliating Giles, he was mistaken. Giles was fascinated by the strengths and weaknesses of the two-masted lugger rig of *The Ruddy Fox* and welcomed the opportunity to get a direct feel for them.

The wind had picked up a bit during the afternoon, so they made good time returning to the Bay of Quiberon. As they came around the headland beyond which the bay opened up, Giles saw that the French frigate was still at anchor.

"Can you sail a course to keep quite close to her, Captain Creasey?"

"That I can. Indeed, it would seem strange if I seemed to be steering clear of her. Much more suspicious. You go forward, Captain, and adjust that jib sheet* so that it draws a bit better. Then you can lean on the rail, in the way we *real* sailors do when we have nothing else to do, and look at her. It would be strange if you did not."

Giles did as the smuggler suggested. On the frigate, it must be the equivalent of whatever the French called the second dog watch. Many of the crew members were on deck, but they did not seem to be involved in any work to do with the frigate.

Mr. Macreau snorted as he joined Giles at the rail. "What a pig-sty! They have been here for some time. Why hasn't their first lieutenant made sure that everything is neat and stowed properly, Bristol fashion?"

Giles laughed. "You would hardly expect a French ship to be Bristol Fashion, Mr. Macreau. Surely your countrymen would not strive for a level defined by an English port."

"Maybe not. But I am horrified that the ship is not neater. Maybe it would be understandable under the republicans, but now I would expect better order."

"Well, it may be to our advantage if we have to take her. That sort of sloppiness may extend to things like proper watchkeeping and alertness of lookouts."

"I suppose that you are right, sir."

They had hardly finished examing the French frigate when Captain Creasey started issuing orders. It was almost low tide. They were about to join the pack of ships waiting for the flood to ease enough so that it would be safe to traverse the entrance.

"Do you need a pilot here, Captain Creasey?" Giles asked.

"No. I used one the first time, and it turned out not to be necessary -- quite the contrary. He put me aground halfway to Vannes. I can get *The Ruddy Fox* to the quay there by myself.

"Now, everyone, here we go. I'll be steering a course, so standby to adjust the sails smartly to changes in the wind."

Captain Creasey had maneuvred *The Ruddy Fox* into the middle of the pack of ships that were now making for the entrance. In moments the current grabbed them and pulled them through the opening, while the wind that was abeam let the rudder still bite to keep the lugger on course. Giles realized that Captain Creasey must have been through this passage many times before. He also realized that he was now fully committed to this adventure. It would be at least six hours and more likely twelve before *The Ruddy Fox* could leave the Gulf of Morbihan.

Chapter VIII

The Ruddy Fox slowed as the current weakened after she had passed through the narrow passage into the Gulf of Morbihan. Ahead lay three islands with narrow passes between them and the shore. Captain Creasey confidently steered towards the southernmost channel.

"These are only the first of a large number of islands in here," Captain Creasey informed Giles. "I'd guess it's only about eight miles as the crow flies to Vannes, but we will have to pick our way, so we will be going a much longer distance in total, though the current should help us. Luckily the wind is holding. There is a very narrow entrance to get to Vannes, which is slightly upriver from the Gulf. If we don't get there in good time, we will have to wait for the next tide."

The wind did hold steady, and Captain Creasey threaded *The Ruddy Fox* skillfully between the islands on their way to the town. The early July sun had set as they came to the narrow passage that the Captain said led to Vannes, but daylight lingered. The tide was still flooding, and the wind held steady from the southeast so that he could bring his ship through the passage and up to a quay in the town under sail.

Giles threw a line to one of the idlers on the dock. In minutes the lugger was snugged down for the night, moored in a town in Napoleon's France. Close ahead of her, a large merchant ship was docked. Giles thought it resembled the troop transports with which he had tangled in Ireland on his last voyage. When everything was shipshape, Captain Creasey suggested that they go ashore. There was a tavern farther up the quay, and he wanted a drink. It would also be an excellent place to learn what was going on by overhearing other people's conversations, especially if the Englishmen all pretended not to know French.

Giles and Lieutenant Marceau accompanied Captain Creasy as he walked along the quay. All three had the rolling gait of sailors, and it did not take much play-acting for them to appear to be three men who were off for some relaxation after a voyage. Their steps took them right past the merchantman they had noted earlier. Her name was *Marie Dumoulin*. There was an army-uniformed, armed sentry standing guard over the gangplank. His presence strongly suggested that the ship was indeed a military transport. They could see no sign of a watchman on the deck of the vessel.

A few steps farther took them to a tavern. It was almost full, with a mixture of working men and military officers. Giles led the way to a table next to one where a man in an elaborate military uniform was talking with someone who looked as if he might be a merchant ship's captain. The trio sat down, and Giles signaled to the waiter.

"Garkon," he announced loudly. "Wine – vine – rudge – for." and he held up three fingers.

The waiter did not seem to be surprised by being addressed in what could only be considered the most fractured of French. "Bon," he announced. He scurried off and soon returned with three tankards of red wine. Giles sipped his and found it surprisingly enjoyable. He remarked on it to the others, who both responded in English.

Lieutenant Marceau had taken the seat closest to the two French officers. Giles and Captain Creasy started talking about the cargo they hoped to get in loud voices while the lieutenant seemed to be concentrating on his wine while adding the odd comment to the others. He could hear the conversation at the next table very well.

The two French drinkers seemed to be in no hurry to leave, while the English contingent seemed to be more interested in drinking than in conversing, though they did have some talk and some joking that could get to be quite boisterous at times. They were well into their second mugs of wine before the French pair became rowdy. The sea captain stood up and declared something in a loud voice, shrugged his shoulders in a very Gallic way, and marched out of the tavern. The French officer sat back and drained his glass. Then he too departed.

The English group did not react immediately. Instead, Giles started telling a joke, in rather bad taste, that produced howls of laughter from all three and caught the attention of other patrons of the tavern. Mr. Marceau leaned forward and said, quite loudly, "I have a much better one than that."

"Let's hear it," responded Captain Creasey, "but not so loud. We are foreigners here and don't want to cause a disturbance."

They all leaned forward as Mr. Marceau started to talk.

"That ship will be loading supplies tomorrow and soldiers the next day. The ship's captain said that they would sail early in the morning the day after that, so they could get through the bottleneck before the tide turned. That is what got them so agitated. The colonel said that they should sail the minute his soldiers were loaded, and the captain told him that that couldn't be done because of the tides. But he wanted the soldiers on board and settled in before daylight faded to avoid chaos."

"Did they talk about where they were going?" Giles asked.

"Not directly. However, the colonel complained bitterly about how small this force was relative to the one that that damned Englishman had destroyed. Only he didn't say 'maudit,' which is 'damned' but something much stronger. So it might well be Ireland that is their destination."

"Did they say much of anything about that frigate at the exit to Morbihan?"

"Yes. It is waiting to accompany this transport when it emerges from the entrance. That is one reason that the time is set for leaving here. *L'Aventure de Marseille* -- that is the name of the frigate -- will be expecting this ship and will get underway according to the scheduled time based on the tides.

"They also talked about the seventy-four we saw. She is called *La Ville de Nantes*. They mentioned that she has recently been launched in Lorient, as you guessed, Captain Giles. Her crew is not totally inexperienced; many of them have been transferred from other ships. She is supposed to sail with the other two ships, but both men were skeptical that she would be ready to do so.

"Now, let's laugh noisily as if I am delivering the punch-line of a good joke."

All three broke into rather forced and artificial laughter that soon turned to genuine guffaws as they realized how ludicrous was their humor in the midst of an enemy tavern.

"Thank you, Mr. Marceau," Giles said as he wiped the tears of laughter from his eyes. "We have learned far more than I expected. Captain Creasey, I think we should leave Vannes at once."

"Not so fast, Captain Giles. If we leave now, it will be noticed and may set off all sorts of alarms with the French. I am here to get a cargo, and I have to find out tomorrow if there is one. We can probably leave in the afternoon, not before. That will give you plenty of time to get ready for the transport's exit."

"I suppose that you are right."

"I know that I am, and it is my lugger! Now we had better be quiet for a while before leaving this pub."

They settled down to their drinking again. Giles was having trouble keeping up with Captain Creasey. He had never been a heavy drinker and would much prefer to keep his wits about him. But it would be suspicious if he did not keep pace with his captain, especially as Captain Creasey would be paying the bill.

Luckily for Giles, it was not long before a well-dressed man came up to their table and sat down. "Captain Creasey, it is good to see you again," he began in heavily accented English. "Are you looking for a cargo?"

"Yes, M. Saint Clair, that is why I am here. What do you have for me."

"Some Armagnac. Fine quality. Excellent spirits. Sell it to your *maudit* nobility. Very good price. Special for you."

"Oh, why?"

"It is barrels, not tubs*. Most of you English captains won't take barrels, too hard to move. Get caught by your *gendarmes* if have barrels."

"I'll need to taste it."

"Of course, Captain Creasey, of course. Is in warehouse on this quay. You sample it now if you wish. Get your friends' opinions. Excellent stuff. Good price, too."

"All right. Let's go. Come along, you two." Captain Creasey was again enjoying treating Giles as one of his seamen whom he could order about.

They went a fair distance down the quay before they came to a warehouse. It had a small entry door set into the large doors that would give access to wagons. M. Saint Clair produced a key and opened the lock. "Wait a minute while I get a light," he said.

Their guide stepped into the building, and soon they heard him strike a flint. The sound was followed by the glow of a candle. "Come in now," M. Saint Sinclair's voice came from inside the warehouse.

M. Saint Clair guided them over to the opposite side of the warehouse, where some barrels were stacked in the corner. "Pick any one of these barrels to sample, Captain Creasey. All same quality as you can see from the writing on them."

Creasey picked one in the third row, just high enough that it would be a nuisance to tap but not so high that a ladder would be required. Mr. Saint Clair, who was a rather short man, did not appear pleased with the choice but went ahead without complaint. It took him only moments to produce a well-filled glass, which he gave to Captain Creasey.

"Not bad," the lugger captain said, after several gulps which he washed about in his mouth. "It might do if the price is right. Here, you men, give me your opinion. But take the next glasses from another barrel."

M. Saint Clair did not seem happy about providing the common seamen with good liquor, but he did draw two more glasses from barrels that Captain Creasey selected. Both Mr. Marceau and Giles probably had more refined palates than Captain Creasey, but luckily both refrained from showing their expertise. Both took a gulp rather than a sip but only swallowed a portion so that they could make some sort of evaluation. It was, indeed, a very superior brandy, as good as any that Giles had ever tasted. He did realize that his judgment might be affected by the amount of wine he had already consumed and the crude way he took his sample of the liquor.

"Good stuff, Captain Creasey," Giles stated, gulping down the rest of the contents of his glass. Mr. Marceau nodded vigorously but said nothing. He knew that his French accent might be picked up by the French trader.

Captain Creasey started the long process of bargaining over the price. He could take the whole lot but wanted them at a favorable price. Although M. Saint Clair wished to get them off his hands, he was holding out for a better price. In the end, they shook hands on the price. M. Saint Clair would have them delivered to *The Ruddy Fox* first thing in the morning.

"That is excellent brandy you have bought at a very low price, Captain Creasey," Giles remarked when they were out of sight of M. Saint Clair.

"It certainly is," chimed in Mr. Marceau. "As good as any I have tasted. Why do you suppose that it is in Vannes, which is a long way from Gascony where it is made?"

"I am sure that the cargo is stolen in one way or another. Possibly a pirate masquerading as a privateer, in which case I am afraid that the fate of the original ship and its crew is unspeakable. More likely, though, the original ship's captain concocted the story of being taken by an English privateer. He would say that his captor did not want the ship but did steal the cargo and let him go after transferring the cargo to his own vessel. The French captain would come in here to quietly sell the cargo before reporting it stolen. He would have come in here because no one would expect this to be a port for shipping brandy, and it is very obscure. I imagine that he sold the cargo to St. Clair and sailed off again. Since the brandy is covered, no doubt, by insurance and the insurer will treat the loss as a typical cost in wartime, no one has much incentive to examine the transaction very closely. Saint Clair, however, would like the evidence to disappear from Vannes, and he hadn't known that only honest traders would take barrels of the stuff. That is why he sold it to me cheap.

"Now, we had better get back to the ship. That brandy will arrive at dawn, and Monsieur Saint Clair will want me to sail as soon as possible, just as you desire, Captain Giles."

The following morning, as the sun was rising, a dray loaded with barrels pulled by two huge horses drew up alongside *The Ruddy Fox*. Early though it was, and despite Giles's thick head, Captain Creasey had already had the hatch covers removed and a tackle rigged to the end of the main gaff. Each barrel was roped, hauled up from the cart, and lowered into the hold where it was stowed securely. Though they were in a hurry, there were no slip-ups, to the frustration of various idlers who were watching the work, several of whom were hoping for a broken barrel to allow them to sample the contents of the cargo. A pause was called while the dray went back for a second load, and then the remaining barrels were loaded. The hatch covers were fixed in place, and *The Ruddy Fox* was ready to sail. They need not have hurried; it would be another hour before the tide turned; they could not leave the port until they had a favorable current.

Sometime after *The Ruddy Fox* started loading, carts began to come to the *Marie Dumoulin* to fill her holds. That activity was still in progress as the crew of the English ship sat back to wait for the change of tide. The army officer, whom they had seen and heard the previous night, sauntered down the quay to look at *The Ruddy Fox*.

"Hey, Englishmen," he hailed the crew of the lugger. "Where you take your cargo?"

"Harksmouth in England."

"Ah, smugglers. Good business. Brings us gold and gets you rosbeefs drunk."

"I suppose you could look at it that way," said Giles amiably.

"Do you know that man Gille?"

"Who?"

"Gille. The English captain who destroyed our Irish expedition."

"Oh, Giles, Captain Giles. No, I have never met him."

"Have you heard where he is operating?"

"No. I would not be surprised if he is still in England. He is an important man, a viscount, you know."

"No. I didn't. I was hoping to learn that he would not interfere with our latest doings."

"I don't know what he is, but I, of course, hope that he does hinder you."

The French officer shrugged his shoulders in a typical Gallic way and returned to the *Marie Dumoulin*.

The wind was from the south-southeast, and it would have been impossible for *The Ruddy Fox* to have sailed close enough to the wind to have navigated the narrow passage to the main body of water of the Gulf of Morhiban. However, the ebbing tide, assisted by the river's currents that passed through Vannes, made it possible to use long poles to push the lugger away from the dock and down the river so that they could escape from the harbor. After they reached the broader stretch of water, they were able to turn westward and sail among the islands in the Gulf to get to the entrance.

They reached the passage to Quiberon Bay while the ebb tide could still sweep them through the final gap. The *Ruddy Fox* arrived just in time, for the current had slowed so much that Captain Creasy could not rely on it to carry his ship through the passage. The wind, which had been getting steadily lighter, failed completely. They were becalmed half a cable or so from the entrance. If something didn't change soon, they would be drawn back into the Gulf on the rising tide. Captain Creasey debated whether to anchor or to break out the sweeps so that they could crawl away to safer waters. He had almost concluded that anchoring was the more sensible course of action when the wind sprang up from the east-northeast. If it held, *The Ruddy Fox* should be able to clear the headland that marked the end of the bay in which the French frigate still was at anchor.

It was a close thing. As the lugger left the beginning grip of the flood tide, she passed quite close to the French ship, close enough that Giles could read her name, *L'Aventure de Marseille*. Everything about her was just as he had expected: no substantive change from when he had last passed her. He scrutinized the frigate, calculating the best way to capture her that evening on the cutting-out* operation that he was beginning to plan.

Glaucus was waiting for *The Ruddy Fox* in a bay three headlands along from the cove that was harboring the French frigate. Before leaving on the Ruddy Fox for Vannes, Giles had ordered Mr. Correll to sail *Glaucus* eastward when he parted company with *The Ruddy Fox*, getting out of sight of land in the process. *Glaucus* was to return on the following day to this bay. As *The Ruddy Fox* continued east along the coast, she found *Glaucus* anchored just where Giles had expected her to be.

Giles and Lieutenant Marceau transferred to the British frigate, but Giles was not through with *The Ruddy Fox*. Captain Creasey's first cargo was still in *Glaucus*'s holds. The trip to Vannes had been almost too successful. The load of barrels of brandy picked up in Vannes prevented the lugger from taking back her original cargo. Giles had to pay Captain Creasey for the goods now in *Glaucus*'s hold and hope that he could find another British ship to whom he might sell the cargo.

After parting with *The Ruddy Fox*, *Glaucus* headed offshore once more, hoping that doing so might quiet any unease that her presence was causing on board the French frigate. She would return after sundown and capture *L'Aventure de Marseille*. Giles's plan was simple. There would be no moon that night. In the dark, *Glaucus* would not be seen as she sailed in behind the first headland that defined the bay in which the enemy frigate was anchored. Loading as many men as they could into *Glaucus*'s boats, Mr. Corell and Mr. Marceau would row around the headland during the middle watch when men tended to be most drowsy, board the French frigate, and subdue the crew. If all went well, Mr. Corell would raise the French frigate's anchor and sail to where *Glaucus* would be waiting. The French officers and crew would then be taken ashore to a convenient beach where they would be guarded by *Glaucus*'s marines until four bells of the morning watch. Then the marines would rejoin *Glaucus* in preparation for the next step of the plan. While the prisoners were being dealt with, *L'Aventure de Marseille*, now in British hands, would return to her original position and anchor in the place where they had captured her. When the sun rose, it would appear that the French frigate had not moved in the night and was still awaiting the arrival of some other ship. *Glaucus* would be out of sight behind the headland, but the topmast of *L'Aventure de Marseille* would be visible from the English frigate's topmast.

The plan worked without a hitch. By dawn, *L'Aventure de Marseille* was in Mr. Correll's hands, at anchor just where it had been the night before. It was cleared for action, though without boarding nets* rigged and with gunports closed.

As the sun rose, the wind backed into the southeast. It should keep rising, aided by the land breeze that the sun would produce. It would be a good wind for the *Marie Dumoulin* to leave the Gulf of Morbihan and start her voyage to Ireland. Giles had a trusted lookout watching the top of the French frigate's mast, waiting for the signal. Mr. Correll on *L'Aventure de Marseille* focused his lookout's attention on the gap where the French transport ship should soon appear.

Giles's plan had not taken any account of the French seventy-four. He had figured that she was too raw, and her crew was too inexperienced to interfere with his capture of the *Marie Dumoulin*. Unfortunately, he had underrated the ship of the line. She also had been waiting for the appearance of the transport carrying the troops that were intended to make the token invasion of Ireland. From her position at the head of the Quiberon Bay, the ship of the line could see farther into the Gulf of Morbihan than could either of the frigates. Before Mr. Correll realized that his prey was about to appear, she got underway and headed towards the entrance. The lookout on *L'Aventure de Marseille* failed to report that the warship was getting underway.

When Mr. Correll heard that the *Marie Dumoulin* was coming through the entrance, he signaled the news to *Glaucus* and ordered that the anchor on his ship be raised. Giles made the same command for his frigate. *Glaucus* got underway as quickly as possible. When she cleared the headland, Giles saw immediately that the French seventy-four might interfere with Mr. Correll's successful capture of the *Marie Dumoulin* if that action required any substantial time. *Glaucus* would have to buy extra time for her.

The French ship-of-the-line was close-hauled as it struggled against the wind. On that tack*, she would still be two cables downwind from the entrance when she came as near to it as she could safely get. Mr. Correll might succeed in taking the *Marie Dumoulin*, but the seventy-four was faster than the merchant ship. *Glaucus* would have to delay the French warship enough that Mr. Correll in the captured French transport could get far enough away that the French battleship would have difficulty catching up with her before dark.

Giles had to gamble. If *Glaucus* were to set enough sail to run downwind on a course to intercept the French battleship, there was a danger that something aloft would carry away, most likely a sail would rip, or a line would break. That would slow him enough that he would be ineffective. If he didn't, the stronger ship might get close enough to fire on *L'Aventure de Marseille* and so prevent her from capturing her prey. On the courses the two vessels were sailing, the French broadside would not be able to hit *Glaucus* unless the large ship turned downwind. Her doing so would provide enough time for Mr. Correll to capture the French transport.

Glaucus's bow chasers were much more potent than was usual for frigates, and they could do significant damage when fired into an enemy, even one as large as a seventy-four. The enemy started to turn. She appeared to have figured that she could deal with the English frigate coming at her and still have time to handle the other two ships.

"Mr. Fisher," Giles bellowed to the midshipman in charge of the bow chasers. "Fire when you bear."

"Bear off a bit so that the bow chasers can hit her," Giles instructed the helmsman. Mr. Fisher's cannon roared out.

"All hands, prepare to tack* – helm alee!" Giles bellowed.

Glaucus spun around just in time as her opponent's broadside fired. It was aimed where the frigate would have been if she had not come up into the wind.

"Helmsman, keep your helm to larboard. Mr. Fisher, we will circle to cross her stern."

Round *Glaucus* came. The French ship dithered about what to do. If she held her course or turned into the wind, *Glaucus*'s starboard broadside could rake* her. If she turned downwind, she would expose her stern to Glaucus's larboard guns. To make matters worse, she was getting close to the shore to the north of the entrance to the Gulf of Morbihan – too far north to be able to seek refuge in the inland sea.

The French ship turned downwind. *Glaucus* poured her broadside into the stern of her opponent. The seventy-four continued to turn so that she could come onto the larboard tack. Giles debated tacking. It would put him well to windward of the French ship, provided that *Glaucus* did not miss stays*, but his full circle had slowed his frigate, and she might well fail to pass through the eye of the wind. That would leave him far from his opponent, quite possibly far enough behind her that he would not be able to catch up in time.

Glaucus wore around and came onto the same tack as the French warship. The French were now ahead of the English and to windward of them. That didn't worry Giles. His ship was faster than his opponent's and could sail closer to the wind. The maneuvering had lost the French seventy-four sea room. On this tack, there was no hope of her escaping Quiberon Bay. She would have to make at least one more tack, and that would still put her far to leeward of the *Marie Dumoulin*.

Giles intended to delay the French seventy-four even more. He idly compared this adventure with a bullfight he had once seen in Minorca. His opponent was the bull who could destroy him if he was caught by it. He was the bullfighter who danced almost into range to inflict damage and then withdrew to wait for a better chance. It was exhilarating; he hoped it would end the way that the bullfight had.

Giles and *Glaucus* had the upper hand despite the great difference in power between the frigate and the seventy-four. From her position close on the stern of her adversary, her uniquely powerful bow chasers kept up a steady fire on the French ship. Already her stern stood gaping open, all the windows and fine woodwork gone, and the balls were flying along the deck, causing havoc farther forward on the gun deck. Giles ordered one of the guns depressed to increase the chances of striking his opponent's rudder. If that happened, she would be helpless.

La Ville de Nantes was trapped in a hopeless dilemma, especially as cannonballs from *Glaucus* had put her pop-gun stern chasers out of commission. It would take forever to try to haul any of her broadside guns to the stern as replacements and to strengthen sufficiently the area on the quarter-deck so that they could be fired safely. As a result, shifting her cannon was not a choice for the French ship. If seventy-four tried to tack to bring her guns to bear on her tormentor, Giles would cross her stern to pour a full broadside into her stern, possibly crippling her. If she did succeed in coming about, he could take up the same position on her quarter again. The same would be true if Giles's opponent tried to turn downwind. Finally, she could not keep to her present course because, before long, she would run aground on the Quiberon peninsula. While she might be able to anchor there and await a favorable wind to try to elude her tormentor, that would guarantee that the transport loaded with troops could not be rescued. In the end, she decided to wear* instead of tacking. The maneuver put her farther from the captured ship than ever. However, the wind was rising and was backing somewhat into the east. That would drive her deeper into the bay, but it should mean that she could escape on the next tack. The stronger wind did have the benefit to the French that *Glaucus*'s gunnery was much less accurate because the frigate was pitching more, and so she was doing less significant damage to her opponent.

The two ships raced back across the Bay of Quiberon. *Glaucus* was now more like a dog herding a reluctant cow to its barn than a bullfighter frustrating his adversary, but it was just as effective. The end came quickly. The change in the wind meant that *La Ville de Nantes* would have to go about soon. She was now too close to the shore to make wearing a choice; she would have to tack into the wind, despite the tattered condition of her sails as a result of some of *Glaucus*'s shots going high.

Giles saw what was about to happen. *Glaucus* immediately tacked to be out of range of *La Ville de Nantes* when she altered course. It was as well that he did, for it placed him well out of range of the seventy-four as she tried to escape the trap into which he had driven her. The French ship turned into the wind, but she missed stays, unable to come all the way around. She wallowed for several minutes drifting towards the land with her sails flapping. She fell back onto her previous tack. Before she could try again to turn, she ran aground on a rocky outcrop that ran into the ocean between two wide beaches. With the waves now pounding her, she would not last much longer. Giles reckoned that many of those members of her crew who could not swim would be dead before help could arrive. There was nothing he could do about it.

Giles put *Glaucus* on a course that would take her out of the Bay of Quiberon so that he could follow the two ships that had already gone to seek the British squadron off Brest. It always pained him to witness the end of a proud ship and the inevitable death of so many seamen. After a battle, he took no joy in the death of the enemy, even as he keenly felt how alive he still was.

Giles wondered if he could ever fully explain these feelings to Daphne. It was an aspect of his life he hoped she would never experience and so might never fully understand, even though she had got a taste of naval warfare on *Glaucus*'s maiden voyage. For now, though, he would simply have to carry on. He ordered that the stove be relit so that that the crew could have their belated dinner with an extra tot of rum. Then he went below to see what his servant would find for him to eat and to add to his letter to his wife, the continuous communication that he kept adding to each day until he had a chance to mail it. He was too tired even to notice how the tone had changed from the previous night's entry.

Chapter IX

The colorful fields of late July lined the road as the Ashton carriage neared Dipton Hall on its return from London. Some were in crops, giving varied hues and textures to the scene depending on which plants were growing in the various fields. Others were pasture for cattle or sheep, with many of the animals grazing in them. How the crops and livestock were developing as the summer wore on was a source of endless interest for Daphne. London had been exciting, but she found deeper satisfaction from her familiar countryside.

She paid particular attention to two large fields just across the road from the turnoff to Dipton Hall's drive. While Giles was at home, they had heard that the land was for sale and he had enthusiastically suggested that they should buy the property. Now she was studying how it was being used.

The estate to which the fields had belonged, Long Acres House, had been shrinking for some time. Finally, just these two fields were left, apart from the park around the house itself. The new owner, a barrister called Pennington, had reached an age where the hurly-burly of the courts no longer attracted him. He was not interested in farming the land, or even in renting it to some tenant-farmer. In any case, the fields had been so severely neglected that they could only be rented for a pittance of what they would be worth if they had been adequately maintained, but the old owner had not been interested in investing in the land.

Daphne had bought the acres very cheaply, but they would need draining and other improvements before they would be very productive. In the meantime, Mr. Griffiths, the stable master at Dipton Hall, who was in charge of all aspects of Giles and Daphne's venture in breeding and training hunters, was using the fields. He wanted to start training some of his colts by putting them over different sections of the hedges between the fields and over fences and barriers build for the purpose in preparation for the more serious training that would occur in the fall when the other fields in the area had been harvested. The ends of each field were fenced off temporarily so that cattle and sheep could graze and enrich the soil. Giles had been sure that the three types of dung would be beneficial to the fertility of the ground.

Daphne's thoughts turned to more domestic matters when the carriage turned into Dipton Hall's drive. Would Bernard be there to greet her, or would she have to venture into Nanny Weaver's domain? The nanny felt that it was beneath the dignity of gentlewomen, especially titled ones such as Daphne, to see their offspring more than once a day for an hour before dinner. Daphne's opinion was quite the opposite, and she was not amused when her father pointed out to her that Nanny Weaver had been in charge of Daphne when she was young with no ill effects. Daphne could hardly dispute that, but she was determined that her son would see much more of his parents when he was a child than she had seen of hers. She recalled fondly how she had induced Giles to take a real interest in his son and get genuine pleasure from playing with him on the nursery floor, despite the scowls from Nanny Weaver.

When the carriage drew up to the portico, Daphne was not surprised to see Steves, the butler, exiting the main door so that he could greet her as soon as she had emerged from the carriage. She knew that, when she was away, he stationed one of the maids at a first-floor window to warn him when the Ashton carriage put in an appearance.

After Daphne had been helped from the carriage by a footman, she turned to Steves, who clearly had a message that he regarded as urgent.

"My lady, Mr. Moorhouse wishes you to visit him as soon as possible or to have me send someone to let him know you have returned. He was very flustered about something, my lady. Would you like me to send a footman to tell him that you have arrived?"

"No, Steves. It is not like my father to send such a request unless things are very serious. I will go immediately."

Daphne reboarded the carriage. In minutes it was swaying down the drive, going as fast as the coachman thought was safe. They went only a short distance before they turned into the drive leading to Dipton Manor, Daphne's father's house, where she had grown up. Tisdale, Mr. Moorhouse's butler, came out to welcome her as the carriage entered the circle in front of the manor house. He was followed immediately by his master. Even as a footman handed her from the carriage, Daphne saw that her father's face lacked the broad smile with which he usually greeted her.

Daphne rushed to embrace her father. As always, she had neglected the proprieties of how to behave in front of servants, but none of those present was shocked. They had known Daphne since she was a young lady, in some cases all her life, and would expect no restraint from her.

"Father, what is the matter?" Daphne demanded.

It was a sign of how disturbed Mr. Moorhouse was that he answered her immediately rather than diverting the conversation to discover how her activities had been going. "It's my older brother, George, your uncle. I have received a letter from his lawyer. It contained terrible news...."

Mr. Moorhouse seemed to be unable to continue.

"Father, what news? Is Uncle George dead?" Daphne asked.

"No, no, but it may even be worse than that."

"What has happened?"

"Apoplexy. George woke up three days ago unable to move one of his arms and one of his legs, and he has been unable to speak coherently. There is no one in Birmingham to look after him except his housekeeper and butler, and they do not know what to do about the situation. Daphne, I don't know either. What should I do?"

"Oh, dear. But you aren't close to Uncle George, are you? You hardly ever mention him or say that you would like to see him. I think I have only met him once. I can scarcely remember him. I don't know anything about him except that he owns a gun-making factory in Birmingham."

"I know. I have lived quite apart from George all these years. I hardly knew him even when I was growing up since he was so much older than I. But somehow, I have hoped to get to know him and find out more about my father as I got older. Unfortunately, I haven't acted on those wishes. I have been postponing getting in touch with him until a more convenient time. Now it may be too late. I know I should have visited him."

"Well, he could have visited you, just as well."

"Not really, your grandfather wanted me to be a gentleman, and George was reluctant to see me because tradesmen don't visit the gentry.

"I really should go to Birmingham and see this lawyer about George's affairs. He asked me to do so in the letter that brought the news — some matters concerning the factory and my brother's house that he needs to consult me about. I don't want to go to Birmingham. It has many bad memories for me. And now I have to. And with you in your state, I can't even ask you to accompany me."

"Don't be ridiculous. I am only pregnant, not feeble. Mr. Jackson urges me not to limit my activities until much nearer the time. We must go to Birmingham at once. Family is family, even if they are not close and don't get on together very well. The fact that he may not be a gentleman is irrelevant: you did not bring me up to be a snob!"

"Shouldn't your brother Geoffrey be the one to go? He is George's heir, after all."

"Geoffrey may be needed and should come certainly, but he has the children who are too young for this sort of thing, and he'll have to arrange matters in Winchester before he can go to Birmingham. Anyway, he may not even have heard yet about Uncle George, and he is not much good at acting decisively. Your Uncle George needs someone who can.

"We should go soon. Tomorrow, in fact. Even a day or two may be critical. Come to dinner tonight so we can discuss what may need to be done. I will ask Mr. Jackson to come to dine too. Now I have to change and get ready for tomorrow. You must write to Geoffrey to let him know about Uncle George and that we are going at once.

"William, drive me back to Dipton Hall," Daphne ordered the coachman as a footman assisted her into the carriage.

If Steves was surprised to see Daphne back at Dipton Hall so soon, he did not show it. He similarly accepted without comment that there would be two more for dinner, and he would inform Mrs. Darling, the cook. All that the change of plans meant for the staff at Dipton Hall was that dinner in the servant's hall might be a bit plainer than usual.

Daphne rushed upstairs to tell Betsey to get ready for a trip of several days to Birmingham. Then, even before changing, she went to the nursery to see her son. She played with him for quite a while before she had to prepare for dinner.

Mr. Jackson, the apothecary, was undoubtedly a gentleman, but not on the level of men like Mr. Moorhouse or even Dipton's curate. The only person at dinner who appreciated such distinctions was Steves, who was very much a snob, but even he had become reconciled to the fact that Daphne paid little attention to gradations of status while Viscount Ashton cared even less.

The conversation focused on Mr. Moorhouse's brother and apoplexy. Mr. Jackson was very knowledgeable about the subject, though he said there were far more puzzles and things he did not understand about the ailment than matters he believed he knew. Long-term effects varied widely. However, from the information he had, the apothecary suspected that, at best, a partial recovery might be hoped for in George Moorhouse's case. Many problems might be lessened with time, but full recovery from a severe seizure was unlikely.

Mr. Jackson also could not rule out the possibility that the patient might suffer another attack that could well be fatal. It was highly likely that George Moorhouse would need to be cared for on a continuous basis by people more experienced in dealing with the severely ill than were his present servants. Mr. Moorhouse and Daphne should not be surprised to find that he had no stamina initially, but his energy should increase with time, though it also was not likely ever to reach the level he had enjoyed before this event.

Daphne and her father left the next day in the Ashton traveling carriage. Daphne brought Elsie while Mr. Moorhouse was accompanied by his valet. They spent the night at an inn in Banbury, where they had a large meal in a separate dining room. Daphne learned it was only about fifty miles further to Birmingham, but Mr. Moorhouse did not think they had time for frivolous sightseeing in the town since a long climb up to Birmingham would make the going slow. Daphne was most annoyed. She threatened not to leave until she had seen Banbury Cross. She could remember her mother reciting the nursery rhyme to her as a little girl, and here she was in Banbury itself! She was only dissuaded from holding up the party when the innkeeper solemnly swore that Banbury Cross had ceased to exist more than one hundred years earlier.

Late in the afternoon, after many dreary uphill miles, the city came in sight. Its most noticeable feature was smokestacks from which black coal smoke emerged to join a black pall that was concentrated over the eastern part of the city. Hundreds of smaller chimneys contributed to the cloud, resulting from fires for cooking and heating, for it was an unseasonably chilly evening.

Daphne was struck by how new many of the buildings they passed seemed to be as well as how grimy they were. It was entirely different from Dipton village, which had been shrinking for years, or Ameschester, where most structures were many, many years old. In both those cases, the structures were darkened mainly by time, not by smoke. She also noticed how busy were the streets, and that, instead of a quiet river as in Ameschester, the waterway they crossed was a canal lined on each side by long, narrow boats. She wondered how many of them were used for smuggling. Her experiences with the use of the waterway at Ameschester, which went by a property she had recently acquired, suggested that undoubtedly some were.

Mr. Moorhouse complained that everything was very different from when he lived in Birmingham, and he even had to order the coachman to enquire how to get to St. Paul's Square, where his brother's house was located. The coach turned left off the main street. After a short distance, it entered a large square which was notable for a beautiful brick church topped with a white steeple, very different from the ancient churches that Daphne knew from Dipton and surrounding parishes. The church sat in the middle of a large, grassy churchyard where gravestones were not crowded together and looked to be fairly new. The outer sides of the square were lined with red-brick houses with white trim of the style of only a few years past. The coach halted in front of one of them. The door of the house opened to allow a butler to exit with a footman who rushed to open the carriage door.

Daphne and Mr. Moorhouse emerged from the carriage feeling a bit stiff after being confined for a long time in the swaying vehicle. The butler directed them into a pleasant drawing room with high ceilings, large windows, and an imposing fireplace surround that represented what had been the height of elegance a few years back. A fire of wood logs rather than coal was burning in the grate with the flames dancing cheerily. Daphne reflected sardonically that her uncle George might not be a gentleman, but he undoubtedly lived as one.

The butler fussed about telling them that their rooms had been aired and that the lawyer, Mr. Arbinathy, was already being sent for and would explain the legal situation. Tea would be served to them as soon as possible. Regrettably, he had not been informed when they would arrive. Daphne noticed that the butler was extremely nervous, and it dawned on her that he was worried about getting a reference from people who did not know him if the house had to be closed.

"I must see my brother." Mr. Moorhouse announced.

"Yes, sir. He is in the morning room with his caretaker, Mrs. Dugmore. She was hired by Mr. Arbinathy to look after the master. Wouldn't you prefer to visit Mr. Moorhouse after you have had your tea?"

"No, I want to see him immediately."

"Yes, sir. This way, sir – and madam."

Daphne had made it very clear that she would accompany her father. They were led into another room that was in shadow now, not only because it faced east but also because the drapes were half-drawn. This room was also well furnished.

Despite its being summer, a wood fire was smoldering in the grate. Sitting near it in a Bath chair, wrapped in a blanket, was an elderly man with a large bandage wound about his head. He did not raise his head from a slumped position when his visitors entered the room though his eyes moved up and followed Daphne and her father as they approached his chair. He grunted some sounds that were incomprehensible.

"Oh, Uncle George, do you remember me?" Daphne asked. "I'm your niece, Daphne, but we haven't seen each other in ages. I was horrified to learn what has happened to you."

George Moorhouse made some more noises as his eyes turned to his brother.

"George, this is a sorry state in which we find you," Mr. Moorhouse commented. "Know that we will do everything we can to ease your lot. You and I have not been close over the years, I know, but we are brothers, and I do owe you all the ties of family."

George attempted to reply, or that seemed to be the proper interpretation of his unintelligible grunts and his waving his right arm.

"Stop that, Mr. Moorhouse," ordered the woman standing behind the chair, presumably the caregiver. "You'll do yourself more damage getting excited that way. I've told you to keep still!"

For the first time, Daphne wondered about the bandage on her uncle's head.

"Quincy, why is my uncle's head bandaged?"

"Oh, my lady, when he had his seizure, he must have been standing up. In falling over, he gave his head a nasty bang on the fireguard."

Daphne turned to Quincy. "Get something hard to write on and some paper and a pencil."

She turned back to the invalid. "Uncle, I know that you are trying to say something and are having difficulty. Let's see if you can still write despite what has happened to you."

The butler quickly complied with Daphne's request. While Mrs. Dugmore looked on with displeasure, Daphne helped her uncle so that the writing board was lodged firmly on his lap in a place where he could write comfortably with the pencil – that is, if he could write at all. George Moorhouse took the pencil from Daphne and wrote, in a very shaky hand, "Welcome. Thank you, niece. No one else thought of this."

The writing was wobbly, to say the least, and it wandered over the page, but it was entirely legible.

"George was always very left-handed," remarked Mr. Moorhouse. "His tutor and our father tried to make him right-handed, but it never worked, and his writing with his right hand was awful, wasn't it, George? Just like now. It is a very encouraging sign, George, that your writing with your right hand is no worse than it ever was."

"How are you feeling, Uncle George? Are you in pain?" Daphne asked.

"No. I can't speak or move most of my body. I might as well be dead," wrote the invalid.

"Nonsense. With proper care, you still have a lot to live for."

"My business. I can't manage my works."

"Don't worry, George," Mr. Moorhouse broke in. "I'll make sure that it is all taken care of."

This remark seemed to increase George's distress. He wrote, "You have never been good at managing anything, Daniel."

"That's true," Mr. Moorhouse confessed. "But Daphne makes up for all my shortcomings in that area and more. You'll see."

It was clear that George was tiring rapidly. Daphne was about to add her assurances to her father's when she noticed that her uncle was asleep.

"I think we should leave him for a bit," Daphne declared. "Mr. Jackson said that initially, after a seizure like this, people tire very easily."

Tea, accompanied by hot buttered scones with strawberry jam, appeared in short order when they returned to the drawing-room. Apparently, the cook had anticipated the possibility that her skills might be put to the test. Moments later, the butler introduced Mr. Arbinathy. A rotund, red-faced man bustled into the room, rubbing his hands like a tailor trying to accommodate a difficult customer. "Lady Ashton, Mr. Moorhouse," he began unctuously, "I am so sorry about the illness of Mr. Moorhouse ... ugh ...ugh... Mr. George Moorhouse ... a great man struck down."

"Now, Mr. Moorhouse, as I told you in my letter, your brother had a minor seizure some time ago. He had me prepare a power of attorney in case he suffered a more serious apoplexy and could not handle his own affairs. I am afraid that is what has come to pass. May I proceed to read the document he left with instructions for you?"

Mr. Moorhouse, not at all overwhelmed by the rush of information, nodded his head.

Mr. Arbinathy produced some folded papers sealed with wax. He asked Mr. Moorhouse to break the seal and note the date under it. Daphne was puzzled by this request, and it piqued her interest. The seal and the date below it were meaningless since they could have been added at any time. Was there something strange going on?

The power of attorney was a lengthy document for the simplicity of its terms, and Mr. Arbinathy read it in a dull monotone. If this was intended to lull his audience into not paying close attention to the contents, it failed utterly with both Daphne and her father. The document had many seemingly redundant terms and clauses that lengthened the reading considerably, but its central provision was that everything was put into Mr. Moorhouse's hands, but with some explicit instructions about what he should do. The power of attorney stated that Mr. George Moorhouse's assets were the House, on freehold property and with no liens against it, the contents of the house, and other personal effects. These items were listed in an inventory that was part of the document and which Mr. Arbinathy insisted on reading in the same monotonous voice. He must be being paid by the word, Daphne thought. This section of the document finished by saying that Mr. Moorhouse had complete discretion in how he handled this part of his mandate.

Next, the document proceeded to other matters, almost as an afterthought, it seemed. Its main content concerned the business known as Moorhouse and Son with all its assets and liabilities, including loans and assets held by the bank, including Mr. Moorhouse's personal deposit and securities held for safe-keeping in the bank's vault. These items were not listed at all. The power of attorney specified that the maintenance and running of the enterprise and use of the financial assets should be handled by Mr. Arbinathy. He would also handle all legal matters, including common-law requirements, as they applied to Mr. Moorhouse's affairs. Furthermore, Mr. Abernathy was to have full discretion about the use of any profits from Moorhouse and Son and income from the assets. For these services, Mr. Arbinathy could charge the fees that he judged appropriate.

"Do you have a copy of this document, Mr. Arbinathy?" asked Mr. Moorhouse when the solicitor had finally ended his reading.

"Oh, yes. We always make a copy." He produced a document that was less impressively sealed than the first one and offered it to Mr. Moorhouse.

"Did you read to us from the original?"

"Yes."

"Then, that is the one I will keep. We will have to study this material, I think, and then see you tomorrow. Thank you, Mr. Arbinathy. I hope you will bring the books of Moorhouse and Company with you tomorrow. Come at nine o'clock sharp."

"But the books are very large and heavy, and anyway, since I am placed in charge of running the business, there is no need for you to see the accounts," Mr. Arbinathy protested.

"I suppose the records are heavy. However, I need to see the books since I am the person in charge of my brother's affairs until he gets better, even if he did leave the running of Moorhouse and Son in your hands. Get someone to help you with the records and bring them tomorrow."

Mr. Moorhouse rose to indicate firmly that the interview was over. Daphne was amazed at this abrupt dismissal of the lawyer. It was not like her very courteous father at all. She was about to ask him about it when the butler returned from seeing Mr. Arbinathy out of the door.

"I am afraid I did not get your name," Mr. Moorhouse said, addressing the butler.

"Quincy, sir."

"Tell me, Quincy, did your master have a desk?"

"Yes, sir, it is in his smoking room."

"And does it have a locking drawer?"

"Yes, sir."

"And do you have a key to that drawer?"

"No, sir. It was also not among the items in Mr. Moorhouse's pockets when he fell ill."

"Wasn't it? Did you undress him?"

"No, sir, of course not. When he had the seizure, the first thing I did was summon Mr. Arbinathy. He brought Mrs. Dugmore with him, and she undressed him and provided me with the contents of his pockets."

"It is a pity that the key has been misplaced. Please arrange, Quincy, for a hammer and chisel to be available in the smoking room before Mr. Arbinathy arrives tomorrow. I will want one of the town constables to be on hand too, but he can wait below stairs until we need him."

Daphne was puzzled by her father's behavior. What could he have in mind? It wasn't like him to act so crisply.

Mr. Moorhouse provided the answer before Daphne could question him.

"Daphne, that man, Arbinathy, is a crook. I don't know what George's power of attorney really said, but that tedious document is not it. Not only would my brother not give the running of Moorhouse and Son to a solicitor, but he also would not leave such vague instructions about what was to be done with it. Moorhouse and Son is his heart and soul. The seal on the document itself reveals that it was applied after George had had the seizure."

"How do you know that."

"It is complicated. I shall explain later. However, knowing how George was as a young man, I would be astonished if the real document is not in the drawer of his desk. We will just have to see if we can catch Mr. Arbinathy red-handed tomorrow."

"Don't you think you should ask Uncle George before tomorrow and tell him your suggestions?"

"But he is asleep. I don't want to wake him."

"Mr. Jackson said that in these cases, in the early days, a patient is likely to take a lot of naps, and it does no harm to wake them."

"Then, let's ask him."

Daphne and her father returned to the room where they had left George. He was all alone, still sitting in his Bath chair, though the writing materials had been taken and put on a table. He was awake.

"Uncle George," Daphne began, after making sure that he could again write. "Are you strong enough to answer a few questions?"

"Yes," her uncle wrote.

"George, did you give Mr. Arbinathy authority to run Moorhouse and Sons in your power of attorney?" asked Daniel Moorhouse.

"Of course not! Ludicrous!" The invalid broke the lead of his pencil writing the exclamation mark. Daphne handed him a new one.

"Where did you put the real document?"

"Desk drawer."

"Good, that is what we wanted to know," said Daphne.

At that moment, Mrs. Dugmore entered the room.

"What are you doing, waking my patient, and getting him all worked up!"

"He was awake, Mrs. Dugmore," Daphne responded mildly.

"That does not matter. I am in charge here! I think you should both leave now."

George became very agitated at that remark. Daphne turned to him, asking, "What is the matter, Uncle George."

He started to write furiously on his piece of paper.

Mrs. Dugmore strode forward and snatched the paper from him. "I said you should not upset my patient."

Daphne stared at her for several moments, having never been addressed in those tones by a servant. "Give me that paper at once."

The caregiver crumpled up the page but then did hand it to Daphne, who smoothed it out and read out loud, "Get rid of that woman. I hate her. Anyone else would be better."

"Uncle George, I will do as you wish. Mrs. Dugmore, ring for Quincey." Daphne ordered.

When the butler appeared, Daphne addressed him. "Quincey, I believe that you said that Mr. Arbinathy hired Mrs. Dugmore."

"Yes, my lady."

"Mrs. Dugmore, you are dismissed without a reference from us. Since Mr. Arbinathy hired you without consulting my father, you can see him about your wages. Quincey, Mrs. Dugmore is leaving this house right now. Let her collect her things and make sure that she takes nothing else. Oh, and ask the housekeeper to come here."

The butler did not succeed in hiding his delight at the first part of his orders. The second part was fulfilled immediately, suggesting to Daphne that the housekeeper might have been listening outside the door.

"This is Mrs. Beamish, my lady," Quincey introduced the woman. "She is the housekeeper here."

"Mrs. Beamish, I have dismissed Mrs. Dugmore. I am afraid that entails* more work for you and your staff."

"That is no problem, my lady. I think we will all be glad to see the back of that woman! Might I make a suggestion, my lady?"

"Of course."

"Before I became housekeeper, the position was held by another woman who left to be married. Her husband was a good worker, but he lost his job soon after their first child was born. To help make ends meet, Mrs. Hopley – that is her name – became a wet nurse. That work has ended now. Unfortunately, Mrs. Hopley lost her husband and her child to the flu that we had here last winter, and she now has only been able to find temporary positions. She is at a loose end and would be free to nurse Mr. Moorehouse, I believe."

"That sounds like a good idea. Can you arrange for this woman to come here?"

Mrs. Beamish blushed and looked embarrassed. "In truth, my lady, Mrs. Hopley is in my sitting room right now. I asked her here to have tea and a natter with me today."

Daphne did not ask whether this was in anticipation that Mrs. Dugmore's tenure was about to end. Instead, she said, "That's good news, Mrs. Beamish. Uncle George, what do you think of the suggestion?"

"Get her," was the response written on a fresh piece of paper.

"Mrs. Beamish, please ask Mrs. Hopley to come here," Daphne ordered.

Mrs. Hopley turned out to be a substantial woman with a face whose lines told of a tendency to smile frequently and to frown seldomly. She curtseyed quickly to Daphne and Daniel Moorhouse and separately to George.

"Mrs. Hopley," Daphne began. "You no doubt have heard that Mr. Moorhouse suffered an apoplectic seizure and that it has left him partially paralyzed and unable to talk. However, he can write. Are you able to read?"

"Yes, my lady. Mr. Moorhouse has always made sure that anyone who works for him can learn to read and write if they do not already have those skills."

"Good. Now, Mr. Moorhouse needs looking after continuously. Mrs. Beamish has suggested that you might be available to fill our requirements, at least until a long-term solution is found. I hope you might be interested in taking the position."

"I would be delighted to, my lady, provided that that is what Mr. Moorehouse wants."

George started writing before Daphne could ask him what he wanted. His statement was brief: "Hire her!"

Daphne suggested that Mrs. Hopley begin the position immediately. Arranging for the replacement of Mrs. Dugmore had so tired George that he was again asleep in his Bath chair before Daphne had finished laying out what she expected of the new caregiver.

Daphne still did not know what had made her father realize that Mr. Arbinathy was dishonest. Despite her curiosity, her father refused to say anything more about his suspicions. Dinner awaited them, but it was an unusually silent meal. Both were wondering what provisions they needed to make for their incapacitated relative, but they could do little without more knowledge of the possibilities. The cloud that Mr. Moorhouse had cast over the lawyer meant that they could not even consider how much they could leave in his hands to see to Mr. George Moorhouse's welfare. Daphne had been impressed by her father's atypically efficient style in handling the matter of the power of attorney, but he refused to say anything more about his suspicions.

Chapter X

Daphne and her father were up early in preparation for the return of Mr. Arbinathy to St. Paul's Square. Quincey had arranged for the constable to be on hand, and, for good measure, he had asked the night watchman to join the constable in the servant's hall. When Quincey reported these actions to Mr. Daniel Moorhouse, the butler mentioned that the gentleman who had served Quincey's master as a solicitor for a very long time had been forced by illness to give up his practice. Mr. Arbinathy had only come on the scene after his master's first seizure, and Quincey had a low opinion of him. Mr. Moorhouse was surprised: it was very unusual for even a senior servant to voice his opinion about one gentleman to another member of the gentry.

Mr. Arbinathy arrived at a quarter past nine. Mr. Moorhead had earlier directed Quincey to show the lawyer into the smoking room where Daphne and he would be waiting. He also wanted to have a couple of burly footmen present, whom Quincey should supply.

"Mr. Arbinathy, you are late," Mr. Moorhouse opened the conversation.

"I was detained by other business."

"You were, were you? Did you bring the books?"

"No. As you know, the power of attorney gives me unfettered control of Moorhouse and Son. In view of that fact, I saw no reason to show you the books."

"Don't you? We will see about that later. Now, about what you are claiming about those pieces of paper you produced yesterday, I am afraid that we cannot allow your fraudulent document to stand. Quincey, would you break open the desk drawer since the key has disappeared."

The butler signaled to one of the footmen who used a chisel to pry open the desk drawer. Inside were two documents, each sealed with a ribbon and a blob of wax and with prominent writing telling what they were. The top one read 'Will of George Moorhouse, Esq.' The one below it said 'Power of Attorney.'

"Ah, that's what we are looking for," said Mr. Moorhouse picking up the second document. "Please observe, Mr. Arbinathy, that the seals are unbroken, not that it matters much. Let's see what this version says."

Mr. Moorhouse used a penknife to remove the seal and open the document. He scanned it until he was partway through and then looked at the final page where the power of attorney had been signed by George Moorhouse, dated, and witnessed by Mr. Arbinathy.

"Ah, yes." Mr. Moorhouse remarked. "As I expected, the provisions in this document differ significantly from the ones you presented to us yesterday, Mr. Arbinathy. This one states that I should manage the affairs of Moorhouse and Son as well as all personal matters. It suggests that I can rely on the works' manager, a Mr. Hugh Bottomly, for help and advice to make sure that the enterprise is run efficiently. Nothing about you, I am afraid, Mr. Arbinathy. Your name appears in the document only as a witness. How do you account for the difference?"

The lawyer had lost color and had looked horrified when the new power of attorney was found, but he quickly regained his composure.

"Why that is simple, Mr. Moorhouse. What you have there is an earlier version of the power of attorney. Mr.

George Moorhouse had second thoughts about putting you in charge of the business. He had me prepare the later one which I gave to you yesterday, and he must have forgotten to destroy that one when it became irrelevant. You will notice that the date of that one is several days earlier than the one I left with you."

"Yes, I noted that. It is very odd, isn't it? The one you produced yesterday was sealed even before the newly discovered one was dated and supposedly signed."

"That's nonsense. There is no basis for such a silly claim. The date it was signed and witnessed is certainly later. How can you claim that it was sealed earlier?"

"Not sealed earlier? Not sealed at all , though old seals have been attached to your version. I imagine that you must have forged my brother's signature, though you didn't do it very well. The seals, however, give you away."

"What are you talking about?"

"My brother has always been a most ingenious metal worker. Years ago, he invented a sealing ring that has the date built into it, very unobtrusively. The magic of the device was that the date could be moved forward but could not be moved back. George was in the habit of moving the date forward every day. You can see the date on the seal between the butts of the two stacked muskets in the impression in the wax. You will see that the date on the seal on the power of attorney we just found in the desk is the same as the date on which the document was signed. The seal on that travesty you produced yesterday predates both the day the real one was signed and the date on your version. If that isn't enough to convince anyone, the signatures do not look very much alike. Your version hardly resembles the signatures that I have been observing for years on letters from George and other examples of his writing that I am sure that we can find."

"But he had a seizure and could not write very well. The document I read yesterday is the final one and gives me full power."

"Is it, and does it? Let's ask George himself."

Mr. Arbinathy laughed. "You forget, Mr. Daniel Moorhouse, that Mr. George Moorhouse is no longer able to talk."

"True, Mr. Arbinathy, but he is able to write. Quincy, bring your master here together with his writing materials.

"Of course, Mr. Arbinathy, since George can communicate, the question of which is the true power of attorney may be moot since we can determine his current wishes. However, attempted fraud is not a matter that can be overlooked."

At that point, Quincy wheeled in the master of the house. Daphne helped him to arrange his writing supplies.

"George," Mr. Moorhouse started. "Did your power of attorney give Mr. Arbinathy the power to run your business?"

Only part of George's face reacted to this question, and the watchers were not sure what the grimaces signified. But there was no doubt about his written response, "Of course not! Daniel is in charge of everything, the house, the company, the consols, everything!" In writing the exclamation mark, George broke the pencil lead and put a hole in the paper.

"That's pretty clear, isn't it? Quincey, would you ask the constable to come here."

"What does he have to do with anything?" demanded Mr. Arbinathy though the distress on his face revealed that he knew what was in store for him.

"The constable will, of course, be arresting you so that the magistrates can bind you over for trial."

The constable, together with the night watchman, entered.

Mr. Moorhouse explained the situation. Then he ordered, "Take this man to the magistrates. He is charged with fraud and various other things."

"Daphne, we need a lawyer to make sure that the right charges are brought. George, do you know of one nearby?"

Unfortunately, the recent excitement had proven too much for George, and he was fast asleep.

"Quincy, do you know of any lawyers close to here?" Daphne asked.

"Yes, my lady, Mr. Throgmorton, who lives across the square, is a celebrated solicitor with a large practice. He might even be at home now since he likes to start late and work late."

"Good. Send a footman to enquire if he is free at the moment. No, on second thought, I shall go myself. Summon Betsey immediately."

Moments later, Daphne and Betsey, accompanied by a footman to show them the appropriate address, were on their way. The house was similar in style and size to George Moorhouse's residence. The knock on the door was answered by a footman.

"Is Mr. Throgmorton at home? I need to see him on some legal matters pertaining to your neighbor, Mr. George Moorhouse," Daphne said, handing the servant one of her visiting cards.

He glanced at it. "I shall see, my lady. Please come in while I ask."

The entrance where they waited was lavishly furnished, though not, Daphne thought, in the very best taste. After only a few moments, the servant returned and led Daphne into Mr. Throgmorton's library. It was a dark room, with deep brown bookcases entirely filled with leather-bound books, whose bindings did not always match each other. Daphne's immediate impression was that this space was not just a showroom; here was the library of someone who loved books. Rising from a desk near the window was a tall, gray-haired man.

"Lady Ashton. This is an honor. What can I do for you?"

"It's about my uncle George – Mr. Moorhouse."

"Oh, yes. I was very sorry to hear about his attack. He has been a pillar of Birmingham manufacturing. How can I help?"

Daphne outlined what had happened with Mr. Arbinathy.

"You are right to come and see me. Arbinathy has been a disgrace to our profession. Your uncle, for a long time, used a very old, well-established firm of solicitors. Unfortunately, the principals, two excellent lawyers, brothers, grew old. They had no sons to follow in the business. Then one of them died, and most of their business got transferred to other solicitors, some indeed to me. George was always very loyal to anyone he worked with. So even when Arbinathy took over the remaining practice, George didn't take his business elsewhere. Of course, he had just had his first seizure and did not want to be concerned with the problems of changing solicitors.

"I'll come with you immediately. It is important to get all the relevant facts pinned down as quickly as possible so that there is no way some tricky barrister can get Arbinathy off at the assizes."

Mr. Throgmorton only needed his silver-headed cane before being ready to accompany Daphne to George Moorhouse's residence. The walking stick, Daphne discovered, was for show, not for support. Once inside, Mr. Throgmorton was the soul of efficiency. He took detailed notes of the answers to the questions that he asked of everyone who had witnessed Arbinathy's performances so that he could draw up affidavits for their signatures. This even included a quizzing of George Moorhouse, both to verify his intentions in the power of attorney and to confirm how he wanted his affairs to be handled. The solicitor was entirely unbothered about his new client's inability to speak.

"I'll have all the necessary papers written out by my clerks and shall return late this afternoon to make sure that all the documents are correct and can be signed and witnessed. We'll nail this man. He should hang!"

"Father," Daphne said after Mr. Throgmorton had left, "we should make sure that Uncle George's business is functioning properly in his absence. You heard him say that you are in charge for the time being."

"Oh, no! I have always hated the metalworks. That's why my father decided that I should be a gentleman. He said, just like my brother did, that I was useless in the enterprise. I don't think I can go back and be involved in the shop again, not after so deliberately leaving it behind me."

"Well, someone has to take care of the shop, you know. If for no other reason than that the people working there have to be informed about Uncle George's condition."

"Can't you go for me?"

"What? I don't know anything at all about manufacturing."

"You don't have to. George must have someone who can run things when he is away. You would only need to tell them what is the current state of affairs."

"As if I knew what that is."

"You know it as well as I do. Please, Daphne, it would bring back too many painful memories of never fitting in for me to return to the workshop."

"All right, since you feel that strongly about it. I suppose that Quincey can tell me where the workshop is."

"I am sure that he can. Do you want to go now?"

"Yes. I don't see any point in postponing it."

Quincey had Daphne's carriage called and gave the coachman detailed instructions as to how to get from St. Paul's Square to the works which were located at the edge of the Jewelry District, Daphne learned, though that information enlightened her not at all. The location proved to be a grimy brick building on which there was a large, faded sign saying "Moorhouse and Son." The sign had not been repainted in some time, and Daphne thought that she could just make out a final 's' on 'Son.' Was this a mute reminder that, at one time, her grandfather had hoped that his younger son, her father, would also go into the business?

The main entrance was near the west end of the building, though there were, farther along, huge double doors that could be opened, presumably to enable large loads to enter the facility. A modest, ordinary door gave immediate entrance to a good-sized office where several clerks were hard at work. The man nearest the door looked up when Daphne led the way inside. He seemed to be startled that a well-dressed lady should be entering the factory, followed by her maid.

"Can I help you, ma'am?" he asked in a tone that indicated that he doubted that he could provide any useful service.

"I believe that you can. I am Mr. Moorhouse's niece. You have heard that he is ill, no doubt. I have come to see how the company is faring in his absence."

"The short answer, my lady, is very well. The orders keep coming in, we keep making the guns, and the payments are received as quickly as can be expected, though. as always, they are slower for our fine pistols and hunting firearms than for the others. But, my lady, you will have to talk to the works manager, Mr. Bottomly, about how things are going. I am just the head clerk.

"Jake," said the head clerk to a man at the desk nearest the door leading farther into the establishment. "See if you can find Mr. Bottomly and tell him that Lady Ashton is here."

"I am surprised, Mr...." Daphne began.

"Shearer, ma'am, Geordie Shearer,"

"Mr. Shearer," Daphne continued, "I am surprised that you know who I am. My father has been estranged from his brother for a long time."

"Oh, yes. We know that. Over the years, Mr. Moorhouse has had few kind words to say about his brother Daniel. However, ma'am, you are another matter altogether. He was pleased as punch when he got word that you were going to marry the famous Captain Giles, even though he refused to attend the wedding, saying he would be out of place. And we hear every time that Captain Giles – for that is what the papers tend to call him even though everyone knows that he is now a Viscount – that Captain Giles is in the news, about how you are married to the hero. Mr. Moorhouse retells the story with great pride, making sure that we know how he is related through his niece. I also have to say that when there was a piece in the paper about how you were involved in putting down smuggling, your uncle was over the moon. Some of us even laid wagers about whether it would make him stop buying free-trade spirits. So I had no trouble guessing who you were when you mentioned that Mr. Moorhouse is your uncle or how to address you.

"Enough of that, my lady. Here is Mr. Bottomly. May I present Mr. Hugh Bottomly to you, my lady? Hugh, this is Viscountess Ashton, about whom we have heard so much from Mr. Moorhouse. She was asking, on behalf of her uncle, about the state of the business."

"Your ladyship, it is a great pleasure to meet you. What can I do for you?"

"Well, Mr. Bottomly, first and foremost, I need any news that might set my uncle's worries at rest. Or, of course, anything else that should concern him. You may not have heard, but his intellectual facilities still seem to be sharp, and he can communicate by writing. Unfortunately, he is terribly handicapped physically, and he is unable to speak coherently. He will certainly understand any reports I give him, though he will tire very quickly. I would also like to understand the business a bit since I may, for a time, be the intermediary between you and him. It would help if I knew what you and he were talking about."

"Very good, my lady. Let me show you around the shop floor so that you can see what we are doing. It may give you a feeling for some of our problems. As you know,

Moorhouse and Son has always been in the gun business. Not the great artillery cannon, you understand, but the finer examples of firearms. Shotguns and rifles for hunting by gentlemen and also pistols. We have developed some very exclusive lines of pistols, especially Queen Anne pistols, where Mr. Moorhouse has made several improvements."

"Queen Anne pistols?" Daphne queried since she had no idea what they might be. Mr. Bottomly was more than happy to explain to someone – a lady and aristocrat at that – who showed an interest in what was, after all, his life's work. He explained that the Queen Anne pistol was a breech-loading pistol with a rifled barrel, giving it unparalleled accuracy and ease of loading. It was first developed almost one hundred years previously during the reign of Queen Anne, hence the name.

"What is rifling?" Daphne asked. Mr. Bottomly explained how ridges in the barrel made the bullet spin which produced much more accuracy. He also told her how being able to load at the back of the barrel, what he called breech-loading, made it easier to place the correct amount of powder in just the right place. As a result, the Queen Anne pistol was much more accurate than its rivals. Though she didn't quite understand what the advantages of this design were, Daphne was intrigued that her uncle had made improvements.

"So are rifles also made the same way?" Daphne asked.

"No, my lady."

"Why not?

Unfortunately, she did not understand the answer. It had something to do with cleaning the gun between shots. When she asked whether soldiers used rifles made by Moorhouse and Son, she was told that they were used only by special brigades where accuracy was more important than the rate of fire because a rifle took much longer to load.

"Of course, the pistols and the hunting guns are almost a sideline now, though we take great pride in them and in finding the best materials to adorn them and finishing them as elegantly as possible."

"What is the rest of the business?" Daphne asked.

"Primarily turning out muskets for the Army, the East India Company, and the Navy. The latter might interest you the most. Your husband's marines may use our guns. They would use the naval type, of course, and we are one of the biggest makers of them."

"If rifles are so much more accurate, why don't the soldiers and marines use them?" Daphne wondered.

"Some army units are armed with them, but rifles take too long to load. I don't know why the Marines have not adopted them, but it is probably for the same reason. I have heard that the purpose of their initial volley is to make the enemy keep their heads down. After that, quickness of firing is more important than accuracy. I guess if you fire onto a crowded deck, you are likely to hit someone, even if he is not the person you are aiming at. You can still be pleased with the result."

Mr. Bottomly took Daphne all over the factory, which was far larger than she had expected. At various places, he introduced her to particular workers who seemed to be in charge of important sections. Daphne had the impression of a very smoothly running operation that could probably keep on running in the same way for a good long time. She was relieved. Maybe having Uncle George severely handicapped would not be quite as large a problem as she had feared. She was struck by the fact that the area of the factory that was devoted to muskets and ordinary rifles was much larger than that concerned with making fine weapons. When she remarked on this observation to Mr. Bottomly, his reply was tinged with sadness.

"Yes, we particularly pride ourselves on the best of our firearms. That is, after all, how the firm began. But for a long time now, the real money-makers are the guns for war. Even our standard pistols are crude items. We make them as well as we can, but they are not works of art, even though I swear that they are the best of their kind. We can only hope that this war continues. When it ends, we are going to have to shrink our operations and lay off a lot of talented workers. I know that Mr. Moorhouse has been worrying about it."

"Well," Daphne responded. "Captain Giles is afraid that this war will continue to drag on for a very long time, so at least that is good for your workers."

"Yes, my lady, but there would be many other uses for our metal-working skills and equipment even if we couldn't sell muskets. We started making Brown Besses years and years ago when we were selling a special version to the East India Company. Moorhouse and Son will be alright in the future, but we will certainly miss Mr. Moorhouse, and one always worries what might happen if ownership should change. It has been very much Mr. Moorhouse's own firm for as long as most of us can remember."

"There is one thing before I leave, Mr. Bottomly."

"Yes, my lady."

"I would like you to make me a pair of Queen Anne pistols for my husband. He only uses crude shipboard pistols and claims that they are so unreliable that their only use is to make a big bang, and then he can throw them at his opponents. I would like him to have ones that are more accurate and well made, even if he then throws them at the enemy."

"So not dueling pistols, my lady?"

"Heavens no. He has enough encounters with danger without taking on any artificial disputes. It would be a way for me to say that I understand that he has to go in harm's way, and I support him in his need to serve."

"Very good, my lady. We can certainly make him the finest pistols that have ever gone to sea. Is there any hurry, or can we take our time to make them both perfect and beautiful?"

"It will be months, I am sorry to say before he is in England again."

Daphne returned to St. Paul's Square, relieved that she would not have to take over the management of the factory to keep it running profitably until it could be sold. That is what she had feared when she set out, though she only realized after learning about the situation how much that worry had been preying on her mind. Now, all that would have to be resolved was what provisions had to be made for her uncle. Even that was not as problematic as she had feared it would be when she had first heard that he was incapacitated and unable to communicate.

Mr. Daniel Moorhouse had been worried about the same things, but, in his case, he had been horrified by the notion that he might have to be responsible for the plant. He did not want to ask Daphne to take on running the business, but he was well aware that he did not have the talent to manage it, especially not from Dipton. He most certainly did not want to move to Birmingham. Now Daphne could reassure him that he need not worry.

Daphne and her father sat down to discuss the matter. George was again asleep, and they met in the drawing-room without him.

Daphne outlined what she had learned at the plant and concluded by saying, "Father, the only thing we need to decide now is what to do with Uncle George."

"What are you thinking about that problem, Daphne?"

"We could leave him here, being waited on by his servants. Or we could take him to Dipton. All his life has been at the factory, and he cannot go there now. You may have noticed that no one visits him here. Won't he be very lonely and bored here in Birmingham? As I see it, the alternative is that we take him to Dipton when we go back. He could stay with you or with me. We can make sure that he is well looked after."

"I suppose that you are right. I hadn't really thought about the implications of George's being all alone here, crippled so badly. Yes, I suppose that I should let bygones be bygones. He resented that he was not a gentleman and never would be, while our father set me up as one. Thinking about him made me feel embarrassed that I was supposed to be the gentleman, especially as I knew that he had many more talents than me. So we shunned each other. Now is the time to change that. But we will need someone to look after him properly if he moves to Dipton."

"Yes, that will be a problem. But surely we can solve it. I think, though, that we should ask Uncle George what he would like before getting into the details of our plans. There is certainly some way we can accommodate him if he wishes to come to Dipton."

George was awake when they went into the morning room, sitting in his Bath chair and staring out the window at the garden. The new nurse, Mrs. Hopley, looked up at the sound of the door opening and said,

"Mr. Moorhouse, I will attend to some things that need doing while your brother and niece are here. I am sure they will call me at once if you need anything."

Daphne and Daniel Moorhouse explained to George what they had been considering. Daphne had expected that he would find it a bit confusing, but he understood immediately.

"I don't want to stay here. Not the way I am. There won't be any friends visiting, and I won't have any interests now that I can't go to the factory every day," George wrote.

"So you would like to come to Dipton?"

"Definitely. Daniel's house might be better than yours, Daphne. I know you are very busy. Maybe it is time we got to know each other, Daniel." George wrote.

"That will be wonderful, George. I am looking forward to it, too," said Daniel.

"Can I take Mrs. Hopley with me? She is wonderful, and she talks properly."

Daphne suspected that George really meant that the new nurse talked with a Warwickshire accent and used terms he was used to. "We'll have to see if she wants to come. After all, uncle, she may not want to leave Birmingham."

Mrs. Hopley was summoned and appeared immediately. Would she be interested in taking care of Mr. Moorhouse in Dipton even though it was in the country and quite some distance to the south of Birmingham? She would. Her husband and her children had all died of the flu in the past winter, leaving her struggling to make her way. Nursing jobs were not readily available, and the people offering them were often not considerate employers. In the short time during which she had been working for Mr. Moorhouse again, she had come to like him more than when he was not crippled, and the servants in his house spoke highly of the reputation of Mr. George Moorhouse and his niece.

Daphne was delighted. She hired Mrs. Hopley on the spot, though, much to the new employee's surprise, she undertook to pay her fare to return to Birmingham if either side was unhappy with the situation. Mrs. Hopley was almost struck dumb by this last term. It was unheard of. Had she thought about it, Mrs. Hopley would have expected that, if she were dismissed or unhappy enough to want to leave, she would be turned out of doors without any provision for where she might go. She didn't tell Daphne that she would have taken the position even under such conditions. Daphne was well aware that the terms she offered were unusual. She had found in the past that treating servants with consideration worked wonders in the quality of service they provided.

Everything that needed to be done in Birmingham had been done. Daphne and her father could return the next day to Dipton. George's carriage and coachman would come with them, together with Mrs. Hopley. Daphne was amazed at how smoothly and quickly it had all fallen into place. It was only after dinner, when she was ascending the stairs to her bedroom, that Daphne realized that there was a large gap in how they had handled George's affairs. Decisions about the house on St. Paul's Square would have to be made. Further reflection assured her that while this was true, it was too early to spring those decisions on her uncle. Let him settle into Dipton, and then they could approach the subject.

Daphne sat at the table in her bedroom after Betsey had been dismissed. It was her time of day to write to Giles. She always did it before bed, and the time spent was always the most precious minutes of the day. This time there was so much to tell him! It wasn't until she got to the part about where her Uncle would live that she realized that she had not considered what Giles's wishes might be. She knew that he would welcome her uncle into his household. After all, he had taken in without question his half-sister and her daughters when he first acquired Dipton Hall, even though what little he knew of them at the time he did not like. She also knew that he was even more delighted than she had been when his relatives had found marriages that would take them away from his house. She knew that he would prefer to return to Dipton without her uncle living under the same roof. It was lucky that they had decided that Dipton Manor would be the best place for him rather than Dipton Hall.

Lord, how she missed him! Since he had sailed, she had received one letter that ended with his finding the Admiral after his successes in the Bay of Quiberon. She might get another one if he happened to meet a homeward-bound ship. Otherwise, she would have to wait until he returned from Africa. She had known before she married Giles about the long separations with hardly any news which were the fate of naval wives. She couldn't imagine wanting to be married to any other man. However, it seemed to be getting more and more difficult, no matter how busy she kept, to stay at home waiting for news of him and worrying that he might be ill or might perish. Would Giles be home in time for the birth of this child that she was carrying? She wouldn't let any of these feelings seep into her letter, though she would, of course, make it very clear how much she missed him.

Chapter XI

It was hot, horribly hot. The thermometer in Giles's cabin said that it was 82° on Fahrenheit's scale, but it seemed to be much warmer on deck. The sun was almost straight above them as the noon sights were being taken. The only shade on the quarterdeck was the narrow sliver coming from the billow of the mizzen topsail. Giles looked on in amusement as the midshipmen and master's mates tried to handle the extreme angle they were trying to measure accurately.

Giles remembered all too well learning navigational skills when he was a midshipman. It had been the hardest part of his training. However, old Mr. Swales, the master who had elucidated for Giles the mysteries of using celestial bodies, a sextant, an accurate timepiece, and various tables to determine location, had been sufficiently rigorous that the skills remained with him still. He often joined the midshipmen at the noon exercise to show that the captain they all respected could determine the ship's position, so they had no excuse for not being able to do the same. Unlike the master, who sometimes used the night sky for determining the longitude as well as the latitude of the ship, Giles limited his endeavors only to the noon exercise. Today, it was too hot even to do that.

"Mr. Bush," Giles addressed the youngest of the midshipmen. "What have you discovered about our position?"

"Sir, we are at 65°14' North. I haven't had a chance to calculate our longitude yet, sir. I looked up today's latitude offset before I came on deck."

"I see. That is very discouraging. Your figure puts us somewhere in Iceland, which is not at all where I hoped we would be. Mr. Fisher, where do you put us?"

"24° 02' North, sir."

"That sounds about right, Mr. Fisher. Is it, Mr. Brooks?"

"Yes, sir. Mr. Fisher agrees with me within a few minutes. I am afraid that Mr. Bush must have taken the reciprocal of the reading to get his result."

"It is difficult, I know, Mr. Bush, but you should get better with practice. Well done, Mr. Fisher. Mr. Brooks, let me know exactly where we are when you complete the calculations."

"Aye, aye, sir. By my pocket watch, I'd say that we are fifteen leagues* off the coast of Africa. That smudge on the eastern horizon is coming from the land, I believe. It is hard to know with the heat producing strange things. I'll get a more exact reading when I consult the chronometers."

"Very good. Continue on this course, Mr. Hendricks, until we see land more clearly."

Giles went below. *Glaucus* was nearing the destination of this voyage. She had made reasonably rapid progress after leaving the captured French vessels with Admiral Throgmorton. The Admiral had expressed glee that Giles had frustrated the French once more, a reception that was quite different, Giles was sure, from how he would have been greeted by the Admiral's predecessor. This admiral had even volunteered to supply officers and seamen to see the two captures to Portsmouth so that *Glaucus* could continue south with a full crew.

Glaucus had visited Lisbon on her way south to find out if the British ambassador or the East India Company agent had any more news about the captures of East Indiamen and the kidnappings of their passengers and officers. Unfortunately, they knew nothing that Giles had not already heard, but the Company factor in Lisbon had proven to be very useful anyway. He had pointed out that there was no British consul in Kamlakesh as far as he knew and that the town was sufficiently isolated that it would be entirely possible that there was no one who spoke English in the town. The agent understood that the locals, including presumably the Bey himself, talked some dialect of Arabic. If Giles did not have an Arabic speaker on board, he might have trouble communicating.

Giles recognized the validity of the warning. When he asked if the factor had any ideas on how to overcome the problem, he learned that there was a man in the Company's employ in Lisbon who had been to Kamlakesh at least once. The employee was called Sidi Mohammed, and he had shown himself to be a dedicated and intelligent worker. Mr. Mohammed was from Casablanca originally and spoke the appropriate dialect fluently, while his command of English was laudable. Giles agreed that Mr. Mohammed sounded like just the person he needed, especially as he had no other way to find someone suitable in the short time before he had to leave Lisbon. It was to be Mr. Mohammed as the translator, or else no one at all since Giles intended to make no other stops on his way to Kamlakesh.

"What should this Mr. Mohammed be paid?" Giles asked the factor.

The answer was that the East India Company would continue to pay his stipend. While Giles realized that this meant that the man would be spying on him for the Company, he could see no drawback to that.

Mr. Mohammad was a swarthy individual with a pronounced, hooked nose. He spoke in a high voice with a distinctly Kentish accent. He turned out to be a lively addition to the wardroom. Giles had been afraid that there might be difficulties with the newcomer joining with his other officers and sharing meals with them, for young Englishmen were known to have a very disdainful outlook on foreigners, especially ones who were not European. He had mentioned his fear to Mr. Miller, whom Giles suspected would be one of his officers who would be least welcoming to the translator, and asked him to set a good example for the other officers in how to show respect to a colleague. Later, Mr. Miller reported that Mr. Mohammad fitted very well into the officers' living space. He was, indeed, an asset, bringing new tales and perspectives. While some had resented having a foreigner foisted on them, they had all come to accept his presence. Some even thought he was an excellent addition to their company.

Glaucus was now steering southeast on the northeast trade wind, making about three knots. The smudge on the horizon grew steadily more pronounced. Finally, the lookout at the masthead called down, "Land Ho. Three points to larboard."

Subsequent calls told that the lookout could see a low hill. Next, he announced that, to the right of the hill, he could see a headland with land continuing to starboard, possibly a league beyond it. This cry was what Giles would expect if *Glaucus* were approaching Kamlakesh. He turned to the master and clapped him on the back. "Well done, Mr. Brooks. You have brought us to exactly the right place."

According to Giles's and the Master's scanty knowledge, Kamlakesh was sited on a short narrow inlet that paralleled the outer shore. It was shielded from the ocean by a hill, or maybe a large sand dune so that vessels approaching from the north or west could not see it. Glaucus would have to get around the headland before they could assess what they might be able to do to bring pressure on the Bey to release his captures and his captives.

"Mr. Bush," Giles said to the youngest midshipman. "Join the lookout and learn from what he sees and how he reports it. And make any comments you think that he has not made that are relevant. I should remind you, however, that he is one of the best lookouts on board. He is the sort of man to put at the masthead when you are expecting complicated sightings."

A half-hour passed before the next cry from the lookout, "I can just make out a thin tower behind the hill – make that four towers."

Mr. Bush could not restrain himself. His young voice broke as he called down to the deck, "Sir, they look like the towers in pictures of Mohammadan Churchs."

"He must mean mosques," remarked Mr. Mohammad.

Glaucus sailed on in the light wind. The next hail from the masthead galvanized everyone on deck. "Ship emerging from behind the headland. No, there are two, no three ships. Many ships."

"What do they look like?" bellowed Giles.

"Can't tell for sure," replied the lookout. "Could be galleys."

Giles realized that he had not told Mr. Bush to take a telescope aloft with him, so he could probably make out even less about the ships than the lookout who was known to have extra-sharp eyesight. Though it was not what a captain was supposed to do, no one would feel hurt when he grabbed the telescope and started up the ratlines himself. He had far more experience than any of them, and he was responsible for all the decisions that might be made based on what was coming into sight.

Before going aloft, Giles ordered, "Clear for action. Have the guns in my cabin set up as stern-chasers, but do not remove the windows yet. Also, don't open the ports for the bow chasers. We'll keep them as a surprise."

After giving those orders, Giles would not be needed on deck for several minutes. Instead of going below, he turned to the mainmast shrouds* and started aloft with his telescope slung on a strap over his shoulder. Up and up *Glaucus*'s rigging he went, avoiding the lubber's hole* for the quicker route to his destination. He was only slightly out of breath when he joined the lookout and Mr. Bush. He promptly put the telescope to his eye. He soon found the ships in question and focused on one of them.

What Giles saw was a strange craft. It was being rowed like a galley, but it had a broader beam than the galleys which he had seen in the Mediterranean and at St. Petersburg. Furthermore, it had a short mast sticking up in the middle of the boat while the long spars of a lateen-rig were lying on the gangway between the banks of oars. In the bow was mounted a cannon, a nine-pounder, he would guess. Large enough to do serious damage to *Glaucus* if it was allowed to pound away at his ship for any length of time. Scanning across the other ships emerging from the inlet, Giles saw that they were all the same awkward hybrid of lateen-rigged sailboats and Mediterranean galleys.

A total of twelve of these unusual craft had emerged from whatever lay beyond the spit of land. Even as he watched, the lead ship started to turn towards him. The others also changed course, but only after they had proceeded some distance from the headland. Giles suspected that the spit of land must continue underwater for some way and that the strange craft did not turn until they were sure of missing it. If *Glaucus* were to venture around that point, he would have to make sure that they gave it a wide berth and have men in the chains to sound frequently.

The flotilla turned towards *Glaucus*. Each of the vessels had a significant number of men on deck who appeared to be armed. Also, there were eight oars in the water on each side, and two men pulled each one. Giles wondered if the men pulling the oars were galley slaves or free fighters. If the ships were galleys like the ones he had seen in the Mediterranean, he would know the answer, but here, and with a different type of vessel, he could not be sure. It would make a tremendous difference if any of these craft got close enough to *Glaucus* to try to board. If the oarsmen were free to join the attack, the numbers of men against him could be overwhelming. There would be an extra thirty-two men to deal with from each boat. That would be enough to make quite a difference in a boarding attempt, especially if the modified galleys could all hook on to *Glaucus* at the same time so that *Glaucus*'s broadside guns would be useless. At the present distance, even with the aid of the telescope, Giles could not determine precisely what the situation was, though he did think that he could see the glint of chains on the rowers' benches. All he could do about the danger was to make sure that none of the vessels got close enough to board his frigate.

There was nothing more he could learn while at the masthead. Telling the lookout and the midshipman to keep their eyes open for the appearance of other ships, he went down to the deck.

Glaucus and the hybrid craft converged rapidly. The rowboats were moving faster than the frigate. The noise of drums beating the pace of the oars became audible on

Glaucus's quarter deck. While it was still out of range of the frigate, the flotilla broke into four groups. One set of four vessels backed their oars and seemed to be waiting for *Glaucus* to come up with them. Another group of four increased the beat of their drums and began to go faster than the others. These boats veered to starboard of *Glaucus* in a wide arc around her. It was not hard to guess that this group intended to get right astern of the frigate. The remaining four ships split into two pairs and diverged, with one pair aiming to come level with *Glaucus* at a generous distance to starboard and the other one on a course that would place them off her larboard beam.

Giles presumed that he was observing maneuvres of the type of craft that had been taking the East Indiamen. He could safely treat them as enemies. He could also guess what their strategy would be. With the four groups forming a diamond about *Glaucus*, those ahead and behind the frigate could open fire to rake her with impunity. If she turned to bring her broadsides to bear on those two groups, they would dart away while the other pair could now hit his ship with impunity. Well, if that was their intention, they were in for a surprise.

The galleys, for that was how Giles was thinking of the enemy since they were not using their sails, formed up just as he had anticipated. When the groups were just out of range of the frigate, the ones astern turned and picked up their pace to close with the frigate. The ones ahead now resumed rowing hard towards her while the ones abeam maintained their position relative to Giles's ship so that they were keeping pace with her.

Giles bided his time. He wanted the enemy to be close before he sprang his trap. The fore and aft galleys were converging on *Glaucus* as she maintained her course. If they wondered why she did not turn to bring her guns to bear on them, their puzzlement was not enough to make them deviate from their plans. The guns in the galleys' bows held their fire, obviously hoping that their initial shots would be devastating.

Before the enemy could fire, Giles ordered the stern ports that masqueraded as windows and the bow ports, which hid the strength of *Glaucus*'s bow chasers, to open and for the guns to fire as they bore. The response to his command was immediate. As the ports rose, the guns were run out. Only a few moments were required to adjust the aim and the elevation that the gun captains had already judged reasonably accurately. The guns boomed out. Their crews were ready to prepare the cannon as quickly as possible for their next blast the minute their recoils had been stopped. The officers in charge were the only members of the gun teams who looked to see where the shots had landed. They promptly ordered adjustments for the next salvo.

The surprise had been more effective than Giles had hoped. The first salvo had hit five of the craft. In each case, they were now in dire straights. The damage produced by *Glaucus*'s guns, as well as the unexpected nature of the gunfire, had caused confusion on board the galleys. The ones that had been hit were at least temporarily out of the fight. The remaining three enemy craft, one astern and two in front, had been rendered ineffective, and their shots had missed Glaucus because of the disturbance caused by the cannonballs. They seemed to be uncertain about whether to press home their attacks or to veer away to avoid the next blast. Two of them decided to fire while the other one, which was the only vessel left unharmed in the group astern of *Glaucus*, took the less daring approach of trying to move into the quadrant where none of Glaucus's balls could reach them. Even that one was not successful. It had become the target of all four of the stern guns, and it was blown out of the water before it could get away. In front, one of the enemy ships had its cannon hit just before it fired, while the other one had its larboard set of rowers mowed down by a shot. That forced the galley to veer to larboard so that, even though its gun did fire, the shot went wide.

Only a few minutes had been required to change the situation completely. The eight attacking craft all had been put out of action. They were shattered and either had sunk or were in danger of sinking. Before Giles could express his satisfaction with the quality of *Glaucus*'s gunnery, he must give orders to prevent more lives from being lost.

"Mr. Brooks, back the mainsail," Giles ordered. "Mr. Miller, get our boats in the water to rescue any survivors. Have the crews armed in case they meet resistance. Bosun, make sure each boat has tools to undo the chains of the galley slaves. Mr. Marceau, Mr. Stewart, Mr. Dunsmuir, Take command of our boats. Mr. Macauley, have your marines stand at the bow and the taffrail* to shoot any of the enemy who want to keep attacking us. Dr. Maclean, you can expect to receive some injured members of the enemy that you should patch up as well as you can. Mr. Bush, keep an eye on the other four galleys and let me know if any show hostile intentions."

Giles realized that there was nothing more that needed his attention. He could only wait for the results of his commands before his next steps could be taken. He had been surprised at how well coordinated had been the enemy's attack. It must have been the tactic used to capture the East Indiamen so easily, and so it must have been well-practiced.

The unprovoked attack resolved some of the puzzles that surrounded Giles's mission. Kamlakesh should be treated as hostile. Before *Glaucus* had arrived, it had not been clear whether the Bey was harboring the pirates or only supplying a convenient way for the thugs to dispose of their booty. It was now evident that the boats were based in Kamlakesh. They had emerged as a coordinated group once *Glaucus* had been sighted. The lookout involved on land must have been on the hill that shielded Kamlakesh from the ocean, and so the observer's presence would be known to the Bey's officials whether he was another pirate or one of the Bey's soldiers. Giles should feel free to destroy the pirates' lair if he could.

Having this question answered still left other problems for Giles. Should Kamlakesh itself be treated as an outlaw state, or did he have to worry about its being part of a larger entity or country? In the latter case, might his attacking be construed as starting a war between Britain and another legitimate kingdom? Nobody had mentioned these problems when Giles had been sent to clean up the situation created by the piracy, but now he had to worry about them. If the Bey of Kamlakesh was indeed a vassal of the Sultan of Casablanca, would he be overstepping his mandate by attacking the town, or should he limit his endeavors to the waterfront in front of the walls? If Giles could get the East Indiaman and the hostages back by negotiation, he reckoned that he should do as little damage to the town and its citizens as he could. Otherwise, he should feel free to do whatever harm he thought would advance his purpose. If the Government or the Admiralty chose to question his decision, that would be a problem for them. He shouldn't be guided by that danger

Giles's reverie was broken by the return of the first boatload of survivors. They were not an impressive-looking bunch, many of them wounded, probably by splinters that had sprayed about when a cannonball had hit their craft. They all seemed to be stunned. However, several of them appeared to be happier about boarding the frigate than the rest. The less dejected men had manacles on their wrists, presumably because the men from *Glaucus* had not had a chance to remove their fetters in the hurry to save lives. These people must be galley slaves. Giles ordered that they be separated from the other bedraggled survivors.

"Mr. Mohammed," Giles called. "Find out what you can about these prisoners and whether they are independent pirates or working for the Bey. Try speaking to them in English first, and if that doesn't produce information, speak in the local language, but do so in a way that sounds as if you are an Englishman who understands and speaks their language only with difficulty. That way, you may overhear them talking among themselves when they presume that you won't understand them. We had better give you an English name – let's see – Mr. Cornwell – while we are in the presence of enemies whom we may have to release.

"Mr. Shearer, strike the manacles off the second group of prisoners. Mr. Stewart, see if any of those people speak English or a language that one of our sailors knows.

"Mr. Miller. We'll get underway again as soon as everyone is aboard. Don't worry about the flotsam. Head a couple of cables off the end of that point ahead of us. Two men in the chains as soon as we get close to it. Once we are past it, we may have a better idea of what we are up against. Keep the ship closed up at action stations, but shut the windows and gun ports."

Giles again found himself with nothing to do while his subordinates were busy. The boats were still rescuing people clinging to the remains of the galleys, and the officers who were not involved in the rescue operation or directing the bringing on board survivors were carrying out his orders for dealing with the unfortunate men now on his ship.

He turned his attention to the four unharmed galleys. They were still heading towards the land beyond the end of the peninsula on a course that would again give the point a wide berth. He had the impression that they had speeded up the pace of their rowing from what they had used in approaching *Glaucus*. What lay around that headland? Were the galleys seeking the haven of a well-fortified port? Were they attempting to alert and join up with more ships so that another attack could be made on *Glaucus*? Or were they racing to get home before he could come after them? If the latter possibility was true, Giles felt that it reflected the panic caused by the destruction of their sister ships, so he could ignore them. In the present wind, the frigate had no hope of overhauling the galleys before they had passed the headland and were safe in Kamlakesh. There was nothing to be done about them right away.

Glaucus soon resumed her course towards the land with her boats back on board or trailing behind. Mr. Stewart was the first officer to report about the survivors.

"Captain Giles," he announced excitedly. "About half the galley slaves we rescued are British or European sailors, captured by the pirates. Many are from the East India Company, but also some others are our countrymen who were on other ships which the pirates captured, and a few are from other countries, Spain particularly, but also Holland and Italy. They were caught by the pirates who captured their ships. They were made slaves when no one would ransom them. We'll have to keep them well away from the pirates, sir. They want to kill their captors with their bare hands. The rest of the galley slaves are convicted criminals from Kamlakesh.

"The slaves tell me, sir, that there are three captured ships in Kamlakesh at present, one East Indiaman, and two smaller ships, one Spanish and one Dutch."

"We'll have to keep the British and the other Europeans with us, I suppose, until we find some other way to get them home," Giles declared. "I wonder what to do with the other galley-slaves. They are not exactly people whom I want to have on board. I don't suppose that you were able to communicate with them."

"No, sir. I imagine that some of the rescued sailors may have learned some of their language."

"Maybe. I think that we will wait for Mr. Mohammed to finish with the pirates and then he can talk with them. He may have suggestions. By the way, we are calling him 'Mr. Cornwell' when the prisoners might overhear us, and he is pretending not to speak much of their language. Now, Mr. Stewart, I would like you to write down the names of all the men from the English ships and what were their ratings. Then try to do the same with all the ones from other countries. How many are there, anyway?"

"Only twenty-one British, sir, and thirty-two of the others. The slaughter among the galley slaves was terrible. Many of them must have drowned, pulled down by their chains when their boats broke up or were swamped. Fifty-six pirates were captured, sir. The rest either continued trying to fight and were killed, or else they drowned. The marines are guarding those people."

"Good. One more thing, Mr. Stewart, before you do anything else. Ask these people what lies behind that headland and in Kamlakesh, especially at the harbor. I want to know what we can expect to find when we get there."

"Aye, aye, sir."

"Mr. Miller, Mr. Macauley," Giles called. "When we get close to the headland, but before we can see what's behind it, we will take the prisoners ashore. Make sure they have no hidden arms."

That left Giles with the dilemma of what do to with the thirty-two surviving slaves who had been sentenced to the galleys as punishment for crimes. Could he, in humanity, also set them ashore with the pirates? He did not want any extra men aboard who would need water and food when he was far from friendly ports, but he could hardly turn them loose if the result would be their execution. Luckily, at that point, Mr. Mohammed stepped away from the group and came to report.

"Sir, I have some news. Most of the group I talked to are common criminals, convicted of theft and such crimes."

"What will happen to them if we return them to Kamlakesh?"

"They will be enslaved again, maybe in the galleys, maybe as workers of one sort or another."

"So, we can set them ashore without worry that they will be killed?"

"Yes, sir. I might mention that most of them would have been sentenced to hang or be transported if they had been in England. There are exceptions, however."

"Oh?"

"Yes, sir. A while back, the Bey of Kamlakesh was overthrown by his nephew, who is now the Bey. That event marks the change in the nature of the piracy against the East India Company. The former Bey was killed, as were some of his principal ministers. However, two of the galley slaves were officials in his court and were sentenced for letting their dislike of the present Bey be known. They may be helpful by still knowing some of the ins and outs of the government. One other prisoner is a very high-ranking man who was kept on by the new Bey when he took over. This man had rivals, who accused him of looking with too much interest at the Bey's principal wife. The price of that indiscretion, which he denies, was to be sent to the galleys. He might be a big help in negotiating with the Bey if that is what we have to do. We would have to pay him for his help by taking him somewhere where he would be safe."

"All right, we had better separate those three from the others whom I am going to set ashore with the pirates we captured."

"Might I suggest that we keep another one of the galley slaves, sir? Crooks often know the details of their towns far better than court officials, and that may be useful in dealing with the Bey."

"Very well. Choose the one who will be most helpful to us. We'll promise to take all four of them somewhere where they may begin again.

"Mr. Miller," Giles called to the first lieutenant, "we will be putting the galley slaves from Kamlakesh ashore with the pirates, except for the four that Mr. Cornwell will point out to you."

Lieutenant Miller looked puzzled by who 'Mr. Cornwell' might be until he noticed that Giles was pointing at Mr. Mohammed to make his meaning clear.

Giles had had some of his immediate dilemmas resolved, especially what he would do with the various groups that he had aboard as a result of the fight against the galleys. Now he would get rid of most of them and then proceed to sail past the headland and explore what lay beyond it. It would be some time before *Glaucus* came abreast of the point so that he could see what was in the inlet that slanted northwards toward Kamlakesh.

Giles retired to his cabin. He now had a lot more to tell Daphne in the ongoing letter, and he needed to relax from the strain of the attack and its aftermath. The crew would know that all was well with the captain and the ship when the sounds of his violin wafted up from the open scuttle airing his cabin, even though Giles knew that several of them claimed that it sounded like he was torturing cats. That they were not serious about this claim was revealed by the fact that they all tended to drift towards the source of the sound rather than away from it.

Chapter XII

Giles's longed-for retreat to his cabin for the soothing pleasures it promised was frustrated by Mr. Stewart. "Captain, there is something essential that I discovered from questioning one of the English slaves whom we rescued! You will want to hear what he has to say right away!"

"Yes?" Giles was amused. It was easy to forget just how young Mr. Stewart was because he was so competent in his role as acting third lieutenant. Here the eager youngster predominated over the trustworthy officer in the excited way in which he was addressing his superior.

"This man is what we would call a master's mate, or even possibly a master, on *Gloriana*. That is the East Indiaman the pirates have captured most recently. He says that he can draw us a plan of how that ship and two others are moored. He says that they are tied up on the inside of a sort of a mole that acts as a breakwater to protect the harbor. The Kamlakeshis only have a harbor watch on the ships, one man for each one."

"What is the significance of that, Mr. Stewart?"

"Well, sir, the man thinks that a cutting-out operation against the three vessels would work tonight, especially if we don't go beyond that headland so that no one in Kamlakesh knows that we are aware of the position of these ships. He says he knows what the hazards in getting at them are. Sir, wouldn't it be wonderful if we could capture them without a fight?"

"Yes, it would be, Mr. Stewart. Let me talk to this man who you discovered.

"Mr. Miller, Mr. Brooks," Giles called to these two officers before interviewing the man Mr. Stewart had discovered. "Do not go beyond that headland. Instead, back the mainsail while we are sending the prisoners ashore. Then head out to sea again, close-hauled as if we were slinking away having been attacked, afraid of what may lie behind the headland."

Mr. Stewart came back in a couple of minutes with one of the rescued slaves. He looked older than Giles and was gaunt, possibly from lack of nourishment while he was a galley slave. His face featured a long, tangled beard, and his hair hung down in dirty strands. He did not give the appearance of being a responsible sea officer, but, Giles reflected, who would look the part after a period as a galley slave to a merciless pirate band?

"Captain Giles," the acting lieutenant announced. "May I introduce Mr. Lassiter of the East India Company. He can tell us about the harbor in Kamlakesh."

"Welcome aboard, Mr. Lassiter. I'll be grateful for any help that you can give us."

"Captain, I am the grateful one. I don't know how we came to be so out of position when we were captured, though I have my suspicions. Captain Moudley seemed to be terribly offended by the treatment he received from the pirates, though it was nothing like what I got when it turned out that I had no one to ransom me. It almost seemed that Captain Moudley expected to be captured and then treated well. He was ranting about how other captured captains had been treated as princes. Almost as if he had been hoping to be captured by the pirates. We certainly did not put up any sort of a fight."

"Mr. Stewart tells me that you know a lot about the harbor at Kamlakesh and how we might recapture some of the pirates' takings."

"Yes, sir. It might help if I could sketch out the harbor and its features instead of just talking about them."

A makeshift table was quickly positioned while a pencil and some paper were being brought. While that was going on, Giles introduced the man from the East Indiaman to

Glaucus's master, Mr. Brooks. Something in the latter's bearing indicated that he did not equate the navigator with either a master or even a master's mate in the Navy.

Mr. Lassiter spoke as he drew. "Kamlakesh is on this inlet that runs along the coast. The headland over there marks the opening. As we proceed along the inside of this peninsula," Mr. Lassiter continued, sketching as he talked, "there is a little bay like this." He outlined a bay that formed a semicircle before another headland, in turn, took the inside shore of the peninsula to where it continued farther to the north.

"Kamlakesh was founded, I am told," Mr. Lassiter continued, "by the Portuguese. They established a fort here a couple of hundred years ago, about here." He drew a rough rectangle along the northern shore of the little bay. "The walls are made of sandstone, I think, and look to be about fifteen feet high. Atop them is a small battery of guns, very old cannon, I would guess, and not very powerful ones. Not the big ones you now see in batteries designed to protect harbors.

"Along here," he continued, "the Portuguese built a mole with a breakwater on one side and a quay on the other. There isn't much tide here, so there is no problem mooring alongside the mole. That's where the pirates keep their captured vessels. My ship, *Gloriana*, an East Indiaman, is here, nearest the end of the mole. Then comes a French brig and, finally, a Dutch barque. They usually have only a single watchman on board each one at night.

"Next, in this corner, where the mole joins the land, the pirate galleys are moored. Not so many now, but the four that got away from you are probably there as well as six others that were not ready to attack you for one reason or another. They all will have their slaves on board, but only one guard is on each of them at night, but only on the ones moored next to the dock. At least, that was their practice in the past. They may still be doing so since the leader of the pirates was killed on the galley in which I was chained.

"There is another quay over here, in front of the fortress. That is where the fishing boats are tied, and there are usually also some small trading vessels. There weren't any this morning."

"Are you suggesting that we could recapture the three regular ships, Mr. Lassiter?" Giles asked.

"Yes, sir, unless, of course, they suspect that you are coming to take them, which would make it a good deal more hazardous."

"Could we also deal with the pirate vessels, do you suppose?"

"I hadn't thought about it – yes, I think you could if you could persuade the slaves on board to row the boats out. You would probably need one of us and someone who speaks Arabic for each boat if you want to get their support quickly."

Dr. Maclean approached the little group, as Mr. Lasssiter was finishing his description.

"Thank you, Mr. Lassiter," Giles said. "I will think about it. Dr. Maclean, do you have an injuries report?"

"Yes, sir. One of our men, Jasper, received a nasty slash on his arm. I have cleaned it and sewn it up. If it does not putrify, he will recover soon. I did the best I could to patch up the wounded pirates, but eight of them have died, and the survival of several others is still in question. Three of the slaves died after they were brought aboard. Four others have serious wounds. I had to amputate the leg of one of them, I am afraid. Whether he or the others will survive is up to God. The conditions on the rowing decks must have been awful. Shall I tip the dead pirates over the side?"

"Let me think. No. We'll take them and the other corpses out to sea and give them proper burials. The watchers from Kamlakesh may well have telescopes, and it should help to convince them that we will not be attacking them immediately. Mr. Miller, did you hear me?"

"Yes, sir."

"Then carry out that plan."

"Aye, aye, sir."

"Next, I want all officers and petty officers to gather here so we can plan what we will be doing."

The group assembled near the taffrail.

"There are three merchant ships moored on the mole in front of Kamlakesh," Giles began. "At night, they only have a single watchman on board each one. Here is a sketch that Mr. Lassiter from the East Indiaman drew for us. I intend to capture the three vessels. To complicate matters, the pirates moor their craft at the end of the breakwater, here. They should not be a problem, but we should try to keep quiet so that we don't alert them to our presence until the three ships are in our hands. I also hope to destroy the pirate galleys if it turns out that we can do so safely.

"The First Lieutenant would normally lead such an expedition, but I am sorry to tell you, Mr. Miller, that I shall be in charge."

"But, sir, surely it is my privilege to lead such attacks so that I may advance my career towards getting posted."

"It would be, normally, Mr. Miller, I know. However, if things do not go as I hope, we may be fighting the Bey's men. He is nothing but an outlaw who lives off the proceeds of piracy, but he is, at least nominally, under the Sultan of Casablanca. This raid could be interpreted as going to war with a foreign kingdom, and, especially if the attack doesn't work, the commander of the landing force may find himself in very hot water. On balance, it is better if I take direct command.

"I want to try to fool them into believing that we are going away or at least considering our options before attacking them. Our actions should, at least, indicate a level of caution that would suggest that nothing will happen tonight. So, Mr. Miller and Mr. Brooks, we are going to sail westward until almost sunset. See what you can do to have us go slowly without it being clear what we are doing to someone watching from the shore. We are going to hold a burial service before the sun sets. When it is full dark, we will reverse and sail back.

"I want to reach the headland, which is hiding the way into Kamlakesh, by midnight. Then we will take to the boats: my barge, the longboat under Mr. Marceau, Mr. Stewart will have the cutter, and Mr. Dunsmuir will have the longboat we 'borrowed' from the French frigate. I will capture *Gloriana*. That's the name of the East Indiaman. Mr. Marceau will take the French ship, and, Mr. Dunsmuir, the Dutch one is your responsibility. Mr. Macauley, you will take a file of marines in Mr. Stewart's boat and stand ready to help any of us who are having trouble. Otherwise, I will want you to keep an eye out for the pirates trying something to counter our actions. Finally, if all goes well, we will try to destroy the remaining pirate galleys before we leave. Now, Mr. Stewart, using your knowledge of the former galley slaves, select ones who were on the merchant ships we are going to capture to join our cutting-out operation. Put them in the boats that will be directed at the ones in which they sailed.

"Yes, Mr. Mohammed?" Giles concluded by addressing the East India Company man, who seemed very eager to say something.

"Captain Giles, if you are going to try to capture the pirate ships, may I suggest that I come along. I don't think you want to sink them with all the slaves chained on board, and taking them to sea will be easier if I can tell them what is going on. Some of the men we rescued should be included since they are familiar with the operation of those boats."

"Well thought of, Mr. Mohammed! And thank you for volunteering. See to it with Mr. Stewart. They can also go in his boat with Mr. Macauley and the marines.

"Any questions?"

"Sir," said Mr. Brooks. "If we drag a sail behind us while we are going out to sea, we can have all sails set and still be going very slowly. I am sure that we can set the drag without being seen from the shore. That way, we can be surer of being able to return by midnight, even if the wind drops."

"Good idea, Mr. Brooks. See to it with the officer of the watch."

The meeting broke up with some excited chatter about the upcoming adventure. With the exception of Mr. Brooks, they were all young enough to treat the planned recapture of the three ships as an adventure. It promised plenty of excitement to further break up the boredom of their long ocean voyage.

Giles went to his cabin to sleep. He would be up all night and needed to be alert when leading the adventure. He had learned, starting from his first days as a midshipman, that it was wise to grab sleep whenever the opportunity presented itself, especially when broken nights were anticipated.

"Wake me at one bell of the second dog-watch," he instructed his servant. In moments he was asleep, just as if he had not a worry in the world. He woke ready to conduct the burial and to go on to capture the merchantmen according to plan.

All was prepared for the funeral when Giles emerged on the quarter deck. In the waist of the ship, the corpses had been lined up, ready to be deep-sixed as he was reading the service. The crew was assembled, looking serious about witnessing the time-honored ceremony.

The last of the weighted-down bodies splashed into the ocean as the sun was setting. *Glaucus* resumed her course away from Kamlakesh. Giles looked towards the land. On the top of the hill that hid the town from view, he saw the glint of the last rays of the sun reflected, he guessed, from a telescope.

"Mr. Miller, hold this course for a while after the sun has gone," Giles ordered before rushing down to his cabin.

The stern windows had been left open for the cool evening air. Giles grabbed his telescope and looked through one of the windows, keeping back in the shadows so that there would be no danger of the watcher spotting him. He focused on the spot where he had seen the glint. Yes, he was right. There was a man, dressed in a white robe, lying on the ground and leveling a telescope at *Glaucus*. Giles had been watching for only a few minutes when the watcher rose, shrugged, and turned to walk away. Giles waited until his head had disappeared behind the hill before going on deck again.

"Mr. Miller, get that drag back on board. Then wear around and come onto the course to take us just clear of the headland. We are no longer under observation."

Glaucus sprang forward as a jerk on a line converted the heavy sail from being a sea anchor to being merely an inconvenience. It was hoisted back on board with water pouring from it. The frigate reversed course.

Glaucus began to make the most of the light breeze. It was, Giles reflected, just as well that he had ordered the use of the drag. Otherwise, they would have been very late getting to the place where the boats were to be launched.

The twilight deepened, and the stars seemed to gain in brilliance as *Glaucus* glided smoothly through the small waves that the light breeze generated, rising and falling gently with the long ocean swell that was not pronounced on the lee side of Africa. Giles had worried that the wind might veer to make it impossible to reach their object on one tack. Instead, it had backed very slightly, if it had changed direction at all. It was also blowing strongly enough that sound would not carry very far over the water. There was every chance that there would be no warning of their presence to people in Kamlakesh.

By Mr. Brooks's reckoning, *Glaucus* reached the point at which the boats were to leave slightly after eight bells were rung to signify midnight. It was a clear night, the stars alone providing illumination for the activity. Moonrise was not until a few minutes after five bells. Giles was counting on the moon to provide more straightforward navigation of the captured ships when it came time for them to leave Kamlakesh's harbor.

The rowers in the four boats did not rush, stroking smoothly in time with each other without any splashes as the oars dipped into the water; Giles did not want them to be exhausted when the time came to seize the ships. After an hour of toiling, he had the oarsmen change places with other sailors whom he had brought. The destination of the little fleet was clear. It showed ahead as a black stripe between the starry sky with pinpricks of light reflected by the water, which was ruffled by the light breeze. Finally, *Glaucus*'s boats reached the end of the mole. The approach had gone without incident. The enemy should have no inkling about what was about to befall them.

Looking to the east, Giles could see the first hint that the moon was about to rise. He signaled for the boats to proceed with the attack. His crew was to be the first to try to capture a merchantman. He relieved Carstairs at the helm; his coxswain would be the best man to be the first man to board the East Indiaman. When he was a midshipman, Giles had persuaded the thief who was now his cockswain that serving in the navy was preferable to being delivered to the authorities to be hung or transported to Australia. It had been a good choice. Carstairs was followed by Jenkins, another one-time Cockney pickpocket.

The only sound heard by the men of Giles's barge after Carstairs and Jenkins boarded the East Indiaman was a muffled thump. A couple of moments later, Jenkins peered over the side at the barge.

"All clear," he whispered down. "Only a night-watchman. We've dealt with him."

Most of the crew of Giles's longboat surged onto the deck of *Gloriana,* making as little noise as they could as they prepared to take the ship to sea. Giles stayed in his barge and directed the remaining crew to row as quietly as possible to the next vessel, which was the French brig. Mr. Marceau leaned over the ship's side to say in a low voice, "She is ours now."

Something went wrong with Mr. Dunmuir's attempt to capture the Dutch barque in silence. Just when it seemed that all three targets had been taken without anyone noticing, a loud cry, followed by a solid-sounding thump, broke the silence. Everyone froze, wondering what would be the consequence of this shout.

The noise elicited a loud cry from farther along the quay where the pirate ships were moored. Giles's hope for an undetected capture of stolen vessels had been frustrated.

The situation was saved by Mr. Mohammed. He was aboard Mr. Stewart's longboat, which was sheltering in the shadow of the Dutch ship. In a loud, slurred voice, he yelled a string of words. They were answered from the galleys by a seemingly light-hearted yell, to which Mr. Mohammed replied in words that must have been a curse, recognizable from the tone even though no one among the attackers understood a word of what he said. His bluster was followed by a laugh from the galley and a teasing sounding shout.

Silence followed. Giles signaled everyone to remain still. They waited for ten minutes before starting the next phase of their attack. Though it was asking a lot of the marines from whom stealth was rarely required, Giles's plan called for them to land silently and form up beside the Dutch barque. The pirate galleys were berthed along the landward end of the mole, with each one having three or four others rafted up to them. There was room for eight on the quay with up to six more rafted together alongside each of the ones on the mole. Of course, many of the ships that had formerly been moored in this space had been sent to the bottom earlier in the day. How many would be tied up alongside after the havoc that *Glaucus* had rendered to their numbers and how many were still rafted was anyone's guess.

The pattern for protecting the galleys at night, Giles had been informed, was for a watchman to be stationed in each of the vessels tied to the mole, with no guards on any of the ones rafted farther out. The pirates counted on their slaves' shackles to keep them docile. That was why there had been only one guard for each string of boats with that man stationed on the galley next to the mole. Giles hoped that that was still the case. His plan was to overwhelm the watchmen, seize the boats and row them out of the inlet along with the recaptured ships. It would be best if he could do it without alarming the rest of the pirates who presumably were somewhere in Kamlakesh.

Central to Giles's plan for capturing the pirate galleys was his coxswain, Carstairs. His career as a pickpocket made him the perfect choice to use to silence an opponent with no fuss. Carstairs had recruited several others of *Glaucus*'s crew with similar nefarious occupations, which had all relied on stealth. They were assigned the task of silencing the watchmen on the galleys with no noise. A very trying few minutes faced Giles as the chosen men moved silently along the quay towards their targets. When the one who had been assigned the last of the moored galleys reached his position, he would make the sound of an angry goshawk. That would be the signal for a simultaneous attack on each of the galleys.

Giles found himself holding his breath as the designated attackers crept towards their targets. A soft, ugly cry coming from the end of the mole, which Giles presumed was supposed to represent a goshawk's call, broke the silence. The attack should begin at once. The only indication that the operation was underway came immediately after the goshawk's cry. It was the unmistakable blast of a musket, coming from the third galley in line.

The need for stealth had evaporated; Giles's attackers surged onto their targets. All the pirate vessels were in the control of the men from *Glaucus* in a matter of minutes. The victors wasted no time in going to their assigned places. The former galley slaves who were part of the raid told the ones still chained to the prizes what was happening and what they had to do to gain their freedom.

The rising moon provided more illumination, making it easier for the galleys to cast off from each other and to unship their oars. Soon they were all at sea. Giles ran along the mole to *Gloriana* and gave orders to leave. Everything was ready. Immediately the men high on the spars dropped the sails while others on deck and on the mole took in the mooring lines. The sails were sheeted home, and the captured ship was underway. The French brig and the Italian barque were equally quick in leaving their berths.

Things were not going as smoothly on the captured galleys. There seemed to be a major problem with getting the slaves to row in a smooth rhythm. Mr. Bush, who was on the leading boat, solved the problem by ordering that the drum be used to set the pace as it was in normal operations. The confusion was ended. His galley cut through the water as it was designed to do. Drumbeats were the method of coordinating their strokes with which the rowers were familiar. All the other galleys followed Mr. Bush's lead. Soon all the captured vessels were rowing smoothly to the rhythm of their drums.

The boom of drums in the quiet harbor, Giles reflected, would surely produce a reaction from the town, even though the firing of the musket had yet to create any visible activity. He had only a short time to wait. Torches appeared on the quay at the base of the wall protecting Kamlakesh. Giles could see a group of men on the other side of the harbor trying to make out what was happening. They all set off running along the seafront to get to the mole. It would do them no good: Giles had taken all the boats. The only watercraft which remained in Kamlakesh were a cluster of fishing boats and two or three small coasting vessels that were tied up in front of the town. Even if they set to sea, they would only be an irritant in the successful taking of all the essential vessels. There was now no way in which the forces of Kamlakesh could interfere with Giles's seizing the means and rewards of their piracy.

The progress of Giles's little group of ships down the inlet was restricted to the speed of the slowest vessel. This slowpoke was the Dutch barque, possibly because it was the one for which the fewest men familiar with that ship had been among the liberated slaves. At first, Giles thought that he might have to tow her out, but before he could issue the appropriate orders, the barque's crew found a way to get more speed from her.

Mr. Miller, who had spent a sleepless night on *Glaucus* waiting for news of the raid, had the impression that the flotilla was hardly moving after it had first been spotted coming around the end of the mole. Indeed, dawn was at hand before they came up to the frigate. Giles ordered the ships to anchor close to *Glaucus* and the galleys to tie up on each side of her.

Freeing the galley slaves was the first task to be performed. The shackles were opened, and the men taken aboard the *Glaucus*. There they had to be fed. As with the men whom Giles had liberated earlier, they were starving. He ordered that a substantial meal be provided and then told Mr. Dunsmuir and Mr. Mohammed to separate them into two groups as they had the previous captives. He had no use for the galleys themselves. He ordered that they be sunk as soon as they had been searched for anything that might be useful.

"Mr. Miller," Giles addressed his first lieutenant. "Go over to the East Indiaman and gauge what she has aboard her and how much of a crew would be needed to sail her on a lengthy voyage."

He gave the equivalent orders to Mr. Marceau and Mr. Stewart to evaluate the French and Dutch ships. Then he was free of immediate duties, so he could ruminate on what his next step should be. The primary problem remaining after he had liberated the East Indiaman was how to pry loose from the claws of the Bey of Kamlakesh the British citizens who were being held hostage. While, implicitly, his orders had concerned only gentlefolk and officers of the East India Company, Giles was also resolved to free any British seamen or other civilians who had been enslaved. He did not have explicit authority to pay for the most important people to be freed, though he was sure that the East India Company would arrange for their ransoms if he failed. However, he wanted to release all hostages, both ones held in the hope of ransom and others who had been enslaved because they were thought to be valueless as hostages.

Giles decided to strike while the iron was hot. Even before the liberated slaves had been sorted into those to be set ashore and the ones to remain with their rescuers, he ordered *Glaucus* to sail up the inlet until they were close to Kamlakesh. There the frigate hove to. Giles took his barge and the longboat to see if he could arrange a parley with the Bey of Kamlakesh. He asked Mr. Mohammed to accompany him to act as a translator. He divided Mr. Macauley's marines among the two boats with orders to have their muskets loaded and primed. The pair of boats set off towards the town under a white flag that Mr. Mohmmed assured Giles would be recognized as a flag of truce.

The boats headed towards the entrance in the city's walls from which men had emerged the previous evening. The rowers in Giles's barge maintained a steady, unhurried pace. Giles had no doubt that the news of *Glaucus*'s approach to the town had been spread throughout Kamlakesh, and his leaving the frigate should soon prompt a response. He was right. When their boat was halfway to the quay, the city gate opened, and a troop of men in white robes carrying muskets emerged. They were followed by a paladin carried by eight men in which sat a richly dressed, chubby man who was, in turn, followed by other robed men. Was this person the Bey, or was he some other high-level functionary? If the latter was the case, Giles hoped he had the authority to bargain, though he suspected that it was unlikely that he would get an immediate response to his demands.

The Bey, if that is who he was, remained on his throne. He started talking to a man who was more elaborately dressed than the others who accompanied him, though his clothes seemed simple in comparison to the man in the paladin.

"I think that it would be good tactics to interrupt that discussion," Mr. Mohammed addressed Giles.

"You're right," Giles agreed. "Tell them that I demand to speak to the Bey."

Mr. Mohammed, who turned out to have a much louder voice than Giles would have expected, rose from his seat in the boat and called out a long, emphatic-sounding speech in Arabic. Among the many words that were incomprehensible to him, Giles did recognize 'Richard Giles,' 'Ashton,' and '*Glaucus*.'

"What were you saying, Mr. Mohammed?" Giles asked.

"I told him that King George of Great Britain had sent the renowned captain Sir Richard Giles, Viscount of Ashton, in his ship, *Glaucus*, to retrieve all hostages that the Bey has captured illegally. He was not prepared to talk to some flunky but must talk with the Bey himself."

"Good. It looks as if they are ready to respond."

The chubby man with whom the man on the throne had been speaking stepped forward and shouted a long and angry-sounding speech. When the Arab spokesman concluded, Mr. Mohammad took a moment to gather his thoughts about the best way to report the conversation.

"The man on the carrying chair is indeed the Bey. He rejects your request completely, complaining that you are the pirate taking ships that were already in his control. The prisoners will only be released when the money he demands for them is paid."

"Tell him that I will wait only for a brief while for him to come to his senses. Otherwise, my king's navy and I will annihilate his fortifications. I will also make him and his family slaves, except that I will execute the most important of them, if the British hostages are not treated in the most proper way."

Giles's response must have angered the Bey. The minute that Mr. Mohammed finished speaking, the Bey called out what must have been an order to the soldiers who accompanied him. They leveled their muskets and fired a volley at Giles's boat. Whether it was poor training or because the boat was beyond the range of the ancient guns, none of the shots came near the launch; the water many yards short of it erupted in numerous little splashes.

Mr. Macauley looked at Giles, who nodded. The marines then pointed their already loaded muskets at the shore and fired. Their Brown Bess muskets were notoriously inaccurate, but they did fire a large ball that could do serious harm if it struck someone even at the limit of its range. The quay was within the range of the marines. Several of their musket-balls found targets in the closely packed men around the Bey of Kamlakesh. The most notable of the hits was on one of the men supporting the Bey's throne. It hit the man in the leg, knocking him down. In falling, he made untenable the position of the other man who was supporting that corner of the Bey's elaborate conveyance. The second man was knocked down by the first one, and down came that corner of the Bey's portable throne. The Bey was thrown to the ground. Some of his lackeys immediately picked him up and rushed back through the gate to disappear into Kamlakesh. The gate was slammed shut as soon as the last man had fled through it. Two bodies remained on the quay. One marked the place where a musket ball had shattered the leg of the man who had been helping to hold up the Bey. The other white hump was a soldier who had tripped and then been trampled by his comrades.

Giles ordered his boats to stay in the same places to see if the Bey or his minions would reopen negotiations. However, the gate remained closed. Soon they could see movement on the ramparts of the wall facing the harbor. It was pierced at regular intervals with gun embrasures. Behind these openings, Giles could make out guns. When he examined them through his telescope, they appeared to be bronze cannon, much tarnished by age and elaborately decorated even at the muzzle. The guns must, he thought, date back to the time when the Portuguese had established a fortified base here to facilitate their trade.

Both Giles and Mr. Macauley knew that the chance of a cannonball hitting a small boat at such a distance was very small. Nevertheless, Giles did give the order to start to row away, but only slowly, as if the firing from the guns was not a worry.

The first of the guns barked. It had looked to Giles as if the cannon was at maximum elevation. He expected the ball to go over his boat. Instead, it plopped into the water just beyond the mole. Another gun fired, with no more impressive a result. The same lack of success marked the firing of the other cannon.

"They must be using really bad gunpowder," Lieutenant Macauley called across to Giles.

"Or maybe they are using cannonballs that are too small." He replied.

It was a long time before the guns fired again, and again the shots fell well short of Giles's boats, and few were in a line such that they could have come close to their targets even if they had gone farther. These guns would not prevent *Glaucus* from getting close to the fortifications of Kamlakesh. She could safely bombard the city.

Giles ordered a return to his frigate. He would try again to get a parlay, but not on the next day. In the meantime, he would place his ship so that no vessel could enter or leave the town. He would wait several days for a response from Kamlakesh. Possibly the Bey would be more willing to negotiate when he realized that he was now sealed off from the sea.

Once on board *Glaucus*, Giles made a point of praising the accuracy of the marines. The men who had been chosen to go on the expedition were all in good spirits recounting how their shots had tumbled the fat dignitary to the ground. They, of course, had no worries about what would happen next, as Giles did. He retired to his cabin. Daphne would want to be told about today's events while they were still fresh in his mind, even though it would be a long time before she would get to read about them. That thought reminded him that she was probably working on mastering the first of the Beethoven sonatas they had acquired in London. He had better put in some time working on the music, now that there was nothing much else for him to do. He needed a lot of practice if he expected to keep up with her once they were reunited.

Chapter XIII

The summer was progressing smoothly, Daphne realized, as her carriage approached Dipton. It seemed that the corn looked just a little bit riper, and the lambs appeared to be stronger than when she had left only a few days ago. Would the reports from her managers be favorable? So much could go wrong, especially when she was responsible for not only Giles's large estate but also her father's. She had yet to go to Ashton to see the property there, which went with the title she enjoyed, though she did get regular reports about it. What would happen financially when the Earl of Camshire's holdings were added to Giles's present ones?

Major Stoner would want to discuss the canal shipment business. He was fully capable of managing it by himself or with the assistance of Captain Bush, but he seemed to consider Daphne his colonel or possibly general to whom regular reports were required and whose approval was necessary. She should really try to think of Captain Bush as Sir Toby, if only for his finacée's satisfaction. The thoughts of all the tasks, which she would have to undertake, reminded her that she now had to try to straighten out her uncle's business affairs. At least, he would be able to do much of the work himself since they had discovered that he could communicate by writing, but his participation would still require the aid of her father or someone else. Given how adept her father was at business, the someone else was likely to be her.

All these worries were for another day. Today, she would relax at home. A nice hot bath to remove the grime of the journey from Birmingham, followed by time in the nursery with Bernard, and then a good dinner with no guests, followed by an early night. She hated to admit it even to herself, but bumping over the hard-packed roads of summer, despite being in the best of carriages, was a tiring business.

Only two of the steps in her plan came to fruition.

The bath was heaven though Betsey seemed to be a bit out of sorts as she got it ready and made sure that large, fluffy towels were available when Daphne emerged from the tub. Berns was glad to see her. Despite Nanny Weaver's disapproval of his mother's getting down on the floor, Daphne did just that. She even helped him when he indicated that he wanted to stand. That went well, and he was able to remain upright for several seconds. As soon as he sat down, he wanted to try standing again, and it became a game to see how long the infant could stand after she had helped him up before he plopped down amid a burst of laughter.

Nanny Weaver was getting more and more distressed. Parents should see their children only for limited amounts of time and only in the most decorous manner. It would be her task to calm him down after his mother had got him all excited. She was even embarrassed that she had learned from Daphne the fun of raucous playing with Master Bernard and sometimes indulged in it herself.

"My lady," she announced. "You are exhausting Master Bernard and getting him so excited that he will have trouble settling for his meal and his next sleep."

Her annoyance was clear in the way she addressed Daphne. Having been Daphne's nanny, she usually addressed her mistress by her first name when they were in private. Daphne complied with the suggestion that she stop playing with her son only after she had continued long enough to show who was in charge. Then she picked up the squealing infant, kissed him, and returned him to the nanny.

The deviation from Daphne's plans arrived as she was changing after her romp in the nursery. Steves came to the door of her dressing room to tell Betsey to inform her mistress that the Countess of Camshire had arrived and wished to see her urgently. Daphne ordered Betsey to have Steves tell her mother-in-law that she would be down to greet her ladyship as soon as she could. Lady Clara was, of course, to stay in the rooms which she preferred to all others in Dipton Hall.

Daphne was puzzled by the Countess's arriving unannounced. Though Lady Clara was a frequent visitor and was always welcome, her invariable practice had been to write well in advance to say that she was coming to Dipton. Her mother-in-law was usually a stickler for proper etiquette, though Daphne's influence was getting her to unbend a bit. What could be the reason for this departure from her usual pattern?

Daphne descended the main staircase to find that the Countess had already gone to her dressing room to change from her journey. While she was waiting for her mother-in-law to appear, Daphne asked Steves to ask Nanny Weaver to bring Berns to the drawing-room. She knew that, like Nanny Weaver, this was how the Countess believed children should be seen by their parents rather than by their going to the nursery to play, though that was what Daphne usually did. There is where the Countess found them with Daphne again on the floor playing a silly game that had Berns laughing and crawling vigorously all over the rug as Daphne moved various animal toys around. His nap must have been short, but he was not acting sleepy or cranky.

Lady Clara joined them on the floor, even though she had once told Daphne that she had never done so when her own sons were small. Only when Daphne had introduced her to this way of enjoying children and demonstrated that there was no irreparable loss of dignity involved, did the Countess begin to participate. She was now as keen on getting down to his level as Bernard was to have her there. Unfortunately, all too soon, Nanny Weaver insisted that the child not be allowed to get too excited and carted him off to the nursery.

Only when the nanny and her charge had left, and the two ladies were seated more decorously in chairs, with tea provided by the ever mindful Steves, did Daphne introduce the subject of Lady Clara's visit.

"Lady Clara, it is always a great pleasure to welcome you to Dipton Hall. I am afraid that your note must have gone astray. Otherwise, I would have welcomed you properly."

"No need to apologize, dear. I didn't have time to write in advance. I have received a terrible letter from Camshire. I want your advice about it."

"What did it say?" Daphne asked.

"Here, I would like you to read it," replied the Countess fumbling in her reticule for the missive. She handed it to Daphne, who opened it and read:

> Wife:
>
> I am writing to inform you that my fool of a doctor tells me that I have at best four more weeks to live. He may be wrong, of course; he often is. However, I am in such pain that I will be happy to go.
>
> I have, for some time, been taking steps to ensure that my financial affairs are settled as much in the way I want as my rotten father's entail will allow. I have also been shifting as much money as I could acquire into consols in the name of my long-term

companion, Mistress Marilyn Montrose. Mistress Montrose has provided me with pleasure and services that you, my wife, never would. She joined me when she was already highly skilled in the arts of love and conversation, and she has provided me with much exciting satisfaction, far more than I ever received from you. I should have known what to expect from you based on my experience with Carolyn, my first wife, but you were even less responsive to my advances. Mistress Montrose quite rectified that emptiness in my pleasures. I will leave to her the house we live in, free and clear, together with the consols I mentioned earlier. It is fair payment for her services.

I am happy to say that I have compromised the income from lands in the Camshire entail as much as I have been able to. As a result, your widow's portion will be far less than you expect, though far more than I would choose to leave you if there were no entailments. Of course, this reduction in your expectations is only fair since I expected to get considerable financial benefits from marrying you that never materialized. Your father shut me out in a most unfair way.

I would be leaving this earth happier if Richard – I will not call him Ashton, for he lacks all the spirit of my true eldest son – were not so weak-minded that he will undoubtedly support you just as he did my daughter Marianne. I am sure that my son David would have a much keener awareness of his own interest.

My will specifies that I am to be buried at Ashbury Abbey. It pleases me to know that my son must keep his ties to the place where I am buried because, unknown to him, I have renewed the entail on all my lands. I have done everything that I can to make it an unproductive place, which he cannot even sell.

I realize you will not genuinely mourn my passing. It gives me pleasure, however, to know that you will have to pretend to do so by the conventions of our class.

The letter was signed 'Camshire' in a very shaky scrawl. The rest had been neatly written in the round, characterless hand that indicated it was the work of someone who had come to literacy only after reaching maturity and was little practiced in writing.

"What a horrible man!" Daphne exclaimed when she had finished reading. "It's improper for me to say, I know, but you will be well rid of him!"

"I certainly will be. I am very sad about it. I never loved him, but it was supposed to be a great marriage when I agreed to marry him. He was always complaining about me and was very stingy about everything except clothes for functions where he hoped to advance his own interests or a stylish carriage to demonstrate how affluent he was. He asserted his rights over me without warning, whenever he wanted, and then complained that I was not willing to do unspeakable things with him. Luckily, he stopped soon after David was born.

Everyone knew that he was having affairs with other women. He never tried to hide it. In fact, he boasted about what he was doing. Then he took up with that woman, and everybody knew about it too. And now, he has done me out of my dower rights."

Lady Clara burst into tears at that last statement. Daphne let her weep for a few minutes before stating, "Don't be upset. We'll set it right – at least the way he has been stealing from you to set up that woman, whoever she is."

"I don't see how you can. He has already spent the money on that doxy."

"Who is she, anyway?"

"She was a courtesan. Expert in pleasing men – in all ways, if you take my meaning. I suppose she was somewhat like Lady Hamilton. Maybe not so accomplished, but then Camshire is no Admiral Nelson, is he? She got Camshire to set her up in a house in Norfolk. He has several times told me that she would do things to him that I wouldn't, though I have no idea what he was talking about. In some ways, I was relieved not to have to put up with him anymore, but it was very humiliating when he flaunted her all over the place so that all my acquaintances knew about her. I have no idea what she did to him that cast such a complete spell."

Daphne had a fair idea about what this Mrs. Montrose could do to keep the Earl's attention. Daphne had inadvertently found out more than she had wanted to know when she was extricating from the claws of a celebrated madam Giles's inheritance from his half brother. There had been strong hints about some of the things that the whoremonger and her 'ladies' provided to their customers to extract money from them. Daphne had been smart enough to figure out what they might be talking about. No one had ever told her before how to pleasure a man, nor that a couple could enhance their love-making if they only knew how. She had explored these insights with Giles. After his initial shock at her suggestions, he became an eager partner as they explored each others' bodies in ways that earlier she had never even guessed existed, nor would she have imagined that they could convey such pleasure. Maybe it was sinful what they were doing, but it certainly had cemented their relationship as nothing else could have.

Daphne could hardly tell her mother-in-law about those discoveries. It would probably disgust and embarrass her, and the prospects of it being useful knowledge for Lady Clara to acquire were remote. Instead, she turned to the more practical aspects of the situation.

"Lady Clara, you are not to worry about your dower rights. If Camshire has succeeded in ruining the income of Ashbury Abbey and other properties – and he may not have done all that much damage – Richard is bound to set it right. Knowing him, he will not allow your portion to fall. As you are aware, he gives me full authority to make that sort of commitment. However, first, we should do all that we can to frustrate the Earl's schemes. I will get to work on undoing the Earl's work right away."

"But, Daphne, you are busy – and have another child on the way."

"True, but I am not just sitting around waiting for the baby to arrive. Mr. Jackson thinks that is the worst thing that women who are with child can do, even though it is usually recommended for pregnant gentlewomen. I have to take a day or two to recover from my trip to Birmingham and make sure that my uncle is properly settled, but then I can go to London to consult our solicitors and others about what can be done."

"You have only just returned from Birmingham? Oh, I shouldn't have come. And what's this about your uncle?"

"Of course you should have come, even though I am busy. I like to be active, as you know."

Daphne went on to explain what had happened to her uncle and why they had thought it best to bring him to Dipton

Manor. The Countess was distressed to hear about Daphne's uncle's predicament, though Daphne noted with some private amusement that Lady Clara's concern seemed to be as much for her father's having an invalid placed in his care as it was for her uncle. Not for the first time, Daphne wondered whether a romance would bloom between her father and her mother-in-law when the later became free to consider a liaison.

"I will send word for my solicitor in Ameschester, Mr. Snodgrass, to call on us tomorrow morning. He may have some ideas. Then, if necessary, I shall go to London to see our solicitors there. Richard's agent, Mr. Edwards, is likely to know of lawyers who are very good at getting around entails and so understand how to prevent his ruining you. You, of course, are welcome to come with me or to stay here while we sort the problems out. I imagine that we would be welcome at your sister's, Lady Struthers's, house.

"There is one thing that I would like you to do, Lady Clara. I want you to copy out the exact wording of the parts of that letter which concern how Camshire intends to do you out of your portion. I will show it to the lawyers, but they do not need to see the insults that are also included in that letter. I leave it to your judgment what is relevant and what is not."

Steves announced dinner at that moment. When they were seated kitty-corner to each other in the small dining room, the Countess was still brooding about her problems, so Daphne had to carry the conversation. Most of it was about Birmingham and the situation she had found there. Even as she talked, she realized how little she really knew about the gun-making business. Had she bitten off more than she could chew in taking on some responsibility for seeing that Morehouse and Son remained viable?

Lady Clara was not paying overly much attention to what Daphne was saying, only giving one word remarks to keep the conversation going. Daphne noted that her mother-in-law was consuming much more wine than was usual. When Daphne paused, the Countess broke in.

"I often think I would have been better not to have married the Earl at all. There have been some good times, I confess. If I hadn't married him, I would never have given birth to Richard and David, and they have been a joy to me, especially Richard. Being married to the Earl of Camshire wasn't all bad at the beginning, even though the marriage was never a love match. I enjoyed being a Society hostess in the early days and being in charge of Ashbury Abbey when there was still some money. But it was never a truly happy marriage."

Daphne decided it would be good for Lady Clara to ramble on so that she could let out her long-repressed ideas. The story was a sad one. Clara Delacourt was the fifth daughter of a nobleman of excellent lineage and connections, though, in recent times, their wealth had become much diminished, and her father was hastening the problem with extravagant expenditure and unwise investments in various money-making schemes. In many ways, Lady Clara's father had been just like her husband.

Lady Clara had been unlucky in the season in which she came out. She had never been a great beauty but was undoubtedly attractive. However, in those days, she was shy and lacked confidence. She had attracted one highly desirable suitor, but he had lost interest when he discovered that her dowry would be small. It took another two years before, finally, she attracted a serious suitor. The Earl of Camshire directed his attentions at her. He was, of course, a good deal older than she, and he had three children, by his previous marriage, whom he thought, in some vague sort of way, needed another mother. It turned out that he had paid so little attention to his offspring that he thought they were a great deal younger than they were in fact.

Lady Clara had appeared to the Earl to be a very suitable choice to fill his requirements. She was good-looking and not at all assertive. At that point in the narrative, Daphne wondered if her mother-in-law was deluded or whether her trials and tribulations over the years had made her change. In Daphne's experience, the Countess had always seemed very determined to get her way. This tendency had been particularly evident in their early encounters, but Daphne still, at times, had to manage their relationship so that it appeared that she was allowing the Countess to assert herself even when Daphne was adjusting only a little to her mother-in-law's wishes.

Lady Clara's marriage was more a business deal than a romance. The Earl had never cared much for his bride personally, though he had insisted forcefully and, at first, frequently, on his marital rights. Those encounters had produced Richard and his younger brother David. They, and not her husband, had become the center of Lady Clara's life for a time. However, Richard had been sent away to sea at a young age, and for years she had seen far too little of him. She had seen more of David, though he often stayed with friends for large parts of his vacations after he had gone to public school and then university, so, in fact, she had seen little of either of her sons after they had ceased to be small children.

The Earl had become steadily more complaining and avaricious as his fortunes declined. His allowance to his wife became hopelessly meager if she was to run their big houses on what he provided. He had galloped through her dowry until there was nothing left, and he continually complained at how stingy her father had been.

Lady Clara's maternal grandfather had realized the unfortunate situation in which she had found herself. He established a fund that would make up for the inadequacies of her husband's provisions for her. He had not transferred the money to the Earl, knowing that then his granddaughter would benefit little from it. Instead, the fund was set up as a trust for Lady Clara's benefit, managed by her father's solicitor to give her a stipend to spend as she wished. Of course, when the Earl learned of this fund, he had cut back what he gave her still further, but the money from the trust fund was still adequate and, of course, more predictable than the amounts provided by her husband.

Though the Countess had never had a happy relationship with the Earl, it had been quite tolerable while he was having some good fortune in his various ventures. However, as his financial disasters became more numerous than his successes, and his word was considered less and less trustworthy, his income shrank. He responded by becoming involved in shadier and shadier ventures. As a result, his reputation, and, by association, that of Lady Clara worsened. Friends stopped writing. Invitations to visit became rarer. Then her situation was completely shattered when the Earl took up with Mistress Montrose.

"Who was she?" Daphne broke in.

The Countess was reluctant to speak of this woman, but, with a little prompting, the story emerged. Mrs. Montrose was a courtesan, a very successful one by all accounts, though maybe not as talented as some of the most well-known of the breed. According to the rumors that some acquaintances had gleefully told to Lady Clara, this trumped-up doxy was rapidly losing her allure as she aged. She had latched onto the Earl of Camshire as, allegedly, her last hope. She had somehow mesmerized him completely. Having ensnared the Earl, he had set her up in an elegant house near Norwich to which she had retired. That house was where the Earl was now most likely to be found, enjoying the benefits of being the support of a talented whore, though Lady Clara's 'friends' had made sure to tell her of the rumors that Mrs. Montrose was not above entertaining other admirers when the Earl had to be away.

The result of this courtesan getting her claws into Lady Clara's husband was that he was now determined to ruin his wife as far as it was possible, according to the letter that Lady Clara had shown Daphne. His taking up with the whore and the rumors that woman had spread about Lady Clara's inadequacies, retold so nastily by the Countess's acquaintances, had already cost her most of her friends. Now she was warmly welcomed with complete support only at her sister Gillian's house in London and at Dipton Hall.

Daphne's sympathies went out to her mother-in-law. However, in her view, sympathy was not enough. Concrete action was required to try to frustrate the worst of the Earl's intentions. She had to convince the Countess that they could take steps to minimize the damage he was doing, and maybe even get a bit of revenge. She had already sent for her solicitor, but she guessed that she needed the more experienced lawyers in London. She knew that she and her mother-in-law would be welcome at the mansion of the Countess's sister Gillian, Lady Struthers.

Lady Clara retired as soon as dinner was over, claiming exhaustion as a reason for not lingering at table or in the drawing-room. Daphne was also tired, but, before she went upstairs, she arranged for Griffiths, an ex-cavalryman, to take their fastest horse to London immediately to warn Lady Struthers that Daphne and the Countess would be visiting.

The following morning, Mr. Snodgrass, the solicitor, arrived from Ameschester. He had, at various times, helped

Daphne with legal problems. He listened carefully, taking notes as the story unfolded, while Daphne explained how the Earl was trying to impoverish his wife and, incidentally, lower the value of Giles's inheritance.

Mr. Snodgrass asked several questions for clarification as Daphne's report on the problem went on, but made no substantive comments. When she had finished, he gave his initial opinions.

"Property matters among the landed gentry, including entails, form a large part of my practice. Entails are always good for my business. Though they are all basically the same, there are subtle differences that can have significant effects on how restrictive they are, and, because of these complications, many solicitors benefit greatly from matters related to them. I suppose that entails are meant to ensure that the next generation – as represented by the eldest son – will maintain the estate he inherits while still being able to enjoy its benefits and make reasonable provisions for any daughters or other sons. For many families, it is a tradition that the entail on the property keeps on being renewed from generation to generation automatically, but in many cases, the owner of an entailed property will try to get around the restrictions, though surprisingly often he will then entail the property more restrictively so that his heirs cannot use the same devices.

"I cannot say, however, that I have ever encountered such a despicable way of trying to destroy the value of an entailed property or to avoid the proper provision for a widow. Did the Earl place an entail on his properties to limit their use by his heirs?"

"Yes, he did," replied the Countess. "I heard him tell his first son, Peter, who was the Viscount Ashton before my son Richard, that, since Lord Camshire had been restrained and greatly inconvenienced in using his inheritance, he would impose even stricter limitations on his son. Of course, in Peter's case, that was a critical measure to take if the property were to keep its value while he owned it."

"I see. I have to confess that this case is a bit out of my experience. If you want my help, my lady, I would have to see all the relevant documents. I suspect something might be done to stop your husband from further eroding the value of the properties, and possibly to recover some of the money he has transferred to this Mrs. Montrose, though undoubtedly that would have to be resolved in court. However, exactly what would be the most efficacious manner in which to proceed is something that is beyond my own competence since I have never handled a case quite like this one.

"I would suggest that you consult with a more expert solicitor, one who has more experience in dealing with the various local variations of the interpretation of documents that are relevant to the properties involved. As you may know, while it is the case that the law is reasonably uniform as it applies to most of the gentry, it tends to vary in strange ways when peers of the realm are involved. What is the law depends, I am sad to say, on how much interest the nobleman and his first son have. The interpretations also may differ in different counties.

"I can recommend a good friend of mine in London who is part of a large group specializing in just this sort of problem. Geoffrey Hazleton is his name. I articled with his father and got to know him quite well, though I then decided that I would be happier here in Ameschester rather than in London. Mr. Hazleton's rooms are in Chancery Lane, just off the Strand. I will write a letter of introduction to him if you believe that you would be better off to have him and his associates look into this matter for you rather than me."

"I think that we should do that, given what you have said about your limited experience in this sort of case," Daphne said after only a glance at the Countess. "I was thinking of going up to London tomorrow, to visit Lady Camshire's sister, Lady Struthers, if it should prove to be desirable to visit London on this matter."

"In that case, I shall give you a letter of introduction to take with you. You can send it round to Mr. Hazleton when you arrive. I am sure that he will see you as quickly as possible."

"Do you think that he will be able to see us immediately?" Daphne asked.

Mr. Snodgrass laughed. "I am afraid, my lady, that you have yet to realize how prized any professional man would be to have as clients a countess and a viscountess, the first the sister to the wife of a powerful member of the Government and the second married to a future earl who is also a prominent war-hero. My friend will see you just as soon as he can. If possible, he will clear his calendar for your consultation to take place immediately or to wait on you at Struthers House at once if that is more convenient."

The meeting with Mr. Snodgrass had used up much of the morning. As the solicitor left, Steves discretely let Daphne know that several of the men who were in charge of various aspects of the running of Dipton Hall wanted to see her. Daphne reflected, not for the first time, that she really should find an overall manager to whom these people could report so that she need deal only with the most pressing matters. However, she reflected, she enjoyed the contact with those more closely involved in what was happening, and so herself knowing what was going on in more detail. She had found it very difficult already to surrender some of her control to managers, and she would not let go of all of her making direct decisions about what should be done at Dipton Hall. She did, however, find time to direct Steves to ask her father and uncle to come to dinner and detailing to him what changes were needed to make sure that the invalid would feel at home. She hoped that the presence of her father might ease some of the gloom that surrounded the Countess. She had suspected that when the Countess was free, and a conventional period of mourning had passed, her father might marry Lady Clara. It could, however, radically alter this expectation if Lady Clara realized that tending to Daphne's crippled uncle might be involved in such a development.

When the last of the men she had to see about running her estate had left, Steves entered to announce yet another arrival. This one was the painter, Mr. Findlay. Daphne had forgotten all about how he was supposed to come to Dipton Hall to start work on the paintings she wanted, landscapes of some of the finer views on her estate as well as family portraits. Well, she was just too busy right now to sit for him. Besides which, recently, pregnancy had been good for neither her figure nor her complexion. Mr. Findlay would have to start on the landscapes and prepare the backgrounds of the portraits in anticipation of their subjects being available to sit for them. He would have to stay with her father. With Giles away, she wanted to give the gossipy women of the neighborhood and of society no pretense for speculating on what the painter might be doing. On her visit to London, she had discovered that society ladies were sure that portrait painters were all too ready to seduce women, or at least to get them to pose in the nude. Daphne wanted no rumors to start, no matter how unfounded they might be.

Daphne had steves show Mr. Findlay in so that she could explain the situation to him, though she only told him the part about how busy she was. He was welcome to stay with her father and to work on the landscapes. She would invite him to dine when things were less hectic. She didn't mention that that would not occur until Giles was home.

When Daphne's Uncle George was wheeled into the parlor before dinner, Daphne at once recognized the schoolroom slate that rested in his lap. Writing on it would be easier than on a pad. Who in the world had found it among the things that had been put away at Dipton Manor and realized that it would be an improvement over using a pad and paper?

Introductions to the Countess resulted in George Moorhouse demonstrating that he had already mastered the art of jamming the slate on his lap so that he could write on it and then using his good hand to show the result to others. Daphne hoped that this achievement would go a long way to relieving her mother-in-law's doubts about including an invalid in their group.

Uncle George's value in a gathering was demonstrated in the middle of dinner. Daphne and the Countess had been telling of the actions of the Earl in trying to reduce the productivity of his lands to hurt her future income. Mr. George Moorhouse became a bit agitated and started writing on his slate. "Tell the tenants not to pay their rents until the Earl is dead," was his suggestion.

When everyone had read this message, he wrote, "Tell them to use the rent funds to restore their land in the ways that he should have done."

Mr. Daniel Moorhouse was the first to get the idea. "Are you saying, George, that this would starve the Earl of money while, at the same time, it would revive the income the Countess will receive?"

"Yes," was the written reply.

"But can't he just throw the tenants off their land for not paying rent?"

"In principle, but they have rights. They can tie up the Earl in court for not fulfilling them. If the Earl is about to die, he will be dead long before he can foreclose."

"Good point, Uncle George," said Daphne. "And as representing the future Earl and the influence he will inherit as it applies to doings concerning Ashbury Abbey, I can tell the local magistrates that it would be wise of them to go slow. They may be Lord Camshire's lackeys now, but they won't stay in their positions if Giles isn't happy with them."

"What a good idea," broke in the Countess. "I confess that I have boasted enough about Richard and how Daphne can handle all his affairs while he is at sea, that they will know that she speaks for him. I will write to my steward and tell him to implement this suggestion. He knows who will soon be in charge and will do as I say, even though it goes against the Earl's wishes. I know that he wants to keep his position after the Earl dies. Thank you very much, Mr. Moorhouse, for thinking of the solution. I now realize how beneficial it is to have a man of business in our circle."

It was hard to know since Daphne's uncle's face was somewhat frozen as a result of his ailment, but Daphne would have sworn that he was surprised and delighted by the Countess's words. Daphne had guessed that her uncle had been dreading the meeting, which her father had welcomed without thinking of his brother's feelings. Uncle George would know the low opinion held by the landed gentry of men who made their living by owning a factory, no matter how much talent was required to do so, or how much money it brought in.

The Countess had ceased to be horrified at Daphne's unique custom of not leading the ladies from the dining room to the drawing-room when there was only a small family gathering or a few close friends at dinner. Steves was, of course, still conflicted about this shocking variation on custom, but he was beginning to appreciate how popular it was with the dinner guests. He had even stocked the cellar with some cordials which many women preferred to port. The liquor lifted the gloom that had enveloped the Countess, and she told some stories of a light-hearted nature about life in Amesbury Abbey.

When the party broke up – Mr. George Moorhouse had been showing signs of dozing off in his Bath chair – the Countess insisted on at once writing a note to the estate manager at Ashbury Abbey to have him tell the tenants to stop paying rent and to use the money to improve their fields. Daphne allowed her mother-in-law to add that Viscountess Ashton wholeheartedly endorsed the instruction. Knowing that the future Earl's wife approved of the scheme would help to allay any fears he had about following the Countess's instructions without consulting the Earl.

As Betsey helped her mistress prepare for bed, Daphne reflected that she was excited about going to London, even though she had just returned from Birmingham. It wasn't that life at Dipton Hall was boring. Quite the contrary. But it was exciting to be part of larger matters as well and to be able to arrange things to help others. Of course, assisting the Countess would also enhance Giles's fortune and her son Bernard's inheritance. It was strange to be thinking of the child she played with on the nursery floor having an estate that needed protecting. However, Ashbury Abbey would be his eventually since the Earl had slapped a strict entail on his property, more to spite Giles than with any real desire to guarantee the well-being of a grandson he had never met.

The baby inside her took that moment to start kicking. She smiled at this signal that he -- or she -- was alive and vigorous, even though the movement in her womb was distinctly uncomfortable. She would have to try to persuade

Giles that her baby's inheritance, if the child she carried turned out to be a boy, would be substantial even though, of course, Berns would get the lion's share of Giles's estate.

Good heavens, how her life had changed! Three years ago, Miss Daphne Moorhouse, destined for a contented spinsterhood, would never have envisaged having thoughts about the inheritances of her children. When Giles had swept her off her feet and changed all her plans, he was then only a third son with no expectations of inheriting any property at all. It was still the dashing sea captain who had first charmed her for whom she was longing. Becoming the heir to the Earldom had not changed him significantly. How would his becoming the Earl alter their lives?

How she wished he would return soon! Certainly, dealing with issues surrounding the present Earl's illness and death would be easier if he were here, but that was not why she wanted him home. Simply put, she missed him, and she missed him more and more as time went on. Where was he now, and what was he doing? It had been such a long time since she had received a letter from him!

Chapter XIV

The hot African night, tempered only slightly by a land breeze, drove most of *Glaucus*'s crew on deck to sleep in various places, some of them using their hammocks to provide pillows. Despite Mr. Miller's horror at this interruption of the strict rules of the ship, Giles allowed the practice, making clear that it was an exception that was allowed only in this abnormal situation.

Glaucus was anchored right off the headland that marked the beginning of the inlet in which Kamlakesh was hidden. Giles was giving time for the Bey of Kamlakesh to evaluate the situation that he faced before again approaching him. With *Glaucus* in her present position, no ships could enter or leave the inlet. Already, he had seized many fishing boats, keeping the cargos to provide welcome supplements to his crew's meals, while preventing the fish from reaching the town. In each case, he put the fishermen ashore and sank the vessels. He had also captured a small Spanish trading vessel with a cargo of metal goods destined for Kamlakesh. Everyone on the captured vessel spoke some incomprehensible form of Spanish, probably from the Canary Islands, so Giles's curiosity about the sort of cargo the ship was intending to pick up in Kamlakesh went unanswered. Mr. Mohammed believed that much of Kamlakesh's supplies arrived by overland caravans rather than by sea, though he had no idea what the camels carried or what Kamlakesh supplied to traders in return.

Two weeks, Giles reckoned, should be enough time to make the Bey recognize the advantages of giving in to Giles's demands before *Glaucus* could wreak havoc on the town. However, he suspected that he might have to demonstrate more explicitly just how he could harm the Bey's citadel. Mr. Miller might have preferred more days to get everything not only ship-shape but perfect aboard the frigate. Nevertheless, Giles knew that that was the preference of all first lieutenants whose responsibility was to make sure that everything was in top condition. They could always find things that needed to be done if they had more time. Giles had to weigh the advantages of delay against the fact that waiting reduced the frigate's supplies.

Giles ordered Mr. Miller to clear for action and get underway at two bells of the morning watch when he could count on the sea breeze to agree with the prevailing trade winds to allow him to sail up the Kamlakesh Inlet easily. The frigate proceeded sedately up the channel, rounded into the wind, and anchored a couple of hundred yards off the mole. Mr. Miller attached a spring line to the anchor cable so that Giles could adjust the direction in which his ship was pointing, guaranteeing that he could make the broadside guns cover any part of the waterfront of Kamlakesh. The position which Giles had chosen was beyond the range of the ancient cannon mounted on the city walls. *Glaucus* could hit the fortifications easily, and she might be able to fire cannonballs above them into the city while there was no danger that the guns of Kamlakesh could strike his frigate. The next step in the show that Giles was putting on was to raise the gunport lids and run out the guns.

Giles was in no rush to try to enter into negotiations with the Bey. Let the man twiddle his thumbs until Giles was ready to make a move. Of course, the Bey could also play that game, but Giles still felt that lack of haste would advance his cause. He spent a leisurely five minutes on the quarterdeck, scrutinizing the ramparts. He was wearing ordinary working clothes, which would probably not advertise his status to the uninformed observer. In the same vein, Giles next climbed the mainmast to see what he could learn from that vantage point. From the cross-trees, he could easily see over the ramparts. Immediately behind the walls, extending a short distance into the town, he saw roofs of tenements in an area that, even from the masthead, did not look to be well maintained, with narrow, twisting streets being the norm. Kamlakesh was built on a slight hill. As one went up the slope, it appeared that the houses became more luxurious. At the top of the hill, there was a large palace, with what looked like marble pillars and a stone wall surrounding it. That must be the Bey's palace.

There were two mosques near the top of the hill, each one marked by four thin minarets. Neither mosque was particularly close to the palace, but the one closest to it had a more prosperous look. A straight street ran from the gate in the wall facing the harbor to the palace with a wide, ornate metal gate where the road entered the Bey's compound.

Giles returned to the deck in time to begin the next phase of his plan. First, the marines, in full dress uniform, climbed down into the longboat, followed by Lieutenant Macauley, also in full dress despite the heat. Midshipman Bush, in his best uniform, was in command of the vessel. While the marine lieutenant was leaving *Glaucus*, one of the sailors played a military sounding salute on his trumpet, a feature suggested by Mr. Miller as being much more likely to impress than the shrill call of the bosun's pipe which was the Navy's usual musical instrument. Next, Carstairs brought the captain's barge around from the side of *Glaucus* away from the town. Its crew were dressed in their smart uniforms, usually worn only to impress other naval ships at anchor at Spithead or the Nore*. They were intended to demonstrate that *Glaucus* was a crack frigate. Giles was in his best uniform with the star and ribbon of the Order of the Bath on his chest, glad that he had thought to get tropical clothing before sailing. Otherwise, he would have been silently cursing the pomp he had ordered because he would have been wearing his warm woolen uniform coat. He descended into his barge while the trumpet played another fanfare.

The two boats took up station a hundred yards away from the quay in front of the gateway. When there was no immediate response from the town, *Glaucus* fired a signal gun. Someone in Kamlakesh was watching for almost at once a file of soldiers emerged through the gate, followed by several officials. The Bey and his palanquin were not part of the procession.

Giles had told Mr. Mohammad to state that they had come to get the hostages. He should announce that time was up. Giles would not tolerate further delays. Refusal, after the Bey had fired at the frigate earlier, would be considered an act of war. If the hostages were not released immediately, *Glaucus* would have to demonstrate her command of the situation.

It took far more words in Arabic than in English to send the message. Giles suspected that Mr. Mohammed had greatly embellished his words. The translator's speech was followed by a lengthy address from the most richly dressed of the officials.

Mr. Mohammad summarized the lengthy reply when the official had finished: "He says 'no.' We have no business being here. They want compensation for injuring the Bey's attendant. If we don't leave immediately, they will sink our ship."

"Will they, indeed!"

Giles took off his hat and waved it at Mr. Miller on *Glaucus*. That was the signal for the broadside to fire. The hat was hardly on Giles's head again when the first gun boomed out. It had been aimed at one of the gun embrasures on the wall, but missed. It did crash into the wall next to the opening and dislodged a large part of the parapet. Almost immediately, *Glaucus*'s next gun fired. Again, part of the wall was demolished. The Bey's gunners must also have been prepared for all their guns now fired, but their balls fell short of *Glaucus,* as Giles had predicted based on their previous experience. On and on, the frigate's guns roared out, usually causing damage to the wall. In one instance, the shot hit an enemy gun as it was being readied to fire. There was a loud clang as the ball hit the cannon, followed immediately by an explosion as some spark must have ignited the gunpowder in the cartridge about to be rammed down the barrel.

When the last of *Glaucus*'s guns had fired, the first one fired again. One by one, the rest of the broadside sent their balls into the wall. For the third round of firing, Giles had ordered that the guns be tilted to their maximum elevation and fire over the wall into the town. Of course, from his barge, he could not judge what the effect was, but he imagined that it would cause panic if the cannonballs were striking among the wealthier houses that he had seen from the masthead. Even if they were only hitting the tenements near the wall, pandemonium would ensue, and the Bey's control would be shaken.

Although Giles could not see what damage these last eighteen cannonballs had done in the town, the earlier thirty-six had revealed that the wall could not resist a sustained barrage. Large parts of the parapet had collapsed. There was a gap in one place, which went far lower than the parapet, where a large part of the wall had disintegrated. Another shot had hit the wall just above the gate with the result that a considerable amount of rubble was piled up on the road below.

Giles hoped that all this damage might be enough to change the Bey's mind. The party sent to talk with Giles had not left the quay before the bombardment began, and it had had to huddle at the water's edge to avoid falling rocks. Its members started to stand up when it became clear that there would not be a fourth set of shots coming their way. Undoubtedly they now appreciated the damage that *Glaucus* could do to the town.

"Mr. Mohammed," Giles ordered. "Get the attention of those men on the quay. Tell them that I am giving the Bey twenty-four hours to reconsider his position. If he does not agree with our terms, I shall proceed to annihilate his defenses. Mr. Mohammad bellowed the translation of Giles's message. He got only a sulky reply from the Bey's spokesman before the group from Kamalesh turned to try to find a way through the rubble at the gateway.

"What did that man say," Giles demanded.

"It was a crude way to tell us to mind our own business," was the reply. "It is not fit for translation."

Back on board *Glaucus*, with the hands sent to dinner, and having changed into more comfortable clothes, Giles realized that he was still too on edge much to enjoy his meal. Instead, he climbed the mast to survey the town again. Aloft, he found Hector, a man renowned for having some of the sharpest eyes on *Glaucus*.

"What are you doing up here, Hector?" Giles asked. "Did Mr. Miller send you aloft?"

"No, sir, I was up here spotting the fall of shot when we were firing on the town over there, but now I am just enjoying the breeze, such as it is. I told Jim Sexton that I would take the first part of his watch."

"Did you see the results of our shots?"

"Oh, yes, sir. It was easy with the guns firing one at a time."

Hector broke off to survey the horizon all around. It remained clear. With that task out of the way, he resumed the conversation with his captain. "You can see the wreckage we caused to their guns and platform from up here better than from the deck."

Hector was right. Giles could see that parts of the walkway behind the parapet of the wall had broken off. More pounding from *Glaucus*'s guns might well open breaches in the walls, or even turn them into dirt heaps.

"What about the third set of shots. Did they do much damage?" Giles asked.

"It's hard to tell. You can see some damage to the roofs near the wall. Look there and there." Hector directed Giles's attention to the places to which he was referring. "Many of the shots fell farther up the hill in those gardens so I couldn't tell what they had hit. There was one place with a sort of domed roof that was hit directly. You can see it over there. It is the building where a large part of the roof has collapsed."

Giles followed Hector's pointing finger and saw the damage to which he was referring. The damaged roof was to one side of a small grove of palm trees. It was on what must be an opulent residence. Giles was delighted. Putting holes in the roofs of tenements where the poor might be living, or even destroying parts of the town wall might not have much effect on the Bey, who would guess that Giles did not have enough men to capture the town. Damage to the properties of the wealthy, by contrast, might bring pressure on the Bey to bend to Giles's demands.

Giles returned to the deck and gestured for Mr. Miller to join him.

"We will stay anchored here, Mr. Miller, until we receive a response from the Bey. If we haven't heard anything by nightfall, rig the boarding nets, and set many lookouts. I think that the Arabs have hardly any boats left, but keep a sharp eye out during the night in case any do approach. Have the gunner select the best balls for four rounds per gun tomorrow in case we need them."

There was no response from the town during the day, nor any during the evening. At about five bells of the first watch, a small boat was sighted rowing quietly towards *Glaucus*. Giles ordered that it be allowed to come to the entry port, and the people in the boat should be permitted to board.

"Even if they are whores, sir?" asked Mr. Stewart, who was officer of the watch.

"Of course not," replied Giles in a tone that suggested that there was no need for such a question, even though he had forgotten that Mr. Stewart had hit on the most likely reason for a surreptitious approach of a small craft to an anchored ship. It was also one to which, in more normal anchorages, Giles would have turned a blind eye.

The boat turned out to contain four men in robes whose quality and embroidery suggested wealth. Giles and Mr. Mohammed met them as they reached the deck. The first one aboard was also the first to speak, in a long speech during which he pointed at the other three men. Mr. Mohammed's translation was considerably shorter.

"The spokesman says that the tallest man is the son of the former Bey. The other three are well-off leaders in Kamlakesh. The spokesman owns the villa whose roof one of our cannonballs hit today. They all have property in the area that we have shown we can hit. They want our help to overthrow the Bey."

"I see," said Giles. "Let us go to my cabin so that we can learn what they have in mind. I suppose that I should not offer them a drink, some wine or something, since they must be Mohammadans."

"I doubt that they are going to refuse a drink. Many highly-placed Arabs do not follow the Prophet's teachings in the way that they insist that others do. Offer it to them and see what they say."

Giles led the way to his cabin and sat at the head of the table while the visitors took seats around it. He offered them some Madeira. Everyone accepted, except Mr. Mohammad. They took large initial gulps of the wine when it had been poured. Only then did they get down to business.

The story the visitors told was straightforward. The new Bey had felt it politic not to dispatch the last Bey's son as part of his coup, at least not while he was still establishing his position with the other powerful men of Kamlakesh and getting them to accept him. The leader of the four men was the son of the displaced potentate. The other three men supported him because they had been the men who had been the chief ministers in the previous regime. The new Bey was letting them live, even allowing them to enjoy some of the benefits of their former positions and had not confiscated their wealth, as yet. This treatment was not due to his leniency, they believed. The new Bey was only biding his time while he consolidated his power. Then they could expect to be dealt with very harshly.

One of the reasons for the overthrow of the previous regime was the belief that the terms on which captured ships and their passengers were released had been too generous. The new Bey was sure that they could acquire much more money from the piracy Kamlakesh fostered. This had not turned out to be the case so far, and now, with *Glaucus*'s presence causing significant damage first to the pirate fleet and then to the town itself, much of the support for the new regime had vanished.

This was all very interesting, Giles remarked, but what did the delegation want.

It took a while for his visitors' desires to emerge as they skirted around the subject of their treachery in elliptical ways. In summary, the Bey's power was normally maintained by a corps of janissaries, whose sole purpose was to protect the ruler, and by the crews of the pirate vessels based on Kamlakesh. It was because the leader of the janissaries had been persuaded that the previous Bey was not extracting nearly as much money from piracy as he believed could be obtained that he had joined the rebels in their revolt. His decision had led to the past Bey's overthrow. Now the support of the pirates had largely evaporated since Giles had so completely defeated them. The town guard did not want to take sides. They presently supported the new Bey, but they would not object to his removal though they would not help with it. The janisaries still were loyal to the current Bey. They would have to be dealt with if another coup d'état were to succeed, for they had not been persuaded to change their loyalty. Without neutralizing their power, the new Bey could not be unseated.

The janissaries were a small group whose job was to guard the Bey and his Palace. The present Bey had dug in his heels about submitting to Giles's demands, claiming that *Glaucus* could not long remain so far from her base and did not have the power to conquer the city. He would lose prestige if he gave in, and the houses that *Glaucus* could demolish were held by only a fraction of the wealthy and influential in the city. The Pretender to the Beyship would have the support of most of the prominent men of Kamlakesh, tacit support only, for overthrowing the present Bey provided that the pretender could kill the current Bey prisoner, or kill him, and capture the palace.

"What do you want from me?" Giles asked after the background situation had been outlined.

More hemming and hawing was the response to this question. Much probing and questioning by Mr. Mohammad were required before the answer became clear. They wanted Giles to provide his marines and members of his crew to capture the Bey's palace and to take the palace guard prisoners. That would be a necessary first step if a coup d'état were to succeed.

"You want me to take the palace? Is it fortified?" Giles asked with a sharp tone.

Yes, it had a high wall around it, a thick one with battlements above it. The only way in was through a gateway which had a couple of heavy, iron gates that barred entrance effectively. The Bey's palace sounded more like a castle than a mansion.

"So, you want me to use a handful of men to attack a well-defended castle in the hope of overthrowing the Bey?" Giles asked in disbelief.

"No," came Mr. Mohammad's translation of the response. "There is a secret tunnel from the Pretender Bey's residence into the harem of the Palace. They say that we can use that to get inside and take the janissaries by surprise. Half the guard will be patrolling on the walls, and the rest can be taken by surprise. When that happens, they expect the ones on the walls to surrender since we will have captured the Bey."

Giles had some more questions, and the answers made him ever more inclined to join the visitors in the venture. Otherwise, he appeared to be in a stalemate. His guns could do damage, but not such that the Bey would give up his prospect of getting great wealth from ransoms. The Bey had no way to move Giles from his present position. While she controlled the inlet, *Glaucus* could prevent Kamlakesh from providing any more support to the pirates, but she could not stay indefinitely.

"If we are going to do it, let's do it tonight," Giles said. "I suggest that we commence at two bells, which is one o'clock in the morning to those who do not know navy terms. That is when I will bring my marines and some of my crew to the quay in front of the ruined gate. I noticed that some workmen were clearing a path through the rubble there today, so we should be able to proceed into the town without trouble."

The offer, when Mr. Mohammad had translated it, took the visitors by surprise. They conferred together for several minutes before the leader gave his reply. "They do not think they can be ready so soon. He suggests doing it tomorrow."

"Tell him that in that case, I shall have to bombard the town in the same way as I did today. Otherwise, it may seem very peculiar to the Bey that I have not again reminded him noisily of my presence, and, given the extra time, he may be able to take steps to frustrate us."

This remark led to another discussion among the visitors. "They agree to do it tonight," said Mr. Mohammad, "though they are not very happy about it. I overheard them saying something about not having enough time to plan properly, but I have no idea what they were getting at."

"I picked up something there too," Giles remarked. "It may just have been that they realized that what they have proposed is going to happen. They won't be able to pull back if they have any doubts. I've had that feeling often enough when committing to an undertaking."

"Let's hope that is what it is." Mr. Mohammad didn't sound convinced.

It didn't take Giles long to prepare his shipmates for the night's excursion into Kamlakesh. He warned Mr. Macauley to have his marines ready and then picked a small contingent of his crew members. In doing so, he concentrated on men from the big cities, London, Edinburgh, and Birmingham mostly, who would know better than country-dwellers how to move about poorly lit streets, ones probably piled with garbage or other hazards. Many of the men he chose had been pickpockets or housebreakers who were used to taking decisive action when danger threatened.

Giles had his party take to their boats soon after midnight so that they would have plenty of time to row quietly to the quay where they would arrive at two bells. There was no moon, but he could make out enough in the dark so that they docked right in front of the town gate. There they were met by the four conspirators who had hatched the plot with Giles in *Glaucus*'s cabin. The locals carried torches and had lanterns as well. They were accompanied by a few other men whom Giles guessed were trusted servants. The man who wanted to be Bey led the way along what was probably one of the main streets of the city, the roadway which rose in a straight line from the gate at the quay to the palace that Giles had seen earlier. The marines marched in step until Mr. Macauley told them to break step so that it would not be so obvious that a military contingent had arrived and was moving towards the palace. Partway up the hill, the Pretender stopped to point out a partly collapsed hovel with a cannonball in its rubble.

"He is calling our attention to one of the buildings we hit today so that we can see how effective we have been," Mr. Mohammad explained to Giles.

They continued to ascend the road. Near the gates of the palace, the Pretender turned to one door in the wall that now lined the street. He knocked on it in some sort of code. The door opened, and they went into a large courtyard. They crossed the space to where two ornate, filigreed gates were opened for them. A large domed entryway came next, but here the effect was spoiled by a gaping hole in the roof. Rubble from the ceiling had been swept to one side, but not yet removed.

"Another of the results of your bombardment," explained Mr. Mohammad following a lengthy tirade by one of the Pretender's associates. "I suspect that one is the hit that made them want to stop your firing at them."

Under the dome, there was a large pool with a raised stone border around it. The Pretender strode over to the edge of the pool and gestured to one of his attendants. The man went forward and bent down. He slipped his hand into a space where the floor met the border. The opening must have served as a concealed handle for, with a grunt, the attendant pulled on it. A large section of the pavement swung up to reveal a flight of stairs going down into darkness. A hand gesture by one of the Pretender's companions made a couple of lantern bearers come forward to light the stairs. A short speech followed given by the would-be Bey.

"He says," reported Mr. Mohammed, "that this is the secret tunnel leading into the Bey's Palace. It emerges in the anteroom of the harem. That place is almost always empty, for it is used to separate the women from the guards beyond. Only the Bey is allowed to enter even the anteroom, except, of course, for some slaves who clean it or who cross it to take supplies for the harem. There is a long story about the construction of this way into the palace, but we have no time for it now and or to hear about how closely the women are guarded."

Giles agreed with that sentiment.

A torch-bearer led the way as they descended a flight of stairs. Then he started along a low, flat tunnel. Giles guessed that it was passing beneath the mansion because, after a while, it began to rise steeply. Giles was silently counting the steps they were taking. He felt very uncomfortable entombed in the narrow, dark tunnel. If anything happened, there would be no escape. Suddenly he started having grave doubts about the wisdom of this venture. However, if treachery against him rather than the Bey was afoot, it was too late for him to do anything about it. After four hundred and thirty-seven steps, the tunnel again flattened out. A further short distance took them to a flight of stairs leading upwards.

"At the top of these stairs is a door," Mr. Mohammed translated a whispered statement by the Kamlakeshi leader. "It gives directly into a chamber that separates the harem from the guardroom. There is a locked door across the room from where we will emerge. The door is used traditionally only by the Bey when he visits, though the present one often brings his henchmen to enjoy some of the pleasures on offer inside. To the left is another door. It leads to the janissaries' guardroom. When we are in the first room, we should surge into that room, catch them off-guard, and kill them all. Then we can deal with the rest of the Bey's guards."

"Men," Giles said in a conversational-level voice, "You heard what he said. Now, only kill people if it is necessary. We want to defeat them with a minimum of bloodshed."

Mr. Mohammad decided not to translate this statement into Arabic. The force from *Glaucus* lined up outside the door. The leading members were the sailors whom Giles believed would be the best men at subduing any resistance when his group charged through the door. Behind them came the marines who would overwhelm the bulk of the men by their presence with loaded and cocked muskets. The other seamen came last, with their task being to disarm the cowed janissaries.

Giles signaled for the attack to begin. The door at the top of the stairs was quietly opened, and the raiders proceeded through it as silently as they could. It was doubtful if this care was required. From beyond double doors to their left came sounds indicating that a raucous party was underway.

When all of Giles's party had filed into the anteroom, he gave the signal to attack. The double doors crashed open as the sailors burst into the guard room. They were greeted by a scene of debauchery. Clouds of sweet-smelling smoke could be traced back to many hookahs on which some of the guards were puffing. Others were waving bottles that Giles doubted contained no alcohol. Still others were cavorting with houris dressed in diaphanous trousers and tops or even less clothing. It was a scene from many sailors' wildest dreams. Giles feared that discipline would break down. As it turned out, his fears were groundless.

All the revelers froze in surprise as the doors crashed open. Carstairs and his contingent made quick work of disarming those who still had weapons at hand. Only one man tried to use his curved sword; a quick cutlass slash killed him. After that, none of the others attempted resistance.

By the time the janissaries recovered from their shock, they faced the loaded and cocked muskets of the marines. Giles realized that he should have had his men bring coils of rope to tie up his captives, for he was now faced with the dilemma of how to guard so many men when his own force was required for the next step in taking control of the city. The sailors solved the problem. A jumble of belts and discarded clothing, both male and female, quickly and effectively bound all the guards. Some of the women were cowering helplessly in a corner, but others were voicing their opinions on this interruption to the party. A backhand from a large, former ruffian who had escaped well-deserved punishment in England by volunteering for the navy, silenced her. He was not the only one of Giles men who looked villainous, and the rest of the women rapidly became docile.

Giles was proud, though surprised, by the conduct of his men. When he had first seen what lay behind the guardroom doors, he was afraid that his men might join the orgy, ignoring their duty. That did not happen, though he suspected that several sailors had handled some of the women more physically than was called for as they herded them into a group and checked for arms. Now his men were ready for the remaining palace guards who had been patrolling the wall and grounds. There weren't nearly as many of them still at large as there had been guards who now had been rendered harmless.

Mr. Mohammad informed Giles after he had conferred with their guides that the guard was scheduled to change in another ten minutes. These armed men would have to be killed or captured for the takeover to be complete. Giles reassembled his men before the door to the guardroom away from the anteroom to the harem. He had been told that this door led to the palace grounds. He chose several of the sailors and a few of the marines to stay behind to make sure that the captives did not escape. Then he intended to go out of the room to capture the remaining guards.

Before Giles could order his group to proceed through the door so that they could complete their task, it was opened for them. Standing outside were the remaining guardsmen ready to enter the festivities inside, quite unready to meet an armed and well-trained force. Without hesitation, the sailors attacked the new set of guards, using their knives to kill them or to render them docile. The fight lasted only a few minutes, after which the new captives were herded into the guardroom to join the others.

Mr. Mohammad told Giles that the reason the second group of guards had appeared right where, from the attackers' point of view, it was convenient for them to be, was that they had become impatient to be relieved so that they could take part in the orgy. There might still be a few guards who took their duty more seriously, so Giles's contingent should check the gates and walls of the palace for any guards remaining at their proper places. It did not take long for Carstairs to conduct the inspection. He returned to say that there were no guards at the palace gate or on its walls. Mr. Mohammad relayed this news to the Pretender.

"He says," the translator announced, "that all that remains to be done now is to take the current Bey prisoner together with his henchmen. He asks that you leave sufficient men here to guarantee that the guards that we have captured do not escape and that you bring the rest of your men to confront the Bey."

Giles gave the orders, leaving Mr. Macauley and the marines where they were. The rest of his group followed the Pretender back into the anteroom and then turned left to pass through the Bey's entrance to the harem antechamber. As they snuck through a series of corridors, Giles was amazed at the labyrinth that was the Bey's palace. He was glad that his guides seemed to know exactly where they were going. He doubted that he could easily find his way back to the guardroom. Finally, the small party stopped before a double doorway. It was distinguished from others only by an unusually ornate door frame. The Pretender opened the door and rushed in. Giles was right behind him. In the light from a lantern, Giles could see a man lying on a bed under an elaborate canopy. Before he could do more than take in the scene, the Pretender had rushed to the bed and plunged a knife into the man. Frantically, the victim was stabbed over and over until there could be no doubt that he was dead.

"The Bey is dead," proclaimed Mr. Mohammad. "That man is now the Bey of Kamlakesh."

To Giles's surprise, the clerk from the East India Company knelt and kissed the new Bey's feet.

"Why did you do that, Mr. Mohammad?" Giles asked.

"Captain Giles, I have left the Company's service, and, therefore, yours too. I have taken a superior post with the Bey, who will treat me with respect. I never get that from the Company. I am always just a native who has uppity airs and speaks with a strange accent. Useful, maybe, but definitely inferior to any English man. Here things will be different, I hope."

At this point, one of the men from Kamlakesh, who had been accompanying the Bey when he was only the Pretender, came into the room and addressed the new Bey. After the messenger had finished, the Bey turned to Mr. Mohammad, "He says," reported Mr. Mohammad gleefully, "that the city guard is here now. They have taken control of the palace as well as the city. Your services are no longer needed, Captain Giles. The Bey thanks you for your assistance, but now you must leave. Members of the Kamlakesh guard will accompany you to the quay to make sure that you do."

"What about the hostages? They must be handed over to me immediately."

Another exchange took place between Mr. Mohammad and the Bey. "The Bey regrets to say that you must have misunderstood. Of course, the hostages will only be turned over when their ransoms are paid. However, you will be glad to hear that the prices have been set at the old rates, the ones in effect before the usurping Bey came to power. He says that since you have already stolen the East Indiaman, you should regard recovering the ship as fulfilling any obligation to you that you feel that he is under. You can return to Kamlakesh when you have arranged for the funds so that the hostages can be sent back to England.

"The Bey does warn you against bombarding Kamlakesh again since the hostages will be moved to buildings that are within *Glaucus*'s range. Any concerted bombardment will be certain to kill many of them. He adds that you should be grateful that he has not had your head chopped off since you have destroyed many of the pirate vessels that brought wealth to the city and stolen three of his prizes, and wrecked some palaces. The Bey is being lenient only because of the assistance you have given him. Otherwise, he would enslave you and all your crew right now."

"What?...What?" Giles was rendered speechless by this sudden turn of events. However, he saw no alternative to agreeing to have his party return to *Glaucus* though he was fuming inside for having been played as a fool. His group formed up and set off out through the palace gates and down the road to the harbor, trailed by a strong contingent of the Kamlakesh Guard. The small British force then boarded their boats and returned to their ship.

Giles slept little for the rest of the night. He did not even find solace in writing to Daphne. While he had told her of his worries and fears in his previous letters to her, he had never had to confess to such a debacle. He realized that he was lucky that his trusting the Pretender had not resulted in his men as well as himself being held as further hostages or enslaved in Kamlakesh's typical handling of captives whom they thought would have little value otherwise. He suspected that the only reason that it had not happened was because the new Bey realized that retaliation for seizing a captain of the royal navy and part of his crew would produce much quicker and more damaging retribution than Kamlakesh's interrupting the voyages of East Indiamen had done so far.

Such thoughts did not help Giles decide what to do next, or weaken his chagrin at the way that the Bey had tricked him. The fact was that he had never found himself in such a disgraceful and troubling situation before. He felt that if he thought carefully for a while, he should be able to find some way out of the awkward position that had been forced on him. Could he write to Daphne before he had found a way to extricate himself with honor? He was tempted to wait until he had emerged victorious from his embarrassment at the hands of the Bey. However, he thought better of that idea in a moment. They had resolved to share everything, both the good and the bad. She would want to know about what had happened and have a record of his thoughts and experiences while they were fresh. He knew that she would always be on his side without reservations.

Chapter XV

Mr. Hazelton, the solicitor who was the expert on entails, arrived at Struthers House promptly at nine o'clock. He was a rotund, middle-aged man whose ruddy countenance suggested that he enjoyed social occasions with alcohol rather than much outdoor exercise. As Mr. Snodgrassl had suggested, this authority on the law had been most happy to wait on Lady Camshire and Lady Ashton at the specified time.

Lord Struthers had presumed that he would be meeting with the solicitor to see what could be done about his brother-in-law's financial treatment of Lady Camshire, but the meeting would then have had to be postponed because he had pressing duties to perform as a member of the government. When Daphne explained that speed was of the essence in preventing the Earl of Camshire doing further damage to the Countess's interests, Lord Struthers reluctantly agreed that the meeting with Mr. Hazelton should go ahead without him.

Lord Struthers had not endeared himself to the other ladies when he expressed the opinion that there was nothing to be done, though Daphne realized that he was probably right. Problems of property and income were gentlemen's matters, not suitable for ladies, were at the heart of his beliefs. That prejudice did not prevent her uncle-in-law's opinion from being correct in this instance. Nevertheless, she would persevere. So she told Lord Struthers that it might be a good idea for the ladies to start the discussion with Mr. Hazelton. If they got no satisfaction, Lord Struthers could step in, but Daphne did not think he could alter the conclusions of Mr. Hazelton.

They met in Struthers House's morning room. It was a tastefully decorated room which was filled with the morning light, not at all in tone with the dingy details of how the Earl of Camshire was treating his wife and ruining the value of the properties to which the entails in question applied.

Mr. Hazelton appeared to be surprised that Lord Struthers was not present. Nevertheless, he listened as Daphne explained the problem, even though he silently gave the impression that he was expecting only a somewhat muddled explanation from a lady. Though Lady Struthers and Lady Clara were also at the meeting, they were of little assistance at making the solicitor understand the essence of the difficulties in which Lady Clara found her herself.

The lawyer had expected a man to tell him what the problem was. However, when Daphne began to speak, he soon was hiding his wonder at how precisely Daphne outlined the situation. Nor did he seem by the end to still be uncomfortable in having a lady describe so accurately a problem stemming from the atrocious behavior of a peer of the realm.

When Daphne had finished, Mr. Hazelton asked a few questions, largely ones related to the fund that Lady Clara had access to as a result of her grandfather's appreciation of the character of the Earl of Camshire. Then he sat back for several minutes, collecting his thoughts before speaking. Daphne's patience was almost exhausted when he finally began.

"I am not sure, my ladies, that there is much I can do to help you, though I appreciate how unjust the Earl's behavior must appear to be. The problem is that the seeming injustice stems from the presumption in law that a husband knows best in all material aspects of life affecting his wife. I must say that, in my opinion, the presumption works very well, though I am aware of instances where ladies would appear to have more acumen in worldly matters than their husbands and others where one must doubt that the husbands truly have their wives' interests at heart. You see, for all three of you, my ladies, the law treats you as *'femes coverts,'* covered women, as opposed to uncovered or, as we say, *'feme sole,'* a term which applies to widows and unmarried ladies with no male guardian, such as a spinster or a governess. Ladies still living at home with their fathers are usually considered *femes covert*. The terms come from the French, of course, though now those people don't know how to pronounce or spell the words correctly in their own language. I am told that the distinction between *covert* and *sole* has been abolished as part of the lawless, bloody French Revolution, which, as you know, Lady Ashton, your husband is trying to undo. I don't know the present situation in France, but I hope that their new-fangled Emperor will restore *coverture*. It will certainly return when that upstart 'Emperor' Napoleon is put in his place."

"Yes, but how is this *coverture* relevant here?" Daphne demanded.

"It is presumed that everything material in your life, Lady Camshire, is handled by your husband and that you can only act with his permission. That even holds for any number of purchases you might make by and for yourselves, my ladies, because the law presumes that each of your husbands approves them and could withdraw that approval if he pleased. Indeed, that particular presumption is binding unless he publically specifies that his wife is acting without his permission. As a result, a man may expressly limit what his wife can spend on various items, usually with the threat that he will not allow her to buy anything at all if she does not comply. In your case, Lady Camshire, there is an exception for the fund that your grandfather set up in your name and which, I imagine, is managed by your uncle or cousin on your behalf. It is presumed that such trustees approve any expenditures, explicitly or implicitly."

Lady Clara nodded her head that she supposed that this was the case. Daphne realized that her mother-in-law saw nothing peculiar in the arrangements.

"To summarize," the solicitor continued, "when push comes to shove, everything to do with property or the spending of income is in the man's hands, as it should be, never in the woman's. So if he wants, the Earl can dispose of his income or his wealth as he sees fit, or take on debts, without informing or consulting you or paying any attention to what you may say. Of course, there are some ladies who, I am told, use their tongues to induce their husbands to do what they desire by nagging them, but even that is because, in law, he is allowing it, not because they have any right to do so. If she doesn't obey him, he is allowed to beat her.

"When the Earl of Camshire dies, Lady Camshire," Mr. Hazelton continued, "you will be a *feme sole* instead of being a *feme covert*, and you will have considerable rights of your own over the property of your deceased husband, but that is irrelevant now since he is still alive and, according to the law, presumed to be making valid decisions on your behalf. Even that letter, which you showed me, despite the malice it exhibits, does not, in my opinion, change that presumption. Not only is the law not on your side, but, in practice, it is believed that peers have particular acumen in handling material matters. No judge would be willing to set aside a nobleman's decisions unless they were very demonstrably mad.

"Your options in this situation are very limited, I am afraid. Indeed, I do not believe that there is anything that you can do. For instance, even your suggestion that tenants withhold rents until the Earl dies could land you in trouble by the law. That may be mitigated by the consideration that the suggestion comes in the name of Lord Ashton, I presume, and the other fact that the Earl is at death's door.

"There is something, Lady Ashton, that you, or rather your husband, can do which might hamper that Earl's ability to reduce further the value of Viscount Ashton's inheritance."

"What is that?" Daphne asked.

"You can arrange for notices to be posted that Lord Ashton will not recognize any debts incurred by his father after the date of the notice," replied the solicitor. "I would not be surprised to learn that the Earl is still able to borrow sizeable sums of money, even though he cannot pledge any of his property as security for a loan because of the entail. It is widely known that Viscount Ashton paid the debts of his deceased brother when he inherited the title, even though some of them could easily have been repudiated. All London knows about that action, I am afraid, Lady Ashton. Lenders may easily be presuming that Lord Ashton will take the same steps about debts incurred by his father. Such notices, of course, would have to be placed on orders of Viscount Ashton, and I understand that he is away at present."

"Yes. He is currently at sea, and he is unlikely to return soon. He has, of course, made arrangements that his affairs can be dealt with. In practice, I decide what needs to be done, but, formally, notices such as the ones which you describe would be placed by his prize agent, Mr. Edwards, on my instructions."

"Very good. I suggest that you instruct Mr. Edwards to do so as soon as possible. That will hinder the Earl a bit, but it will not recover any of the money that he has already succeeded in diverting from what should be Lord Ashton's inheritance and, by doing so, Lady Camshire's share through her dower rights. I imagine that you, Lady Camshire, feel particularly aggrieved by the fortune that he has transferred to this Mrs. Montrose. However, I can think of nothing you can do about that now. However, there is one step that you and Lord Ashton might take on the Earl's death which could undo that."

"Oh, what do you have in mind?" asked Daphne, sounding rather surprised. She had thought that the money was lost for good.

"You can sue to get the funds back after he is dead, saying that the Earl was not of sound mind when he made the transfer. Therefore he could not make proper decisions, in particular giving the house and money to that courtesan."

"What chance would such an action have of succeeding?" asked a very dubious-sounding Daphne.

"Better than you might think. The Earl's behavior has been so scandalous that the usual protections coming from peers joining together to enshrine their rights, no matter how badly their priveledges may have been abused, might not be at work in this case. I admit that it is a long shot, and it would be using up a lot of the universal goodwill that Viscount Aston has earned for himself."

"I am not certain that my husband would be willing to undertake such a suit. He has been very embarrassed by some of his father's failings and might rather wish that his outrageous behavior, in this case, be forgotten. Especially as the scandal, which arose from my successfully frustrating the dubious aspects of his half-brother's association with a brothel has caused him much distress, even though he wholeheartedly supported my actions when he learned of them. A suit of this sort would keep drawing attention to the embarrassment my father-in-law has caused both to Lady Clara and to my husband. Is there nothing else that you can suggest to counter either the despicable way he is hurting Lady Clara and my husband or the shocking way he has been supporting this ... this ..."

"I think the word you are looking for is 'whore,' my dear," interposed Lady Struthers sweetly, much to Daphne's surprise. It was not a word which she expected the noblewoman ever to use since women of polite society were apt to pretend that such creatures did not exist.

"I am afraid that is correct, Lady Ashton," replied Mr. Hazelton. "As you know from your own experiences, many of our greatest peers consort with courtesans and ladies of the night. I am afraid that injured wives have no recourse in such situations except to harangue their spouses. Usually, I would guess, to no avail."

Daphne was annoyed at Mr. Hazelton again alluding to her clash with a prominent madam while she was rescuing some of the inheritance that Giles had received from his half-brother from a bawd's clutches. The story, Daphne had learned, was all too common gossip among the society of London and those who imitated them, but she would prefer that it not be mentioned even if it could not be forgotten.

"Thank you very much for your help, Mr. Hazelton. Please send your account to Mr. Edwards, my *husband's* agent."

Mr. Hazelton knew when he was dismissed. He also sensed that he was unlikely to get any further business from Lady Ashton or the other two peeresses. He cemented that conclusion by rising abruptly and giving a rather surly good-day to the three ladies.

"What a waste of time that was!" Daphne exclaimed when the lawyer had left. "I didn't want a lecture on being covered or alone. I wanted a solution to the problem."

"I am not sure there is one, dear," said Lady Struthers. "I am afraid that that is just the way things are. I know that I have never been bothered by how Lord Struthers is in charge of everything. He always listens to me before making his decisions; at least he does if they affect me.

"Now, Daphne and Clara, I know that this has been a disappointing morning for us all, and it would be easy to become discouraged because of it. I suggest we go shopping and have luncheon in a teahouse to pick up our spirits."

Lady Clara seemed as keen as Lady Struthers on the proposed outing, so Daphne went along even though purposeless shopping was not high on her list of pleasures. They set out into a pleasant summer day, not too hot if they did not walk overly quickly. Just being out of the house was a pleasure after sitting all morning through Mr. Hazelton's explications of property and inheritance laws. The three ladies maids who trailed them did not seem as happy to be out in the warm weather in their black uniforms.

Lady Struthers led them down shady streets heading south from Struthers House. At one point, they detoured into a large square. In its center was a well-kept garden, surrounded by a wrought-iron fence, in which some nursemaids were sitting with infants in baskets, while older children played under the watchful eyes of nannies. All of the houses surrounding the square were well maintained, and some looked quite luxurious. They all featured the large windows that had been fashionable for some time now. Lady Clara, who had been walking with her head down, concentrating on her problems and on how the lawyer had suggested no effective way out, looked around and said, "Oh, Gillian! Isn't that Camshire House?"

"Of course it is," Lady Struthers replied. "I thought, dear, that it might cheer you up to see it."

"It was a wonderful place, and I had a good time there until Camshire lost his money and restricted how much we could entertain. In the end, I became quite ashamed of his penny-pinching and was quite relieved when he said I could come to London for only a couple of weeks of the Season. It was a very nice house. I can remember Richard and David playing in the square, just like those children are doing now."

The memory cheered Lady Clara up, and it seemed to relieve some of the gloom that had descended on her after the meeting with Mr. Hazelton. She pointed out to Daphne some of the features of the square and mentioned which houses had been occupied by prominent families, and wondered if they were still living there.

"I wonder if Richard will want to have a townhouse when he becomes the Earl," she said, a bit wistfully. Daphne was startled. She had never contemplated the implications of Giles's assuming the title to which was attached a seat in the House of Lords. If Giles took the obligations of his rank seriously, he would have to spend time in London during the Season. She knew, of course, that Ashbury Abbey, the Earls' traditional home, came with the title, but she was sure that Giles would want to continue to have Dipton Hall as his principal residence. The thought reminded her that she had yet to inspect Ashton Place, which Giles had inherited from his elder half-brother.

The three ladies concluded their walk at Hatchard's bookshop. Lady Struthers was a great devourer of novels and wanted some more. She had an almost full bookcase of them in her dressing room because Lord Struthers would not allow them in his library. It was restricted, he claimed, to serious books. Daphne had teased him that *A Pilgrim's Progress* was really just a novel, and so it should also be banished from the shelves of her uncle's favorite room.

In browsing around the shop while her aunt made her selections, Daphne chanced upon a book that most certainly did not seem to be frivolous. On the cover was inscribed '*A Vindication of the Rights of Woman: with Strictures on Political and Moral Subjects.*' Its author was listed as Mary Wollstonecraft, a name that Daphne vaguely recalled as belonging to the author of a scandalous novel published quite some time ago. When she asked Lady Struthers about this writer, her aunt replied it had stirred up quite a controversy at the time. Her husband had forbidden her to read it, though he himself had not read it and was basing his stricture on gossip. Lady Struthers confided that she had bought the book anyway. It was one of her early additions to her little library of novels. She had heard of the work that Daphne had discovered. She recalled that it had also been controversial when it came out and that there was some sort of scandal about the author, though she couldn't remember the details.

Daphne decided on the spot that she should buy the book. It might well illuminate her feelings about the injustice done to Lady Clara by her husband's unbridled behavior. Lady Struthers also felt that she should get a copy, even though she was afraid that it might be hard slogging to read, unlike the novels which she favored, though she did remember that the author's tale had been fascinating. Lady Clara, though not much of a reader, felt that she also should acquire the book to see if it would illuminate her situation.

Lord Struthers returned from Whitehall in good time to change for dinner. "How did your meeting with the solicitor go. Daphne?" he asked.

Lady Struthers had insisted that Daphne address her as Aunt Gillian and her husband as Uncle Geoffrey, while she always referred to Viscount Ashton as 'Richard.' Daphne was delighted with the recognition that, in marrying Giles, she had been welcomed into an extended family. While it had taken a while to warm to the Countess of Camshire, the rapport with Lady Struthers had come as soon as she met her.

"I am sorry to say that Mr. Hazelton had nothing useful for us. It seems that we have no recourse. All he could suggest is that I place notices in the appropriate places saying that Giles will not pay his father's debts when he becomes the Earl. That might do some good, I suppose, but it does not get to the heart of the problem."

"Which is?" asked Lord Struthers politely.

"It is the money that Camshire has squandered on that doxy, Mrs. Montrose."

"Ah, yes, I imagine that that is the case. Money spent cannot usually be recovered, and certainly not by a wife getting back sums spent by her husband on pleasure, no matter how dubious that expenditure may be morally."

"I find it particularly horrid that he has bought her a house in Norfolk with, I suspect, money borrowed that Richard will feel obligated to repay."

"Yes, I can see that, certainly. Did you say that Camshire bought it for this woman, free and clear?"

"That is my understanding."

"Well," said Lord Struthers, "that does surprise me. Usually, when men set up establishments for their courtesans, they retain title to the property. That is if they buy the properties. It is more common in such circumstances for the men to rent the property usually on a short-term lease, and give them a fixed allowance in line with their needs. I know from the chap who handles Lord Nelson's affairs that that is what the Admiral has done for Lady Hamilton."

"I don't see that that matters in this case, but Lady Clara heard that Lord Camshire had bought the place in which he has established that whore."

"Is that your understanding, Clara?" asked Lord Struthers.

"Yes, it is, Geoffrey. I was astonished when I heard that he had purchased it for her since it did not sound like Camshire at all," said the Earl's wife.

"I am surprised for the same reason. There are three ways in which a man can provide a house for his paramour. The first is to give her money to buy it, in which case it will be held in her name if she is not married. That sounds unlikely, especially knowing your husband's character, Clara.

"The second is to lease it for her rather than buy it. That is probably the most common arrangement. If that is the case, the lease may well end with Camshire's death. If it doesn't, I imagine that Richard should be able to wriggle out of it easily and cheaply.

"The third is that he bought it outright for this Mrs. Montrose. He may not have transferred title to her, and implicitly he might expect the arrangement to end with his death. Otherwise, he may intend to leave it to her in his will. I can't be sure, of course, without seeing the relevant documents, but very stringent entails can include treating any property, real property that is, purchased by the person in question as also being covered by the entail, even though he did not receive it directly from an inheritance as long as the money used can be related to the income from land covered by the entail. That is, he cannot sell it without the explicit consent of his heir, and, in some cases, not even then. I would not be surprised to learn that the entail on the Camshire estate is of the most stringent kind since I know that the twenty-first Earl of Camshire loathed his son and so would have imposed as constraining an entail on his property as was possible.

"The twenty-second earl, your husband's father, Clara, also did not trust how his eldest son was turning out. His lands were already entailed; it was a family tradition, I believe. However, as I said, his father made it even more restrictive. He strengthened the entail applying to his son so that any real property his offspring acquired would also be entailed. I know about this provision, because soon after his father died, Camshire's first wife wanted to move from their townhouse in St. James to the newly more fashionable area of Mayfair. The Earl agreed. In those days, he had yet to go through much of the fortune that was in the ownership of consuls and shares of the various sound companies that his father had left to him. Camshire, of course, could not sell the St. James's house, but he could lease it on very favorable terms to Green's Club. He even obtained a lifetime membership in the club for himself and his eldest son as part of the arrangement. That is why Green's has never thrown him out, though I imagine now that his account is well overdue, they may not let him charge any more items to his account. I don't know whether the provision of that part of the entail applies to Richard now. It certainly doesn't apply to any of his present holdings since he got them all through his own efforts. Anyway, the stronger restriction became general knowledge when Camshire wanted to sell the Mayfair residence. In checking the relevant documents, the solicitor handling the transaction discovered that the terms of the entail meant that the Earl could not sell Camshire House in Mayfair as he wanted to. Your husband has never been a discreet man, Clara, so he ranted and raved about the injustice of the entail. As a result, everyone knows about it."

"That is very interesting, Uncle Geoffrey," Daphne said, "but how is it relevant to Lady Clara's problem with Mrs. Montrose's having wound Lord Camshire around her little finger?"

"I was thinking, Daphne, that it is very unlike a man like Camshire to give up real property when he doesn't need to. He is not an open-handed man. He may have given consols or cash to this harlot free and clear – presumably for services rendered – just to annoy Clara. He may have left the house in Norfolk to her in his will for the same reason, but to transfer the title of the house to her does not sound like him, and even if he did, it would be against the entail. If he tries to leave it to her in his will, you should be able to stop the transfer. Only if he gave her cash to buy the property without his name appearing on the title at all could you not recover the property – whatever it is. Of course, you may then still be burdened with the problem of what to do with it, if it is entailed in the same way when it passes to Richard."

"I wonder how we can find out whether Mrs. Montrose truly owns the house," Daphne said.

"I don't know," replied Lord Struthers. "There must be records of who owns all real property somewhere. I will ask my solicitor to find out for you."

"Talking about what Camshire owns," said Lady Struthers. "I have heard that the merchant who has rented Camshire House – I don't remember his name – may want to give up the lease."

"Why would he wish to do that?" Lady Clara wondered. "Isn't it still an excellent house in a very fashionable location. These merchant people always seem to have plenty of money and like to rub shoulders with their betters."

"The rumor – I got it from my lady's maid, Doris, who got it from the lady's maid of Lady Stanstead, whose house is right next to Camshire House – is that the tenants feel uncomfortable in Camshire House because their neighbors shun them for being in trade. They want to buy their own place in Fitzrovia. If they do give up the lease after Camshire dies, then you may want to use it as your townhouse, Daphne. You will certainly need one with Richard being in the House of Lords."

"I had never thought of having a separate residence in London," Daphne confessed. "I am not sure that our using Camshire House, even if it is available, would be fair. The rent on the place must be significant. If it is rented out, thirty percent will be Lady Clara's by right, and ensuring that she gets what should be hers is what this is all about. Of course, Giles can be counted on to support his mother fully, but that is not the same as her having her own income. Of course, all this is speculation until we learn what is in the entail exactly, for Lord Camshire may have changed it, while we also don't know what exactly is in his will."

At that point, Lady Struthers indicated that she thought that the conversation was at an end by rising and leading the three ladies into the drawing-room. Lord Struthers was not a great drinker even in company, and he did not enjoy drinking by himself. He joined the ladies after only partially drinking one glass of port.

"Daphne, I don't quite understand why you put so much emphasis on Clara's having her own funds. Surely she knows that Richard will provide for all her needs. A more open and generous chap I don't know, totally unlike his father. Even if he were to die, and a sailor's life is more precarious than most men's, his heir will be young Bernard, and you will surely be able to guarantee Clara's well-being."

"I know that you may not understand, Uncle Geoffrey. I don't think many men would see what is at stake, no matter how well-intentioned they are towards women. There is a difference between having income as one's own and having it as a gift from someone else. It may be only a symbolic difference, but I think it is important. I am lucky since Giles is happy to have me participate in making decisions, and have me make them when he is away, but I only do it by his permission as the lawyer this morning made abundantly clear. I don't have any independence myself while he has it all, in principle. That difference matters, not so much to me specifically, but because it reflects how most women's intelligence is undervalued."

"I don't understand, Daphne, my dear. It is only natural for men to be in charge of a family. It is only the unfortunate women who do not have a man to count on that have rights over themselves and their property. That is how it should be," Lord Struthers affirmed his belief in the way things were. Daphne realized that he had never really thought about the subject.

"I am not sure that I can agree with you there, Uncle. I think that we women should be recognized more explicitly as individuals who are separate persons from their husbands rather than the way we are considered now."

"You do sound a bit radical, Daphne," said Lord Struthers. "Next thing, you will be quoting from that dreadful book, whose title I cannot remember offhand, that claims that women have rights that are not currently recognized."

"Maybe I will," said Daphne, not at all amused by the condescending tone that Lord Struthers had adopted. "I bought a copy of it today at Hatchard's."

"Did you indeed," responded Lord Struthers. "I wonder how much you will get out of it."

"I bought one too," chimed in Lady Struthers, "and so did Clara."

"Well, well, well. You do surprise me! I suggest, Gillian, that you return it unread to Hatchard's."

"Are you forbidding me to read it, Lord Struthers?" Lady Struthers demanded fiercely.

"Of course not, my dear. We already have a copy in my library, next to that dangerous tract about the rights of men. You can, of course, read anything you want that is in my library, or to buy anything that appeals to you. It just seems silly to me to have two copies of any work in the library."

The conversation turned to other matters. Daphne retired soon after. She had difficulty writing her letter to Giles, telling him about the events of the day. She had no trouble describing the efforts around trying to protect Lady Clara's interests and how they hoped to foil Camshire's intentions. She found that it was more difficult when it came to telling about the volume that she had bought in Hatchard's, and hesitated about what, if anything, to tell her husband of her opinions that surrounded the lack of independent status for noblewomen. She knew that he took for granted his lawful position in the family. It had never galled her until now, and, even now, it was just a general feeling that the present situation was unfair to her sex; she didn't have any complaint against Giles himself. However, she had to realize that she and Giles had had no serious disagreements, ones which he had every right to settle by fiat. In fact, he had been very tolerant of her expanding business interests arising from her distaste for the smugglers. If he had been different and had forbidden such activities, truly forbidden and not just argued against them, how would she have felt? Of course, she would obey him, but maybe the 'of course' wasn't really as it should be. Lord Struthers, she knew, was not a tyrant in his own household, but Lady Clara had once commented on how skillfully her sister managed her husband to get him to agree to what she wanted. Was that really how it should be?

These were disturbing thoughts, and she was having trouble with her letter from thinking about them. She couldn't raise them with Giles, not in a letter! What would he think? Wouldn't it distress him? No, she couldn't suggest the topic while he was away. She wouldn't even mention her purchase of the book on women's rights. Would she be content when he returned to have him have the last word on every important decision concerning their property or the raising of their children? But what other alternative was there? Surely someone had to be in charge, and a decision had to be made when there was disagreement that could not be bridged. Still, it seemed unfair that husbands always could have things their way, but Daphne had no solution to the problem. How in the world had she got into a position to raise these questions for which she had no answers? Should she even read the book which she had bought or simply presume that things were the way God had ordained as so many people believed?

None of these questions made it into the letter to Giles. Instead, she wrote about what she had learned about entails. She did mention that she felt his mother should have her own funds even if her husband had left her inadequately provided for and should not be beholden even to her son for the security of her old age, even though both Giles and Daphne would be delighted if she lived close to them or even in the same mansion.

She finished the letter by mentioning that she had seen Camshire House and what Lord Struthers had told her about it. Would they really need a townhouse when he became a member of the House of Lords? If so, should it be the one he had known while his father still used it, or should they continue to rent it to others and get a place for themselves which did not have such memories so that Lady Clara would get some of the income to which she was entitled?

The last half-page, as always, was not about news, but about her feelings. She wished that Giles were home. That feeling she made very clear. She was careful, however, not to put pressure on him to leave the sea. He was, she knew, compelled to do his duty, even though his love of the sea was fading somewhat. Nevertheless, she would not pressure him to give it up, because then he might always blame her for losing his primary role in life. She knew that she would be happier if he came ashore because that was what he wanted, not because she desired it. All this talk of entails and wills involving his father, however, made her guess that Giles would feel it his duty to take on the responsibilities that came with his earldom, even if many peers ignored them completely. As she fell asleep, after completing her letter, Daphne was horrified to realize that she positively wished for the early demise of the Earl of Camshire.

Chapter XVI

Dawn found Giles staring out the stern windows of his cabin, lost in thought. He was still smarting from the way he had been played for a fool by the latest Bey of Kamlakesh and by Mr. Mohammed. He was not, however, going to give up. It was only a question of what do do next. Would firing on the palaces of the rich be enough to bring the new Bey to heel? Was the threat that Glaucus would endanger the hostages by doing so believable? Probably not: the Bey would also calculate that placing his hostages in harm's way was foolish since a dead hostage had no value, either monetarily or as a way of preventing an attack. For the latter to be effective, the Bey would have to be much more explicit about where the hostages were. Anyway, the chances of hitting them were slight, so Giles might be expected to turn the town into rubble while figuring that the danger to the hostages would not be acceptable. Military commanders were not known to be very sensitive to risks to civilians when they had to attack. Anyway, the chief hostages were probably deep into the plot to extract money from the East India Company. Why shouldn't they be put in harm's way in order to remove the problem they had created?

His mind made up, Giles went on deck. His first task was to talk to Mr. Abbott, the gunner. He wanted him to make up cartridges of gunpowder that contained as much as possible, given the sort of powder they had on *Glaucus*. Then

Giles wanted the gunner to choose the best cannonballs in terms of going the farthest when fired. Next, Giles called Mr. Miller and Mr. Brooks to him. *Glaucus* was anchored close to the quay in front of the walls of Kamlakesh with a spring attached to the anchor cable so that the aim of the cannon could be adjusted. But was it the best place from which to lob cannonballs onto the palaces of the prominent citizens of Kamlakesh, or should they be closer to or farther away from the quay? The conclusion the trio reached was that they were in about as good a place as they could guess at without firing some balls to see just where the frigate would be better placed.

Mr. Miller had a suggestion to improve their chances of hitting their targets. The starboard side of the ship faced the city. If they ran out the larboard guns and lashed them in that position, *Glaucus* would be tipped over to larboard, and the maximum elevation of the cannon would be increased. Mr. Brooks pointed out that rowing out a second anchor would give more stability to the direction in which the frigate was pointing. Giles took that idea and pushed it farther. Instead, he decided to run cables to the land and the mole, which would do the job of maintaining *Glaucus*'s aim even easier and more precise

Everything was ready by three bells of the forenoon watch. Giles went aloft with Mr. Stewart and Mr. Bush. He would give the orders that aimed the guns. The others would watch for the fall of shot to determine where next they should aim. Giles called down instructions so that the cannon lined up with the roof of what he now knew to be the Bey's Palace. Giles had planned a full broadside of eighteen shots in his first bombardment, but he realized that firing the guns simultaneously, while undoubtedly very impressive, would not be the most effective way to hit the best targets After the first one gun fired, he ordered that the gun captains try to fire when the frigate was listing farthest to larboard as a result of the recoil from firing shot before it in the order.

When everything was ready below him, Giles bellowed open fire. The first gun roared out. Then the next and the next until all eighteen guns had sent their cannonballs into the town. Giles and his officers then put their heads together to evaluate what damage had been done to the town. The first ball had fired true and had come very close to its target. Giles and the others agreed that it must have hit somewhere very close to the line along which they had been aiming. He thought that it had hit the roof of the Bey's palace. Because of some trees obstructing the view, they could not be sure just where it had hit, but they knew it had probably hit the roof because of the dust and stones thrown up by the cannonball strike.

The other shots had sprayed unpredictably over quite a large area of the town, judging by the signs of hits that they could discern. For purposes of doing random damage to Kamlakesh, this was satisfactory. However, Giles felt it would have been better to have been able to hit more nearly a specific area, especially or near the Bey's Palace, since he guessed that that would be considered most serious by the men who now controlled the town.

The first shot had been very satisfactory. The others had been less so. The problem had been both the elevation of the guns, determining how far a ball could go, and also where the cannon was actually pointing when it fired. After the first shot, *Glaucus* had been struggling against the cables that were supposed to be holding her steady, so that the gunners had great difficulty judging the elevation when their cannon fired, and no one could predict very accurately just where it would be pointed when it fired.

A conference followed on deck when the three officers who had been aloft were joined by the First Lieutenant and the Master. They agreed on a different way to bombard the town. This process would be slower, but it might be more effective. Mr. Brooks pointed out that the longer time that it would take to fire eighteen shots might have the advantage of automatically drawing out the time during which the men of Kamlakesh would have to worry about the possibility of their properties being hit, or even of getting killed themselves. The lengthened suspense might well lead to extra pressure being put on the Bey to give in to Giles's demands.

After they had decided how next to bombard the town, Mr. Miller suggested that it might be a good idea to call for another parlay before the subsequent bombardment. The message was to call for Mr. Mohammed to tell them whether the Bey was happy to have *Glaucus* continue to its next step in the destruction of Kamlakesh or whether he wanted to free the prisoners. Mr. Brooks could deliver the message with the aid of the speaking trumpet since he was renowned for communicating with the masthead in a roaring storm without even having to use the speaking horn. Giles suggested that the message include the statement that *Glaucus* would wait for an answer for an hour before starting the bombardment again.

Mr. Abbott fired a signal gun. Mr. Brooks bellowed out his message. Then dinner for the hands was piped, and the officers who were off-duty retired to the wardroom to enjoy their meal. Giles, as usual, ate alone, bothered by doubts that these plans would have no better effect on accomplishing his mission than had his previous attempts. Could there be a way of storming the town and rescuing the hostages without too much loss of life? About one thing he was resolved: he was not now going to sail away with his tail between his legs, even if he had already recaptured an East Indiaman and put a large crimp into continuing piracy based on Kamlakesh.

Giles waited a full hour and more before going on deck again. This time they would fire a ball from one of the cannons and then wait for the ship to settle down before another one was fired. This time they would use just one gun, the one that Mr. Abbott figured was the most accurate. Again he would be using the best balls and carefully measured cartridges. Even though it should be much easier to determine where the shots landed, Giles once again took Mr. Stewart and Mr. Bush aloft to try to see where the cannonball fell. As Giles knew from the previous bombardments, it was not easy to determine exactly where a shot must have landed or to determine what damage it had done.

The first shot banged out. There was now a longer wait before the next one fired. Giles and his two companions now had ample time to guess exactly where it landed. They agreed that it must have hit the Bey's palace again, made more likely since it was clear that it had knocked a branch from a tree that was right in front of the palace. The cannonballs were falling mainly near the palace. It was hard to determine just what damage they were doing, especially as there were many empty spaces around and within the building where a cannonball would do little harm. Of course, some balls still went astray, one of them putting a hole that they could see clearly on a dome of a wealthy house. This bombardment was undoubtedly doing what Giles hoped it would. It was hurting the rich of Kamlakesh rather than the poor.

After the gun ceased blasting away, Giles had Mr. Brooks again extend an invitation to parlay. Still there was no response from Kamlakesh. Giles wondered how long it would take to bring the Bey to his senses or for pressure on him from others who were being harmed to force him to negotiate.

However, he had read enough history to know that leaders in situations such as the one with which the Bey was now confronted could be stubborn and proud even when it was against their best interests. He hoped that that was not the case here. *Glaucus* did not have enough powder and shot on board to flatten Kamlakesh. She could not even spend on the city all that she carried if she were to have enough to be capable of meeting challenges that might arise on the voyage home. Despite these gloomy thoughts, he ordered the next bombardment to commence when an hour had passed since Mr. Brooks had issued his invitation.

This bombardment produced significantly more encouraging results than had the previous one. After two more shots struck the Bey's palace, a third one was followed by a massive cloud of dust that suggested that it had resulted in the collapse of a good part of the structure. In addition, a ball that had struck something behind a small grove of fruit trees must have started a fire, for soon a column of smoke was observed coming from where the ball must have struck. It was followed by flickers of flames that were visible even in the full sunlight that bathed the target. It must have been the property of a wealthy man to have been able to use precious land in the town for such a frivolous purpose. Surely, that hit alone should increase the pressure on the Bey to comply with Giles's demands.

Giles had Mr.Brooks hail the town once more when the bombardment had finished. This time, he was to indicate that *Glaucus* was finished for the day, but that the firing would start again the following morning if they had not received a positive message from the Bey.

As nightfall approached, the First Lieutenant approached Giles. "Captain, I believe that we should rig the boarding nets."

"Why, Mr. Miller? We have pretty well destroyed the boats that the Kamlakeshi could use to approach us. I don't think we are in danger of being swarmed by swimmers, though I suppose that we might double the lookouts just in case."

"I wasn't really thinking about a possible attack, sir. Rather, I wanted to find another task for the crew. Only the officers and the men handling one gun have had much activity today. Our people need more tasks to do, and we have not practiced setting the boarding nets* for some time."

"That makes sense. Carry on, Mr. Miller."

The sun set, but quiet did not descend on *Glaucus* at once. The boarding nets had been set and the lookouts set, but the crew, by and large, remained on deck, yarning or working on carvings, or listening to the captain who was playing his violin with the sounds drifting through the scuttles to entertain everyone. There had been various arguments on board about how good he was, and whether he would be ready to play with Lady Ashton when he returned to England. Daphne had established, on her few visits to Giles's ships, a stellar reputation for being capable of anything. Most of the crew felt that nothing was too good for her, including the captain's playing of the violin. Amid this relaxation, a lookout suddenly left his post to address Mr. Harris, who was the officer of the watch.

"Mr. Miller, sir," the seaman reported, "there is a swimmer nearing the starboard quarter."

"Let's see. Mr. Bush, please inform the captain that a swimmer has been sighted approaching the starboard quarter."

Without pausing for Giles to come on deck, as he was sure to do after receiving such a message, Mr. Miller went across the quarter-deck to peer over the starboard rail. There was, indeed, a man swimming towards *Glaucus* with the easy stroke of someone who knew the water and was conserving his energy while making good progress towards his destination. Few onboard *Glaucus* could have done as well while swimming. Giles arrived on the scene and immediately took charge.

"Mr. Miller, raise that boarding net so that he can approach the ship. You can swim, can you not, McAlister?"

"Yes, sir," replied the topman whom Giles had addressed.

"Lower the entry ladder, Mr. Miller, to the water. McAlister, go to its end and help that man aboard."

Giles then turned to the lookout. "you saw him first, didn't you, Jenkins?"

"Aye, sir."

"Well done! It is often not easy to see that a swimmer is approaching a ship."

McAlister, in the meantime, had gone to the end of the ladder. The swimmer altered course to come to his position. McAlister helped him out of the water and signaled for him to precede him up the ladder.

As he emerged onto the deck, the bedraggled swimmer was the focus of all eyes. He was a young, slim, blond fellow, quite thin but not emaciated. He was dressed in what looked like a feminine top designed to hold breasts. Soaked as it now was, it clung to his chest, revealing that he had none. He wore a pair of baggy trousers gathered at the ankles that the water had rendered almost transparent as well as plastering them to his skin. He might have seemed effeminate, but he was, without doubt, a young man.

The Master at Arms took charge of the man as he emerged, dripping, onto the deck. He escorted him to Giles, who had resisted the temptation to be at the entry port to avoid showing too much curiosity about the visitor. The man had deep-brown colored skin almost everywhere in sight. It was only his blond hair that suggested he might be European, but that could be sun bleach, Giles supposed.

"Do you speak English?" was Giles's first question.

"Yes, sir."

"What is your name, and why did you come here?"

"Samuel Gentry, sir. I was an apprentice-mate on *The Glory of the East* when she was taken by pirates."

Giles recognized the name of the ship as one of the East Indiamen, which had already been ransomed under the former regime. He had understood that all the European employees of the East India Company had been exchanged. He was becoming suspicious. If what he suspected were true, it might be better to continue the interview in his cabin.

"We'll continue this discussion below," he announced. "Mr. Miller, please come too."

When he reached his cabin, Giles tossed his hat on a couch and sat behind his table with Gentry positioned in front of it so that the bright stern windows were behind the captain. He signaled to Mr. Miller to stand at the end of the table. He took some time looking at Gentry without speaking though he was staring at the man. He noticed that in addition to his bizarre costume, the man was wearing gold rings on his ankles and wrists. The jewelry looked too small to slip off and had little rings attached to them suggesting that they were shackles that could be locked as restraints if wanted.

"I thought that all the English people on *The Glory of the East* had been ransomed. Why weren't you?"

"Because of Pasha Abraham. He is now Bey Abraham because of the events a night ago. When my ship arrived here, he made me his personal servant, really his slave. As you may know, sir, except for the passengers and the officers of *The Glory of the East*, we were all enslaved. Even so, I heard that the other members of the crew were released when John Company* paid the Bey's demands, except, of course, for the Indian servants and some of the Indian seamen. Pasha Abraham had found me too attractive to release me when the other English prisoners were freed. He told me that he struck my name off the list because, he had claimed, I had died of a fever. The pasha had selected me for private use. After he found me pleasing, I had no contact with the other slaves from our ship, so I guess that the Company must have bought his story. Captain Richards couldn't have cared less whether I had lived or died," Gentry concluded bitterly.

"Captain Richards?" queried Giles.

"The captain of *The Glory of the East*, sir. He always presumed that I was a molly-boy because of my looks. But I am not like that."

"You aren't?" Giles asked skeptically. "You mean that Pasha Abraham dressed you like that, even with gold shackles, for no reason at all?"

"No, of course not, sir. He gave me no choice. Either I did what he wanted, or he would give me over to his guards to use as they wanted. He described just what they would do. Servicing him sounded like a better alternative. I even became skilled at it so that he wouldn't get rid of me anyway."

"I see," said Giles, though, in fact, he did not and was revolted by the whole business. One didn't grow up in the gunrooms and wardrooms of the Royal Navy without realizing that some men enjoyed relations with other men either as a substitute for female company or even for itself, but it had never appealed to him nor could he understand the attraction.

Giles had been suspicious of the arrival of Gentry since he had first come aboard. Pasha Abraham and Mr. Mohammed had already disastrously fooled him. Samuel Gentry did not look as if he had been badly treated while he was a slave -- if he had been one. Had he been forced to submit to the disgusting desires of the Pasha, or had he been a willing participant in the perversions? Could this be another attempt to manipulate the Captain of *Glaucus* to forward the interests of the new Bey?

"Why are you here, Gentry? What do you want of us?"

"I hope that you will take 'me with you when you leave Kamlakesh. With no one knowing or even caring that I have been enslaved, you are my only hope of regaining my freedom. I would also like to help you to defeat Pasha Abraham and to get what you require from him. I have been much abused by him."

"Oh? You look quite healthy to me."

"I suppose that I must. After he showed me what would happen if I did not comply with his wishes, I was well fed and required to maintain myself in good shape."

Giles realized at this point that it might be wise if he probed more deeply to find out whether this man was another decoy. He suspected that the man in his peculiar costume had been used in revolting ways by his owner. Giles had no way of knowing how willing a participant in such activities the young man had been; he was aware that many men enjoyed such activities even though they pretended disgust.

"What is the situation in Kamlakesh now?" Giles asked.

"I don't know precisely. Pasha Abraham has met more opposition than he expected, he told me. He had to break off his latest pleasuring himself with me because of men complaining that the bombardment was ruining their mansions, and he had to stop it. He had to release all the hostages since you were doing more damage than they were worth.

"Pasha Abraham left me then. I took the chance to get away. There were a lot of angry people outside the palace. After dark, I was able to escape in the confusion. I wrapped a robe around myself so that my status would not be evident. I didn't waste any time getting to the water and swimming out here."

"What do you know about where are the people he is holding hostage?"

"They used to be held in a wing of the Bey's Palace, I think. After Pasha Abraham became Bey, he had them put in shackles. When you started firing at us, he had to interrupt our time together to order that they be taken somewhere beyond where your cannonballs could fall. It was very frustrating, getting interrupted by that," Gentry added peevishly.

"Do you know where they were taken?"

"Yes, Pasha Abraham directed that they be kept in another palace of his which you couldn't hit. He was going there himself since it could be defended better than the Bey's palace after you had knocked it to pieces. He didn't take me with him. I don't know why he didn't want me after all I had done for him," Gentry concluded.

"How did you communicate with your Pasha?"

"I learned to speak Arabic very quickly. If I hadn't, he might have soon lost interest in me. Nothing like the threats that hung over my head to make such a determined pupil! Once I started to learn, listening to conversations, and picking out what they meant, let me learn more. I have a good ear, so the accent was not too much of a problem. That is how I know more than he suspected by listening to what he was saying. I was not as good at talking as I was at listening, so he thought I had not learned much. He would beat me for it or do other, more awful things to me."

"You say that things are chaotic in the town now."

"They were when I left. I think that a lot of prominent men want Pasha Abraham to turn the hostages over to you before you can destroy even more of their palaces."

"Do you know how to get to the place where the hostages are being kept?" Giles asked, a plan forming in his mind even as he spoke.

"Yes -- no. You can't make me go back there."

"Yes, I can. And if there is any treachery, I won't hesitate to kill you.

"Mr. Macauley, I'll need your marines armed with muskets and bayonets. Mr. Miller, arm the watch off duty with muskets and cutlasses. Have the boats ready to ferry us ashore. I am going to rescue the hostages."

The two officers complied, Mr. Miller knowing that it would be futile to protest that he should lead the expedition. He may not have been too disappointed. Giles's previous venture into the town had been remarkably unsuccessful. If

Mr. Miller had been in charge of such a fiasco, it would have seriously hurt his chances for promotion.

In short order, the landing party was ready, and the boats were ferrying them ashore. When all the party was on land, Giles, Mr. Macauley, and his marines led them through the rubble of the gate. Samuel Gentry attempted to find a place in the rear, but Giles was not going to allow that. He told Mr. Macauley to assign a marine to make sure that their informant was with the leaders. Up the main street, they proceeded, first through the undamaged poor quarter, then into wealthier parts where the effects of the bombardment became evident. The damage reached a maximum at the palace of the Bey, where they had been so ignominiously outwitted. Soon after that, there was no more damage. Next, they came to the walls that surrounded another luxurious property. There was a mob outside the stout main gate, whose thick doors were tightly shut. Gentry confirmed that this was their destination

Giles evaluated the scene at a glance. "Mr. Stewart," he addressed the acting lieutenant who was part of the expedition. "Take some of your people back to where there were some beams on the road and select a couple to use as battering rams. Gentry, order that mob to disperse."

Samuel Gentry had been given clothes more suitable to his status than the ones he had been wearing when he swam out to *Glaucus*. In a surprisingly loud voice, he gave a series of orders in Arabic, which had the effect of getting the mob to break up and drift away.

Mr. Stewart returned with his battering rams. The seemingly stout gates broke open at the third time the beams slammed into them. The marines did not rush in. Instead, with their muskets held vertically, they marched through the gates and spread out immediately. The few people who were in the courtyard fell to their knees, obviously hoping to avert being slaughtered. Without pausing, Lieutenant Macauley detailed a couple of his men to herd them into a corner.

The main door to the palace was locked, but it quickly yielded to the battering rams. The entry hall was empty.

"Where do you expect us to find your former master?" Giles asked Gentry.

He pointed to a set of double doors. They were locked, but a blow from a musket butt broke them open. Inside the new Bey, accompanied by Mr. Mohammed, waited for them. Behind them were several Europeans, quite well dressed. The Bey was dressed to impress with gold embroidery on his white robe, and a belt decorated with emeralds and diamonds. In the belt was a bejeweled ceremonial knife, which, Giles noted, had a wicked-looking steel blade.

The Bey growled something, which Mr. Mohammad translated, "The Bey presumes you have come to pay the ransom for these people.

"Don't be ridiculous, you traitor." We will take the hostages, some of whom are, I presume, behind you."

"That is all we have," said Mr. Mohammad.

"Is it? I know you are lying, Mohammad. It will go easier on you if you cooperate with me."

Before the traitor could reply, one of the Europeans spoke up, "I am Captain Howard of *The Star of Madras*. A few of the less important people are elsewhere in the town. It will be very dangerous to try to get them. I demand that you take us to your ship immediately before the mob gets out of control again."

"Do you, Captain Howard? I am not leaving until we have freed all the captives. Where are they?"

"Oh, there are only a few scattered all over the place. Like that creature with you, many seem to be happy to be here and will be reluctant to leave."

"That's nonsense, you traitor," burst out Samuel Gentry. "There are many of the well-to-do Englishmen in the palace. And far more are held in the slave pens, those who probably would not be ransomed, and some women to whom some Pasha had taken an interest."

The Bey said something to which Mr. Mohammad responded, and the Bey said something else while pointing to Samuel Gentry. Something snapped in the East Indiaman apprentice. With a savage growl, he lept on the Bey, knocking him over. In a moment he had seized the knife from the aristocrat's belt, grabbed him by the private parts, and took one swift cut of the knife. Blood squirted from his victim. Gentry shook his hand from the enveloping robes and waved over his head the severed member of his victim. He then seemed to realize what he did.

"Throw me in irons if you wish, Captain Giles. I am content to have evened my score with the man who turned me into his plaything."

. "Mr. Macauley," ordered Giles, "take some marines with you to search this palace for hostages. Mohammad, tell the Bey that he won't see a doctor unless he quickly tells us where the hostages and slaves are kept. If you don't co-operate, I'll have you castrated too and left to be at the pleasure of whoever is in charge here. Now, Gentry, do you have any idea where the people from our ships who were enslaved might be."

"Yes sir, as far as those who are slaves of the town. But individual slaves, especially females who are serving in particular houses, may be anywhere."

The Bey had been only too happy to co-operate in the hope that something could be done about his wound. He had detailed his knowledge of where the hostages were held.

"Mr. Stewart," Giles gave his next order, "Take a dozen seamen with you and some marines. Take Gentry with you too, and collect the slaves the Bey has told us about. Also, any others whose location Gentry may know. As you are going about the town, have Mr. Gentry call out regularly that all slaves must be brought out of the houses immediately."

Dr. Maclean had asked Giles that he be allowed to join the party out of curiosity but indicating that his services might be needed if armed opposition was encountered. Now Giles told him to attend to the Bey. Giles had fulfilled his promise to the Bey by asking the doctor to do what he could. Of course, the man might die anyway, or, as a despised eunuch, he could be overthrown quickly.

"There is not much I can do except to sew him up. His manhood is gone, and he may die of infection," the medical man informed Giles.

"Do the best you can. It undoubtedly would be better if that man remains a living example of what happens when you try to seize Englishmen."

Dr. Maclean had the ex-Bey lie down on the floor. Without much ceremony, he slashed away the elaborate pantaloons which had clothed his lower body. He staunched the bleeding and sewed up the ugly wound left by Gentry's knife. By then, the patient had passed out. The good doctor waited for his patient to recover consciousness before he poured some run over the area to finish clearing it before bandaging it. The bandage came from one of the former Bey's attendants, who was only to happy to comply when Dr. Maclean indicated by a gesture that, otherwise, he would see about performing the same operation on the man that Gentry had done so crudely on the Bey.

It did not take long before the results of the searches began to appear. Lieutenant Macauley had found several East India officials and passengers in a large room in the palace as well as the captains of the French and Dutch ships. Giles sent the squad of marines out into the town to further the work that Mr. Stewart was doing. Within an hour, groups of minor hostages and household slaves were being brought to the courtyard of the palace. Then, Mr. Mohammad and Gentry led the way to where the slave pens were. It was lucky that they had the marines with them, for once the slaves realized that they were being freed, they became a very unruly lot. Mr. Macauley and Mr. Stewart quickly separated the Europeans from the others and brought the Europeans to the palace. On the way, they were joined by many household slaves and servants, most of them women. With the other slaves roaming free and set on revenge, and with a power struggle about to break out among the leaders of Kamlakesh, Giles realized that he had done all he could with his small force.

Dawn had broken while the search for captives had been going on. While the marines stood guard, the released people were ferried in several boatloads to *Glaucus*. She was badly overloaded by the time the last of the marines were aboard. Giles had the anchor raised. Using the beginning of the land-breeze, *Glaucus* was able to leave Kamlakesh. Looking back, he saw smoke rising in various parts of the town. He guessed that old scores were being settled among various factions because Kamlakesh's government had broken down. Inevitably, additional property damage would result.

The sporadic sound of muskets shots indicated that there would be a further, significant loss of life.

In this breeze, it would be some time before *Glaucus* would come up with the three rescued ships that were anchored at the mouth of Kamlakesh Inlet. Giles put to work all his officers who were not immediately involved in sailing the frigate sorting the seamen from the landsmen and the important officers of the East India Company and prominent passengers of the captured ships from the rest in preparation for dividing them among his little fleet.

With all his orders given, Giles retreated to his cabin, nursing a splitting headache. How in the world was he to deal with all these passengers? Were there enough provisions in the four ships to feed them on minimum rations? He would undoubtedly have complaints from the East India Company officers and officials as well as their other wealthy passengers. He knew that he might have exceeded his orders, but that was not likely to have repercussions. He just dreaded having to deal with all these people on the journey home.

How he wished that he could confide in Daphne right now! She would have good suggestions, he knew, and she would undoubtedly be on his side. Even writing to her would be a comfort. It would clear his mind and clarify the possibilities open to him. Just thinking about her would calm him. Out came the already very long letter to her. Despite his headache, he would detail his thoughts to her at least until the time when *Glaucus* met with the other three ships. After that, he should be heading home.

Chapter XVII

Daphne and Lady Clara returned to Dipton in the middle of the afternoon, a couple of days after the dinner at which the subject of the rights of women had been raised. Daphne had found that she could not read while traveling in a coach because trying to do so gave her a headache. As soon as Betsey had finished helping her to change from her traveling clothes, and she had had a brief visit with Bernard in the nursery, Daphne ordered her maid to find the volume. She settled down on a chaise longue, with her feet up, to start reading the work.

Daphne was amazed that the author, *Mary Wollstonecraft, began her book by talking about the education of women. It was a subject that Daphne had never thought about. Her own, she knew, had been unusual. Her governess had been at odds with Daphne about what was suitable for a young lady to learn. Geometry was the subject that had produced a change from the usual education of young women. Her governess had believed it to be utterly unsuitable for young ladies, mainly, Daphne suspected, because her mentor understood little mathematics and no geometry. She had instructed Daphne in arithmetic, though only in addition and subtraction. She had not seemed to understand multiplication, and division had been quite beyond her. Mr. Moorhouse had quite different ideas about what his daughter should learn. If Daphne was interested in geometry, then she should be taught it, even though her father's grasp of the subject was only slightly better than the governess's.*

After her father had dismissed the governess, Mr. Moorhouse had been content to let Daphne follow any intellectual interests she might have, buying her books on mathematics and, when she became interested in what was happening on his property, treatises on agriculture and estate management. A smattering of history and philosophy, chosen seemingly at random, and some literary classics, including many Shakespeare plays, had completed her education. If she found a book boring or too dense, she had dropped it. Her time spent reading had diminished as she became interested in the management of her father's estate, especially as she did set aside a certain amount of time for practicing the piano.

Daphne knew that her father's permissive indifference was an unusual approach to education. While growing up, she had had few contemporary female friends, but she was aware that their schooling was concerned with what she thought of as trivial matters. As she got to know more gentlewomen and gentlemen, she realized that she knew more in many areas that she considered to be important than did the women, but that she had less broad knowledge than many of the men. However, not liking the feeling of not understanding what the men might be alluding to in conversation made her search out further books for enlightenment. She was lucky that Mr. Moorhouse not only had an extensive collection, but he was also quite ready to order any works that Daphne wanted. He also paid for her subscription to the Ameschester lending library and made sure that she could go there whenever she wanted.

A kick from her womb reminded her that she would soon have another baby. Would it be a girl or a boy? If it were a girl, what would her education be like? A boy's education would be straightforward. As a second son, he would be tutored before going to school and then on to university or into the inns of court or even to sea as a midshipman. But a girl's upbringing? Girls didn't have the same opportunities as their brothers. Daphne knew that they were often strongly discouraged from pursuing interests similar to what a boy would learn. That wasn't right! She wouldn't allow it to happen if the baby turned out to be a girl! She turned back to her book, and the baby gave another kick as if to concur with her decision.

She continued reading for some time. She acknowledged to herself the cogency of many of the author's arguments but also felt that they hardly applied to her, though they might describe other women. Early on in the book, she found the phrase, "some women govern their husbands without degrading themselves, because intellect will always govern." Possibly, she thought, but she didn't want to 'govern' Giles, but only to participate in his activities and she had achieved that without effort. Of course, she could not go to sea, though she had heard that some captains' wives did so, and also fulfill her role as the overseer of their properties and land-based interests. How did her having established the anti-smuggling canal service square with the author's views of women's place? Was she such a complete exception to the role and activities of women? Surely not.

Such contemplation was all very well, she thought, but she had tasks to perform. She should invite her father and his brother to dinner. She had somewhat left things in that area hanging when she dashed off to London with Lady Clara. There were matters to discuss about her uncle's business and his settling into life at Dipton Manor. She had even said that she would have a look at the books of Moorhead and Son, a task he found very difficult to do after his seizure. She had the documents, including the latest reports that had arrived from Birmingham by post. Careful examination of them would give her a much better idea of how the business was doing even though she knew almost nothing *about how guns were made. In addition, she should plan to take a trip to inspect Ashton Place before the baby made such an excursion impossible. She had entirely neglected Giles's property at Ashton, which he had inherited from his half-brother. Taking time to do that would make her other tasks more pressing. Mary Wollstonecraft could wait for a time when she had less to do.*

Somewhat reluctantly, Daphne heaved herself into a standing position. She was still quite agile but was aware that she was becoming less mobile as the child she was carrying got larger. However, she still had quite some time before the baby was likely to insist on being born.

Daphne settled at the desk in her workroom and soon was absorbed in what the accounts told her about the business. The dry figures still let her imagine the workshop. Materials came in and had to be paid for, people worked in the plant and were paid. Guns were produced from material supplied to the company and shipped out of the establishment, or picked up by customers, and paid for. The accounts at which she was looking covered only recent times, but that was the period that concerned her.

She soon spotted some changes. The pattern appeared to change a few days after her uncle's seizure. Usually, deliveries of metal had been made weekly. When he fell ill, a couple of days were missed before a delivery was made by a different company at a higher price. The following week, the same new company made the delivery. It was also at the higher rate. Soon after, a larger quantity of material had been received, and the higher amount had then become standard.

Further tracking of the progress of the company showed that the larger orders continued. They had, in fact, increased still farther. The number of guns produced had at first dropped a little and then resumed at the former rate.

Other expenses had remained the same, but then the bill for workers increased significantly. It looked as if new people had been taken on, but the output had exceeded the earlier level only enough to make up the shortfall that had occurred right after the changes. The output figures then stabilized at their previous levels. The accounts showed no increase in the number of muskets and rifles produced for the government, and that was the bulk of the business. It now cost more to manufacture them. Daphne was puzzled by the change. She wondered what had caused it. She would ask her uncle at dinner if he had any ideas.

At that point, the dressing gong sounded. Steves was reminding her that it was time to change for dinner. Daphne wasn't sure why she always changed for dinner when her father and her uncle would be the only guests, but it was such a routine custom that she wouldn't think of abandoning it, even though it was a time-consuming nuisance and her daytime gown was quite adequate for the evening events.

Daphne was in the parlor with Lady Clara when Mr. Moorhouse and his brother came in with one of the footmen pushing the invalid's bath chair. There had been no change in Daphne's uncle's condition, but he had been learning new tricks to deal with his disability. He was also thinking about whether there was some way in which he could find a way of propelling his bath chair himself using his one good arm and one good leg. He also, his bother reported, was making progress on using sequences of the grunts he was capable of sounding to get the servants to do what he wanted.

Conversation at dinner centered on the recent trip to London. Only when the cloth* had been drawn, and Daphne and Lady Clara had not left the room to let the men indulge in port, did Daphne raise the subject of her uncle's business.

"Uncle George, I spent some time examining the records of Moorhouse and Son before dinner. I am puzzled by one thing."

Daphne paused to get a reaction from her uncle, but then she remembered that he could only communicate by writing.

"Soon after your seizure, the supplier of iron or steel and other metals changed. The new materials were more expensive and were bought in larger quantities, yet no more guns were produced. They were sold for the same old price. Do you know what happened?"

Her uncle applied himself to his slate. "No," he wrote. "Cobbler and Triscott the suppliers. Asked Geordie Shearer to find out what happened. He didn't know. Cobbler won't talk to him. Won't deal with ordinary workers. I don't know the new suppliers, Nick Flinch and Co. Geordie hadn't heard of them. New company? Wouldn't talk to Geordie. Claimed had contract as exclusive supplier of our metals. Don't know where that came from. Metal inferior quality. Wastage reason for using more."

"What should we do about it, Uncle?"

"Don't know," George wrote. "Need someone in Birmingham to look into the matter. Agent used to be Arbinathy. Don't use him!!"

Daphne saw that her uncle was getting more and more upset at the situation. She could understand how helpless he must feel with his business going downhill and no ability to change it himself. Her father had surprised her in dealing with Mr. Arbinathy, but he had no head for business. Her brother, Geoffrey, was very reluctant to have anything to do with the Birmingham factory business. He was a stubborn sort. He also had said he wanted nothing to do with Dipton Manor. He had said that he was content with his bookshop in Reading.

She could see only one solution. She would have to go to Birmingham again. There was the difficulty that she was a woman, and, therefore, she would have trouble being taken seriously by whoever was ruining the business. Maybe she could call on Mr. Throgmorton, the solicitor who lived on the square where her uncle's house was located, for help. He had been friendly and supportive on her last visit to Birmingham. Yes, she should visit Birmingham again. It should be done as soon as possible to minimize the damage being done to her uncle's business. She could stay at his house in the city. She should send news so that the housekeeper could open up some rooms for her. She should also contact Mr. Throgmorton.

The other diners had noticed that Daphne had become abstracted after her interchange with her uncle. "Daphne," said her father, "what are you thinking about?"

"I think I should go to Birmingham as soon as possible to straighten out this mess."

"Do you have to? Can't we use some agent or someone else."

"No, I don't think so. The people working in the plant know me and so will be more helpful than they would be to a stranger. We haven't even talked to Geoffrey about the plant, though I still think he should inherit it. Maybe there is room in Birmingham for him to open a bookshop there."

"I suppose you are right, Daphne, about the business," conceded Mr. Moorhouse. "Geoffrey wants no part of it or of me for that matter, but I should be the one to go, not you."

"Nonsense, father, You have always said that you have no head for such things. Uncle George needs you here.

I'll leave the day after tomorrow. With luck, I will only be gone a week or so."

That settled the matter. The next day, Daphne dealt with anything in Dipton that couldn't wait, and the following morning she departed for Birmingham in her carriage with Betsey. It was not the adventure that her first visit to the midlands city had been since this was not the first time she had traveled to her uncle's house, but there were still many new things to see.

When the carriage pulled up in front of her uncle's house in St. Paul's Square, Daphne took a few moments to look around. It was larger than the square in London in which Camshire House was located, and it had a church in its center rather than a garden, but it could be considered just as elegant, she felt. She noted Mr. Throgmorton's house but thought that she should find out more about the problems at Moorhouse and Son before requesting his advice or services.

Even before she was helped from the carriage by a postilion, the door to her uncle's house opened. Quincy, her uncle's butler, must have had his eye open for her arrival. She was about to greet him when Mr. Throgmorton interrupted her. He had been walking towards his own house and happened to arrive just as Daphne was being helped from the carriage.

"Lady Ashton. It is good to see you again. How is your uncle?" he asked.

"As well as can be hoped for after his seizure, Mr. Throgmorton. If anything, he is getting better and more able to cope with his disabilities."

"I am glad to hear it. And what brings you to Birmingham, my lady?"

Daphne explained how problems with Moorhouse and Son had necessitated her visit. Mr. Throgmorton was sympathetic. "If I can be of any assistance, my lady, let me know. I am acquainted with most of the leading manufacturers in the city."

"That is very good of you, Mr. Throgmorton. Thank you."

"I see that you have just arrived. You must be tired. Don't let me keep you." Mr. Throgmorton made a bow and proceeded on his way.

Daphne felt almost smothered by the attention she received from the servants at her uncle's house. She understood it. They were all worried about their positions and whether they could get good references if they were dismissed. They all enquired about her uncle's health and also tried to make sure that Daphne had everything she wanted. Betsey mentioned that she was getting more assistance straightening out Daphne's things than she had ever received in other houses.

This treatment by the servants brought to the forefront of Daphne's attention that some decisions, possibly painful decisions, had to be made about her uncle's house and business. Could her brother Geoffrey step in to keep things going, with at least general oversight of the company? His bookshop in Winchester was his great love, but possibly Birmingham needed a bookshop of the sort he had developed. Anyway, there was nothing to be done about those matters right now. A wash and change of clothes and dinner, followed by a long sleep, was what she needed.

The following morning, Daphne, with Betsey in tow, arrived at Moorhouse and Sons at nine-thirty without any prior warning. She wanted to surprise the men who were running the plant to see if their reaction would tell her anything suspicious. It did not.

Geordie Shearer looked up when the door opened and sprang to his feet.

"Lady Ashton. Thank heavens that you are here. I wrote to Mr. Moorhouse about our problems. Everything is going to hell, and I don't know what to do. How is Mr. Moorhouse?"

"I am sorry to say that he is much the same as when he left Birmingham, though he is coping with his incapacity better. Now tell me about the difficulties here."

"Gladly, but I think I should get Mr. Bottomly since he knows most about what is happening on the factory floor. However, we don't know exactly why we have these problems or what to do about them. Neither of us can run the plant by ourselves. We need some sort of manager to fill in for Mr. Moorhouse."

Hugh Bottomly entered at that point. Someone must have gone to get the plant foreman as soon as Daphne came through the office door.

"Lady Ashton, I am so glad to see you. As we wrote to Mr. Moorhouse, things have not been going well since he left. We didn't want to worry him, of course, but we did hint that something needed to be done."

"What is the trouble?"

"It is the quality of the metal we have been receiving. We used to get it from a very reliable firm. But that suddenly stopped just after you had been here. Instead, a new company, Prittship and Company, showed up with our order. The teamsters who were delivering the load came with a senior figure from the new firm. When I said I didn't think we had ordered anything from their firm, the office-type man pulled out a sheet of paper, which was an order to deliver the material signed by Mr. Arbinathy, the solicitor who was in charge after Mr. Moorhouse had his seizure. I wasn't happy with it, but there was nothing I could do except accept the load. I did call around later in the day to our previous suppliers, but they rebuffed my questions with great rudeness. They were not willing to discuss why they were not providing our metal, but the man I talked with did suggest that I speak to Mr. Arbinathy about the matter. The lawyer hasn't been here since then, and his office was closed when I went there, so I have not had a chance to ask him about what was happening."

"There was one strange thing about that piece of paper," Geordie Shearer broke in. "It instructed me to draw up a draft in the name of Mr. Arbinathy, and he would arrange payment of the suppliers. I wasn't happy about this arrangement, but there it was in writing by someone who had been put in charge by the owner. I didn't want to trouble Mr. Moorhouse in his condition. I have handled subsequent invoices in the same way.

"Oh, dear," Daphne said. "We had to get rid of Mr. Arbinathy. His power of attorney was bogus, and he was to have nothing further to do with any of my uncle's affairs. He was arrested. Didn't you hear about it?"

"No, my lady. No one informed us."

Daphne was horrified. In their concerns about how to take care of her uncle, her father and she had forgotten to inform those in charge of the day-to-day operations of the company. Mr. Arbinathy had stolen a march on them. Daphne suddenly realized that her presumption that the crooked lawyer was in prison must have been incorrect. Had the local magistrates been in league with him? Had they let him go or freed him on the promise of attending court when it was held?

Whatever the situation about him might be, she would have to deal with its consequences. She should also talk to Mr. Throgmorton about making sure that Mr. Arbinathy would have no further opportunity to ruin her uncle's business.

"I did try to ask at Cobbler and Triscott about it," said Hugh Bottomly, "but Mr. Cobbler wouldn't talk to me. He was, in fact, very rude, saying that, with Mr. Arbinathy in charge, he wanted nothing to do with us, ever. Of course, he is well known for not liking to talk to ordinary workmen, except to give them orders."

"Do I understand that the new supplies are not as good?" Daphne changed the subject.

"Yes, my lady. They are shoddy stuff. Some we have had to discard completely. Others we had to resmelt to get rid of the defects. Even then, I'm not entirely happy with the results. The material is suitable for our muskets after our efforts, but we have to be extra selective to get material for our rifles and other guns. The extra work has meant that we have had to take on more hands. Geordie has been complaining about how the costs are increasing. Most of our work is for the army or the navy, on a contract basis that specifies the prices, so we can't raise them. We do need someone who can arrange for further contracts; the work for our present ones is almost finished."

Mr. Bottomly then explained in some detail how the poor quality material had to be dealt with, especially in the forge. Daphne was intrigued. Here was a chance to learn about a process about which she knew nothing. It was precisely the sort of thing that fascinated her. Her many questions revealed that fact.

"I think I understand where the quality of metal fits in," Daphne said when Mr. Bottomly's lecture ended. "I wish I had time to stay for more instruction. Maybe some other time. For now, let's get this mess straightened out. First off, accept no more shipments from this Prittship and Company, and, Geordie, make no more payments to Mr. Arbinathy. I'll see what I can do about Cobbler and Triscott. I am finding that a lot of people love to talk with titled people who won't give ordinary men the time of day. Of course, he may hate dealing with a woman even more than dealing with a working man. I will let you know the outcome. Do you have someone who can tell my coachman how to get there?"

"The boy can show him, my lady. Tommy, go with Lady Ashton to direct the coachman to Cobbler and Triscott."

The metal supply company occupied a large space some distance away, probably near what had been the edge of the city before Birmingham had started to expand so quickly. The yard had a high, solid, brick wall all around it, which was pierced by a gate that was wide enough to let massive wagons through. Near the entrance was a small brick building, in a modern style, much better maintained than the wall surrounding the yard.

Daphne sent Betsey into the building with her card and the message that Lady Ashton wanted to speak to the managing partner. Moments later, a senior clerk accompanied by a youth came bustling out.

"Lady Ashton," the clerk said unctuously, "It is an honor to have you visit. Mr. Cobbler will be delighted to see you. Gerald," he said to the boy, "assist her ladyship to alight. Hurry up now."

Daphne descended from the carriage in as haughty and self-confident a manner as she could muster. The clerk led her to the door and then stood aside so that she could enter first.

"Mr. Cobbler will see you at once, my lady," said the factotum, moving across the reception area to a door which he threw open, announcing, "Viscountess Ashton to see you, Mr. Cobbler."

Daphne hid her amusement well. Since acquiring a title by marrying Giles, she had found that some people were so awed by encountering people who were in the upper class, and therefore especially deserving, that they would do anything for them. Bottomly's remark on how he had been treated at Cobbler and Triscott had given her the hint that her present, haughty performance might get her farther than would being her usual, unpretentious self.

"Mr. Cobbler," Daphne began after the pleasantries had been exchanged. "I am here about Moorhouse and Sons. As you may know, my uncle, Mr. George Moorhouse, suffered a severe seizure, which has rendered him incapable of managing his company. I am in Birmingham to try to straighten out some problems that have arisen, largely, I believe, thanks to a dishonest lawyer, Mr. Arbinathy. As a consequence of his involvement, I understand that you have ceased making deliveries to the Moorhouse and Son. I hope that I can persuade you to restore the service. Incidentally, in case you doubt my word, I have here a power of attorney signed by my uncle authorizing me to handle the affairs of his company."

"I am sure that the document is unnecessary, my lady, at least here. Mr. Moorhouse was not only a customer but also a good friend. He often mentioned that he was very proud of you. I cannot believe that you had any part of what happened after his seizure."

"Just what did happen, Mr. Cobbler, if I may ask."

"I don't know all that went on at Moorhouse and Son. What I do know is that that man Arbinathy came to me soon after Mr. Moorhouse fell ill to say that he was in charge of the company. I found it unlikely, I must tell you, but he did have a power of attorney, and I recognized Mr. Moorhouse's signature on it.

"Arbinathy stated that he was unhappy with our rates and demanded that I slice them a lot. He also hinted that he would reward me himself if I complied with his wishes. The cut he wanted was substantial, but I would not lose from the arrangement, but I would make very, very little. I told him 'no'; it had been a just contract which I had negotiated with Mr. Moorhouse, fair to both parties, and that I was horrified at the side payment the man hinted would be mine if I co-operated with him. I can tell you, my lady, that Cobbler and Triscott does not do business on such terms. He persisted, even threatening me, so I told him to leave.

"A few days later, Mr. Bottomly tried to see me, but I don't do business with mere plant foremen, especially when they are working for a blackguard such as that Arbinathy."

"Quite understandable," Daphne lied. "Now that we know what Mr. Arbinathy was up to, I hope you will consider making the same deliveries on the same terms again."

"Normally, I wouldn't think of it, my lady, not after Arbinathy's behavior. However, George Moorhouse is a good friend, and you have enough problems with Moorhouse and Son without having to negotiate a new contract with me. Yes, I will be happy to do so, especially as I am honored to do a favor for a celebrated lady whose husband, the Viscount Ashton, is such a well-known war-hero. Just tell your bookkeeper to pay the invoices in the usual way. Normally, delivery would be tomorrow. Is that acceptable?"

"Yes, indeed it is."

Daphne wanted to leave at that point and get on with other tasks at hand, but instead, she had to be polite to make sure that the deliveries would not meet any arbitrary snag. Mr. Cobbler wanted her to understand how happy he was to be dealing with such distinguished people, how excellent was his company's service and how Mr. and Mrs. Cobbler were becoming more and more prominent members of Birmingham society. All this with an implied wish to get her approval and move closer to her orbit.

"Pompous fool," Daphne muttered under her breath, as she climbed back into her carriage. The boy who had been sent with her by Mr. Bottomly was still with them. He could direct them to her next stop, which was Prittship and Company, the outfit presently making the deliveries. She wasn't looking forward to dealing with such crooks, but she also had to prevent them from making any more deliveries.

Prittship and Co. had only a wooden shack as an office. When Betsey took Daphne's card in, a large, ungainly man emerged and came to the carriage. Luckily the coachman had recognized that the man would be no help and quickly descended from his bench to open the carriage door.

"Lady Ashton," the man said, in a clipped, midlands accent. "George Prittship. Do come into my office."

The office was only one room with desks for two clerks and another one for Mr. Prittship. He quickly cleared off a chair for Daphne. She explained that she represented Moorhouse and Son.

"Lady Ashton, I have to tell you that I am not happy about our dealings with Moorhouse and Son."

"Why ever not? I know that Moorhouse and Son has not been happy with the quality of your materials nor the price."

"The objection to the quality I can understand, my lady. I warned your Mr. Arbinathy that we served cruder trades than fine firearms, and he would not likely be happy with what I could send for the price on which he insisted. In fact, he made it so low that I wasn't at all sure that I should take the contract. We make hardly any money from it."

"How can that be? Our records show that the price is much more than our former supplier charged."

"What? Well, we certainly didn't get it. Here, Gonner," he addressed one of the clerks, "show Lady Ashton our records on the Moorhouse account."

Daphne scanned the ledger that the clerk opened for her. It showed that the recorded payments were far less than the sums entered by Geordie Shearer in Moorhouse and Son's books. How could this be?

"So, these record the payments from Moorhouse and Sons as issued by their chief clerk?" Daphne asked.

"Yes," said Mr. Prittship. "Well, not directly from Moorhouse and Son, no. It is a very usual situation, but so is Mr. Arbinathy's management of the company. We send our invoices to Mr. Arbinathy's chambers. After a few days, he issues a bank draft on an account at Lloyd's Bank."

"So the transaction goes through Mr. Arbinathy, and the money does not come directly from Moorhouse and Son?" Daphne asked.

"That's the way it is. Very unusual, I must say, but so is the current situation at Moorhouse and Son."

"Thank you, Mr. Prittship. This situation is very awkward. I fear that you have been involved in a scheme to drain money from my uncle's firm. I will try to mitigate the harm he has done us, and, hopefully, I will see that Mr.

Arbinathy is punished with the full weight of the law. Hanging him would not even be enough for the depths of … of … of thievery to which he has descended. I am sorry for all the inconvenience we have caused you."

"I'm glad you have straightened it out. As I said, it was a bad agreement, and I am happy to be out of it. Of course, if Moorhouse and Son needs lower-grade metals at any time, I will be happy to supply them, and at very competitive rates."

"I'll keep that in mind, Mr. Prittship. Now I must get on with the next steps of straightening out this mess."

Daphne had her carriage return to Moorhouse and Son, where she confirmed how Mr. Arbinathy had been stealing from the firm. Then she went to Lloyd's Bank, on which the bank draughts had been drawn. She wanted to make sure that Mr. Arbinathy would have no more access to the money of Moorhouse and Son. She would also seek the bank's advice on how to recover any of the money he had stolen.

The news at the bank was not good. Arbinathy had withdrawn large sums from the account of Moorhouse and Son. The bank claimed that the paper-work was all correct for him to have the authority to take the money. Now they could stop all transactions concerning Mr. Arbinathy, but they had no way to recover any of the money that had been stolen. The banker did suggest that Daphne visit the magistrates to lay charges against Mr. Arbinathy. She did so.

"This man should hang, my lady," was the magistrate's opinion, "but we have to catch him first. I will send some constables to his house and place of business, and if they do not find him, I shall issue a bulletin to be posted throughout the kingdom for his arrest. Might I suggest, my lady, that you need someone to manage the company? Mr.

Shearer and Mr. Bottomly are no doubt excellent men, but you need someone with the experience and capability to manage your uncle's company in his place."

Daphne was tired. She had done enough for that day. She told the coachman to take her back to her uncle's house. He complied, but the day was not over. As she alighted from her carriage in front of the house on St. Paul's Square, Mr. Throgmorton was again walking by.

"Lady Ashton, I hope that you have had a satisfactory day."

"A tiring one, at any rate. I have found out so much."

Daphne launched into a summary of all she had discovered. Then she continued about the problems she was facing.

"Now I have to find someone who can manage the business for my uncle," she declared. "I need a man who can be in Birmingham and can assume overall charge of all aspects of the enterprise. Doing pretty much what Uncle George was handling before he had that miserable seizure. Can you suggest anyone?"

"I am afraid not. However, I have an idea. Tonight, after dinner, I am hosting a small group of people. They are some of the members of our Lunar Society here in Birmingham. We are a group of leading citizens with a curiosity about scientific matters and engineering, as well as philosophy in general. Several members own manufacturing plants in the metal-working trades. They might be of help. I think you would enjoy talking with them anyway."

"But are women allowed?"

"Oh, yes, we have a few female members. We are not the Masons, even though several of our members are also members of the Masonic Order. Women are most certainly welcome in our club. Unfortunately, not many of the fair sex seem to be interested in the subjects that fascinate us. I am sure, Lady Ashton, that you will fit in. The get-together is at seven o'clock. I do hope you will come."

Daphne was delighted to accept. The idea of being included in a group indulging in after-dinner conversation about serious matters rather than local trivia, which was the usual practice of ladies after they had withdrawn from the dinner table in Dipton and elsewhere, delighted her. Furthermore, it might help her solve her principal dilemma for dealing with Moorhouse and Son. That was finding a capable manager.

The soirée had already started when Daphne arrived at Mr. Throgmorton's house. He introduced her to the various people who were there already. She was amazed. She had heard of several of the people who had won fame for their engineering and manufacturing innovations. To her surprise, several of these people with lofty reputations had heard not only of Giles but also of her for her challenging the illicit barge trade. When they had heard about what she had been discovering about making guns, they were ready to increase her knowledge, treating her not as some idiot who had to have things explained to her in the simplest of terms, but as someone who could be presumed to ask questions if their talk became too technical or abbreviated. There was no gathering like this in Dipton, Daphne reflected, nor, for that matter, in Ameschester.

One of the men to whom Mr. Throgmorton introduced Daphne owned a metal foundry, a Mr. Adderley. His firm did not produce the materials that Moorhouse and Son usually required, but he was well aware of her uncle's company. When she mentioned her need for a trustworthy manager to take overall charge of the enterprise, Mr. Adderley thought for a moment and said, "I may have just the man for you, if you don't think him too young."

"As long as he has the right experience, his age doesn't matter. How old is he?"

"Graham Adderly, for he is my son, is twenty-seven. He has worked in my plant for nine years, and he has shown a great ability to understand what we do and to manage our workers and foremen. I have been grooming him to take my place, but he has come along so fast that he is ready to assume that role, but I am not willing to give it up."

Daphne did not point out that this paragon was, in fact, older than she was. Instead, she replied.

"I will certainly be happy to consider him, Mr. Adderly. I will, of course, have to meet him. Unfortunately, I should be returning very soon to Dipton. Could your son call on me at my uncle's house tomorrow at nine-thirty?"

"I see you are direct, my lady. That is our way in Birmingham. Yes, I can arrange for Graham to be there. If he cannot, I will send you a note well in advance."

The soirée ran late. When Daphne returned to her uncle's house, she was exhausted. She was also too stimulated by the conversations she had enjoyed to fall asleep immediately. Instead, she sat down to tell Giles all about what had happened during the day. She dwelt, particularly, on the evening at Mr. Throgmorton's house. She knew that her husband would also have enjoyed such a gathering. Surely, there must be such gatherings in London that they could attend when he had to be in town for attendance in the House of Lords, she thought, but then she decided not to include such speculation in this letter. He would not be having such lively get-togethers in the wardroom of *Glaucus*, and she did not want to seem to be emphasizing her pleasures when he was in no position to share them. Of course, she would soon be at Dipton, where the conversation was much more mundane, but her other activities would be much more satisfactory. If only she could share them with Giles in person!

Chapter XVIII

It was near the middle of the forenoon watch when the masthead lookout made the hail that intrigued everyone on *Glaucus*'s deck. It relieved the tedium of another day on the crowded frigate as she worked her way north. The ship had already gone through the dawn ritual of clearing for action. She had then gathered her little flock of vessels, which had scattered during the night, into a tight formation. Then the landsmen had holystoned* the decks. Finally, everyone had been allowed breakfast.

Now the frigate was on a close reach on the larboard tack, with all sails set to the topgallants, closing the coast of Portugal, which was still below the horizon. She had stopped nowhere since leaving Kamlakesh, Giles feeling that Gibraltar was not a suitable place to bring the captives he had rescued. Instead, he was making for Lisbon, where the good offices of the agents of the East India Company might ease his problems of having too many civilians on board his four ships.

"Sail Ho!" was the call. "Three points off the larboard bow…on a starboard reach."

Giles was on deck, taking his morning exercise, pacing alone up and down the weather quarterdeck. He had finally succeeded in getting into the thick heads of the passengers that he did not like conversation at that time in the morning and that they must respect his wishes by keeping to leeward.

"Mr. Bush," he ordered before the officer of the watch could respond to the call. "Take a telescope aloft and tell me what you see." Giles knew that the lookout, a man named Carlyle, was an experienced sailor, notable for his keen eyesight, and he would make sure that the youngest midshipman would not make a fool of himself in reporting what he was seeing.

The teenager climbed the rigging carefully, knowing that all eyes were on him, avoiding the lubber's holes for the more dangerous but quicker route to the top. There Carlyle pointed out to the junior officer the ship that he had sighted. Mr. Bush took his telescope, and, in the way in which he had been taught, pointed the instrument to the left of the point where he could just make out the blob that was a ship's sail, rising and falling into and out of sight as the waves moved *Glaucus* and the other vessel. He slowly moved the telescope to the right until he spotted the sail in the instrument and brought it into focus. He could now make out that it was a sail billowing away from them in a way that must have allowed Carlyle to determine her course. How the lookout had accomplished the determination with the naked eye was beyond the understanding of the youth.

"You, no doubt, have noticed that the cut of the sail is English, Mr. Bush," said Carlyleeven as he continued to scan the ocean all around Glaucus, "as are her other sails that are now coming into view. Don't prove nothing since the Frogs sometimes capture one of our ships."

"Do you think that the ship is a frigate?" prompted the lookout.

"Is she, indeed?" asked Mr. Bush.

Carlyle quickly listed the features of the three sails that were visible intermittently that led him to that conclusion.

Even with the aid of the telescope, the midshipman had missed the telltale features that now he could see.

"Best let them know on deck," prompted the lookout, allowing the callow youth to take credit for what he had observed and its implications.

"Deck there," shouted Mr. Bush, his voice breaking in a most embarrassing way. "The sail is a frigate."

Giles had no doubt about who had actually determined the nature of the strange ship, but the assignment was good training for Mr. Bush. In future, he might be able to make the determination himself when the lookout had weaker vision or less experience than Carlyle.

"Can you see her colors?" the captain bellowed.

"Not yet, sir," the midshipman called back.

"Right answer, sir," Carlyle encouraged the midshipman. "Now, let's look carefully to see if we can make out a banner or flag."

Mr. Bush suspected that the lookout already knew the answer, but was making him see it himself. Through the telescope, he could now see, thanks to Carlyle's prompting, that the strange ship was flying a red, white, and blue banner. Was that the symbol of a French or British ship, or even a Dutch one? He couldn't tell or remember the differences between them. But there was also a flash of a blue flag with something in the upper quarter. The French did not use such flags, nor did the Dutch, he had been told by the Master and other officers in charge of his training. Still, he would temporize in his report.

"Deck, there. The frigate may be showing English colors."

"Now, what do you see, Mr. Bush, sir?" asked Carlyle.

The midshipman stared carefully at the distant topsails but could see nothing.

"Look carefully at the set of her sails. Do you see how they have changed their angle and are pointing more towards us?"

"Yes?"

"Doesn't that indicate that she has altered course to intercept us?"

"Oh, yes, now I see it."

"I think, Mr. Bush, sir, that the Captain might like to know about your observation."

"Of course. Deck there, the frigate has altered course to intercept us."

Giles was glad of the news. Otherwise, he would have had the dilemma of whether to alter *Glaucus*'s course to go more downwind or to ignore the distant sail. This way, he did not have to give up any distance to windward, which might be hard to regain after the ships had met.

"Mr. Miller. We will delay clearing for action and the other preparations for battle until we are closer to avoid inconveniencing the passengers more than necessary."

Time crept forward as the two ships sailed toward each other. It was established that the unknown frigate was flying British colors and a blue ensign indicating that she was under the command of an admiral of the blue.

Even as everyone on board was a twitter about the strange sail, the routine of shipboard life continued. The noon sights were taken and *Glaucus*'s position entered in the log.

The watch changed. The hands went to dinner. Dinner was also served to the wardroom members who were off duty. The meal could hardly be considered a treat. The few special items of food and other luxuries that the officers had brought on board to relieve the tedium of the fare the Navy supplied had long been exhausted. Giles ate some bread and cheese on the quarter-deck so that he could avoid having to dine in his cabin and listen to the complaints and questions of the most distinguished of the people he had rescued. When dinner was finished, the strange ship could be seen much more clearly from the *Glaucus*'s deck.

"Mr. Miller, clear for action. Mr. Bush, signal the prizes to take station off our larboard quarter. Then raise the private signal."

Several minutes were needed before new flags were sighted on the strange ship.

"The response is correct, sir," announced the midshipman. "She is H.M. Frigate *Titan*, 36. Captain Sir George Mersey-Smythe. He is junior to you, sir."

"What do you know of her, Mr. Brooks?" Giles asked. The Master kept abreast of all developments in the navy, swapping information with other masters when they were in port together.

"She was launched in '02, sir. Just in time for the Peace of Amiens. She has seen service in the Chanel Fleet, mainly. No encounters with the enemy, though she took a prize – just one—last year. Sir George is a baronet, inherited the title from his brother. The Mersey-Symthes are a Lancashire family. The title goes back to George II if I remember rightly. Sir George got his step* through influence, with nothing distinguished in his record. He is a bit of a martinet, I hear. Likes to flog."

Giles had hoped that *Titan* had a captain who would be amenable to helping him get his little convoy into Lisbon. Mr. Brooks's summary did not sound encouraging. Distinguished captains were much more likely to be flexible in interpreting their orders liberally than ones who relied on the goodwill of their admiral as well as the influence to keep their commands.

The two frigates continued to close with one another. Soon *Titan* was hull up. Her deck was the subject of close inspection by every telescope on board *Glaucus*. Using false colors was a well-practiced trick, especially by ships that had recently been captured by the enemy. Suddenly Mr. Brooks laughed.

"There's Old Jack Slaughter. He was Master in *Thermopylae* before she was decommissioned in '02. I heard that he had secured a berth in a new frigate, but didn't know which one."

"Are you sure that it is him, Mr. Brooks?" Giles asked.

"Absolutely, sir."

"Then I think that we can delay further preparations for action, Mr. Miller. Indeed, you can start having the crew set things to rights, and the passengers can be let on deck again."

It didn't take much more time for the frigates to converge on each other. Giles ordered *Titan* to take station on her windward quarter and for the captain to come aboard.

Captain Mersey-Smythe, as Giles called him, not being impressed by a minor hereditary title, was a large man about Giles's age with a face on which bad temper had etched unattractive lines. He held himself rigidly as he was piped aboard and saluted the quarter deck. He responded without warmth to Giles's greeting and invitation to adjourn to his cabin.

"What are your orders, Captain Mersey-Smythe?" Giles opened the conversation.

"I am carrying dispatches to Gibraltar about the implications of the changes in the strategic situation," Mersey-Smythe replied somewhat pompously.

"I have been out of touch completely with England for several weeks now, Captain Mersey-Smythe," Giles continued the conversation. "How has the situation changed?"

"Everything has been very confusing," confessed Mersey-Smythe. "You must have heard that Villeneuve and his fleet sailed from Toulon*. He quite gave Nelson the slip again. Villeneuve headed out into the Atlantic after passing Gibraltar and went to the West Indies, we later learned. Nelson finally realized where the French had gone. He went after Villeneuve, but he didn't catch him.

"For some unknown reason, Villeneuve showed up off the north coast of Spain where he picked up some Spanish ships. Admiral Calder discovered them, and they had a battle near Cape Finisterre. For some reason that I don't understand, Calder broke it off at nightfall and did not continue the next day. I don't know what happened to Villeneuve, though rumor has it that he headed to Cadiz, of all places. I don't see how that will help him get together with the main fleet at Brest. I am carrying dispatches to Gibraltar. Maybe they will know there more about what is happening.

"Nelson didn't fall back on the Channel Fleet when Villeneuve got away from him?" Giles said in some surprise.

"No, my admiral felt that Nelson was acting on his own in a very dangerous way."

"And Villeneuve?"

"Any other news?"

Well, the Rochefort Fleet also is at large; I don't know where, somewhere in the Atlantic, I suppose. It may have met up with Villeneuve. If it has, and if the Brest Fleet comes out, our Channel Fleet will have their work cut out for them."

"I imagine they would have."

"Can I ask where you are coming from, Captain Giles, with that intriguing little convoy you have?"

Giles explained in terse sentences his activities in Kamlakesh. He concluded by saying, "So you can see why I have three other ships with me. They are all overcrowded. I am intending to stop in Lisbon to get supplies and to see if the East India Company can help in dealing with the ships and the rescued people."

"Good luck with that, Captain Giles. I would not be surprised if, with the news of the French fleets at sea, and things apparently turning against us a bit, that the Portuguese may be less willing to help or at least to turn a blind eye when our ships use Lisbon. I imagine that they will be reluctant to anger Boney by being seen to help us."

"You may be right, but I cannot ignore the needs of the souls for whom I am responsible."

"Before, we part, Captain Giles, you mentioned that you rescued a large number of seamen in this Kamlakesh place. I am short of crew, very short, what with sickness and injuries that have taken some of my men, and I did not have a full crew when I sailed. Can you let me have some?"

"How many do you need?"

"I am short sixty-four men."

"I see." Giles was delighted about the request. He had far too many passengers on his four ships. Many of them were prime seamen from the East Indiamen, and many of those people were lascars, good seamen all, who had not been ransomed in previous transactions. He would benefit from having them impressed into *Titan*. Strictly speaking, sailors on the Company's ships were exempt from the press. However, if there was to be any objection in this case, it could be countered by the argument that the Company had already abandoned these men.

"Yes, send a recruiting party to the *Gloriana*, that's the East Indiaman, with the letter I shall write to Mr. Miller, my first lieutenant who is in command of her right now. It instructs him to pick fifty lascars to be impressed into *Titan*."

"Your first lieutenant is in charge of the East Indiaman?" Captain Mersey-Smythe queried. "I would have thought that the command would have been restored to her captain."

"It is a long story," Giles responded. "We don't have time for it now. You will want to get on with your duties."

He stood as he uttered these words. Captain Mersey-Smythe had no choice but to rise as well and accompany Giles to the entry port. The decision to take command of the East Indiaman away from its captain, Captain Macintyre, had been a tricky one for Giles. He had reason to suspect that Captain Macintyre had been complicit in the capture of his ship. He had heard from other sources that the cause of some valuable East Indiamen falling prey to Kamlakesh's pirates was that there had been a conspiracy between the masters of the vessels and the pirates so that the ships. After clearing the Cape of Good Hope, the East Indiamen had sailed well to the east of their supposed courses, on routes that the pirates had

had no difficulty intercepting. The captains in captivity had been well treated by the beys of Kamlakesh, supporting the supposition that they were co-conspirators in seizing East India Company ships for ransom.

Captain Macintyre had been very upset when Giles announced that *Glaucus*'s first lieutenant, Mr. Miller, would be in command of *Gloriana*, so much so that Giles had decided that *Gloriana*'s master would be a guest on *Glaucus* rather than traveling on his own ship. Captain Macintyre had proved himself to be an uncongenial passenger.

It did not take long for Captain Mersey-Smythe to acquire his sailors, all of whom had been slaves in Kamlakesh. Giles could only hope that their lot would be better on *Titan*. Mr. Miller would be happy not to have to feed the extra fifty mouths or find them somewhere to sleep.

Giles wondered if the worsening naval situation, especially with French ships loose and supported by ones from France's ally Spain, would have repercussions for his welcome in Lisbon. He understood that the ties between London and Lisbon were both strong and of long-standing, but the threat of attack by Bonaparte or just his Spanish ally must make the Portuguese wary of taking steps that could serve as an excuse for a Spanish or French attack. However, his need for supplies as well as news overrode the attraction of caution, and he ordered his flotilla back onto the course for Lisbon.

Only five minutes after Titan's sails had dipped below the southern horizon, another hail came from the masthead. A ship had been sighted to the northeast. Before long, the unknown vessel altered course to intercept *Glaucus* and cracked on more sail. Giles could guess that she wanted to come up with *Glaucus*, or possibly her merchant ships, as soon as possible. They must appear to the trained eye to be an

English convoy with a frigate escorting the very valuable East Indiaman together with a couple of lesser vessels through the dangerous waters where French or Spanish warships or privateers might be hoping for rich pickings.

Giles's suspicions were soon confirmed by another hail. "Deck, ahoy. The ship is a French frigate, possibly a thirty-six. She has been at sea for some time."

"How long before we meet her, Mr. Brooks?" Giles asked.

"Two, maybe two and a quarter hours, give or take, sir," the Master replied. "If we turn downwind, she will not come up with us before nightfall."

"Yes, but how much time will that waste before we can get back on course safely? No, since we should be evenly matched, we are almost bound to slow her so that the convoy can get away, even if we have bad luck. We will carry on. Mr. Bush, signal to *Titan*, 'Enemy sail to the Northeast.' Return at once."

"But, sir," the midshipman replied rather than giving the usual 'Aye, aye, sir.' "*Titan* is out of sight."

"I know that, but the Frenchman does not. He will presume that I am summoning assistance, and that may make him hesitant to attack us. When you have finished making that message, Mr. Bush, signal to our three ships to take station on our starboard quarter.

"Mr. Brooks, we will hold our course.

"Bosun, pipe 'Clear for Action.' This time I want all the passengers below decks long before we engage."

The French frigate converged rapidly with *Glaucus*. Studying her through his telescope, Giles realized that she was a new ship, but that she had been at sea for about a month.

Her bottom would be clean, and her crew might be somewhat experienced in their duties. She could be a formidable foe.

Giles glanced behind him, where the three merchant ships were stationed. *Gloriana* was less than a cable off *Glaucus*'s quarter. The other two were considerably farther away. He had already given orders that, should the French ship defeat *Glaucus*, they were to head off in different directions so that the enemy would likely only capture one of them. He suspected that Mr. Miller might have other ideas, and they were not bad ones. *Gloriana*, undoubtedly, would be the French ship's next target if she was able to disable or defeat *Glaucus*. Giles could hardly order his lieutenant to risk all his passengers by engaging the French warship, but if *Glaucus* were disabled or, worse still, taken, *Gloriana* would be in no worse a position than if she tried to help *Glaucus*.

Gloriana was painted to give the appearance of a warship with white gunports painted on her black hull. The decoration was supposed to suggest that she had many gun ports, in the way that Nelson liked to have the ships under his command painted. Indeed, at a distance, an inexperienced lookout might mistake her for a ship-of-the-line. In reality, most of the gun-ports were fake, with no cannon behind them; they were not ports at all. In case this charade did not fool an enemy, four of the ports on each side were not false. They had guns behind them, not as big as the ones on a sixty-four would be, but still large enough to do significant damage to a frigate and quite powerful enough to fight off most privateers and pirates. The East-India company also supplied its ships with several stands of muskets and some cutlasses so that their crews could repulse pirates effectively. Mr. Miller and his *Gloriana* could make quite a difference to any fight.

The frigates continued to get ready for battle. The mainsails were furled, and nets rigged to prevent damage from items falling from above. Now only under topsails and spankers, their rate of convergence became slower and waiting for the battle to begin more tedious. Everything was ready on *Glaucus*; all that those on board her could do was wait and try not to show how nervous they were. It must, Giles thought, be much the same on the French ship where they would also be anxiously waiting for the fight to start.

Soon the ships were close enough to each other that tactical decisions had to be made. If each frigate held her present course, the French ship would cross *Glaucus*'s bow with only a quarter of a cable to spare. Giles could not allow that to happen, even though his bow cannon were much stronger than the usual bow chasers. *Glaucus* would be raked by the frigate's broadside, with only his pair of bow chasers to respond. Unless his first two shots were extremely lucky, *Glaucus* would be the ship to suffer the most damage, possibly enough to end the battle right then. It would be pointless for him to turn to larboard. He would still be vulnerable to long-range shots from his opponent before his broadside would bear. His only choice was to turn downwind so that the two ships would come close to each other, side by side, and fight it out broadside to broadside.

Giles gave his orders to Mr. Brooks, who carefully maneuvered the frigate until she came beside the French frigate at a distance of fifty feet. The cannon crashed out on each side, though *Glaucus*'s broadside fired somewhat ahead of her enemy's. Giles noticed with satisfaction that most of the balls were hitting somewhere as clouds of deadly splinters seemed to sweep the enemy's deck. But none of the strikes was fatal; the French ship could easily continue to fight. One of the last shots from her rival did severe and strategic damage to *Glaucus*. It had hit the foretopmast just above the fighting top*. Slowly the mast started to collapse to starboard, taking with it most of the jibs and also collapsing the web of lines that supported the mainmast. *Glaucus* slowed immediately and was dragged into a downwind turn so that most of her next broadside missed her enemy. Until the worst of the damage had been cleared away and emergency repairs made, *Glaucus* would be out of the fight.

Giles looked over towards his enemy, wondering what would be coming next. What he saw astounded him. The French frigate was also in trouble, though not as severe as *Glaucus*'s problems. One of *Glaucus*'s cannonballs had hit the starboard shrouds of her opponent. Most of the lines had been severed, and the remaining ones had been damaged. Her mainmast was in danger of going by the board! Even as he watched, French sailors were climbing the larboard ratlines to furl the sail while another group was trying to adjust the sheets so that the main topsail would put as little pressure as possible on the vulnerable supports of the mast. Her broadside no longer bore on *Glaucus* so that she was effectively also out of the fight until her rigging could be restored. It would now be a race to see which frigate could get underway first. Neither ship had any hope of successfully boarding the other using only her boats.

Giles looked around for his other ships. The French and the Dutch merchantmen were sailing away on their diverging courses. However, *Gloriana* was not leaving. Instead, she was approaching the French frigate. What in the world was Mr. Miller thinking trying to tackle a fully crewed frigate with his motley assortment of men? Indeed, it was quite obvious. Gloriana's four gun ports were open, and the guns run out. Behind her hammock nettings, Giles could see men crouching, probably in anticipation of boarding. Her tops were much smaller than the fighting tops of warships; even so, Giles could see men in them with what looked like rifles. "Did they have muskets up there as well," he wondered.

Clearly, Mr. Miller intended to board the French frigate. With only four guns, he could not hope to win a battle of broadsides. He had a large number of sailors and other passengers on board, but only a handful of hands from *Glaucus* who were adequately trained in boarding maneuvres. If the French kept their heads, it could be a disaster, especially if they could deliver several broadsides into *Gloriana* before she came alongside.

"Bosun," Giles called to Bill Shearer, "Bring all the boats to the entry port. Mr. Bush, Mr. Maclean, select boarding parties, including all the marines, as numerous as the boats can hold. Embark them as soon as you can. Mr. Brooks, you will take command of *Glaucus* while I try to capture that Frenchman."

The crew members designated by the midshipman grabbed cutlasses, pistols, and, in some cases, belaying pins*. They swarmed into the boats as quickly as the craft were brought alongside. Giles hardly had time to take his sword and pistols, which his servant had brought up from his cabin before it was his time to board his launch.

"Row like the devil is on our tails," he bellowed to the crews. Each boat unshipped its oars and started to race towards the enemy ship. The French sailors were already concentrating on the impending encounter with *Gloriana*, so Giles's expedition was not noticed until it had crossed most of the small gap separating the ships.

Giles leaped for the entry batons and found his way onto the main deck of his rival unimpeded. He was quickly followed by Carstairs and the first of the sailors. Some of them had the task of protecting the next men swarming up the sides; others had been designated to drop ropes over the side and secure them so that still more crew members could board quickly. Even as the men from *Glaucus* boarded her, the frigate's guns fell silent, and the enemy crew threw grapnels* onto *Gloriana* to haul her alongside the French ship so that she could be boarded. No doubt, the French wanted to do as little damage as possible to the valuable East Indiaman, whose cargo would be worth a fortune if the ship could be captured more or less intact.

Giles had a significant force on his opponent's deck before any of the French crew realized that their ship was being invaded, and more had come aboard before the fact of their presence had been transmitted to the French officers. With a blood-thirsty roar, Giles's group fell upon the French sailors who were about to board *Gloriana*. The enemy was taken by surprise. Instead of surging forcefully onto the East Indiaman's deck, many of them turned to see what the new threat was. Even those Frenchmen who were hauling in on the grapnel lines paused. However, Mr. Miller recognized what was happening and urged his people to pull on the same ropes so that the two ships would come together.

The men in *Gloriana*'s tops had fired their weapons early with little effect, but they had had time to load again, even the stubborn rifles. They fired just as the two ships came together. The guns shooting from above added to the confusion, especially when one of them hit the French captain in the shoulder. He fell, squirming and howling in pain. At that point, the fight went out of the French. A lieutenant started yelling, "Nous nous rendons! Nous nous rendons!" Almost as soon as it started, the fight was over. *Glaucus* had taken another French frigate.

As Giles gave orders to secure the captured frigate, to assess the damage it had sustained, and to evaluate *Gloriana*'s wounds, he saw that Mr. Brooks had completed the jury-rigging of *Glaucus*. She came alongside the French frigate whose name turned out to be *Nereid*. The other two ships of Giles's flotilla had reversed their courses and now were closer.

"We'll make the needed repairs and get underway as soon as possible for Lisbon."

"Is that wise, sir?" queried Mr. Miller. Giles had had a long struggle to get his first lieutenant to question any suggestion he made. The man had been brought up in the school that believed that captains could do no wrong, even if it were evident that that was what they were achieving.

"Why do you say that, Mr. Miller?" Giles asked, not overly pleased that his subordinate had chosen to question his implied order when they were all tired from the encounter with the French frigate.

"Well, sir, with the news of the aggressive presence of the French navy near Portugal, and that alliance of their neighbor Spain with Napoleon, I would not be surprised if they refused us aid, at least if we want to bring a captured French frigate into their neutral port. I imagine that the Portuguese would not object to our bringing into port a French vessel that had been captured by pirates before we freed it, but I expect that bringing a captured French frigate would make them very nervous about their status as neutrals in our war with France and Spain."

Giles realized that Mr. Miller was right. But how was he to man his little flotilla? The newly captured French frigate would need officers and men to handle her. Luckily, he had had a full crew on *Glaucus,* and she had come through the recent battle with only a few minor injuries, according to Dr. Maclean. The ordinary sailors from the East Indiamen could probably be relied on, but he did not trust the two masters of East Indiamen whom he was bringing back to England, nor their first mates. He suspected that the mates must have been complicit in the capture of their vessels by pirates. If he was right, they might well try to separate from Giles's convoy and try their luck in one of the many small ports that were known to turn a blind eye to pirates' pickings. Giles together with Mr. Miller and Mr. Brooks worked out lists, rather like watch lists, but this time arranging to have adequate crews on all the ships. They carefully took into account that *Glaucus*'s men would be outnumbered on all the ships. By keeping the balance and placement of British marines and seamen in each of the vessels with most emphasis on having British crews on *Nereid* and *Gloriana* Giles felt there was little chance of any of his charges deliberately getting separated, either by stealth or by open revolt, from the convoy and seeking foreign ports.

Luckily, it turned out that *Nereid* carried supplies to see her through a long voyage if necessary. By dividing these stores among the five ships, all the vessels would be adequately stocked to reach the English Channel without hardship, though the fare might be even more restricted than the one-time passengers of the East India Company might like.

Jury-rigging the damaged vessels was completed before long, and the convoy got underway on a course to give Cape Finniestere, at the corner of Spain, a wide berth before turning to head for England. Giles went below. It had been a long and tiring day. Even so, his first job was to write to Daphne. It was only to her that he could confess that he had felt sure that the *Nereid* had defeated *Glaucus*. In his official report, he would give Mr. Miller fulsome praise. Was he about to lose another first lieutenant to well-deserved promotion? Possibly, though Miller was not one of the ablest subordinates with whom he had sailed. He could tell Daphne all these thoughts. Only to her would he confess that he might well have lost *Glaucus* as well as *Gloriana* had Mr. Miller shown the initiative that had saved the situation.

Giles had found that he could not hide his feelings from her, even if he wanted to. Of course, she might not get this letter before he arrived at Dipton. Even so, it was worth writing to her. If the letter had to be delivered by him in person, she would still read it. In the past, she had always insisted on reading any unmailed letters that he had carried home. He had found that it cemented their closeness, for it contained feelings that he would not recall if he told her orally about his most recent voyage.

Chapter XIX

The advanced-summer sun streamed into Daphne's morning room. The windows were wide open, but even so, it was uncomfortably hot. She felt slightly guilty to be stretched out on her chaise longue even though she had every right to indulge herself. Since she had returned from Birmingham two weeks ago, she had had to deal with a myriad of matters connected with the lands of Giles's estates and her father's. The managers whom she had appointed probably did not need as much supervision as she gave them, but she thought that everything ran better when she was on top of the situations.

Graham Adderly had turned out to be everything Daphne could hope for. He had a wide-ranging knowledge of the metal-working business, but he was eager to learn more. He was prepared to learn from Geordie Shearer and Hugh Bottomly and not try to alter things until he had learned from them as well as consulting them. He was quite happy to send weekly reports to Mr. Moorhouse, though he also realized and was untroubled by the fact that Daphne might well be the person reading them and requiring further information or changes. She would give him a six-month trial, and she had negotiated the terms of his employment, which he found satisfactory, while she believed them to be well within the capability of the company to pay.

Now she had to read the latest report. How did she succeed in taking on more duties when she had been intending to have more time for her interests outside of managing things? That thought reminded her that she had to follow up on what had been discovered about her mother-in-law's situation, or, more precisely, about who owned that strumpet's house in Norfolk. Furthermore, her half-brother-in law, Major

Stoner, wanted to talk to her about scheduling the meetings of the Ameschester Hunt, and her stable master had questions about whether Dipton Hall would enter a horse in the upcoming steeplechase. She would like to ride in that, but she couldn't if the baby had not arrived yet. If Giles were home, he would ride his hunter, Dark Paul, but stable hands and professional jockeys were not allowed to participate. Even her own participation would be allowed reluctantly. Women were not supposed to ride in races, but Viscountess Ashton was too important a contributor to the Hunt to be excluded if she wished to participate.

Daphne stood up to go downstairs to her workroom and begin her management duties by dealing with the report from Graham Adderly. She felt wetness between her legs. It was followed by a flood of some sort of fluid that was coming out of her. It couldn't be! Her water had broken at least two weeks early. She wasn't ready to give birth! She had better things to do!

There was no question in Daphne's mind about what was happening. She had already carried one baby to term and knew what was coming. She rang for Betsey; her lady's maid was in the next room and came immediately. Betsey didn't need to be told what was happening. One glance at her mistress let her know that a baby was on its way.

"My lady, should I send for Mr. Jackson and inform Mrs. Wilson that you are about to give birth?"

"Yes, the housekeeper will need to get things ready, and I want Mr. Jackson to be here. He is the only midwife I truly trust."

Suddenly, it seemed that everything was out of Daphne's control. Her bedroom was readied for the birthing. Messengers were sent to warn Mr. Moorhouse of the impending event. Other couriers rode off to inform her half-sister and niece-in-law. In the village, Giles's brother, the vicar, and Giles's close friend, Captain Bush, had to be told. This flurry of activity was spotted by the post-mistress, Mrs. Dumpley, so, very soon, the whole village was aware that Lady Ashton was about to give birth. Daphne was very popular in the area, so innumerable prayers were said for her safe delivery.

Daphne felt that she had become a cog in a smoothly running machine, rather than being the center of attention. Even Betsey, as she helped Daphne out of her soiled gown, chemise, and petticoat and into her specially prepared birthing clothes, seemed to become more impersonal than usual, as if she were dressing a special, helpless doll rather than her usually very-active mistress. Her maid's behavior annoyed Daphne somewhat.

Soon, all was ready and just in time. The first significant contraction hit before Daphne was in position. The next one was not far behind. She had forgotten how very much they hurt, even though she had been through it all with Bernard only about a year previously.

"Bad is it, Daphne?" asked Mr. Jackson sympathetically as he entered the room. "Just keep breathing and pushing when I tell you to, and it will soon be over."

Just as the male midwife stopped talking, another contraction produced an unmuffled yelp from Daphne.

"I'll give you a bit of laudanum now, Daphne," announced Mr. Jackson. "It won't take the pain away, but it will make it more endurable."

The drug did just what Mr. Johnson had promised. Daphne remained aware of the effort and pain of giving birth, but it seemed to matter less. She was somehow divorced from what was going on. It felt at times that she was floating above the birthing process, watching it from above as much as partaking in it painfully. For a few minutes, she thought that she had floated down to the smoking-room to see that her father and Uncle George were there. Could that be Captain Bush slumped in a corner?

These effects of the drug wore off after some time. When Daphne returned fully to the birthing, Mr. Jackson was making encouraging sounds indicating that the conclusion was approaching. "Push when I say, Daphne, but not too hard... That's right ...The baby's head should show up at any moment ... There it is. One last push! ... Good, there we are."

There was another flurry of activity where the baby should be arriving, but Daphne couldn't see anything of it.

"It's a girl!" Mr. Jackson announced. "Mrs. Wilson, clean her up, swaddle her and give her to Lady Ashton."

Daphne wasn't quite sure what happened after the midwife gave these orders. Somehow she had lost track after she heard Mr. Jackson's announcement followed by the howl of a new-born baby reacting to its world. Now she was lying in her bed, in clean sheets, feeling tired, but still excited. Mr. Jackson hovered over her for a moment, checking that everything was all right. Then he was gone for a moment but returned with a huge grin on his face and a baby.

"Here is your daughter, Daphne, a fine, healthy baby girl!"

Daphne looked into the face of the newborn. She had bright blue eyes, just like Giles. She was perfect! There had never been a baby like her! Even before the ladies in attendance could gather round to admire this paragon of babies, she whispered to Betsey to get Nanny Weaver and Bernard. If Giles could not be here, at least her son could be.

Only after Bernard had stared uncomprehendingly at the new arrival was Daphne ready for all the ladies to come and coo over the baby and tell her how well she had done and for them to be followed by the men who had been waiting patiently to come with their congratulations. After placing the bewildered Bernard beside Daphne, Nanny Weaver asked the question that was on everyone's mind.

"Have you and Captain Giles named her yet, my lady?"

"Yes," murmured Daphne, "Christina Arabella Gloriana."

She looked lovingly at her daughter and then at her son and drifted off to sleep.

The next morning Daphne slept very late. It was only the second time she had done so, the previous one being when Bernard was born. She still was tired and sore. Nanny Weaver brought Christina soon after Betsey learned that Daphne was awake. The child was as perfect as she had been earlier. Then Lady Clara sailed in to admire the baby and praise the mother. Only after that did she ask the question that Daphne had been dreading. The baby carried none of her grandmother's names.

"Why did you name the girl Christina Arabella Gloriana, Daphne?"

"Giles and I decided on the name, if it was a girl, before he left. 'Arabella' because that is my mother's name, 'Gloriana' because it was your mother's name. 'Christina' because it is the name of no one in the family, and we liked the sound of it. We'll probably call her 'Chris' of 'Christy' most of the time."

"Very sensible, I must say, though I will probably always call her 'Christina.' I think it is important for a child to have her own name, not have to share it with someone else in the family. I was afraid that Richard would want my name, 'Clara.'

"Now, how are you feeling? You must rest up. Exercise and fresh air can be dangerous for new mothers. I know you didn't go into confinement before Christina was born, but you must be particularly careful now."

"I am intending to get up for a bit after Betsey brings me something to eat."

"You can't possibly do that! I cannot imagine what might happen if you don't rest properly."

Luckily the impending dispute was postponed by Mr. Jackson's being announced.

"Good morning, Daphne, Lady Clara." The Countess glared at the male midwife. She did not approve of him addressing Daphne by her Christian name.

"I'll just have a look at this little girl and her mother to make sure that everything is as it should be."

It only took a couple of moments before the male midwife looked up and said, "Christina is right as rain. No problems here at all. Now let's see to you, Daphne."

Mr. Jackson gave Daphne a relatively superficial examination, though he did check her temperature by his hand and took her pulse. "I see you are carrying out your intention not to nurse the baby, Daphne. All strapped up, unnaturally. Well, it won't do you any harm, but it will be uncomfortable for a while. Now I don't want you to do anything unusually strenuous in the next few days, but you should resume your normal regime. Don't go riding that hunter of yours or, worse still, Captain Giles's one."

The last remark was Mr. Jackson's way of teasing Daphne by recalling an unfortunate incident where she had taken out her husband's unruly horse, only to get into trouble with him.

"Can I go to the baptism of Christina?" Daphne asked.

"And shock half your neighbors? I don't see why not. Certainly, the short walk will do you good."

It was highly unusual for the mother to attend a christening, though not unheard of. The next day, the service took place with the parish curate filling in for the Vicar, the Honorable David Giles, Daphne's brother-in-law, and Christina's uncle. He was off somewhere, probably enhancing his chances of advancing in the Church of England hierarchy. Daphne was disappointed that the ceremony couldn't wait for Giles's return, but she couldn't fly that much in the face of the standard practice. Babies were baptized promptly after birth because they would go straight to hell if they died before the ceremony. Daphne certainly didn't believe that: any God who would condemn a little baby to eternal torture was not one who should be worshipped. Did Giles share that opinion? Daphne realized that she had never discussed the subject with him. When was he coming home?

Usually, christenings were small private affairs. Christina's was an exception. Word had gone throughout the village about when it was going to be held and that, in defiance of custom, Lady Ashton would be there as well as the godparents, who were Captain Bush and Mrs. Bolton, Lady Ashton's half-niece-in-law. The service would be conducted by Lord David's curate. Daphne was quite pleased that he was taking the service rather than her brother-in-law. The curate was a man who showed far more interest in the children of the parish than did The Honorable Reverand David Giles.

When the christening breakfast was over, Daphne retreated to her sitting-room, not her workroom, She was still feeling tired, but she also had no inclination to get on with her various tasks, even though some of them were pressing. She just wanted to lie on her chaise-longue. It also seemed to be an effort to pick up a book, and, when she did, it was not Mrs. Woolstonecraft's treatise but instead one of her novels. In so far as Daphne wanted to read anything at all, this was the sort of work she wanted. She stayed that way all day, even having her meals brought to her.

Daphne started the next day feeling equally lethargic and uninterested in her usual activities. Only visits by Christina and Bernard livened her up a little. By mid-afternoon, Betsey became very worried, so much so that she insisted that Mr. Steves send for Mr. Jackson immediately.

The apothecary came at once. After examining Daphne, he declared, "There is nothing the matter with you, Daphne. Just buck up. You should get back to your usual activities now. What you are experiencing is common with new mothers, though most of them cannot indulge themselves to the extent you are doing. Now stop lounging around! Get back to your usual activities! You can even ride now. I will give you a cordial that should help you regain your enthusiasm, but it is really up to you. Imagine what Captain Giles would think if he found you like this!"

That last remark was the only part of Mr. Jackson's harangue that had any effect on Daphne. No, she didn't want Giles to see her like this. As she was now feeling, she was not the woman he had married. He needed the especially active woman with whom he had fallen in love, not some typical woman lounging around complaining about how hard a life of leisure was. She knew deep down that she would feel better if she was as active as normal. Maybe she would feel better if she just pretended to want to be her usual self. She didn't really like herself the way she was now. Then how could she expect Giles to like her? Of course, he was away somewhere, probably off the coast of Africa, having a fine old time. However, he could show up at any moment without warning. Did she want him to find her like this? No, but she also didn't want Mr. Jackson to think that his lecture had worked.

"Thank you, Mr. Jackson, for the advice. You have no idea what it is like to give birth. You only to observe it. You have no way of knowing what I am feeling. I'll take your cordial, but I don't want you giving me lectures. I want you to leave."

There, she thought, that will put the old quack in his place! She knew that it was unfair to Mr. Jackson, especially as he had induced her to do something, but he had been pompous about what was good for her – even if he had been right. No sooner had the door closed behind him than she turned to Betsey.

"Betsey, I am going into the gardens. Get my bonnet and outdoor boots. I will go by myself."

Once she was dressed, Daphne ordered Steves to place the reports she had received on the table in her workroom about her uncle's business from Graham Adderly. Steves should also make sure that the accounts of the Dipton Barge Company, which Major Stoner had organized and ran for her, were at hand. Then she slipped out onto the back terrace. It was a warm, sunny day with a light breeze carrying a variety of country fragrances that soothed Daphne's soul. She was tempted to sink onto one of the benches to admire her vista, but she resisted. It would be even more satisfying to wander through the flower beds on her way to the little lake that Giles had so enjoyed building when they had refashioned the grounds at Dipton Hall.

As she left the terrace, she started enjoying the extensive lawn bordered by flower beds where many different plants were blooming. How Giles had enjoyed helping to plan them! The altered grounds had been a vast improvement from what Daphne had first observed around Dipton Hall. She could also imagine her children romping on the grass. If she had anything to say about it, they would have a wonderful childhood.

At the water's edge, which Giles had defined sharply with a small stone barrier that separated the lawn from the pool, she sat down, not even thinking of how that might add to Betsy's chores by leaving grass stains on her gown. She took off her shoes and stockings and dangled her toes in the water. She hadn't done that for years, in fact, never since the landscaping had been completed. It felt marvelous, a pure, simple pleasure that made her appreciate what she had even more than she usually did. If Giles came home before the colder weather set in, would he also take off his shoes and stockings to cool his feet? He probably would. She giggled to herself when she thought that he would do so even if, for some unknown reason, he was wearing his full-dress uniform with knee-britches and his cocked hat. Could she get a painter to paint him that way, instead of in the stuffy, formal portrait which would look like every other portrait of an important naval captain? She giggled again at the ridiculous notion but then sobered. That would give his children and great-grandchildren and even the generation after that a far better idea of who their ancestor had been than would the usual representation of forebears that hung, poorly lighted, in the homes of the nobility. It was hard to realize that the vibrant man she had married and she herself were part of a long line that stretched back to the Conquest of men named Giles who had served their country well or ill but always prominently. She really must make arrangements for that painter to visit when Giles was here.

Daphne looked across the pond to where the land rose towards the folly. She had been dubious about including it in their garden, but Giles had felt it would add to the total. It certainly did. Even as she stared at it, she heard one of the hounds of the Hunt, which they had adopted, bark, and a horse neigh from the hunting stud farm they had established. It wasn't the case that everything was her work without Giles lifting his finger about running the estates, as she had been telling herself while moping in her sitting room. When Giles was home, he was her equal partner. Mrs. Woolstonecraft was wrong about her status, even if she was short of formal education. She would do everything to make sure that little Christina would have every opportunity to realize her potential. Of course, it would help if her daughter could find a husband to support her as Daphne had.

Daphne giggled to herself. Now she was acting like every other mother from a good family who wanted to marry off her daughter advantageously, even though her little girl was less than a week old. If Christina had anything like the independence and determination that her mother had enjoyed, she would pick her own husband without assistance from her mother.

A fish came up and nibbled at her toes. It distracted her from her thoughts. Was it a trout? Had the changes to the stream as it flowed through Dipton Hall improved it as an angling spot? Would Giles take up fishing when he had time? He would certainly help by taking some of the burden of managing their estates from Daphne's shoulders. However, like it or not, Giles was busy right now, and it was up to Daphne to see that everything ran smoothly. She had better go back to the house to get on with the tasks she had planned before taking her walk in the grounds.

As often happened, Daphne's intentions were changed by circumstances. As she was striding up the lawn to the house, Betsey came running down the slope to her, waving an envelope.

"My Lady, Mr. Steves thought that I should bring this to you immediately. Lady Camshire has received a similar one."

Daphne broke the seal and started to read the letter immediately. It was from a solicitor in Norwich. The Earl of Camshire was dead. The message then announced that on orders of the executor, whoever that might be, the reading of the Earl's will would take place in the lawyer's office one week from his death. The Earl had died on the previous Friday; now, it was already Tuesday. It would be impossible for Lady Clara and Daphne to get to Norwich that quickly. Was this some last trick of her father-in-law to do in his wife and his sons? Her first inclination was to rush off with Lady Clara to Norwich immediately, but it took her only a minute to realize that that was not a good plan at all.

"Betsey, please go and find out where Lady Camshire is now. Tell her that I want to visit her as soon as possible."

Lady Clara looked up from her copy of the letter as Daphne entered her room. "You have heard the news, haven't you, Daphne? I was expecting it, but it still comes as a shock. No matter that we were estranged, he has been a large part of my life, for good and bad, and so his death leaves a big hole."

"You have my condolences, Lady Clara. I didn't know Camshire, but I can still imagine how hard it is for you to know that he is gone."

"Not that hard, my dear, and 'Camshire' is now Richard's name. It always seemed to me strange how it works, even though I grew up with the practices of nobility. In the blink of an eye, the names the world knows us by change. I am now the Dowager Countess while you, my dear, are the

Countess of Camshire. You probably aren't yet fully accustomed to being Viscountess Ashton.

"I am not going into full mourning for him," Lady Clara continued. "He doesn't deserve it, and I don't want just to keep up appearances. I guess I will, for the funeral, as long as he didn't make some peculiar arrangement for that, but not otherwise."

"I will tell Steves to treat Camshire's passing as the death of a distant relative. He will be a bit shocked, but he did despise the man, I know." Daphne replied.

"What's this about the reading of the will and the 'executor'?" continued lady Clara.

"I don't know, but it does sound fishy," replied Daphne. "We cannot possibly get to Norwich in time. I'll ask our lawyer, Mr. Snodgrass, to come here and advise us. If we act quickly, he may be able to visit this evening."

Daphne wrote a note and gave it to Steves to give to a groom to ride with it to Ameschester on a fast horse. Mr. Snodgrass arrived as Daphne and Lady Clara were sitting down to dinner. Daphne directed the butler to show the lawyer into the small dining room at once.

"Mr. Snodgrass, thank you for coming. Have you dined?"

"No, my lady, I came the instant I got your message. It seemed very urgent."

"It is. Steves, lay another place for Mr. Snodgrass. He will be dining with us. But, Mr. Snodgrass, let us talk of other matters until the cloth is drawn."

Part of Daphne's reason for the stipulation about the subjects to be discussed while dining was to avoid the meal's degenerating into a note-taking by Mr. Snodgrass. Equally important, she did not want him distracted by food as he thought about the meaning and implications of the strange news about the will that had accompanied the notice of death. Mr. Snodgrass was not a good conversationalist, and Lady Clara was too preoccupied with her own thoughts to engage in lively conversation. Daphne had to pry opinions and information out of him. It was a relief when Steves brought the port and cordials of the sort that ladies preferred.

The lawyer read the letter announcing the death and the reading of the will twice over carefully. Then he thought for a few minutes.

"This is really very peculiar, my ladies," he stated. "The letter contains no information about the funeral. Reading the will is usually not announced until the funeral has been held, and it is usually in a location close to where the deceased is to be buried. In the late Earl of Camshire's case, my lady, I would have expected that he would be buried at the church at his principal residence. Of course, there is often a temporary burial, especially in summer, before the final laying to rest is performed."

"Yes. My husband took great pride in the tombs in Ashbury of earlier earls since the abbey church has been the family church of the Earls of Camshire from when it was first built not long after the Norman Conquest. He always talked as if he expected that that would be his final resting place," the Dowager Countess said.

"It is not always the case, of course, that prominent men are buried in their parish churches," Mr. Snodgrass resumed. "For example, many distinguished men have been buried in important churches such as Westminster Abbey or St. Paul's Cathedral or other cathedrals. The funeral may be arranged by the executor or the next of kin, or another close relative. This letter tells us nothing about that, not even where he died, though one can presume it was somewhere in Norfolk. This whole thing strikes me as very peculiar. It is often the practice of people trying to dishonestly get control of parts of an estate to exclude interested parties from the execution of a will until it is too late for them to claim what was supposed to be left to them, or at least diminish the value of what they receive. As they say, possession is nine-tenths of the law."

"What do you suggest that we do, Mr. Snodgrass?"

"We should try to have the probate procedure slowed and make sure that it occurs in the proper venue. Interpretation and execution of wills and testaments come under ecclesiastical law, so they are handled by diocesan courts. Because the late Earl had property in several dioceses, his will should be probated by the archdiocese of Canterbury, not by the diocese of Norwich. The reading scheduled in the letter seems inappropriate, and we should have it postponed and moved to another location. Unfortunately, we do not have much time. It would be quite impossible for me to get to Norwich by Monday, and even more so for you to go. I do know a very able solicitor in Norwich whose practice is mainly concerned with wills and estates. If I could get a letter to him in time, I am sure that he could attend the hearing and put a spoke in their wheel."

"I have just the man to carry the letter," said Daphne. "He is a groom called Geoffreys, a former cavalryman, who is quite prepared to ride night and day to deliver urgent messages for us. He can set out tonight if you can write the letter, Mr. Snodgrass."

"Excellent, my lady. If you can show me to a writing table and provide paper and ink, I can write it now. I brought with me the address of Thomas Chapman, that is my friend's name so that you can send the letter immediately. I will give him Lady Clara's authority to halt the proceedings until proper arrangements are made. He can also find out what provisions have been taken for the deceased's remains."

"Does Lady Clara now have that authority? I thought that married women have no status in almost everything," said Daphne.

"Oh, no, the minute her husband died, Lady Clara ceased to be his wife. She immediately became his widow, the Dowager Countess of Camshire, a feme sole as we say in the law. She can act now on her own behalf, without the need for a man's permission."

The solicitor wrote the letter outlining what they wished Mr. Chapman to do. Daphne sealed it with her own seal as Viscountess of Ashton to give the message extra weight. Geoffreys took it away. He should be in Norwich with plenty of time for the solicitor to act.

Daphne and Lady Clara sipped a final cordial together in the drawing-room. They agreed that they would have to attend the ceremony if Camshire were to be buried at Ashbury Abbey. Somewhat surprisingly, Lady Clara still insisted that she would not go into full mourning for her rotten husband, but now she would not even make an exception for his funeral.

Daphne's letter to Giles that night was full of the news of his father's death and the kerfuffle it had created. How would he be affected, she wondered. He had often said that the world would be better off if his father were dead, but did he actually believe it? How the news she had sent him and had yet to receive a reply was building up! Had he even received any of it? Did he know that he had a marvelous new daughter called Christina? Well, she had married a sailor, and such questions were part of the life she had chosen. What she truly wanted was not mail from him but for him to return home.

Chapter XX

Glaucus came about onto the starboard tack. She probably could fetch the entrance to the Solent on this tack if the wind did not back, but that possibility wasn't relevant. With the persistent easterly wind and two frigates with compromised, jury-rigged masts resulting from their battle, Giles's little flotilla could not proceed by the shorter route to Portsmouth and Spithead. Instead, they would have to continue up the English Channel until they could round the Isle of Wight to get to their destination.

The journey home had seemed intolerably long after *Glaucus*'s victory over *Nereid*. The wind had been dead foul all the way across the Bay of Biscay. It had even seemed to back when they were on the starboard tack and veer while on the larboard one so that, on some days, Mr. Brooks had been unable to claim that *Glaucus* had made any progress towards their destination. The northerlies still blew when they reached the mouth of the English Channel. Giles had hoped that one long larboard tack would bring him to the Solent, but the wind veered into the east when they were halfway there. Giles had been tempted to turn around and head for Plymouth, but he had no guarantee that the favorable wind would hold. Plymouth would be a far worse place than Portsmouth to bring his little flotilla, with all the difficulties that might arise with the East India Company and the Foreign Office when he returned home. They would be more easily handled if he landed in Portsmouth.

Giles feared that his findings about the reason for the Company's losing its ships and his, in effect, starting a war with a Morrocan sub-state would tie him up in endless discussions and explanations of what had happened.

Portsmouth had telegraph communication with the Admiralty in London, which would speed up the process. It was also much closer to both Dipton and London than was the Devonshire harbor. *Glaucus* was finally in sight of her destination. Unfortunately, another wet night at sea would have to be spent before they could reach their anchorage.

Spithead was crammed with vessels. The fleet was in. It would appear that none of the great ships had experienced recent battle, though many showed signs of having been at sea recently. Admiral Carnarvon signaled Giles to take his small collection of vessels directly to the quay in Portsmouth. It would be evident to the Admiral that repairs after the battle had not erased the need for pumping. He added to his terse instructions a more extended signal that had to be spelled out one letter at a time. "Good Lord, Giles. Yet some more captures."

The Port Admiral, who had helped Giles in the past, continued to render assistance. He also had telegraphed the Admiralty to say that *Glaucus* had arrived with a captured French frigate, the East Indiaman *Gloriana*, and two other merchant ships. London telegraphed back, ordering Giles to go to the Admiralty as soon as possible.

"Always the same," thought Giles. "They believe that their concerns are more important than anything else. I'm going to go to London via Dipton, whether they like it or not."

Giles could not leave immediately, however. He had to make arrangements for repairing *Glaucus*. He must find billets for the various passengers he had brought with him. Finally, he had to make provision for each of the ships he had taken. While he was somewhat indifferent to the amounts of prize money they would yield or other compensation to which he was entitled for acquiring the various vessels, his officers and crew most certainly were not.

Another telegraphed message reached him while he was engaged in swearing an affidavit before a magistrate. The sworn statement, which he was making, would result in the captains and other officers of the East Indiamen whom he had brought from Kamlakesh being held for possible trial while all the facts about the capture of their ships were being established.

The new message announced that his father had died. His immediate thought was of his mother and her need for support. Giles knew that Daphne would be providing it, but he couldn't just leave it up to her, could he? Was his mother at Dipton or Ashbury Abbey? Probably at Dipton, and it was on the way to Ashbury Abbey in any case. He would go there immediately.

Giles arranged for a carriage to take him directly to Dipton. There was no direct coach service to Amesbury, and taking a private conveyance that could drive through the night would get him home much sooner. Cost was not a factor in his calculations anymore.

Giles, with Carstairs accompanying him, arrived late the following day at Dipton Hall. He had spent much of the journey ruminating about his father's death. For a very long time, Giles had felt little love for his father, and he had had little to do with his parent for years. He had thought that he would be indifferent to his father's passing, even more indifferent than he would be to becoming the Earl of Camshire, which had never mattered to him. However, now he was swamped with regret that he could never have a positive relationship with the Earl, never known his father as a person, never have the intimacy that he had wanted and never, ever enjoyed.

As the carriage reached the fields around Dipton, Giles's gloom began to dissipate. Now he was where he wanted to be. Dipton was his home. Here Daphne, who was the center of his life, lived. Would she be home, or would she have gone to Ashbury Abbey for the funeral? Or was she unable to travel because of the baby? It was due soon.

Whether his wife was here or not, this was home. Every field and copse and building they passed just confirmed that they were approaching the place where he was happiest. By the time they turned into the drive to Dipton Hall, his mourning for his father was finished.

Giles noticed no signs of mourning on Dipton Hall as the carriage entered the circle before the portico. Steves and a footman emerged. The butler had no way of knowing who was in the carriage, but he was always mindful that an important visitor should be properly greeted. It would not matter if his presence were not needed on any particular occasion. Giles noted that Steves wore a black armband. The footman did not.

"Hasn't the news of my father's death reached Dipton, Steves?" Giles demanded as he stepped from the carriage.

"Yes, my lord, it has."

"Then why isn't the house in mourning?"

"The Dowager Countess ordered it, my lord, the Countess – Lady Daphne -- confirmed that the instruction should be followed. I am wearing my armband since I served the late Earl for a long period in happier times."

Further discussion was prevented by the door of the house opening and Daphne rushing towards the carriage. Giles was used to how she reacted to his arrival after a long separation and braced himself so that he could enfold her in his arms without being knocked over. Steves looked on benignly. Although in Steves's beliefs, such conduct was not appropriate for the nobility, Daphne's happy disregard for the niceties of aristocratic customs had long ago made him make exceptions for her.

"Oh, Giles," Daphne said after giving her husband what most of society would regard as a totally inappropriate kiss and hug. "You're home! I am so glad! I've missed you and need you! Oh, what am I thinking? You must be devastated by your father's death."

"Not really, my love," Giles replied, looking fondly into her eyes. "I did my mourning in the carriage coming here. My father and I never understood each other or liked each other. I am sad that he was not the sort of father I would have wanted, but I don't regret the passing of the father he was. I am surprised that the house is not in mourning."

"That is my doing, Richard," said Lady Clara. She was wearing a black dress, but its possible significance as a mourning gown was denied by white lace at the collar and cuffs. "After the way he treated me towards the end, I have no reason to mourn him. He wasn't worth it."

"Welcome, Mother," Giles greeted her. "If that is how you feel, we will certainly follow your wishes. I hadn't thought that we wouldn't mourn him in public, but you are right. If that is what you want, since Daphne and I agree, it would be hypocritical to go into full mourning. I shall only wear a black armband to signify that I am aware that my father is dead.

"Now, you must tell me all the news. Daphne, you are not pregnant anymore...." Giles didn't know how to finish the sentence. Daphne might have had a miscarriage, or the baby might have been stillborn.

"Oh, Giles, no worries! You have the most adorable daughter. You will love her! I called her 'Christina' as we agreed. You must come and see her at once."

Daphne rushed back into the house with Giles trying to keep up with her and Lady Clara trailing along behind. Straight to the nursery. Nanny Weaver was not too pleased to see Daphne just after Christina had settled down after being fed by the wet nurse, and Bernard had finally dropped off for his nap. Parents, in her view, should have more respect for nursery routines. Still, she knew that protesting to Daphne would be a waste of time. Captain Giles had been away far too long to be likely to accept any delay in seeing his children. He already was somewhat unusual in the interest he had shown in his son, and she should not be surprised at his having a similar interest in his daughter. He was a bit shy about picking the child up, but then he started to make silly sounds and faces that she was still too young to understand. That didn't seem to discourage him at all. Maybe their way of bringing up children wasn't so awful as she had thought. They did remind her a bit of how Mr. and Mrs. Moorhouse had treated Daphne when she was tiny. There was no question that Daphne had turned out all right while Nanny Weaver approved of everything about Captain Giles, even if he didn't now act as she thought an earl should. Even Captain Giles realized that the children had had enough excitement and took Daphne's hand to draw her from the nursery.

Giles, Daphne, and Lady Clara went to the parlor to discuss what should be done about the late Earl's funeral and possessions. There Giles learned about the situation in Norfolk for the first time. He was starting from scratch in understanding everything that had happened in his absence. All Daphne's letters had been sent by the Portsmouth naval mail office to Gibraltar to forward to *Glaucus*, but he had received none of them. He was horrified to hear how his father had been treating his mother and abusing the estate, though he was not at all surprised that the Earl had taken up with a courtesan. He was hardly amazed at how far Daphne had got in finding out what was happening and protecting his and his mother's interests. That was her way. He was also not surprised to realize that she had probably handled the business more promptly and imaginatively than he would have. It was now, presumably, up to him to follow up on the problems, but it would be stupid not to engage with Daphne for every subsequent step on the way to straightening up the muddle.

All three of them concluded that there was nothing to be done until they had further news from Norwich. At that point, Daphne took over. Giles needed to take a bath and change his clothes before dinner. Giles still did not have a valet, and Carstairs had been dropped off at the Dipton Arms to be reunited with his wife. Rather than have him rely on the uncertain services of a footman, Daphne declared, she would supervise his bath and subsequent dressing. All Betsey and the other servants had to do was to set up the bathtub in Giles's dressing room and bring up bucket after bucket of hot and cold water. It would certainly give them more ammunition for gossiping about their master and mistress, but that didn't bother Daphne one iota.

Even Betsey, who knew her mistress's ways inside out, was a bit shocked when Daphne firmly locked the door when the bath was ready. She was not surprised at how long the bath lasted, nor that, when she was summoned to help Daphne dress for dinner, her mistress's gown and shift had not only become wet, but some of the buttons were not in the right holes. Betsey, of course, did not mention her observations, even though she knew from other ladies' maids that such behavior was extremely unusual. What she did know was that a happy mistress led to a contented maid.

Conversation at dinner returned to the dilemmas presented by the Earl's death concerning the will and the details of the entails that applied to his estates. Lady Clara dropped an unintentional bomb when she mentioned that she thought the Earl had had property in other parts of England: London and Yorkshire for sure and possibly Norfolk as well as other counties. Her husband had always been very uncommunicative about his holdings, but he had sometimes mentioned such other properties when he was in his cups. Giles reckoned that this was entirely possible. He knew that the Earls of Camshire had at one time been much more prominent than they were now and had held extensive tracts of land. He thought he had heard this from his father when boasting about how distinguished Giles's family line was. It would be crucial to determine what the various properties were, especially as it would not be past his father to have hidden them hoping to borrow against them if it were not known how stringent were the entails on all his property. Of course, all of them would be included unless Giles's grandfather had made an explicit exception or if the Earl had bought them when he still might have had income not coming from his properties. There might be some such assets purchased from the rewards for favors that the Earl had been able to do to people who paid him before his infamous reputation had ruined that line of business for him. Giles began to understand how important were the efforts of Mr. Snodgrass and the lawyer in Norwich to make sure that the probate of the will was pursued correctly. He congratulated Daphne for thinking that the lawyer could play a useful role and for having thought to have the reading of the will challenged and possibly the will itself. However, he felt that they should also ask the late Earl's London solicitors whether they held a copy of a will and what records they had of the holdings of the Earldom of Camshire.

"I have to go to London to report orally on my activities in Kamlakesh to the Admiralty and to the East India Company. When I do, I will contact my father's solicitors, and I will also have my own London solicitor look into the inheritance. I suppose that I should also find out more about my duties as an earl. I know that I will have a seat in the House of Lords, but I don't know what that is all about. There is no great hurry for any of this; it can wait a few days."

"Can I come with you?" Daphne asked.

"Of course you can. Nanny Weaver, I am sure, can look after the children."

Only after Lady Clara retired did Daphne and Giles have a chance to talk about what interested them more. They had been without news of each other for a long time, and many events had occurred in each of their lives. They talked long into the night and only covered the surface of what they wanted to tell each other.

The Admiralty placed a higher priority on Giles's presence in London than did he. A rider arrived with an order to present himself in two days.

"I don't see why I should go before I want to," Giles complained to Daphne. "I've had a very trying voyage whose purpose was to do a favor for the East India Company and not for fighting the French. It really should have been none of my business as a navy captain, especially as the pirate activity was inspired by the Company's own ships' captains. I've always done what the Admiralty wanted. They can wait a bit."

"You are quite right, of course," Daphne replied. "Those officials are being very unreasonable. However, just think. The Admiralty can be a very vindictive and petty institution. I know you would not be bothered if they took *Glaucus* from you and put you on half-pay. But they are much more likely to take their pique out on your subordinates. You mentioned last night that Mr. Miller is due his step and should be given a ship right away. Young Daniel Stewart should be made a lieutenant, you said, even if he is not yet nineteen. The crew should be given leave, even though it is almost unknown on ships in the middle of a war because of fear of desertion. They could also be transferred as a single group to some ship accompanying prisoners to Australia without ever touching land. You know that the Admiralty is capable of such things out of pure spite, just to show how unimportant its leaders think you are."

Daphne's arguments prevailed. The following day, they went to London.

Mr. Snodgrass arrived at Dipton Hall soon after this decision was made. He had news from Norwich. The solicitor there had attended the scheduled reading of the will and had challenged the document. The will had not been properly witnessed, and it was not written in the late Earl's hand. As a result, it was not valid. A valid last will and testament should be looked for, possibly at Ashbury Abbey or London.

Lady Clara was sure that there was no such document at Ashbury Abbey or with the local solicitor that her husband had used for matters concerning that property. She had enquired even before the wretched letter arrived that had so stirred up her worries. In consequence, there was no need to search at Ashbury Abbey for the will. Giles's intention to ask the London solicitors was a much better idea since she suspected that that was where the document would be found.

Mr. Snodgrass agreed that that was the most promising line of inquiry. He did warn that with one bogus will already having been presented, there might be others. Only the Archdiocesan Court of Canterbury could settle which one was valid if more than one were found that could pass examination.

"What about my father's body?" Giles asked bluntly. He didn't care much about the answer, but he believed the late Earl should be buried properly.

"Ah," Mr. Snodgrass consulted the letter. "He has been buried in the churchyard at St. Michael's on Granfen, in Norfolk. That is the parish church of the place where he died. It is summer, after all, so there is no surprise about a quick burial. Where the late Earl's final resting place will be should be stated in his will. If it isn't specified, you can, if you wish, have his remains moved elsewhere. There is now no hurry for that."

"That sounds satisfactory," said Lady Clara, "Of course, I wasn't present at his burial. If he is buried again, I won't attend the ceremony. I am also not going into mourning for him, no matter what people may think. Let his strumpet wear mourning clothes if she wants to. I do hope that she has suffered a pecuniary loss.

"Richard, I imagine that you can follow the suggestion about contacting his solicitors while you are in London and take any necessary decisions. I think I shall stay here at Dipton, if you agree, Daphne. I want to avoid having to listen to sanctimonious sympathy for my 'loss' arising from the scoundrel's death."

"Of course. You know that you are always welcome here, Lady Clara," Daphne replied. "Giles, you will be busy in London, and I can be helpful. Can I come with you?"

"Of course, my dear. We both know that you are much better than I am in dealing with lawyers and other business. And that way, we can get back here more quickly since we will be able to divide the chores."

Two days later, Daphne and Giles parted company after breakfast at Struthers House. Giles would go to the Admiralty, Daphne, to the chambers of Delancy, Snodgrass, and Foster. The Mr. Snodgrass, who was a cousin of her solicitor in Ameschester, was the member of the firm who had handled the affairs of the Earls of Camshire for a long time. Daphne wondered if the relationship with this firm was about to be broken.

She was shown into Mr. Snodgrass's room immediately.

A short, portly man with gray hair, a large beard, and ruddy cheeks stood to greet her.

"My lady," he greeted Daphne. "Have you not heard of the death of the Earl of Camshire? I see that you are not in mourning."

"No. We have heard. The Dowager Countess felt that she had been so abused by her husband that she could not even pretend to mourn his passing. I share her sentiments."

"That is very brave of you, my lady. You can expect to be condemned in common gossip for not following convention. I can well understand your position. I am afraid that the late Earl, especially in his later years, was not an admirable or even an honorable man. This firm has had no dealings with him for several months since he flatly refused to pay our account."

"I am not surprised to learn of his debt to you. I am sure that Captain Giles will have it paid. What I have come for is to find out whether you have his will or know where it is. A false one was found in Norfolk, where he died, so now we are searching for the genuine one."

"That there was a spurious will doesn't surprise me. We broke with the late Earl of Camshire because he was asking us to devise strategies so that he could effectively sell some of his properties despite the terms of the entails. For all I know, he may have gone through with some of them, using another solicitor and then tried to hide what he had done in his will."

"What was he trying to do?" asked Daphne.

"Some sort of wild scheme to sell ninety-nine year leases to his tenants in exchange for no rent payments during that period. It seemed to me that it was a ludicrous and probably illegal idea, but he may have gone ahead with it. I checked in our records for his will when I heard of his passing. We do have one, but it could have been superseded. It is dated eighteen months ago."

"What steps need to be taken now?" Daphne asked.

"Normally, if we were handling the situation, we would begin by placing notices in the papers asking for any other wills to come forward and to request that all debtors declare their interest by a certain date. The will in our possession names Captain Giles as the executor. If he is to be away again, he should appoint an agent to act for him."

"Can I be that agent?"

"I am afraid that, as a married woman, you cannot. The Dowager Countess could act as the agent of the executor unless she remarried. Of course, we would be happy to act as the agent, and the appointment could state that we are to follow your instructions, my lady, provided that they are within the law. The Earl's solicitor or his prize agent could also act in this regard if he so desires. Mr. Edwards is still his agent, isn't he?"

"Yes. Can I at least ask you now to place the notices you spoke of and to specify dates by which the various steps need to be taken by others and set a date and time for the reading of the will?"

"Yes, you may. It would be desirable if his lordship, the Earl, could be present for the reading, and the Dowager Countess or her agent should also be here. In principle, they can override your instructions, but I am not worried that they will."

"I see. How soon can you schedule the reading of the will?"

"Two days. It would be quite proper, though it might be wise not to take any irreversible steps based on the will until the time specified in the notices has expired."

"Very good, Mr. Snodgras. Please schedule the reading for ten o'clock on the day after tomorrow."

Daphne left the solicitor's chambers, feeling that she had accomplished everything necessary. She would spend the rest of the day shopping with Lady Struthers. She was surprised to realize that visiting a variety of stores and Gunter's famous teashop with Giles's aunt had become one of her favorite activities.

Giles arrived unannounced at the Admiralty. Nevertheless, he was brought to the First Lord, Baron Hatcherly, with no delay.

The First Lord rose to greet him. "Lord Camshire, it is good of you to come so promptly. My condolences. I was saddened to hear of the death of your father. I am surprised that you are not in mourning."

"Lord Hatcherly, thank you. No. My mother feels that my father is not worth mourning, and I agree with her. It's not customary to fail to mark someone's passing in that way, I know, but I think it makes sense in this case. Incidentally, when on Navy business, I much prefer to be called 'Captain Giles.'"

"I understand. I must admit that there must have been a very widespread sigh of relief when it was learned that there would be a new Earl of Camshire. That's something I intend to discuss with you, but first, let's talk about your very successful voyage."

Lord Hatcherly was full of praise for Giles's successes in the Bay of Quiberon, remarking that his crew would be receiving a great deal of money for wrecking the ship of the line as well as prize money and head money for the captured troop-ship and the captured frigate.

"I was quite surprised at how successful your trip to that wretched place in Africa was. What is its name?"

"Kamlakesh, my lord."

"Yes. Hard to get one's tongue around, isn't it? To tell the truth, all I had hoped for was that your showing the flag would induce their Bey, or whatever he calls himself, to go back to the former level of ransom and treatment of prisoners. You went a great deal farther. When I first heard of it in your report, I was afraid of the diplomatic consequences, but the people in the foreign office say that they think your activities should make the Moors respect us more, and there would be no other consequences.

"Your findings about the East India Company certainly put the cat among the pigeons. It seems that they had never considered the possibility of their losses being anything but bad luck. The idea that their captains could have a scheme to enrich themselves at the Company's expense had never occurred to them. Heads will roll, I am sure. I have arranged a meeting with some Company officials for eleven o'clock this morning.

"Now, about your next assignment. Things are very much up in the air at the moment. A lot has happened while you have been away, and the war may have become severely altered. You will recall that the French fleet at Toulon, which Nelson was blockading, gave him the slip. It went to the West Indies. Nelson finally found out where they had gone, sailed west, and missed them again. Villeneuve returned to this side of the ocean and joined up with the Spanish, but not with other French fleets, even though the Rochefort fleet is now at sea somewhere. We don't know why the Brest fleet has not stirred. They have had several opportunities where they could have gotten the whole fleet out with almost no opposition from us.

"That idiot, Calder, caught up with Villeneuve off the north-east corner of Spain. He had a very unsatisfactory fight with the enemy in July, but he broke it off, and he did not resume the battle the next day. Surprisingly the Brest fleet has not tried to come out, even though there have been several occasions when they could have got free with little opposition from us.

"The big change in the war came at the end of August. The camp at Boulogne was abandoned, and the soldiers have disappeared. We have heard some reports that Napoleon's whole army has marched east. Lately, we heard rumors that they had crossed the Rhine near Strasbourg. Equally important, the invasion fleet of small craft in Boulogne and other ports on the Channel seems not to be maintained. All reports agree on it, though none of our naval ships has penetrated the port since you did so a couple of years ago, so we are relying on the reports of rather problematic spies.

"The result is that I am not sure how best to employ you and *Glaucus* right now. You deserve a break, and your crew, unlike most other ones in the navy, I might almost say all other crews, has the reputation of returning from leaves more or less on time. You will want to be with your family, I am sure. Incidentally, we have promoted your first lieutenant to the rank of commander and have found him a nice sloop-of-war. A couple of blind eyes have been turned about your midshipman, what's his name?

"Daniel Stewart, my lord?"

"That's the one. He has been made lieutenant. You are still short a lieutenant since your first lieutenant has been promoted. Are any of your young gentlemen ready to be acting lieutenant?"

"I am afraid not."

"Well, I will have to find one for you unless you can think of someone you want.

"Now, to other, less pressing matters. Since you are now the Earl of Camshire, you are, of course, a member of the House of Lords."

"I suppose I am, yes."

"It's a very responsible position, especially when one shows up in the House regularly, which is what you should do. Unfortunately, many of the other peers do not. I hope you will be different and regularly take part in the debates. His Majesty's Navy needs all the support we can get."

"I suppose it does. But, my lord, I can only vote for what I believe is best. There are many improvements, which would certainly make the Navy more effective, that require Parliamentary authorization."

"Yes, yes, of course. I am sure the Prime Minister will welcome your ideas. Your father, when he wasn't voting solely for his own financial interests, was a Tory. Are you?"

"I don't know. I have never paid much attention to the differences. I think I'll sit on the cross-benches, at least initially. I may be more of a Whig than a Tory."

"We'll have to talk of that later. Incidentally, I would be delighted to arrange for an earl to introduce you to the House at the next sitting or whenever you are available. It is part of the ritual. Tom Foolery, I believe, but then my title is not of ancient provenance as is yours."

The meeting with the officials of the East India Company was not quite the smooth affair that Giles had expected. They were grateful for his recapturing *Gloriana* and rescuing many of their servants and passengers. They were far less happy about his statements that many of the captains of their ships had been involved in a plot to extract money from the Company. They were particularly annoyed when Giles said that he would refuse to keep silent on the matter if they tried to sweep it all under the carpet. When they argued that there was no evidence against any of the captains, Giles laughed at them. He pointed out that the captains' logs and the reports of their officers would detail the consistent difference between the noon sights and chronometer readings that would show how they got off course and altered their paths so that they ran into the arms of the waiting pirates. Records of the captains' bank accounts would list the rewards that followed the payment of ransom by the East India Company. Undoubtedly there would be more evidence if they looked for it. Were the directors of the Company trying to bury it?

The response of the Company officials to these statements was to hint rather explicitly that they would be happy to pay the First Lord and Giles substantial sums to keep the matter unknown and thereby to ignore it. Lord Hatcherly at first seemed to be open to this suggestion, but Giles was infuriated by it and rejected the offer out of hand.

Furthermore, if the Company did not pursue the matter vigorously, he would raise it in the House of Lords.

"I suspect, Captain Giles, that you have just done yourself out of a large payment that they were ready to vote for you for rescuing their ship and people, quite apart from the reward money that we at the Admiralty pried out of them. It will be treated as prize money for the benefit of *Glaucus*, so the lion's share will go to you. Together with the other rewards arising from your latest voyage, you and your crew have done very well. I can't say that being First Lord is anything like as lucrative."

Giles was shocked to hear his superior implicitly mourn not getting a substantial bribe. But he was not in a position to protest the implied corruption. Before his lack of reaction became embarrassing to either of them, the First Lord continued, "I must confess, Captain Giles, that I don't know how best to use *Glaucus* right now. Although Bonaparte seems to have abandoned his plan for invading, our spies cannot be sure. His bloody army has disappeared, though it may be the one reported to have crossed the Rhine. If so, the immediate threat is diminished. Villeneuve is holed up in Cadiz with a large part of the Spanish Fleet. If it ever deigns to come out, the Brest fleet would be a challenge, but without the French army ready to go, that fleet is not much of a threat to our country itself, though it would be a problem for commerce if it ever got loose. I think that our naval focus may have to be directed at the Mediterranean again, maybe under Nelson, though he might be best-used flushing Villeneuve out of Cadiz. But then, he has not had great success so far either in blockading Villeneuve or in bringing him to battle.

"What is the best use of *Glaucus* may not be known for a while. It is not immediately apparent where you would be employed most advantageously in this altered war, partly because we don't understand what Bonaparte intends to do. If

England itself is not in danger right now, we may have to turn our attention to protecting commerce in the Baltic and keeping the countries in the region neutral. You did remarkably well on your Russian voyage, despite that ass of a nobleman we sent as the envoy. Maybe something like that would be best for you. I, myself, think that you should be kept close to home so that you can serve effectively in the House of Lords. I am afraid most members of Parliament, both the Commons and the Lords, do not have much understanding of what a navy can and cannot do.

"Enough of this speculating. For the time being, I do not have an assignment for you. Of course, you remain the captain of *Glaucus*. Give your crew leave, even though that horrifies most of your naval peers. Make sure that every member of your crew is back on board in, say, six weeks from now. We should have a better idea of the situation by then."

Giles soon found himself on the crowded street in front of the Admiralty. Of all the outcomes he had imagined when he arrived at the building that morning, a lengthy leave was not one. Since the start of this war, he had been home only briefly on short leaves or longer ones when he was recovering from wounds. Now he was home indefinitely. He could genuinely share the burdens that Daphne had assumed because of his absence. His time with her would not have a call to return to his ship hanging over their heads, at least not for another six weeks.

Daphne had mentioned that she intended to have lunch with Lady Struthers at Gunter's tea shop before going shopping in the afternoon. Giles would join them there. He could hail a cab or a sedan chair to take him, but it was not a long walk to Mayfair, and he could go faster on foot than in a hired conveyance. Maybe on the way, he should pass through Bond Street, where he might find an appropriate piece of jewelry for his wife to mark his unfettered, if only temporary, freedom from the demands of warfare. He set off down Whitehall with a notable swing to his stride.

Author's Note

The summer of 1805 saw a major turning point of the Napoleonic Wars. The critical event occurred in late August when Napoleon broke camp on the heights overlooking Boulogne and marched what had been the Army of England southeast to the battles of Ulm and Austerlitz. The date when they struck camp is long before the Battle of Trafalgar. The Battle of Finisterre, a debacle that at an earlier time might well have got the British Admiral hung, possibly, finally, decided Napoleon that the French Navy would not be able to sweep the Channel clear of the Royal Navy. More likely, it was the failure of the Brest Fleet to break out and carry out the plan to meet with Villeneuve and proceed to so tie up the Channel Fleet that the invasion of England would have a chance of succeeding.

Part of Napoleon's plans involved Villeneuve rendezvousing with the Brest Fleet off Ireland, which, of course, did not happen. Though plausible in this connection, no intention for France to support even a token uprising in Ireland is known to have been considered. The incident involving such an attempt in this book is pure fiction; Vannes and the Gulf of Morbihan existed more or less as I describe them.

Kamlakesh is completely fictional. Piracy based on Africa, especially Mediterranean Africa, flourished at the time, but there was not, as far as I can discover, a pirate lair on the West African coast.

Birmingham was, of course, a leading center of the Industrial Revolution. It is not widely recognized that it was also an intellectual center of the Enlightenment, especially the more technically oriented aspects of that movement known as the Midlands or Birmingham Enlightenment.

The status of women in this period, both in law and in practice, was as abysmal as I have portrayed it, but there were feminists, possibly better-called proto-feminists, such as Mary Wollstonecraft. While Daphne Giles is fictional, and any actual person did not match her, Daphne's attitudes and willingness to take on traditionally men's roles were not unknown at the time. If any one of my characters is outrageously implausible, it is the hero, Captain Giles, who by now, in a short period, has far exceeded the accomplishments of any of the actual, distinguished, frigate captains of both the Revolutionary and the Napoleonic Wars.

Readers who are interested in reaching me can email me at jgcragg@telus.net. I always enjoy hearing from readers, both those who liked the yarn – they are very encouraging – and those who do not – their criticism suggests ways to improve the next attempt. I might add that reviews given on Amazon are appreciated. Incidentally, reviews on one Amazon site are not usually transferred to another. For instance, Amazon.com often has different reviews from Amazon.uk. It is a point worth considering when buying books and when considering other things that Amazon sells.

Glossary

Admiral Byng's fate — Admiral Byng was executed for lack of aggression for, in Voltaire's words, "pour encourager les autres."

Belay (v.) — Tie down. Regularly used by mariners to also mean stop. Belaying pins were stout, removable rods that were often used as makeshift weapons.

Board(ing) — (1) Refers to attacking another ship by coming side to side so that men from one ship can attack the other one in an attempt to capture it.

(2) in 'on board' it means present on a ship.

Boarding-nets — Loose nets hung from the spars of a ship to prevent enemies climbing aboard from boats.

Brig — A two-masted, square-rigged ship.

Carronade — A short gun, frequently mounted on a slider rather than a wheeled gun carriage, only used for close-in work. They were not usually counted in the number of guns by which a ship was rated.

Close (verb) — Closing with another ship (or fleet) was to sail towards it by the quickest path.

Close to the wind — A ship is sailing close to the wind when it is going upwind as much as it can without stalling. Slang meaning is that the action is almost illegal.

Cloth (drawn) — Refers to the stage of a meal when the final dish had been consumed, the tablecloth had been removed, and the men in attendance gathered together to imbibe liquor stronger than wine, usually accompanied by nuts and fruit. When ladies were present, they withdrew to the drawing room just before the cloth was drawn. It was often a time of more pointed conversation than occurred during the meal.

Consol — A bond issued by the British Government with no stated redemption date, paying the holder a specified amount per annum. The term is short for Consolidated Fund.

Crosstrees — Two horizontal spars at the upper ends of a topmast to which are attached the shrouds of the topgallant mast.

Cutting-out — Entering an enemy harbor in boats to capture a ship and sail her out to sea where the warship would be waiting.

Entail — A provision that the inheritance of real property would go to specified members of a family (or another specified group) usually to the closest male relatives. An entail typically prevented the present owner from leaving the property to someone else, and it was usually put on a property to prevent the immediate heir from dissipating the inheritance but would pass it intact (more or less) to the next generation.

Exemptions — Documents issued to merchant seaman and some other so that they would not be pressed into the navy. Even with them seamen were often forcibly taken from merchant ships to serve in the navy.

Fighting top	A Platform on the mast where the main part met the top mast from which marines could fire their muskets on to the deck of an opposing ship.
Grapnel	A metal hook or set of hooks attached to a line that could be thrown and hook on to the edge of another ship or a wall or other object.
Gunroom	Place where the midshipmen berthed.
Helm alee	Turn a ship into the wind. (It sounds backwards, but originates from the time when ships had tillers which were pushed in the direction opposite to the desired turn.)
Holystone	On naval ships, the decks were scrubbed each morning using sandstone blocks. Since the crew had to perform the task on their knees, they were called holy stones and holystone became the verb to indicate the activity.
John Company	Nickname for the East India Company
Larboard	the left-hand side of the ship looking forward. Opposite of starboard. Now usually called "port."
Lead-line	A thin rope knotted at six-foot intervals with a piece of lead at the end. Used to measure the depth of water under a ship.
Lubber's hole	A hole in the top (q.v.) of a mast so that access can b e gained from below, either to get to the top of to be able to reach the next set of shrouds to clime farther up the masts. Experienced topmen avoided its use when

	climbing the mast, preferring to climb up the ropes on the outside of the top.
The Nore	Anchorage in the Thames estuary off the mouth of the Medway River. A major anchorage for the Royal Navy in the Age of Sail.
Quarterdeck	The outside deck of a ship at the stern.
Raft	Ships or boats are rafted together when they are tied to each other.
Rake (a ship)	Fire a broadside into the bow or stern of an opponent who would not be able to return the fire.
Rout	A large, formal evening gathering. It had a slightly risqué connotation.
Shrouds	A rope ladder formed by short lengths of rope tied tightly between the stays of a mast.
Sheet	A line controlling how much a sail is pulled in.
Stay(s)	(1) A line used to prevent a mast from falling over or being broken in the wind
	(2) Corsets
Step	Promotion from lieutenant to commander.
Spring (line)	A line attached to the anchor cable leading to the aft of the ship that can be used to turn it
Tack	(a) Change the direction in which a ship is sailing and the side of the ship from which the wind is blowing by turning towards the direction from which the wind is blowing.

	(b) (as in larboard of starboard tack) The side of the ship from which the wind is blowing when the ship is going to windward.
Taffrail	Railing at the stern of the quarter deck.
Ton	That part of London society most interested in adhering to the latest fashions.
Toulon	The main French naval base in the Mediterranean. It was under loose blockade both in 1805 and also earlier when it slipped out of the harbor and evaded the Britsih Fleet under Nelson to go to Egypt. Nelson's ability to contain it was no greater in 1805.
Tubs	Liquor was not usually smuggled in regular barrels but in smaller containers, made like a barrel, which could be carried by one man.
Wardroom	The area in a ship used by the commissioned officers of a ship when off-duty.
Watch	(1) Time: A ships day was divided up into fur hour watches with one further divided into two. The watches were

    First watch: 8 p.m.- 12 midnight

    Middle watch: 12 midnight - 4 a.m.

    Morning watch: 4 a.m. – 8 a.m.

    Forenoon watch: 8 a.m. – 12 noon

    Afternoon watch 12 noon – 4 p.m.

First dog watch 4 p.m. – 6 p.m.

Second Dog watch 6 p.m. – 8 p.m.

In each watch, time was marked off in half-hour segments so the one bell of the First watch would be 8:30 p.m., two bells would be 9:00 p.m., and so on.

(2) Division of the crew. The crew was divided (usually) into two watches, the starboard watch and the larboard watch, which alternated when they worked (in normal circumstances) and when they were at leisure or asleep.

(3) the time when officers were on duty. Referred to as "being on watch" or "watch."

(4) Police force on land.

Wear (referring to a ship) The opposite of tack where the maneuver of changing which side of a ship the wind is coming from is accomplished by turning away from the wind. Sometimes spelled ware.

Yellow admiral A Naval officer who has been promoted to the rank of Admiral without being given a command. Largely created to allow the promotion of a captain with less seniority.

Printed in Great Britain
by Amazon